Between Sisters

A Novel

Nina Vida

Crown Publishers, Inc.
New York

F
VID

Published by Crown Publishers, Inc., 201 East 50th Street, New York, New York 10022. Member of the Crown Publishing Group.

Random House, Inc. New York, Toronto, London, Sydney, Auckland

CROWN is a trademark of Crown Publishers, Inc.

Manufactured in the United States of America

Design by Cynthia Dunne

Library of Congress Cataloging-in-Publication Data

Vida, Nina.
    Between sisters: a novel/Nina Vida.
        p.   cm.
    I. Title.
PS3572.I29B48   1996
813'.54—dc20   95–598
                                                          CIP
ISBN 0-517-70071-9

10   9   8   7   6   5   4   3   2   1

First Edition

To Duke

Part
One

1

1965

EVERY SUNDAY WHEN Mama played the organ in Bethany God the Creator Universal Church, it was like God was talking to Lela. Or at least one of his angels. Why, when Lela squeezed her eyes half shut and stuck her eyes right smack on Mama's back, then let them go straight, straight up, not too far, just an itty bit past the tail of a blue satin streamer that kept Mama's brown hair in place, she could see wings growing out of Mama's shoulders. Lela didn't know what angels were really supposed to look like, but surely Mama, sitting up on that platform with her wings as blue as her hair ribbon, was like one.

Lela always swung her feet when she listened to Mama playing the organ. She couldn't help it. Her feet just moved by themselves, as if the music were pushing them. Daddy, who always sat between Lela and Jolene on the satiny wooden church bench, couldn't stand swinging feet and would put his head down close to Lela's and tell her in a sharp voice to keep her feet still or he'd smack her right then and there.

Lela's feet weren't like Daddy's. Daddy had big feet, and he could scare anyone when he stomped around the house on them. Lela's feet weren't like Mama's, either. Mama's feet were wide, and she said it was because she ran barefoot too much when she was a little girl and they got all spread out. Mama liked to tickle the bottoms of Lela's feet in the morning when she helped her get ready for school. Sometimes she even kissed her toes. Mama said Lela's feet were like Elaine's, the girl who was born after Jolene and before Lela. She died six years ago when Lela was only two years old. Lela didn't remember her at all.

Jolene never swung her feet in church. She never did much of anything anywhere. Jolene was weird. Wanting to be alone all the time. Not wanting to talk to anyone. Always pinching up her forehead and biting her lips when you said anything to her. Her feet were a mix of everyone's, Mama always said.

Oh, Mama's playing was so beautiful. All those high notes floating up around the stained-glass pictures and then swooping down toward the floor, where they'd buzz around for a while before they disappeared. And the low notes that sunk themselves so far down into Lela's stomach, she could feel them rumbling there.

Mama never could get through a piece of music without turning to look at Lela to see if she was smiling. Mama was always saying how Lela's smile could melt a Popsicle. Mama never stopped playing, though, when she turned around to look at Lela. Her fingers kept pressing all the right keys and her feet kept sweeping across the wood strips, bouncing on some, slipping past others. It was like magic how her feet stripped those sweet sounds off the wood and tossed them up in the air.

What was that song Mama always played? "Jesus, My Deliverer"? Mama's music was as sweet and smooth as ice cream. Everyone said she was the best there was in the history of organ playing at Bethany God the Creator Universal Church. Not even the organist up at the Catholic church off of Pacific Coast Highway could beat her at organ playing. Everyone said so.

2

JOLENE HADN'T COME out of the bedroom yet. Lela kept watching the bedroom door, waiting to see Jolene's head pop out. The door was open a little, but there was no sign of Jolene's head or any other part of her body. It was like she didn't care that the teacher was there in the living room, didn't care at all what the teacher was saying to Mama.

"As I was saying, Jolene is smart," Miss Thompson said. "She does her assignments on time, completes her homework."

"All the Sweetzers are smart," Mama said. "Those are my people, the Sweetzers. The Benoits are my husband's side. French descent. I couldn't tell you whether they're smart or not. My husband doesn't see his family at all."

Mama had let Miss Thompson sit herself down in the living room when she came in the house. She had tried to steer her to the room off the kitchen with the plastic-covered couch and the television, almost shoved her into the wall with her elbow trying to get her in there, but the teacher had walked right straight into the living room and sat down on the flowered couch. No one ever went in the living room. Just Mama to clean it. And Daddy to check that nothing was messed up, that his cats were all in the same place, that no one had come into the house in the middle of the night and broken one of them. Daddy collected cats. Glass ones, china ones, metal ones, wooden ones. There were even some paper ones. All lined up on shelves that Mama dusted with a feather duster.

"I was good in school, too," Mama said. "But I can tell you I'm not half as smart as my two girls. Would you like some more coffee? I made this pot this morning. You must think I don't know how to boil water, the way it tastes."

"It's fine," Miss Thompson said.

"I can make some more in a minute. It's no trouble. No trouble in

5

the least. My, it must be something special to make you come out on a Saturday to talk to me about my Jolene."

"It's part of my job."

"I don't suppose they pay you for Saturday work."

"You didn't come to parent-teacher conference."

"Donny—that's my husband—doesn't believe in that kind of thing."

"I was hoping to see you on parents' day, at least. I was looking forward to talking to you about Jolene."

"What in the world would you want to say about her? You just said she was smart."

"She's very quiet."

"That wasn't a crime when I was in school. Now, if you were Lela's teacher, I could see you telling me you couldn't figure out a way to keep her from talking. But Jolene? Quiet? Why, quiet's the way you'd want it, I'd think."

"Well, there's quiet, and then there's quiet."

"You're just not used to Jolene. She never did like to talk much. Even when she was a baby she didn't jabber like babies do." Mama turned her head to Lela. "Why don't you go tell Jolene to come out here, honey bunny."

"I'd rather talk to you without her, if that's all right," the teacher said.

"Well, I don't understand. If she's so smart, and it's her nature to be quiet, what's there left to talk about?"

"I'm not sure."

"Well, that's a strange one," Mama said with a laugh.

"I mean, she's so quiet."

"You said that already. My mother was quiet. And my brother Bill. He was quieter than anyone. Never said two words more than he had to."

The teacher was smiling at Lela. Mama kept looking at the teacher's blue jeans and the white socks that curled around her ankles and drooped over her sneakers. Daddy would never let Mama out of the house if she looked like that. Lela liked the way Mama dressed. Mostly she wore a neat skirt and an ironed blouse. And hose, even when she was scrubbing the floor. Right now she was in a dress that had yellow-and-white daisies painted all over it.

"I think I'd like a cup of tea, if you have some," Miss Thompson said.

"I've got teabags," Mama said. "I can boil up some water and stick a bag in it."

"That'll be fine."

Mama hadn't tied her hair up this morning, and it hung loose and fluffy around her neck. She kind of brushed it away with the back of one hand and then stood up and walked into the kitchen.

"Where's your daddy?" Miss Thompson said when Mama was gone.

"Working," Lela said.

Mama was running water into the teapot. Lela could hear it. Splash, splash, splash. It was a sharp sound, like the water was cutting right into the metal. The noise stopped abruptly and Mama stuck her head back out into the living room.

"Is she saying things she oughtn't?" Mama said. "Bothering you?"

"I was just asking about your husband."

"He's away. Be back day after tomorrow. He sells veterinary supplies—you know, flea collars and leashes and disinfectants. Sells to stores, too. Dog bones, dog toys, cat stuff. You can see he's got a thing for cats."

Mama laughed and lifted her loose hair up with two hands and held it above her head for a moment before letting it drop. When she went back into the kitchen, Lela could hear her humming a song, her voice as smooth and sweet as sugar water.

"We don't have a dog," Lela said. "Daddy says they smell bad." She pushed her face close to the teacher's. "You smell good. Mama doesn't wear perfume. Daddy says perfume is dirty, but I like it. It tickles my nose. Sometimes I smell it in the store and it makes me sneeze. But I like it. I wish I had some. Jolene bought a bottle once, but Daddy spilled it out in the backyard. Right on a rosebush. It died."

"Does Jolene talk to you?"

"Sometimes. You have curly hair. My hair curls, too. Feel it."

The teacher touched Lela's head lightly, quickly.

"I wish my hair would go straight down like Mama's does," Lela said. "Jolene ironed it once, but it wouldn't stay."

"You like Jolene, don't you?"

"I had a brother, too. Someone came into the house and shot him, though. A burglar. With a rifle."

Lela sat down on the couch next to the teacher. She had never sat on the couch before. It felt like her winter coat, soft against the underside of her legs. It wasn't cold like the plastic one in the little room off the kitchen.

"The police came. And my aunt Marge from Wichita came with the twins. You can't tell them apart. And my Grandma Renee, she came, too. It was a mess. Mama played the organ. Have you ever seen an angel?"

"No, I don't think so. Have you ever seen one?"

"Once. Pete and Larry. That's their names, my cousins from Wichita."

There was Jolene's head now, showing through the crack in the bedroom door. Lela had never seen Jolene's eyes like that, all scared and watery.

"They brought their comic books with them," Lela said. "They have a thousand comic books, and we read them all, every last one. They were real sad to hear that my brother got shot and killed. Everyone was sad."

"Be right there," Mama called from the kitchen.

"They've got an electric train that takes up one whole room of their house," Lela said. "I played with it once. Have you ever been to Wichita?"

"No, I haven't."

"It's hot there, 'specially in December. That's when we were there. Christmas. Last year. Daddy drove us there in his new Buick. We threw snowballs."

"I thought you said it was hot."

"Oh, that was the time before. I forgot."

Oh, she wished Jolene would either come out here or shut that door. She was making her feel so bad, wondering what it was Miss Thompson wanted to say, what awful thing it was that Jolene had done.

"Aunt Marge is Mama's sister," Lela said. "Mama says she thinks she's smarter than anyone. Mama says she won't even teach her own kids how to sit up straight at the table or to keep their mouth shut when people are tired of hearing them talk. And Grandma Renee's house is a filthy mess, Mama says. Papers everywhere. Did Jolene do something bad?"

Mama was back. "I made the cookies from scratch yesterday," she said. She held the plate out to the teacher, who took a cookie and put it on the napkin on her lap. "My husband won't stand for box mix cookies. You and Lela just go on and talk a little more while I go see if the kettle's boiled yet. Lela's my honey bunny. We talk all the time. She's better company than any grown-up I ever met."

"No, Jolene didn't do anything bad," the teacher said when Mama was gone again. "What grade are you in?"

"Third."

"Does Jolene talk about your daddy to you?"

"Uh-uh."

"Do you like your daddy?"

"Uh-huh."

"That's a pretty dress you're wearing."

"Mama made it. Mama sews all my clothes. Some for my dolls, too. I'm learning to sew. Can you sew?"

"No, I can't. I never learned."

"It's easy. You just turn on the machine. But you got to watch your fingers. You can sew your fingers right to the table if you're not careful. Mama says she did that one time when she wasn't watching. She had to call the police to get her loose." Lela held the thumb of her right hand out for the teacher's inspection. "See there, that's where the needle almost went in one day, but Mama pulled my hand out of the way. It's an old machine. Mama says one of these days Daddy will let her buy a new one, so I won't have to watch my fingers so much."

Mama was back. "I hope these teabags are fresh. No one in the house drinks tea. I make it for Donny sometimes, though, when he has a cold. He says there's nothing like a cup of hot tea to cure a cold."

Miss Thompson sloshed the bag up and down in the cup of hot water, and Mama reached over and sopped up the droplets with a paper napkin. "Got to be careful," she said. "Donny'll kill me if there are drips on this coffee table. He watches everything." Mama smiled. "I don't mean really kill me. You know what I mean."

"Of course," Miss Thompson said. "A figure of speech."

"Oh, Donny's full of figures of speech," Mama said. "You should hear him. I told him he should write a book, he's got so many funny sayings in him. Lela been filling your head with stories, I suppose." Mama sat down on the chair in front of the cat shelf. She sat straight, her slim back not touching the chair at all. "She gets that from me. I love to talk. Don't have much occasion to. Don't see too many people. But when I can, I do."

"She was telling me about your family."

"Oh, them." Mama's face turned sour. "I don't see them much."

"From the way she talks about them, it sounded like you see them all the time." Miss Thompson looked confused now.

"You telling lies again, honey bunny?" Mama said, smiling at Lela.

"I don't know," Lela said.

"Some of the stuff she says is true, you know," Mama said, "but a lot more isn't. She likes to entertain people. My family? Well, now and again my sister Marge calls from Wichita to complain about things. I don't know what she has to complain about, though, she pushes that husband of hers around till he must be dizzy. As for Mama and Daddy, well, Daddy hasn't spoken a word to me since Donny and I got married. Mama sends birthday presents to the girls, though. Donny and my daddy never saw eye to eye on things. Too much alike, I suppose."

"You didn't have a son that got shot and killed?"

"Oh, my heavens, no. I've never had a son." Mama was laughing hard now. "Not that I know of, anyway."

"Oh, Mama." Lela squirmed against Mama's knee.

"I know, honey bunny, I know," Mama said, "but the lady doesn't. You don't want her going away thinking you're a cuckoo bird, do you?"

"She certainly has a vivid imagination," the teacher said.

"I've been trying to break her of lying."

"I don't think it can be classified as lying."

"Donny thinks it can. He beats the living daylights out of her when he catches her at it. Locked her in the garage one whole day when she made up a story about Jolene, made her stay there all day without eating." Mama put her hand out and patted Lela's cheek. "Didn't do a bit of good, did it, sweetie?"

"I don't think that kind of punishment ever works," the teacher said in a more forceful voice.

"Now, don't you go and call child welfare on us, will you." Mama was smiling a sweet smile.

"What kind of story did she make up about Jolene?" the teacher said.

"Oh, Donny just likes to know where Jolene is all the time, and I tell him and tell him that a seventeen-year-old girl can't be telling her father every little thing she does, every little place she goes, every person she sees. My mother interfered with me so bad I could hardly cross the street without getting her permission. It was always, 'Marilee, don't do this; Marilee, don't do that.' I understand perfectly what's going on with Jolene. I mean, I really do. All those hormones backing up in her with nowhere to go. You don't have to tell me about teenage girls. Why, look at you, honey, you look like a teenager yourself."

The teacher blushed and picked at the tops of her drooping socks.

"I told Daddy I saw Jolene talking to a boy," Lela said. "They were standing out in the street, right down at the corner, and the boy had his arm around her like this." Lela put her arms out in a big circle in front of her.

"I don't think Miss Thompson is interested in that, sweetie," Mama said, and she winked at the teacher.

"She was kissing him, too," Lela said. "It was disgusting, his face all in her face. He had his hand back here and he was going like this."

"That's enough, honey," Mama said.

"Well, I'm glad to hear she's got a boyfriend, at least," the teacher said.

"Oh, she doesn't," Mama said. "I guess you can't tell yet when Lela's lying."

"I guess not."

"And as far as Jolene's concerned, she may be quiet, but she's always had the sweetest nature. When she was born you could just look at her and see the goodness. I couldn't stop kissing her. Why, I kissed her and kissed her till Donny said, 'Marilee, you kiss that baby one more time her cheeks'll fall off.' And when she started school, every teacher she ever had said how smart she was, how well behaved. This is the first time I've ever heard anyone even mention Jolene being anything but perfect."

"I'm not saying she's not," the teacher said. "It just seems to me that she's not acting right. This past May as part of my continuing education credits I took a course in identifying teenage suicides, and Jolene fit the profile to a T."

"Suicide?" Mama said. "Jolene? My Jolene?"

"Well, I don't mean Jolene is going to commit suicide. I mean, there are markers, warning signs that—"

"Well, thank you very much. Scared me more than a little there."

"What I meant to say is she fits the profile for teenage suicide. Sometimes I'll look over at her in class and it seems to me she's got a frightened look on her face."

"Jolene? Oh, you've got her mixed up with someone else. Now I'm sure of it."

"Has she ever been to a psychiatrist or psychologist?"

"For being quiet? My heavens."

"For any reason."

"Never. My husband doesn't believe in that sort of thing."

"Well, she seems very depressed to me."

"About what?"

"That's what I thought you might tell me."

"Well, I can't imagine, I really can't."

The teacher didn't speak for a few moments. Mama just stared at her, waiting.

"Some children who've been abused act the way she does," the teacher finally said.

"What?"

"I don't mean any disrespect, but has there ever been anything— I mean, has your husband ever—"

Mama stood up so fast she jiggled the coffee table with her knee and some of Miss Thompson's tea flew out of the cup and onto the lemon-waxed coffee table. Mama didn't even seem to notice the little crystal drops spreading out on top of the shiny wood.

"What a nice visit we've had," Mama said, "and how considerate of you to take up your time thinking about Jolene. And on a Saturday, too."

It was all too mysterious for Lela. Mama's cheeks were flushed and her voice was all quivery. And the teacher looked like she wanted to cry.

"I hope you'll let me help," the teacher said. She stood up, too, and put her hand out toward Mama, tried to touch her arm, but Mama did a little something with her feet to get out of the way. It looked to Lela like she was going to begin to dance, the way she did sometimes when they were alone together in the kitchen. But she didn't dance. She folded her arms and shook her head and started to shiver.

"You don't understand," Mama said. "You just don't understand. How can I explain it to you? How can I talk to someone who wears jeans when they go calling on people? How can I let you know what it means when I say my husband and I are Christian people who fear God's wrath if we break his commandments, who don't smoke or drink or take the Lord's name in vain? Good people. Solid people. My heavens, you've got a nerve."

"I want to help," the teacher said.

"If I thought there was something wrong, something serious, I'd be running for help without you telling me a word about it," Mama said. "Why, I'm Jolene's mama. I'd never let anyone hurt her."

The teacher didn't say another word. She just left. Lela heard the front door close. Very softly. As though the teacher had held the knob in her hand and pulled it slowly toward her.

"What did Jolene do, Mama?" Lela said.

Mama didn't answer. She was standing in the middle of the room, her hands to her flowing hair, staring at Daddy's cat collection like she had never seen it before.

3

"YOU BETTER NOT move," Lela said, "or I'll pin one of these polka dots to your shoulder."

Lela was pinning while Mama measured Jolene's arms.

"You could at least say you like the material, Jolene," Mama said. "Lela and I spent half the morning looking for it in Cloth World. And we weren't looking at the sale material, either, were we, Lela?"

"We were looking for something pretty," Lela said.

Jolene looked like she had Mama's cold cream on her face, it was so white. Lela never remembered Jolene's skin being this white, like there wasn't any blood underneath it, like if you touched it, you'd leave a mark.

"It is pretty," Jolene said.

"All you need is some new clothes to perk you up," Mama said. "I get depressed when I haven't had anything new to wear in a long time."

Mama was so quick with her fingers, pulling out the pins Lela had put in crooked, tucking the seams in so tight on the shoulders that the sleeves stood up like cream puffs instead of collapsed balloons.

"Will you remember me in a year, Jolene?" Lela said.

"I don't feel like any jokes right now," Jolene said.

"This is a good one, sweetie," Mama said.

"I heard it at school," Lela said.

"If you have to," Jolene said.

"Will you?" said Lela.

"Will I what?" Jolene said.

"Remember me in a year."

"I suppose."

"Will you remember me in a month?"

"Okay."

"Will you remember me in a week?"

"Mama."

"Jolene honey, be patient. You were eight once."

Lela could feel the funniness of the joke creeping through her. She could hardly keep from laughing, it was so funny.

"Will you remember me in a month?"

"You said that," Jolene said.

"Okay. Will you remember me in a day?"

"Sure."

"Will you remember me in an hour?"

"All right."

"Knock, knock."

"Who's there?"

"Have you forgotten me already?"

Oh, it was so funny. Mama was smiling. Lela was laughing like she wasn't even the one who told the joke. Jolene still looked as sad as she did before.

"You'd tell me if it was something more than new clothes you needed to give you a lift, wouldn't you, Jolene honey?" Mama said when Lela was finished laughing.

"Sure, Mama," Jolene said. "I'd tell you."

Mama handed Lela the scissors. "Cut me a twenty-four-inch strip for the belt facing, honey bunny, would you."

"Did you do something bad, Jolene?" Lela said as she pulled the material over the kitchen table and began to cut.

"Not like that, sweetie," Mama said. She reached over Lela and guided her hand all the way down the cloth to the end. "It's got to be wide enough to cover. See how I did it?"

"Did you, Jolene?" Lela said. "Do something bad?"

"She's just an English teacher," Jolene said. "You don't have to listen to what she says."

"We didn't, honey, don't worry," Mama said. She was standing close to Jolene now, close enough to hug her. Lela liked it when Mama hugged Jolene. It made her feel good herself. Warm and safe. But she didn't hug her now. She just looked at her and shook her head.

"I like the dress, Mama," Jolene said. "I really do."

"It isn't the dress, honey," Mama said. "It's you. Are you sure you're all right?"

"She's just an English teacher, Mama."

"You'd tell me, wouldn't you?"

"Sure, Mama."

"You know Mama and Daddy love you, we want you to be happy."

Lela walked up close to the two of them, the strip of material trailing behind her on the floor.

"You did kiss that boy," Lela said. "I saw you."

"She spies on me, Mama. I wasn't kissing anyone."

"I know that. You think I don't know that, honey?"

"What does suicide mean?" Lela said.

Mama rescued the strip of material from the floor and slipped it around Jolene's waist. Then she gave Lela a look. Usually when Mama gave her that look, it came with, "You're too young, Lela. I'll explain it when you're grown a little." This time all she said was, "It's just a nasty word, honey bunny, nasty as can be."

Mama always took Lela with her when she went to the gray building on Main Street to pay the water bill. Mama would wait until Lela came home from school, and then they'd walk down Elm Street to Main together. Mama let Lela carry her purse, and they'd always stop on the way at the market next to the bank and have a soda. Mama always drank cherry soda, but Lela liked to try different flavors. When they finished their sodas, they'd walk two more blocks to the gray building and Mama would take money out of her wallet and give it to the lady. Mama's wallet was made of leather and had a picture of a dog on it. Daddy put a ten-dollar bill in the wallet and gave it to Mama for her birthday. Daddy had a whole box of wallets with dogs on them in the closet on the floor behind his shoes.

"You do look hot today," Mama said to the lady behind the counter in the gray building.

"There's no air in here, that's why," the lady said. There were people behind the counter sitting at desks. A few of them were typing on machines. One of them, a man, was sitting with his feet up on a chair, his head back and mouth open, like he was too hot to do anything else. A lady way in the back of the room was talking on the telephone, holding the receiver under her chin and fanning her face with a sheet of paper.

Mama was looking in her purse for something. She already had the wallet with the dog on it in her hand.

"I'm hot, too," Lela said.

"Does she want some water?" the lady asked.

"Oh, no, she's fine. She just had a Coke. We always walk over to pay the bill."

"On a day like this? You could mail it in, you know."

"Oh, I know that. My husband says the exercise does me good."

"I'll bet he'd mail it in."

"It's just this September hot spell. Never fails. The kids go back to school and the summer heat starts. Have you ever noticed how it does that?"

"Couldn't say. This is just my second year in California."

"Well, weather will be weather. Is Janet back there somewhere hiding?" Mama was still busy looking in her purse, holding her lips tucked in against her teeth the way she always did when she was looking for something. "I always pay my bill to Janet."

"She retired last month."

Mama looked up, surprised. "She did what?"

"Retired."

"Why, she didn't tell me that. She told me lots of things about lots of things, but she never told me that."

"They're going to some kind of punch cards or something and I'll be lucky to keep my job, too."

"Here it is." Mama laid an envelope on the counter and pulled a pink piece of paper out of it.

"I'm thirsty, Mama," Lela said, "and my foot itches."

"Oh, sweetie, I'll be through in a minute." Mama smiled at the lady. "She just doesn't have an ounce of patience in her. Has water gone up?"

"Not that I noticed," the lady said.

"My husband thinks the bill's too high."

"It's the heat."

"I told him that."

"You watering every day or every other?"

"Every other. Did Janet say where she was going?"

"She didn't say."

Mama smiled. Lela loved the way Mama smiled, as if she had a secret and she didn't know whether to tell it to you or not.

"Janet and I always talked when I paid my bill. You know how women do, gossip and things. Why, I know probably more about Janet than I do about my own sister. Marge and I aren't close. We used to be. I used to copy everything Marge did. If she wore her hair up, so did I. If she wore her socks stretched up to her knees, so did I. Funny, Janet not telling me she was leaving."

"The punch cards were coming, and it was either retire or get fired, so she retired. I can't say as the water rates went up in the last month. I could check, though, if you want me to."

"Mama . . ."

"Not now, honey bunny." Mama patted Lela's cheek.

"Your hand feels sticky, Mama."

"I must have got cherry soda on it, sweetie."

"We don't even have a Coke machine," the lady said.

"Do you have any children?" Mama said.

There was a gum machine near the door and Lela went over and started to play with the knobs. Sometimes pennies came out onto the metal cup when you fiddled with the knobs long enough.

"A son," the lady said.

"Oh." Mama looked disappointed.

"I wouldn't want a girl to raise. You know what I mean? When they get to a certain age, what do you do with them? Lock 'em up? Follow 'em around? Boys, it doesn't matter what they do."

"Exactly," Mama said. She moved closer to the counter, so her chest was pressing up against the wood. "I've got an older girl," Mama said. "Seventeen. This past year I don't think I even know who she is, she's so changed. I keep trying to think back when I was seventeen, and that mixes me up even more, because that was the year I met my husband, and I don't even remember what it felt like being seventeen before that. He took over and that was that. I was too young, you know. My father about had a fit. I just don't know. It's a funny thing. She doesn't say much, and I just don't know."

"I wouldn't have a girl to save my soul."

"You don't happen to know Janet's home phone, do you?"

"I think she went to Florida. I could find out."

"Florida? Oh. That'd be long distance. My husband doesn't like me talking long distance."

"I could check the rate sheet, see how much water your neighbor used, compare the two, see if there might not be a big difference, then we could send someone out to check the meter, maybe change the gauge. There are things we could do if you're not happy with the bill."

"Oh, no, that's all right," Mama said. "Donny—my husband—doesn't like people tramping through our yard more than they have to."

When they got through paying the bill, they didn't go straight home. Lela didn't recognize the streets here. They had trees with long branches that hung over the sidewalk, and it was cooler than it was at their house, where the trees stuck up in the air and the sidewalk was so hot you could feel it through your shoes.

"Does Jolene talk to you, honey bunny?" Mama said.

"Your nose is red, Mama," Lela said. "It looks funny."

"It's the sun, sweetie. I should have brought a hat. Does she?"

"She tells me to go away."

"I mean about, you know, anything, does she say anything? Think, sweetie."

"Well, she told me she went once to a girl's house and they had a horse there and she got to ride it, and the girl said she could have the horse, but Jolene didn't want it. I told her I'd take it, if she didn't want it, but she said no, it would make a mess in the yard, so I said—"

"No, sweetie, that isn't what I mean."

Mama's nose was really getting red. When they went to the beach and sat on the sand, Mama always wore a hat and a shirt and slacks. Daddy didn't like bathing suits. He only let Jolene and Lela wear shorts and a T-shirt to the beach. Or maybe a sunsuit. But it couldn't be too short in the legs. It had to cover almost to the knee, and the top had to come up almost to the neck. They even went in the water that way.

"Don't step on the cracks, Mama, or you'll break your back."

"I'll be careful." Mama started walking the way Lela was, looking down at her feet and putting them down right in the middle of each square of sidewalk. Mama sometimes came outside in the afternoons when she was through cleaning, and she and Lela would chalk up the sidewalk and play hopscotch together. Mama in her pretty housedress and closed-toe shoes hopping all around in front of the house always made Lela laugh, it was so funny. The neighbor lady once came out and asked Mama to come in for a cup of coffee, but Mama told her that Daddy said drinking coffee in the afternoons meant you had nothing more important to do. The neighbor lady never talked to Mama again. Mama always made sure to hose off the chalk marks on the sidewalk before Daddy got home.

Lela knew where they were now. Daddy sometimes drove them here to pick up Jolene on Fridays when they went out for pizza dinner. It was Jolene's high school. There was the big tower in front that made the school look like a castle in a picture book. The buildings around it didn't look like a castle, though. Long, low, straight buildings with plain doors and some grass and trees in front of them. Lela started to run up the grass, but Mama caught her by the hand and held her back.

"We'll just wait here, sweetie, till Jolene comes out," Mama said.

Mama found a spot under one of the trees for her and Lela to sit on while they waited for Jolene. Mama let Lela take off her shoes and socks because it was so hot. Mama even took off her shoes and was wiggling her stockinged feet in the air to cool them.

"The grass feels good, doesn't it, sweetie?" Mama said.

"It's making my knees green."

"Well, it's a pretty color green. Like limes. I could sure use some limeade now. You know why the grass does that? Because it's alive. Because it wants to. That green on your knees is grass breath."

Lela cupped her hands around a clump of grass and put her nose right in the middle of it. "I can't feel it breathing, Mama."

"You won't if you're expecting it to breathe air at you. Not everything in the world is like everything else, Lela. Some things do things one way, some things do things another way. I've even heard grass talk. Stones, too. And trees. At night sometimes when your daddy's away on a trip, I go out in the yard and I hear everything talking to me at once. Maybe not like you and I are talking now, but in a language all by its own. You just have to listen."

Lela pulled up a blade of grass and held it to her ear. "I can't hear it, Mama."

"Remember when we planted the carnations, and you broke off a stem and you said, Oh, Mama, the carnation's crying because I broke it? Remember that?"

"Uh-huh."

"What kind of sound did it make?"

"I don't remember."

"If you want to hear stones and grass talk, you have to kind of float, sweetie, let yourself go up, up in the sky. Then you'll hear things and see things too wonderful to imagine. You have to be real quiet and just kind of slip out of your body until you're kind of flying over everything. When you do that people get as small as ants, and that's when you can hear the grass talk. Floating's the secret. Sometimes I float when your daddy talks to me. Did you ever do that? Float when someone's talking to you?"

"I can float in the water, Mama. I can float for a year without turning around on my stomach. I can hold my breath, too, for a thousand years, a million years."

"Oh, sweetie, you are the darlingest girl."

A bell was ringing in the tower behind them and kids were starting to appear at the edges of the buildings. Mama got quiet now and kind of sat up on the grass and looked hard through the walkway to the center of the school.

"I see Jolene, Mama," Lela said.

"Where, honey?"

"There, with that boy."

Mama saw them now, too, and Lela thought she'd get mad at the way Jolene was hanging against the boy's chest, her stomach sticking into his. She thought she'd go running across the grass through all those kids and start pulling Jolene away, maybe even yell at her, although Lela couldn't remember Mama ever yelling at anyone.

"See her, Mama, see her?"

"Why, it's just a boy," Mama said, and started to smile. "Our Jolene's lovesick, honey, just all sick with love for that skinny boy, is what's wrong with her."

Mama didn't look mad at all. She looked happy, so happy there were tears rolling out the sides of her eyes. She took Lela by the hand and pulled her up off the grass.

"We can go on home now, sweetie," Mama said. "Don't have to tell Jolene we were here at all."

They always ate at Buddy's Pizza Parlor the night Daddy came home from a selling trip. They always sat at the same table with the same people. Fred Damico, Daddy's friend from high school, who managed the menswear section at Penney's and was building a boat in his backyard, and his wife, Eleanor, and their fourteen-year-old son, Mickey. And, of course, Mama, Jolene, and Lela. Pizza at Buddy's on Friday night. Sawdust on the floor. Cardboard signs with the pizza specials hanging on a clothesline overhead. And the smell. Like vinegar. But sweet. Like sausage. Only peppery. Lela's mouth would start watering about three o'clock on Friday afternoon just thinking about it.

"I want pepperoni and sausage and peppers and—"

"Wait your turn, Lela," Daddy said.

"But I'll forget."

"Listen to Daddy, sweetie," Mama said.

"I hate pepperoni," Mickey said. He was chubby, with a moon-pie face. Lela loved to watch him eat. He once ate two large-size pizzas all by himself before he had to go into the bathroom to throw up.

"Well, I don't," Lela said.

"How's that boat coming?" Daddy said.

"It's coming," Fred said, and his wife chimed in, "We're going to take it to Tahiti when it's finished. Want to come along?"

"What year?" Daddy said.

"Don't be mean, Donny," Eleanor said, and Lela put her hand to her mouth to hide her giggle. No one but Eleanor could talk to Daddy like that and get away with it. Daddy always said Fred missed his chance when he didn't take a belt to her the first time she opened her mouth.

"Jolene's English teacher came to see us while you were gone, Donny," Mama said.

"Mama," Jolene said. She looked like she had been hit in the stomach with a rock.

"Wha'd you say, Marilee?" Daddy said.

Lela tugged at Daddy's sleeve. The waiter had gotten to them and Daddy was telling him what he wanted. "Don't forget, Daddy," Lela said, "pepperoni and sausage and peppers."

"I've got it," Daddy said. He hadn't heard what Mama said.

Jolene looked calmer now. She was looking over at the next table where three boys had just sat down.

"Hey, Jolene," Lela said. "Is that him?"

Jolene didn't answer. She just turned her head back and started studying a dried piece of cheese on the table.

"Looks like your Jolene knows one of those kids over there," Eleanor said.

"She's getting pretty cute," Fred said. "I bet you've got your hands full already."

Daddy's head jerked up so hard Lela could feel the bench jump underneath her.

"I don't know anyone," Jolene said.

Lela tugged at Daddy's sleeve. "That's the boy, Daddy, the one I saw kissing Jolene. That's the one. And I saw her do it at school, too. Mama saw it, too. We saw them at school kissing."

"They weren't exactly kissing, Donny," Mama said. "I'd have stopped them if they were kissing."

"If all she's doing is kissing, I suppose that's all right," Eleanor said. "Look at her, she's blushing something fierce."

"I think she has a fever," Mama said. "She almost didn't come."

Jolene and Daddy were staring at each other now. The boy was coming over to the table. Jolene's neck was shaking with the weight of her head, trying to keep it from moving.

"What's going on here?" Daddy said, and looked right straight at the boy as he walked toward their table.

"Hi, Jolene," the boy said, and he rested his hand on Jolene's shoulder.

"Take your hand off her," Daddy said.

"Donny," Mama said.

"Shut up," Daddy said.

"Maybe it's not the boy I saw," Lela said, sorry she had told anyone about a boy or a kiss or anything else. Not when Jolene was looking like she was going to die right there in front of their eyes.

"What did I do?" the boy said, and put his hands up in the air like Daddy was aiming a gun at him.

"I'm glad I don't have any girls," Fred said.

The boy bent over Jolene and whispered something in her ear, then waved at everyone at the table and went back to his friends.

"Who is he?" Daddy said.

"Just look at her face," Eleanor said.

"That's enough, Eleanor," Fred said.

"I'm just kidding."

"He works at the gas station on PCH and Warner," Jolene said.

"I didn't ask where he worked," Daddy said, and the tone of his voice scared Lela.

"He's just a boy," Mama said.

"Did I ask you, Marilee?" Daddy said. "Did I ask you to open your damn mouth?"

"The party's getting rough," Eleanor said.

Daddy stood up and yanked Jolene by the arm. He pulled her past the table where the boys were sitting, toward the rest rooms in the back. The pizzas had come already and were sitting steaming on the table. No one was eating. Just watching Daddy standing over Jolene in the back of the restaurant, saying something to her that no one could hear.

"Donny believes in disciplining his girls," Mama said.

"Why is Daddy so mad?" Lela said.

"Eat your pizza before it gets cold, sweetie," Mama said.

"I've lost my appetite for at least the next week," Eleanor said.

"Don't be so dramatic," Fred said. "Donny's a little rough, but he knows what he's doing."

"Yeah?" Eleanor said.

"You can't be too careful with girls these days," Mama said, "with all the diseases you hear about."

"Oh, Marilee, you're the limit," Eleanor said.

Daddy and Jolene were back at the table. The three boys had gotten up and left without even placing their order.

No one said a word through dinner. Not even Eleanor, who kept her eyes moving in a circle from Mama to Daddy to Jolene, like she was watching some kind of movie or television show.

In the car on the way home, Jolene sat scrunched in a corner of the car, a napkin from Buddy's jammed against her mouth. Lela kept checking her face to see if she was crying. If she was, there certainly weren't any tears. Just before they pulled into the driveway, Mama said, "I hope it's all right with you, Donny, but I don't want to have Fred and Eleanor with us on pizza night anymore."

Daddy didn't even answer.

4

"I'M THIRSTY," LELA said. "How much longer?"

"Five minutes," Glenn said.

"You keep saying that," Lela said.

There was no air in this car. Not like there was in Daddy's, where cool air came in from secret holes in the upholstery and made you feel like you were sitting in the refrigerator. Glenn had all the windows open, but the air was still hot. And the seats were torn, too, not all smooth like in Daddy's car.

They were kissing again, Glenn's face turned away from the road, his lips all wet in the corner where Jolene's mouth was pressing. They were always kissing. And Glenn was always touching Jolene's chest. Squeezing. It looked like it must have hurt Jolene the way he squeezed her chest, but Jolene never complained, never yelled at him to stop like she did when Daddy did it.

"I'm thirsty," Lela said again.

Glenn pulled his lips away and looked at the road again. The back of his hair was wavy and shiny.

"Daddy puts oil on his hair," Lela said, and touched one of the waves with her fingertips.

"Leave my hair alone," Glenn said.

When Lela first saw Glenn's gray car waiting out in front of Meadowview School, blue and silver arrows painted on the fenders, curtains in the back window, Jolene hopping out in white shorts and a pink blouse, she thought they were there just to give her a ride home. All the kids crowded around, and that made Lela feel real special, like it was her birthday or something. Some of her friends sat on the fenders, but Glenn shooed them off, and then the principal came out and asked Jolene what she was doing there, and Jolene said, "This is my sister. I'm taking her to Bible class."

"Here's a Life Saver," Jolene said. She reached over the backseat and handed Lela the roll. "Suck on one."

They had left Huntington Beach at three-thirty, not even stopping at home to tell Mama they were going anywhere. Just leaving right from out in front of Meadowview School.

"I broke my ankle yesterday," Lela said. The Life Saver didn't help. It just made her mouth dryer.

"You what?" Glenn said.

"I told you, she tells stories," Jolene said.

"We can't take her with us. We can't. I ought to turn around right now and take her back."

"We can't take her back there, I told you that, Glenn."

"You can take me back," Lela said. "I won't tell Daddy anything. Promise. Cross my heart and hope to die."

"We can't take you back there," Jolene said, "and that's all there is to it."

"I didn't even get to tell Mama how I broke my ankle."

"You can write her a letter," Jolene said.

"I stepped in a hole and broke it. In two places."

"Well, I'm not driving all the way to Vegas listening to that crybaby in the backseat," Glenn said.

"I'm not a crybaby," Lela said. "I hopped all the way to school on my ankle. Did I show you the blue mark on my foot, Jolene?"

"I saw it," Jolene said. "It's just a bruise."

"I suppose we could stop in Needles," Glenn said, "rent a room, stay over. We don't have to drive straight through. Someplace with a swimming pool where we can cool off a little."

"It makes me nervous, stopping before we get there," Jolene said.

"A swimming pool?" Lela said. "I want to go in a swimming pool, Jolene."

"When do you think they'll notice you're both gone?" Glenn said.

"I told Mama I was taking Lela to Bible class," Jolene said. "We usually get out about four-thirty. Mama will worry, but she won't do anything. Daddy's working in town this week, so he'll be home about seven. Then they'll know."

"Daddy lets me blow his hair with the dryer," Lela said. "I hold it up with one hand and move it around over his head till all the hair turns dry. Then he puts the oil on and wets it all over again."

"Maybe we'd better stop in Needles," Jolene said.

———————————

The place they stopped at had a big picture of a cactus painted around the front door. While Jolene and Lela waited in the car, Glenn went inside. Walked right through the center of the cactus. It looked to Lela like he was being swallowed up by some huge green monster.

"I don't have a bathing suit," Lela said.

"You can swim in your underwear," Jolene said. "Nobody cares. Look, there's not even anyone here. I don't think there are more than fifty people in the whole town of Needles, anyway. Why should they care about some little girl swimming in a swimming pool in her underwear?"

"Got it," Glenn said. He tossed the key to Jolene.

"What'd they say?" Jolene said as they walked across the gravel to the squat row of green cabins sitting out in the hot sun.

"They said they hoped I enjoyed my stay with my sisters."

"Oh, you," Jolene said, and laughed. "You told them I was your sister?"

Lela skipped up next to Jolene and hugged her around the waist.

"I like when you laugh," she said.

"Time to go in," Jolene said. She and Glenn were on rusty lounge chairs next to the pool, eating candy bars and drinking Cokes from the machine in the parking lot. The rest of the lounge chairs were piled up against the sign that said "No Lifeguard on Duty."

"Just a little bit more," Lela said. She liked the sound of her voice booming out in the dark, sounding like it belonged to someone else.

"Keep your voice down," Glenn said. "They'll kick us out of here if you keep whooping and yelling like a wild Indian."

"I can hold my breath, Jolene," Lela said, trying to whisper loudly enough for Jolene to hear. "Watch." She sat right down next to the bottom step, took a deep breath, and stuck her head under the water. She hoped Jolene was watching. She could feel the water plugging her nose and ears and pulling at her eyelashes. And it hurt her chest, holding all that air in, not letting any out. A little came out anyway, and she opened her eyes and looked at the bubbles it made, all green and shiny in the flickery glare of the pool's bottom light. Maybe she'd die down here, not breathing. Just thinking that made her pop her head up out of the water.

"It's nine o'clock," Jolene said. "I think you're turning into a prune, honey."

"Did you see me?" Lela said.

"You're a wonder."

"A real Olympic swimmer," Glenn said.

Jolene leaned back in the chair again. "Look at those stars," she said.

Lela sat down on the step again. It was still hot out, almost as hot as it had been in the car, but the water felt good. Like a cool cloth on her skin. But slippery. Not a rough cloth, like a washcloth, or anything like that. Lela splashed more quietly now. Maybe if she didn't make so much noise, Jolene wouldn't notice the time, would forget to call her out of the water, would just sit there all night next to Glenn and let Lela soak in that water till she turned into a fish.

There were two beds in the room, and it was just like they were on a vacation, like the time Daddy took them to Yosemite and they all slept in the same room, Daddy and Mama in one bed and Jolene and Lela in the other one.

"I don't have my pajamas," Lela said. She was on her stomach on the bed, watching a cartoon on television.

"You don't need pajamas," Jolene said. "You can sleep in your skirt and blouse. You swam in your underwear, didn't you?"

"You've got to learn to be flexible," Glenn said.

"What's that?" Lela said.

"You don't know what flexible means?"

"She's just a little girl, Glenn," Jolene said.

She and Glenn were sitting on the floor, pouring dried weeds from a plastic bag onto little squares of white paper. "Damn stuff's got seeds as big as boulders in it," Glenn said.

"Do you roll it this way, Glenn?" Jolene said.

"I roll pie crust for Mama," Lela said. She jumped off the bed and kneeled down where Jolene was trying to keep the dried stuffing from falling out of the bits of white paper. "Let me do it, too."

"She thinks it's pie crust, Jolene," Glenn said.

"Just because you know everything, Glenn," Jolene said. "She's just a little girl."

"I'm not," Lela said. "I'm almost nine. In two months. Let me do it, too, Jolene."

"Don't let her touch that, Jolene," Glenn said.

"She can't hurt it," Jolene said.

"I can do it," Lela said.

Glenn pointed to the bed. "Up. Get up there. You're not touching anything."

"You don't have to be rough with her," Jolene said when Lela was back on the bed. "You can talk nice to her. She's really a good little kid. Glenn loves you, Lela honey."

"I don't care," Lela said without turning around. She kept her chin in her hands and her face toward the television, but she felt like any minute she was going to cry.

"I didn't mean anything," Glenn said. "I'm sorry, Lela."

He didn't sound like he was sorry, but his saying he was made Lela feel better.

"Now take a deep drag and hold it," Glenn said, and the smell of something burning made Lela turn and look again.

"Oh, Jolene, Daddy's going to be mad if you smoke that cigarette."

"Daddy's not going to know," Jolene said.

"I want to smoke one, too."

"It's not for you, Lela," Jolene said. "It's for grown-ups."

"You're not a grown-up."

"I nearly am."

Jolene turned the radio on but let Lela keep on watching the cartoon with the sound off. Jolene was giggling now, and the room smelled funnier and funnier.

"There's a liquor store down the street," Glenn said. "I need something to eat. Are you hungry, Jolene?"

"Umm, yes, I'm really hungry."

"So am I," Lela said.

"Bring me back a box of cookies and some potato chips," Jolene said. "And bring Lela another Pepsi."

"And a sugar doughnut," Lela said. Jolene was flat on her back on the floor with her eyes closed.

"What if they don't have sugar doughnuts?" Glenn said.

"I don't care," Lela said.

"I'll get you some beef jerky," Glenn said.

"I don't like beef jerky," Lela said. "Hershey, with nuts."

Glenn brought back a whole bag full of stuff. Cookies and cokes and potato chips and candy bars.

"I've never been so hungry in all my life," Jolene said. She was tearing at a bag of potato chips with her teeth.

"Guy at the liquor store said you get your license at the courthouse on Third Street in Vegas," Glenn said. "Open all night till Sunday. Don't matter when we get there."

When the cartoons were over, there was a movie with a blond girl in it. She was playing twins and had a flat nose and was always getting into trouble. It was a good one and it made Lela laugh in a few places.

But it made her sleepy, too, all that riding all afternoon with no air in the car.

Glenn was on the floor, his head in Jolene's lap. She had her hands down the front of his pants.

"I'm sleepy," Lela said. The movie wasn't over yet, but she couldn't keep her eyes open.

"Then go to sleep," Jolene said. Lela closed her eyes. Jolene had the radio on again, low this time, and she and Glenn were rolling around on the floor. His pants were down below his hips, and Jolene's white shorts were off, and Lela didn't want to look anymore.

Lela didn't think Glenn and Jolene went to bed at all. When she woke up they were smoking some more of the funny-smelling cigarettes.

"I'm hungry," Lela said.

"You're always something," Glenn said.

"I want to go in the swimming pool again, Jolene," Lela said.

"Not now, honey," Jolene said. She had a teeny piece of cigarette pinched in her fingers and was taking quick little puffs of it and then holding her breath before she let out the smoke.

"You're getting real good at that, Jolene," Glenn said.

"It makes me feel good. I'm not afraid of Daddy coming after me anymore."

"Maybe we could give him some marijuana and he'll just go away and leave us alone," Glenn said, and Jolene started giggling again.

"I think we should go home, Jolene, don't you?" Lela said. It was frightening her the way Jolene was acting.

"You can't ever go home," Jolene said.

"For real? For real, Jolene?"

"You're scaring the kid to death," Glenn said.

"I'm just kidding, honey," Jolene said.

5

"JOLENE, JOLENE, LOOK, look," Lela cried.

All the streets were lights. And the buildings. And the sky. The whole place was full of lights. Green and yellow, red and purple, orange and blue. Every color Lela had ever seen. Big postcards of colored lights blinking on and off, every one of them different, all twinkling and flashing, spelling names, drawing pictures.

"I've never seen anything like this in my life," Jolene said.

"I've been to Vegas lots of times," Glenn said. "It's nothing special."

"You've been to so many places, I can't even count them."

"I get around."

Lela rolled the car window down and held her hands out, tried to catch all that brightness. It was like all those lights were breathing in the hot night, their breath making it hotter, trying to fool her into thinking it was daytime, calling to her, every one of them saying, See me, look at me, aren't I pretty, aren't I wonderful.

"Can we stay here, Jolene?" Lela said. "I want to stay here."

"She thinks she's in Disneyland," Glenn said.

"She's never been to Disneyland," Jolene said.

"I don't believe it. Never been to Disneyland?"

"Daddy doesn't believe in it."

"Someone ought to shoot him," Glenn said.

"I thought about it," Jolene said.

It was a big building with a lot of people walking around with papers in their hands. A lot of people laughing and talking. Some of them were carrying flowers and were all dressed up like they were going to a party. Jolene was still in the same white shorts, and Glenn was still in jeans and a Levi's jacket. They went to a door that said

"Marriage Licenses," and Jolene put on some lipstick before Glenn opened it.

"You look beautiful," he said.

There was a line inside, and they had to give their name and wait their turn.

"Is there a swimming pool where we're going?" Lela said.

"There are more pools than people in this town," Glenn said, and right after he said it the woman called his name.

"Driver's license," the woman said. She was wearing a ring on every finger, and her sweater had a snake-looking animal on the front and big square shoulders that seemed to be pulling her right up out of her chair.

"She has a lizard on her sweater, Jolene," Lela said.

"It's a dragon," the woman said. "Who'd want a lizard on their sweater?"

"My sister just likes to talk," Jolene said.

"Here it is," Glenn said, and handed the woman his license.

"Have anything else?"

"My draft card."

"Trying to get married before they send you to Vietnam, are you?"

"Nope. I'll just take Jolene with me if I go to Vietnam."

The woman was pointing at Jolene now. "Identification?"

"She doesn't have a draft card," Glenn said.

"Does she have a driver's license, smart guy?"

Glenn put out his hand to Jolene. "Come on, come on, driver's license."

"I don't have it."

"What do you mean, you don't have it?" Glenn turned sideways a little bit and made his voice low. "The one I got you, the ID I got you, that one."

"I don't have it. I forgot."

"You what?"

"I forgot."

"How could you forget?" His voice was loud now, and everyone in the place was looking at him and Jolene.

"The law in Vegas is," the woman said, "those between the ages of sixteen and eighteen need a parent or guardian present to consent in person, or if not present, must consent by signed, notarized affidavit with date of birth of minor in it. No birth certificate or parental affidavit, no marriage license. That's the law."

"She's eighteen," Glenn said. "Doesn't she look eighteen?"

"Birth certificate?"

"No. I don't even know where it is," Jolene said.

"You'll need a parent or guardian, then."

"We're eloping," Glenn said. "They don't know."

"Then I guess that means you don't have an affidavit from them, either."

"Shit," Glenn said.

They were back now at the row of plastic chairs standing there staring at the bare wall like there was something written there.

"You're taking all day, and I have nothing to do," Lela said. "I want to go home."

"You can't," Jolene said.

"You knew they were going to ask you for proof," Glenn said, and he gave Jolene a dirty look. "I told you that. I said, 'Jolene, don't forget to put that fake ID I got you in your purse.' 'Oh, sure, honey,' you said, 'I won't forget.' Like shit you didn't. What did you think we were doing, anyway, going for a joy ride, going on a picnic?"

"Are we going on a picnic?" Lela said.

"Not now, honey," Jolene said. She looked all sweaty and tired, and there were all kinds of dirt spots on her white shorts.

"I don't believe it," Glenn said. "You heard me tell you to bring your ID. I just don't believe you didn't do it."

"Well, I didn't."

"I have a blister on my foot, Jolene," Lela said. She took off her shoe and sock and examined the little white pearl of skin on the back of her ankle. Jolene knelt down and took Lela's bare foot in her hands.

"Poor baby," she said.

"I'm not a baby," Lela said.

Jolene was acting like a grown-up, staying up as late as she wanted, talking to Lela like she was her mother, not her sister. Calling her "honey" and "baby." She'd even cut Lela's pancakes in the restaurant that morning, and poured the syrup, and made sure she drank her milk.

"You kids trying to get married?" a man said. He just walked up like he knew them.

"She doesn't have any ID," Glenn said.

"I've got driver's licenses, but those take time," the man said. His hair wasn't thick and curly like Glenn's and Daddy's. It was all empty on top, and the skin where the hair wasn't had big brown spots, like pennies, only they weren't that shiny.

"You got time?" the man said.

"We want to get married today," Jolene said. "It's got to be today."

"She needs a paper saying her folks consent," Glenn said.

"That's easy," the man said. He tickled Lela's chin with two fingers and she pulled her head away. Everybody always wanted to tickle her chin. It made her mad sometimes the way they thought they could just come up and touch her like that.

"How much will it cost?" Glenn said. They were almost out of the courthouse and on the sidewalk when he asked it.

"Put your shoe and sock on," Jolene said.

"It hurts to walk on it," Lela said.

"Fifty bucks," the man said. "Can you carry her?"

"I press two fifty," Glenn said. "I can carry a puny kid, I guess."

The man led them down the street from the courthouse, Glenn carrying Lela, and Jolene walking like she didn't feel too well, her shoulders forward and a sweater wrapped around her even though it was still hot out.

"Well, here it is," the man said.

They went into a small house that smelled of onions cooking. The smell made Lela cry.

"I want to go home."

"You can't go home, baby," Jolene said, and smoothed Lela's hair with her hand.

The man's wife gave Lela a cookie and let her sit in the kitchen on a stool at the counter while she ate it. The woman was cooking at the stove and watching a program in a language Lela had never heard before. Jolene and Glenn went into another room with the man, and pretty soon Lela could hear a typewriter click-clacking somewhere.

"Mama fries onions, too," Lela said. "She owns a restaurant, one of those big restaurants with flowers everywhere, and she lets me come and help her cook. Daddy says she's the best cook. We eat there every night. Mama plays the organ while we eat."

The woman was looking at her like she couldn't hear. Lela smiled at her, and the woman smiled back and gave her another cookie.

"Lela been telling you stories?" Jolene said when she and Glenn and the man came back into the kitchen.

"She doesn't speak English," the man said.

Glenn looked happy again and Jolene was smiling.

"Well, I'm sure glad that's taken care of," Glenn said.

"I told you it was easy," the man said.

Glenn picked Lela up and slung her over his shoulder like she was a sack, then tickled her sides till she laughed out loud.

"Did you miss us?" Jolene said, and kissed her cheek.

"Stop, Glenn, stop," Lela said, and she was laughing so much she could hardly breathe.

"She's sure a good-natured girl," the man said.

———————

"Come on, seven. Seven, come on."

Glenn was leaning nearly his whole body onto the green table, shouting and calling out numbers like he was the only one there, even though the place was full of people.

"You'll have to move the kid back farther," one of the men standing behind the table said. "Behind that carpet, on the sidewalk, kid, or the cops'll get you. You want to go to jail?"

Lela looked down at her shoes. They were nearly on the carpet, but she could still see cement in front of the toes of her loafers.

"I could play that game, too," Lela called out to the man. "Want to see?"

"Lela, honey, we'll be right there," Jolene said. She was standing next to Glenn, holding on to his sleeve like she was trying to keep him from crawling right on top of the table.

The whole place smelled the same as when Daddy lit the fireplace for the first time at Thanksgiving and the house filled up with smoke. Mama had to take the curtains down and wash and iron them, they were so black. And Daddy made her leave the windows open for a whole week just to get the smell out.

Glenn was shouting again. It sounded like, "Do it the hard way," or something like that. This whole street was full of places that looked just like this one, all lit up on the outside and dark and full of smoke once you stepped past the carpet line, with people walking around or sitting on high stools at curved tables or dropping coins onto squares in front of spinning wheels. Lela wondered if she could ask to go to the bathroom in the dark back of the place and then run back and stand close to Jolene so no one could see her. It was scary standing out here on the sidewalk, not knowing what Glenn and Jolene were doing or how long it was going to take them to do it.

"Yahoo!" Glenn shrieked.

"Oh, honey, honey," Jolene said, and she grabbed hold of Glenn's hand, and they skipped out onto the sidewalk where Lela was standing.

"Four thousand dollars!" Jolene cried out. "Glenn just won four thousand dollars, honey." Oh, she looked so happy. She was nearly dancing with happiness.

"Let me go back for just one more," Glenn said, and tried to pull himself back into the smoke.

"Oh, no, you don't," Jolene said.

———————————

There were stores in the hotel, lots of them, and Jolene picked one that had a pink dress in the window.

"That's the one I want, Glenn, that one," Jolene said.

They went inside, and the lady made Jolene try on a whole bunch of dresses, even though it was the pink one in the window she said she wanted.

"I'll buy you all the dresses in the place, if you want," Glenn said. "That's how much I love my Jolene."

"You can buy whatever you want," the lady said, "I won't stop you. I'll let you buy the store, if you want."

"Glenn has a job," Jolene said. "In a gas station in Huntington Beach. We're getting married today. He just won four thousand dollars and we're getting married."

"I could buy the store if I felt like it," Glenn said.

The woman went out of the room and came back with an armful of dresses.

"Are we going to sleep here tonight?" Lela said. There weren't any beds in here where Jolene was trying on the dresses, but there was a couch and lots of ashtrays and mirrors and even a platform for Jolene to stand on while she put on one dress after another.

"We're going to sleep upstairs," Jolene said.

"In one of the best rooms in the hotel, too," Glenn said. "There's nothing I wouldn't do for my two best girls."

———————————

The place they went for Jolene and Glenn to get married looked like a church to Lela. It had big pots of flowers that made Glenn start sneezing the minute they walked in. And there were tall stained-glass windows across the whole back wall next to the sign that said "Rest Rooms." There was no altar, though, like in Mama's church, just a desk and a cash register in front of the rows of folding chairs. And there was no organ, just a record player playing a song Lela had heard before but didn't know the words to.

"I miss Mama," Lela said.

"Oh, sweetie, of course you do," Jolene said, and she leaned down and gave Lela a big kiss.

"You're trying to act like Mama," Lela said. "But you aren't."

"She's got you there," Glenn said.

The woman at the cash register waited till Glenn stopped sneezing and blew his nose, then she looked at the papers he showed her, took his money, and rang a little bell, and a man in a brown suit came out of a door near the rest rooms sign and lined Jolene and Glenn up in front of the stained-glass windows.

"Marriage is a sacred institution," the man said.

"Can you make it quick?" Glenn said. "The flowers are killing me."

Lela stood behind Jolene. Everything about Jolene was turning strange. She was like someone else, someone Lela had never met before. She had the pink dress on and was wearing white high-heeled shoes and looked like someone Lela would have to listen to from now on. She looked even more grown-up than Mama.

"I now pronounce you husband and wife. Kiss the bride."

Glenn sneezed and blew his nose again and then kissed Jolene real long on the mouth. When they were through kissing, Jolene turned around, then bent down and hugged Lela.

"I'm married now, Lela. What do you think of that?"

"I think Daddy's going to be mad," Lela said.

———————————

There were two big rooms and a door in between. Glenn and Jolene were by themselves in the other room, and the television was so loud in there Lela could even hear it past the door in her room and into the bathroom. Even when she turned the water on in the bathtub, she could still hear their television.

Jolene had bought them toothbrushes and toothpaste in the store in the lobby. And a sweatshirt for Lela that said "I Love Las Vegas." Lela took off her skirt and blouse and hung them over the towel rack. The blouse looked a little dirty, but it was the underwear, just lying in a heap on the floor, that made her sick. It smelled of chlorine from the pool in Needles. She dropped the underwear into the bathtub, then climbed in after it and sat down.

It was lonely in the bathtub. She kept wishing Jolene would come in and wash her back or tell her what to do with her underwear when she took it out of the water. It was funny how it wasn't as much fun in a bathtub as it was in a swimming pool. Why was that? It was all water. Maybe because this was hot water, and the water in the swimming pool was cold. She turned on the cold-water faucet and let it run till she began to shiver. Maybe it was because there was so much water in a swimming pool and so little in the bathtub.

The television went off in the other room. She could hear a door opening and closing, and then Jolene stuck her head into the bathroom.

"Will you wash my back?" Lela said. "Mama always washes my back."

Jolene dropped to her knees beside the tub. She looked like she wanted to cry.

"Oh, honey, of course I'll wash your back."

Jolene cuddled in the big bed with Lela, and they watched all the programs Lela liked to watch. Jolene was being especially nice, letting Lela skip over the channels with the love stuff on it. Glenn was still downstairs. He'd gone to buy them a hamburger and fries.

"I saw this one before," Lela said. "The dog finds his way home. You'll see. It's really good."

"You like being with me and Glenn, don't you, honey?" Jolene said.

"It's all right," Lela said. "Did you see this one before?"

"I can't remember."

"We can watch what you want."

"Glenn's going to get us an apartment," Jolene said. "Near the beach. One with two bedrooms, so you can have one all to yourself. You won't have to share a room with me."

"Where will you be?"

"In the other room with Glenn. That's what being married is, you know, sleeping together in the same bed in the same bedroom."

"Like Mama and Daddy."

Jolene's cheek began to twitch, and she put a finger where the twitch was and held it there for a second till it stopped.

"We were going to get a place on Main Street near the mortuary before Glenn won all that money," she said.

"That's where they put the dead people," Lela said. "Mama told me that."

"But now we can get a better place, a bigger one, one right on the beach. Well, across PCH, anyway. You just have to watch out for cars, and cross over, and then there you are with your feet in the sand. Not even the people in the Harbour can get that close to the ocean. They've got to go down Warner in a car and park in the state lot. All we're going to do is walk across the street, and there we'll be with our feet in the water."

"How come there's no cartoons?" Lela said, flipping the channels.

"Glenn'll drive you to school every day, and you'll have any color curtains you want in your room. What color do you want your curtains, honey?"

"Ginny James has a four-poster bed," Lela said, "with flowers on the spread that match the curtains. Blue ones with red centers."

"We'll find out where Ginny James's mother bought them, and we'll get the same kind for you."

"Her mother made them."

"I'll find out where she bought the material, and I'll make some, too. You're going to be so happy with us, Lela."

"Glenn doesn't want me," Lela said. "And I'll miss Mama and Daddy."

"Glenn does too want you. He told me over and over that he's so happy you're going to be with us, he just doesn't know what to do about it, he's so happy. And Mama can come over and see you anytime she wants."

Lela looked up at her. "Can Daddy come, too?"

"Well, honey, I don't think Daddy's going to want to."

"Then I don't know if I want to, either."

"There's no wanting about it. You're going to, and that's the end of it."

"You're not my boss," Lela said.

There was a cooking show on, and Lela's neck started to hurt, she was staring so hard at the pot the lady was mixing the white sauce in. Jolene was trying to hug her, but she kept her neck stiff so she couldn't get a good hold on her. Jolene finally just rolled over on the other side of the bed. Lela knew she was looking up at the ceiling. Jolene always was lying in her bed looking up at the ceiling. It wouldn't be Jolene if she didn't do that. Even getting married couldn't change the way Jolene really was.

6

"WHAT THE HELL'S going on here?" Glenn's daddy said. He had come in from the garage when Glenn's mama shrieked.

"They're married, Jim," Glenn's mama said. "They went to Vegas and got married."

"What the hell—"

Lela had seen Glenn's daddy in church. He looked different now, with sawdust in his hair and big wet circles under his arms. She ran over to him and leaned against his knee.

"I broke my foot once," Lela said. "I had to hop to school on one foot."

"Who did what?" Glenn's daddy said. Glenn's daddy's knee was shaking, and the tools hanging from the little white apron around his waist banged against the top of Lela's head.

"Your son and Jolene Benoit got married. Are you turning deaf in your old age?"

"Got what?"

"Married. M-a-r-r-i-e-d."

Lela tried to hold Glenn's daddy's knee in one place the way she did when Daddy got mad at Mama. She had hold of him real tight, but he pried her fingers off like he was peeling a banana. Then he went at Glenn with the hammer he was holding in his hand.

"You rotten punk!"

"Watch out!" Glenn's mama hollered, and she tried to grab the hammer, but Glenn's daddy's arm was like the door in Von's market: once it saw you standing in front of it, it just opened, and there wasn't anything you could do to stop it. Bam! Right into the side of Glenn's face.

"Jeez, Pa!" Glenn said.

Lela watched the hole open up in Glenn's cheek. It started small, with foamy stuff at the edges, and then blood started pouring out.

Jolene was crying now, real loud. Glenn's mama was wailing, too. Glenn just looked surprised, like he never expected his daddy to do a thing like that.

"You didn't have to hit him in the face," Glenn's mama said.

"I'll hit him where I want to hit him."

Glenn's daddy had a round stomach that reminded Lela of Santa Claus, only his hair wasn't white, it was brown, and he had so many freckles on his face, he looked like someone had just dug him out of a sandbox.

"Where did you think you were going to live?" Glenn's daddy said.

Glenn was bleeding all over the gray carpet. A little brown dog had come into the house with Glenn's daddy and was sniffing at the blood. Had its face right down in it, licking it.

"Oh, look what he's doing, yuck," Lela said.

"You don't think," Glenn's daddy said. "That's what's the matter with you. You just don't think. You think with your dick, that's what you think with."

"I had an apartment," Glenn said.

Lela sat down on the carpet and watched the dog lick at the blood. "What's the doggie's name?" she said.

"You take these two home, and you get back here in an hour," Glenn's daddy said.

"We're married," Glenn said. "I told you, we're married. I had an apartment picked out. Everything was set."

"He lost all our money," Jolene said. Lela could tell she was trying hard to stop crying by the way she kept rubbing her little fingers together. She always did that when she was trying not to cry. "I can't go home. I can't go home."

"She's underage, you stupid idiot," Glenn's daddy said.

Glenn didn't look at his daddy's face, just kept his hands stiff at his sides while a string of blood ran down his neck and onto the carpet.

"My father will kill me if I go back there," Jolene said. "You don't know 'im. You just don't know 'im."

"Your father isn't going to kill you," Glenn's mama said. She was fat, fatter than even the woman who had the doughnut shop on the pier, where Daddy would take Lela sometimes on Saturday afternoons. Lela liked the sugar doughnuts. She didn't like the dough inside, just the sugar, and Daddy would laugh at her when she licked the doughnut instead of eating it, and he didn't get mad at her when she gave the shiny, sugarless doughnut piece by piece to the pigeons.

"The doggie's fur is getting bloody," Lela said. "You're going to have a red doggie if you don't watch out."

"Her father will kill her," Glenn said, "and that's no lie. You better listen to what she's saying. She knows him better than anyone."

"That's how they dye the doggies in the circus, you know," Lela said. "They bleed over them, and people think they were born that way, all red. I saw them do it."

Glenn's daddy walked past Glenn's mama into the kitchen and sat down at the chrome-trimmed table and stared at Jolene, who was crying so hard now she couldn't even talk.

"My son's a screw-up," Glenn's daddy said. "And I don't know what all this is about your father."

"She does look awful scared," Glenn's mother said. She had a small rag in her hand and was wiping her nose and face and eyes.

"Her dad does things to her," Glenn said. "He's been doing them since she was little."

"What kind of talk is that?" Glenn's mama said. She tossed the rag onto the bloody spot in front of Glenn and then went into the kitchen and brought back a paper towel for Glenn's face and some Kleenex for Jolene.

"They cut a hole in someone's skin and hold the doggie up to it, and then just bleed right onto it," Lela said. "If I had a doggie, I'd dye him to match the curtains in my bedroom."

Glenn's mama then went and got a spray bottle from under the sink. It had blue water in it.

"Mama has forty-five of those spray bottles in the garage," Lela said. "She gets them free for shopping at Von's. Every time she goes to the store, they give her another free spray bottle. You can clean the toilet and kill bugs with it. I drank a whole bottle once with a hot dog. It didn't even hurt me."

Glenn's mama got down on her knees and started spraying away at the spot and rubbing at it with the rag.

"He goes in her bedroom at night," Glenn said, "gets right in the bed with her and Lela, and while Lela's asleep, he—"

Lela started humming to herself to keep Glenn's voice out of her ears. Glenn's mama stopped spraying.

"I don't want to hear that talk in my house," Glenn's daddy said. He looked like he wouldn't have believed Glenn if Glenn said the house was on fire.

"Let them stay here," Glenn said. "I promise I'll work and save and pay you back, and we'll move out as quick as we can."

"Why didn't you tell someone?" Glenn's mama said. She put her hand on Glenn's daddy's arm and pulled herself up off the floor. She had red spots all around the hem of her dress.

"Who?" Jolene said. "Who was I going to tell?"

"I don't know who." Glenn's mama looked around the room, as though she thought there might be people standing in the corners waiting for Jolene to tell them about Daddy. "My God, how do I know who?" she said, and waved the rag with Glenn's blood, her tears, and the blue carpet cleaner on it toward the ceiling. "Someone. You should have told someone. Your mother. She's the one you should have told."

"Mama's afraid," Jolene said.

"That's the craziest. She's your mama."

"Daddy does whatever he wants."

"I tell Mama everything," Lela said. "I told her about the mouse that got loose in the cafeteria, and everyone was running around, and I saw this black tail, and I ran after it, and I caught it."

"I don't believe any of it," Glenn's daddy said.

"It's a true story," Lela said.

"If I told Mama, then what?" Jolene said. "I don't want to think about what Daddy'd do to Mama if she told him she knew, if she told him to stop."

Glenn's mama's face was turning red, redder than the blood on the carpet that the brown dog was licking at.

"Do you understand what I mean?" Jolene said. "Do you?"

Glenn's mama was studying the carpet now, as if something very interesting were going to happen there. "I don't know what to think."

"It was a big mouse, too," Lela said. "As big as a dog. Bigger than your dog here. Really."

"I've hardly slept this whole past year, wanting to tell Mama about Daddy and afraid of what Daddy'd do to her if I did," Jolene said.

"I'll make some coffee," Glenn's mama said.

"Is that all you've got to say about it?" Glenn said.

"You mind your mouth with your mother," Glenn's daddy said.

"I've got some chocolate cake left over," Glenn's mama said.

"I want some chocolate cake," Lela said.

"I'm not hungry," Glenn said.

"When did you eat last?" his mama said.

"At three."

"I could fix you all sandwiches. That's all I've got in the house. I've got to go to the store. Sandwiches is all I can fix you. My Lord, all I've got is sandwiches. What do you want from me? What in the world do you expect me to say?''

"Chocolate cake's my favorite cake," Lela said. Jolene was shaking the way she did when she had the flu. Lela went and put her arm around her waist and hugged her as hard as she could.

"She's got chocolate cake, Jolene."

"I heard her, honey," Jolene said.

Glenn's mama was looking at Glenn's daddy now, looking at him the way a dog does when he wants you to give him a piece of what you're eating. "They *are* married, Jim," she said.

"What does *that* mean?"

"It means they're married. Let them stay till we find out what's going on."

"Not the little kid. First thing you know, we'll be arrested for kidnapping. I know how that goes. You try to do a good deed, they put you in jail for it."

"I'll be nine in two months," Lela said.

"Oh, no, I'm not saying we should keep the little one," Glenn's mama said. "Marilee would die if we tried to keep her little girl. She's her everything. She'd be over here with the police in two minutes if we try and keep the little girl."

Glenn's mama was acting different now. Quieter. Her voice not as loud. She looked as if she were still thinking over what Jolene had said. "Glenn needs an X-ray," she said. "You might have broke his jaw."

"I didn't feel any bones crack," Glenn's daddy said.

"I'll pay you for everything we eat when I save up some," Glenn said.

Glenn's mama gave his daddy a little slap on the arm with the bloody towel. "Your temper's going to be the death of us," she said.

Jolene waited in the car while Glenn walked Lela up to the porch. The light was on. Daddy's car was in the driveway. Lela had a funny feeling in her stomach, like she should run away and hide. But there was Mama now at the open door, bending down, reaching toward her, starting to kiss her. And then Daddy was right behind her, and he pushed her out of the way.

"Where's Jolene?" he said.

"We're married, Mr. Benoit," Glenn said. "I'm just bringing Lela home. We were going to keep her, but my folks said we couldn't. But

Jolene and I are married now, and you can't do anything about it, and you can't ever see her again. Ever."

"Jolene!" Daddy yelled in the direction of Glenn's car, which was parked at the curb in front of the house, the lights still on and the motor running.

"Let them go," Mama said. "Please, Donny, let them go."

Daddy pushed past Glenn, started running down the walk to the curb. Glenn picked Lela up and ran after him.

"What are you doing with that kid?" Daddy said as Glenn pushed Lela into the backseat again and opened the front door and hopped in behind the wheel.

"You're too crazy to leave her here," Glenn said.

Daddy ran around to the other side of the car where Jolene was sitting. He started pulling on the door handle and yelling. Then he started banging on the window. Jolene was whimpering just like a baby.

"Don't let him get me, Glennie, don't."

"He can go to hell before he gets either one of you," Glenn said. He pushed the gear stick down, and the car bounced away from the curb. Lela got on her knees on the seat and looked out the back window. She could see Daddy's car in the driveway, and the lights were on now, and it was coming after them.

Mama always said a cul-de-sac was the safest place to raise children. There wouldn't be any cars racing through to some intersection, no boys in souped-up hot rods barreling past the house and running over the little kids. Why, they play ball right out in the street, like they were in a park, and I can watch them out the window, she always said. You sure can't get into trouble living on a street with a cul-de-sac at the end of it.

All the neighbors were out now, watching Daddy crash his big Buick into Glenn's little gray car. Every time Daddy hit them, it felt to Lela like she had put her hand on a hot stove. They were going around in circles now, and there was so much noise, all that banging metal, all that screeching from the tires, her ears were ringing. She kept trying to hold herself in one spot, but then Daddy would hit them again, and she'd bounce away into the window or onto the door handle. And on one of the crashes the front seat came loose and bashed right up against her legs, so she couldn't move at all. It was just like a merry-go-round, spinning, spinning. Sometimes she could see Daddy's face through the window when the lights hit just right. His mouth was all tight and mean, but his eyes were happy looking, like he was having a good time crashing Glenn's car to pieces.

There was no place for Glenn to drive to. There was a house and a fence at the end of the street. The safest place to live, Mama always said.

Jolene was screaming, and Glenn was just turning the wheel one direction and then another, and Daddy just kept right after them. Every time it looked like Glenn was going to get past, was going to escape from the safe end of the street, find a way to get to the highway, Daddy was there, crashing, crashing, crashing. Lela's leg hurt now where the seat was resting on it, and she couldn't feel the other side of her body at all. It was as though it belonged to someone else. If she could get her leg free, it would wake up. Maybe it just needed a little jiggle to wake it up.

"Jolene, I'm scared," she cried out. But Jolene had her head down somewhere in the crooked door where Daddy kept crashing, and Glenn wasn't saying anything at all now. He had stopped turning the wheel, and everything was dark, and there wasn't even a sound.

"It's Mama, honey bunny. Speak to Mama, sweetie."

"Mama," Lela said. Her voice sounded to her like a little kitty's, just a meow of a voice.

"Thank God," Mama said.

Everything was white. The walls and the curtains and the metal at the end of the bed. There were lots of people around, too. All bending over her, doing things to her leg and her foot, pressing on her chest, poking at her ribs. Nothing hurt, though. It was just foggy. A white fog all around her head. Maybe she wasn't even there. Maybe she was dead and trying to get back to her body. Maybe Daddy mashed her so flat, she was just a piece of paper stuck on the ceiling, looking down through the fog at all the people.

"You'll have to move back, Mrs. Benoit," a man with an eyeglass in the middle of his forehead said.

"But it's my baby," Mama said. "This is my baby."

There was Jolene. Oh, someone had sewed a seam up the side of Jolene's face. Right up the side. With black thread. Mama always matched the thread to the fabric. Jolene's face was red and white and blue. Why did they use black thread? And her nose looked funny. All red at the tip and turning in a direction Lela had never seen it turn before.

"You can come in for a minute, Glenn," Mama said. "But don't talk to her."

"You're doing enough talking for everyone," the man with the eyeglass said.

"I broke my foot, Jolene," Lela whispered. "I really broke my foot."

"I know you did, sweetie," Jolene said. "Does it hurt?"

"I can't feel it if it does."

"Her ribs are okay," the man with the eyeglass in his head said.

There was a machine next to Lela's head, and clear stuff, clear as water, was running out of a bag and disappearing into the tube stuck in her arm.

"I was dead," Lela said. "Did you see me floating?"

"I sure did," Jolene said.

"You're one hell of a floater," Glenn said.

All Jolene could see was wrong with Glenn was the bandage covering the hole that his daddy made in his cheek. And his hair was messed up. It stuck up at the sides of his face like he had slept on it wrong. And his Levi's jacket was torn in two places on the sleeve. And there was oily gunk all down the front of his pants.

"I'm stitching her and she doesn't even feel it," the man with the eyeglass said. Two women in white dresses had their faces almost into Lela's chest, looking at what the man was doing. It sounded like fish tanks all around her head, bubbling water and swishing sounds.

"My aunt could have her teeth drilled without novocaine," one of the women said. "Had a foot operation and gum surgery with no pain. Some people are like that."

"There's faith healers in our family," Mama said. Lela couldn't see Mama too well, but her voice was bumpy, not smooth like it usually was. "I told Lela she'd never feel pain, no matter what, that pain's just something in your head, not something you feel. I told her that she could put pain in a corner, get rid of it. Or in a box and close it up. You can tell pain to stay where you put it, too, not let it out if you don't want to. I've done it. Remember how I told you to do it, Lela? Remember?"

"The kid's half unconscious, is why she isn't feeling any pain," the man with the eyeglass said.

"Jolene," Lela said. Everything was getting fuzzy and foggy again. Looked like a wool blanket was hanging in front of her eyes and she couldn't even raise her hands to rub the lint out.

"I'm here, sweetie," Jolene said. "I'm right here."

"The bastard tried to kill us," Glenn said.

———————————

Everyone was gone now. Just Mama was left sitting in the chair by the bed, close to where the tube was running into Lela's arm. She kept kissing Lela's cheeks. Oh, Mama's lips were cool, and everything else felt so hot.

"This isn't going to happen again, honey," Mama said. "I promise. I promise. We'll fly right out of here, right out of our bodies, so far up in the sky no one will ever be able to catch us. Are you praying to Jesus to make everything all better?"

"I tried to move my foot before, and I couldn't, Mama."

"Oh, honey, it's all my fault." Mama's hair was messed up, as if she just got out of bed and didn't have time to comb it, and she was wearing house slippers and a bathrobe. She didn't even have her purse with her, just a wad of Kleenex that she kept dabbing at her nose with.

"I want some chocolate cake, Mama. Glenn's mama made chocolate cake."

"I'll bake four chocolate cakes. Five, if you want. And ice cream, there'll be no end to the ice cream you'll eat." Mama was whispering in Lela's ear now, the words coming out of her mouth so fast and low Lela could hardly hear them. Mostly she heard Mama's breath skipping as if she'd been running too fast.

"Glenn has a dog that eats blood, Mama."

"I've been putting money away every week, enough for two bus tickets to wherever we want to go. We'll go to Wichita and stay with Aunt Marge, that's what we'll do. I'll get a job and take care of us. I'll buy a sewing machine and make all our clothes, and we'll have a flower garden and a spot in it for vegetables, and I'll can peas in the summer and make raspberry jelly from our own bushes, and we'll have a happy time and nobody'll ever find us. Nobody. Do you hear me, Lela? Nobody."

"I can hold my breath in the swimming pool, Mama. Jolene said it was fifteen minutes I was holding my breath."

Mama started crying, tears dripping on the tube in Lela's arm. She had her head down on the bed and her brown hair was getting all tangled up in the tube, and she just kept crying and saying, "Oh, my God, oh, my God."

"I like raspberry jelly, Mama. I do." Lela patted Mama's messed hair with the arm that didn't have a tube in it, but Mama wouldn't stop crying, and Lela didn't know what to do to make her stop, and finally the nurse came in and told Mama Lela had to get some sleep, that she was keeping her awake with all that noise she was making, and Mama said she'd stay right there, she wouldn't make a sound, would be quiet as a mouse, wouldn't bother anyone, would just do a little praying, if that was all right, but not out loud, just to herself, kind of moving her lips, is all she was going to do, she said, and she used the wad of Kleenex like it was a comb, tried to make her hair lie down on her head, tried to wipe the tears off the tube, tried to straighten up the sheet, but she couldn't stop crying even though she said she was going to, and the nurse said she had to leave, and Mama started screaming then, and Lela felt like screaming, too, but no sound would come out, and the nurse called the man with the eyeglass, and he took Mama away, and then Lela fell asleep.

7

"Is my mama in there?"

It was a big building, with stairs that went straight up.

"She's in there," Kitty said.

The social worker's name was Kitty, and she had come to the hospital every day to see Lela. She brought her games and read her stories. And asked her questions. And now she was driving into a tunnel beneath the big building, squealing her tires as she went around and around, looking for a parking spot.

"I don't want you to have to walk too far," Kitty said.

"I walked four miles yesterday," Lela said, "from X-ray to the cafeteria, to therapy, and back to my room."

"Four miles?" Kitty laughed. "How do you know it was four miles?"

"There's a parking space over there," Lela said.

Kitty spun into the spot and stopped the engine.

"Will Jolene be there?" Lela said. Kitty turned in the seat, her hand on the door handle. She didn't look like a kitty. She looked like a pony. A pretty one. With long black hair nearly to her waist that she was always swishing back out of her face with her hand.

"You know she won't."

Kitty helped Lela out of the car and steadied her while she got the crutches under her arms. They were a little big for her, and she swung back and forth a few times while Kitty was getting her books and papers out of the car.

"Maybe it was three miles," Lela said.

It was cold in the room, and they all sat around a table, and Mama kept reaching over and touching Lela's cheek with her hand.

"I appreciate your hearing this case in chambers, Your Honor," Kitty said. "I didn't want to scare Lela any more than we had to."

The man she was talking to was in a black bathrobe, but Lela could see his shirt and tie under it and wondered if he slept that way at night and just got up in the morning and put the bathrobe on and went to work.

"Mama once vacuumed the tiger off the wall," Lela said.

"She has a little problem with reality, Your Honor," Kitty said.

"I did," Mama said. "It was a painting Donny bought me in Tijuana. A beautiful velvet painting of a tiger. I vacuumed it, and the whole painting just disappeared."

"Well, that's neither here nor there," the man said, and Kitty cleared her throat and scrunched her eyebrows up like she was real interested in the papers she was reading.

"I brought you some homemade cookies, Lela," Mama said. She patted her purse. "They're right here, in a little bag, for when we're through. Maybe we can find you some milk somewhere, and we'll eat cookies out in the hall and drink milk and—"

"Please try not to get too upset in front of the child," the man in the bathrobe said.

"I'm trying. I'm trying so hard. It's just that—"

"We understand," Kitty said. "These proceedings are never easy."

"Well, if I knew what you were going to do. If you'd at least tell me what was really going to happen."

"That will all become clear in time," the man said. "In due time." He looked over at Kitty. "I think we should hew to some structure, don't you, even though we're going to be as informal as the law allows?"

"Of course," Kitty said.

There was a lady sitting between Mama and Kitty. She was wearing a blue suit with a big white bow under her chin and was typing on a black box that she had on a stand in front of her. Every time someone said something, she pressed some keys down and made little blue marks on a long piece of paper.

Lela got up and hopped over to where the lady with the black box was. It was like a roll of toilet paper, only it wasn't round, it was flat and kept unfolding itself on one side of the box, crawling up a piece of metal, then folding itself onto the other side.

"Can I do that?" Lela said.

"You go to school for two years, you can," the lady said.

"Do you have a report, Miss Dickson?" the man said.

"I do," Kitty said. "Lela, come back over here and sit down."

"She's not bothering me," the lady said, but Lela came back and sat down anyway.

"It's a violent family, Your Honor," Kitty said. "There have been complaints in the past by neighbors of altercations, and some trouble with the older girl at school. Poor attendance, bad attitude."

The man was reading something Kitty had handed him.

"Where's the older girl now?" the man said, looking up from the papers.

"I want a cookie now, Mama," Lela said.

"Can she have one now?" Mama asked.

"Sure," the man said.

Kitty had her papers lined up, and she waited till Mama opened her purse and got out the plastic bag and opened it, and Lela picked out the one she wanted.

"The older girl's name is Jolene, Your Honor," Kitty said. "She's the one who caused the warrant to be issued for Mr. Benoit's arrest. Mr. Benoit is the father, the one who rammed the car Jolene and Lela were riding in."

"Is he in jail?" the man said.

"I don't like raisins very much, Mama," Lela said. "I ate so many raisins one day in the hospital—I think I ate a thousand raisins, fourteen boxes of raisins. I got a stomachache when I was through."

Mama had watery eyes. The water was just rolling around in her eyes like little pools. Just staying there, all filled up, and not dropping over the edges.

"I'll make you chocolate chip next time," Mama said.

"There's a warrant out, but no one can find him," Kitty said.

"And the other girl?"

"We can't find her, either, Your Honor."

"Was she injured?"

"Slightly. She was brought into the hospital, stitched up, and then she and the driver of the car disappeared. She's underage, but they were married in Las Vegas the day before it all happened."

"Hmm," the man said.

He looked at Lela and smiled. "So, little girl, what do you think of all this?"

"All what?" Lela said.

"Of what's happened, what your father did. That."

"Oh, that." Lela shrugged. She didn't know what the man wanted her to say. What did she think? She didn't think.

"Mrs. Benoit is very sincere, but it's clearly the father who domi-nates the family," Kitty said.

"Are you saying I can't take care of my child?" Mama said. "I'd die for my child, if that's what you're saying."

"Now, now," the man said, and the water in Mama's eyes finally dropped over the edges and ran down her cheeks.

"The psychologist calls Mrs. Benoit unstable, as you can see by the report, Your Honor," Kitty said. " 'Subject to the whim of others stronger than she is. On page thirteen. Unable to form opinions of her own. Also claims to have had out-of-body experiences.' "

"What does that mean?" the man said.

"Page sixteen," Kitty said.

"Hmm," the man said.

"I float, is all," Mama said. "Haven't you ever floated out of your-self, just left yourself behind? You know, looking down at yourself? Haven't you ever done that? Like you might have died, only you didn't, you're just out of your body?"

No one answered.

"What's this at page thirty?" the man said. "Communing with rocks and trees?"

"Well, that isn't as simple as you think to explain," Mama said. "You know what the New Testament says, that God created all things in heaven and on earth. Well, rocks and trees are things, and if God says he created them, who am I to say they don't have souls? And if they do, why can't we talk to them, like we do God?"

"Hmm," the man said.

"There are things that are just spirit filled," Mama said. "God planned it that way. He put himself into everything, didn't leave a single blade of grass out. That's all I told the psychologist. She wanted to know my beliefs. I tried to tell her."

"But you did tell her you leave your body?" the man said.

"No," Mama said. "I never said I left my body. I just said it felt like I left my body. And it doesn't happen all the time. Just once in a while. Like in church. You know how strong the spirit of God is in church. Don't you see?"

"Don't cry, Mama," Lela said.

"It's not a good environment, Your Honor," Kitty said. "And the husband probably will return. Anything can happen if he does."

"I hate to do it," the man said, "but she'll have to go to foster care for the time being."

"Aaaaaaah." It sounded like Mama was singing, her voice was so high and she held the note so long.

"Just temporarily," the man said, "till we find your husband. We're interested in the welfare of this child, and we can't know the full picture of what happened, what provoked him to ram his car into another one. As for the other charge, the other—"

"The incest charge?" Kitty said.

"Well, that's open to interpretation, I suppose. The father isn't here to defend himself. I can't rule on that until I talk to him."

Mama followed them all the way down in the elevator to the parking garage. She wouldn't let go of Lela's arm, nearly carried her and the crutches all the way through the dark underground. She squeezed so hard that it was almost a relief when Kitty pulled Lela away and put her in the car. Lela could see her standing there as they drove up the ramp. She had the little plastic bag of cookies in her hand and was waving at Lela with them.

"Marge?"

"Marilee?"

"The line's so clear it's like you're in the other room."

"Are you in trouble, Marilee?"

"How are the boys?"

"Are you calling from the house?"

"I'm right here in my kitchen, Marge, looking out the window to the backyard."

"Does Donny know you're calling me?"

"Donny's not here. How's the weather in Wichita?"

"You're in trouble, aren't you."

"It's been hot here. My God, you can't believe the heat we had in September. But now it's cold, cold as January in Alaska. It's those ocean breezes come off the ocean and get right into your bones."

"I can tell when you're in trouble. Talking fast, like you are now. And calling long distance. Donny'd never let you call long distance if you weren't in some kind of trouble. Are you crying, Marilee? Do you have a cold or are you crying?"

"They're taking Lela away from me."

"Oh, Lord."

"Jolene ran away and got married, and the judge is going to take Lela away from me over something Donny did. I've got money for bus tickets. Can you still get me that job at Wichita Electric?"

"That was ten years ago, Marilee. They've been firing, not hiring.

Jimmy's lucky to have his job. The twins both had their tonsils out, and heating oil's gone up, and I don't know what we'd do if Jimmy lost his job."

"It doesn't have to be high pay. I'll do anything."

"You aren't trained for anything, Marilee. You didn't even graduate high school."

"I'm quick. I can learn things."

"It doesn't matter, because there's no job at Wichita Electric."

"I'll get a job waitressing. I know how to serve food. I could do that."

"I told you ten years ago to leave him, didn't I? That time he pushed you down and broke your collarbone, didn't I say, Marilee, get out of there before he kills you? Didn't I say he'd do more than break your collarbone one of these days? So what did he do now? Break your leg? Your arm? Did he hurt one of the girls? I bet he hurt one of them. Good Lord, Marilee, you don't listen, is what's wrong with you. I told you and told you he was rotten. Why, if Jimmy so much as looked at me crooked, I'd leave him flat. And all you do is take it. Well, I don't know what to say, Marilee, about coming to Wichita, but there's no job at Wichita Electric that Jimmy can get you. And there's no room in this house. I've got my hands full as it is taking care of what I've got."

"This is all the money I can give you," Renee said. She had picked the place to meet, at the Juicee Burger on Venice Boulevard, not far from her house. Marilee had taken two buses to get there from Huntington Beach.

"I didn't mean for you to bring me money, Ma."

"Well, you sounded so desperate on the phone, and not hearing from you since Christmas, I figured what else could it be but money you'd want from me."

Renee dyed her hair red, and it was growing out at the roots so that she had a white halo around her face. She looked as if she had just thrown a housedress on and walked the three blocks to the café from her house. Her house keys were jingling in the pocket of her dress, and she had a pack of cigarettes out on the table and was holding a lit one that had an inch-long ash leaning in a delicate arc toward the table.

"You look thin," Renee said. "You used to have some meat on you. You looked a lot more like me when you had some meat on your bones."

Marilee had put on her best skirt and blouse to come meet her
mother, was even wearing a red-and-blue plaid ribbon that matched
her plaid skirt. "I brought you a picture of the girls taken this last
Fourth of July." She took an envelope out of her purse and laid it on
the table, then slid the picture out so it was in the middle of the table
between her and her mother.

"We had a picnic out in the park and then went over to Main Street
and watched the parade go by, and Donny said, 'Girls, just go over
there where the high school band is going by and I'll take your
picture.' Jolene has her hand up near her face so you can't see just
how pretty she is, but Lela's looking right straight at you. She lost
that tooth last December and it's just now coming in. She's my doll
baby."

Renee looked at the photograph a few seconds, then slid it back
toward Marilee. "They're nowhere as pretty as you and Marge were.
You were the prettiest girls in Culver City. Someone stopped me in
the market when you were five and asked if I wanted to get you in
the movies, you were so pretty. The movies can ruin a child, your pa
said. He wouldn't allow it."

Marilee picked up the picture and stared at it. "My doll baby."

"I wouldn't know. I don't suppose I've seen her twice in her life."

"She's very lively. She talks and talks and tells funny stories and
laughs all the time."

"I never knew you to be so thin. I hardly recognized you coming
in the door. I thought to myself when I saw you out on the sidewalk,
Who could that be that's smiling at me that way?"

Marilee put her hand across the table and took hold of her mother's
fingers. Renee jumped a little at her touch, and the arc of ash blew
across the table.

"The state took Lela away from me, Ma. I don't have my daughter
anymore."

"What in the world are you talking about?"

"I'm talking about Donny."

"Not again. Not like the middle girl. Not like what he did to her."

"Not like Elaine, Ma."

"Then what are you telling me, Marilee?"

"He did things. Bad things. I wasn't paying attention, wasn't taking
care, didn't want to think what I was thinking."

Renee shook her head hard and made a little moaning sound in her
throat. "I don't want to hear it. I'm liable to have a stroke if you
go on."

"They say it's temporary foster care, but then when we go to court for the final custody hearing, they'll say it's too bad, Mrs. Benoit, but you're out of luck, out of kids, out of the picture."

"Why do you always come to me when it's too late? You came running to me when your daughter died, and it was too late then."

"If I have a good place to live, if Lela's in a safe place away from Donny, maybe I'll get her back."

"It's so hot in here," Renee said. "Why's it so hot in here? I have half a mind to go back to the cook and tell him he's driving his customers out of the place with his cooking." She picked up a cigarette and lit it, then put it down again and took a drink of water, then dunked the cigarette in the water and started fanning herself with the plastic menu. "I get a note from you once a year at Christmas, and then you call me and tell me you're in some terrible trouble, and now you're telling me you want to come live with me. After twenty years. Twenty years, Marilee. Like you were a little girl, or something. Like you were an orphan. If you weren't in trouble, you wouldn't even think to pick up the telephone and call me. I'm marrying him, Ma, and that's that, you said. My, it's so hot in here. Between the flashes and the heat, I can't tell the difference. Cold this morning and now it's boiling. It is hot in here, isn't it? All those hamburgers cooking raises the temperature till a person could die of the heat."

"If you do this one thing for me, Ma, I'll never ask for anything else as long as I live."

"Your pa will never let you in the door."

"I won't talk about church or God or Jesus or any of those things that make him so upset. I won't open my mouth one inch and talk about anything that'll make him mad. I'll let him say anything he wants to about Donny and you won't hear a peep from me. I didn't know Donny was going to hit him. He said he wanted to tell Pa we were married, start off on the right foot. I didn't know he was going to start a fight with him, hit him in the face like he did. I'll be perfect. More perfect than perfect. And Lela will be so quiet in the house you won't know there's a little girl there. If I can show the judge Lela's in a safe place, if he sees I'm responsible and can take care of her, maybe he'll let me have her back."

"I can get you a hundred dollars more without your pa finding out about it, but more than that and I won't be able to explain it. I already bought my winter coat and the Christmas presents are all in the hall closet waiting to be wrapped, so every cent has to be accounted for. A hundred more's all I can squeak out without him knowing."

"They're going to take Lela away permanently, Ma, put her in a home somewhere with strange parents, strange things around her. I won't be able to hug her or kiss her every day like I do. I won't be able to tell her stories, make her laugh. I won't have my little girl, Ma."

Renee put her hand on the table and slid across the seat and stood up. "Oh, Marilee, honey, I'm too hot to even think, too hot to go over it with you again, what you should have done and didn't do, what you said to me and to your pa, how you hurt us. It's just too hot to chew it all over again. But you made your bed. That's what I'm trying to tell you, Marilee, you made your bed. Oh, honey, you made an ugly, lumpy, terrible bed, and now you've got to find a way to sleep in it."

8

" I ' L L   C O M E   A N D   check on you once in a while," Kitty said, "see how you're getting along. It's a very nice place, with lots of children and space to play in. They even have a schoolhouse right on the grounds. And there are orange trees and swing sets and slides."

"Do I have to get out of bed?" Lela said.

"Only if you want to."

"Did you bring my paints?" The therapist at the hospital had given Lela a paint box and crayons and paper so she'd have something to do when she went to get her foot soaked in the medicine bath.

"Everything's in the suitcase," Kitty said.

Lela glanced into the backseat. The brown suitcase was bouncing up and down as they drove along the road.

"I'll paint you a picture," Lela said. "A hundred pictures." She looked out the window. It was all green here, with big trees. No more of those houses with the pink roofs and green doors that they passed way back there. Not even any people. Not even any cars. Not even any dogs. Just trees. There were a few mountains, though, way, way up near the white clouds, so far up it looked like they were hiding.

"Where's the ocean?" Lela said.

"We're pretty far from the ocean," Kitty said. "We're in Irvine. Isn't it pretty? Look up there on the hills, can you see the cows?"

"I don't see any."

"Those dark spots on the hills. Can't you see them?"

The hills, green with black dots, looked like someone had emptied raisins out of a box all over them. "Oh, now I see them," Lela said. "But why are they all sitting down? Are they taking a nap? Why don't they stand up?"

"Maybe they're tired."

"Cows don't get tired."

"How do you know? Did you ever ask a cow?"

"I milked a cow once. We owned a farm. 'Old MacDonald had a farm . . .' Do you know that one?"

"Sure."

"My uncle's name is MacDonald. I wanted a glass of milk, so I went and milked a cow. Right into the glass. It was real hard to do it, too, to get the milk to go into the glass. Some of it fell over and hit my shoes. Did you ever milk a cow?"

"Never have."

"Will Mama and Daddy be there, and Jolene and Glenn?"

Kitty didn't answer.

"Where are they?"

"I don't know."

There was a fence, right out in the middle of the trees, a real high one with black squiggly things in it that looked like the curlers in Mama's hot hair machine.

"Mama's hair is pretty," Lela said.

It seemed like they had been driving forever.

———————

"We have eleven children as of last week." June smiled at Lela. "Lela makes twelve." June had a square shape and a full stomach that pressed against the buttons of her blouse.

"An even dozen," Kitty said. "How do you do it?"

"Organization," June said. "You have to have a plan, just like in anything else."

June had put the crutches up against the wall near the kitchen door, too far away for Lela to get at them. She wished she could, though, so she could get over to the refrigerator and open it up and see what was in there. Maybe there was some spaghetti in a pot like Mama made. Or even half a chicken, with the skin shriveled and brown and tasting of garlic.

"I've kept her in the hospital as long as I could," Kitty said. She had all of Lela's things from the hospital in the brown suitcase at her feet.

"No parents?"

"The mother. But she's slightly crazed. The father is a fugitive. A teenage sister, but she's disappeared."

"Some families are so screwed up," June said.

"I like spaghetti," Lela said, and June glanced over at her. The kitchen didn't smell like a kitchen. It smelled like the stuff Mama poured into the washing machine or the medicine they put into the therapy water in the hospital. Maybe both.

"She's an endearing child," June said. "What happened to her foot?"

"Umm, well," Kitty said. "That's the father problem. You know, the fugitive part. I hate to talk in front of her. I'll send you a complete report. I've just been so snowed under I haven't had a chance to do all the paperwork on it. I just wanted to get her here before you changed your mind."

"We are pretty full up."

"It'll just be temporary, until the final custody hearing and placement."

"Well, I always have room for another adorable one."

Through the sparkly windows Lela could see some kids on the swings.

"I broke my foot riding my bike on the sidewalk," Lela said. "Mama says not to ride in the street. There was a hole bigger than this room, bigger than this house, so big—"

"All the particulars are in the report I'll send you," Kitty said.

Lela leaned over and touched Kitty's sleeve. "Did you bring my paints?"

"I told you, everything's in the suitcase," Kitty said.

"You can take the suitcase back with you," June said. "We like to start fresh here, with everything new, right down to their underwear. We like to clean the kids' minds, put fresh ideas in there, try to turn them around, make an imprint."

Lela couldn't tell if June was older than Mama or younger. She didn't have round cheeks. They were flat as a plate, and her nose stuck out so far it made Lela laugh.

"Is something funny?" June said.

"Your nose," Lela said.

"She's not psychiatric, is she?" June said. Lela was sorry she'd said that about the nose, but it did stick out far, and anyway, June didn't look too worried about it.

"Is Mama going to come here, too?" Lela said.

"We have visiting days," June said. She had a pack of cigarettes in her hand.

"Daddy doesn't allow smoking in the house," Lela said. "He once killed a man for lighting a cigarette in the house. Shot him in the kitchen while Mama was making spaghetti."

"We'll have to break her of that habit," June said.

"I think it's a protective mechanism," Kitty said. "If it helps her, I say let it be."

"Are you leaving her in my care?"

"Of course."

"Then I'll handle bad habits."

Lela stood up at the table and looked out at the kids. June got up, too, and got the crutches and handed them to Lela.

"Daddy doesn't allow Mama to wear nail polish, either," Lela said. Kitty's fingertips were painted red, with little white edges.

"I was going to take her out to Chatsworth," Kitty began.

"Oh, no, you wouldn't want to do that," June said. "I hear terrible things about that place. Did you know they've been investigating it?"

"No. Really? I hadn't heard."

"Well, it's all pretty hush-hush, but I think they're going to close them up. Too free a hand with the kids. Marijuana smoking in the dormitories, two pregnancies. I hear it's a real zoo."

June walked ahead of Lela down the hall. Kitty was walking slowly beside her, her hand out in case she fell.

"It's not a good idea babying her that way," June said. She was already in the doorway, watching them. "Let her learn for herself. That's the first step to self-reliance, doing things for yourself."

"My daddy made these crutches," Lela said. "He chopped down a tree in the yard and went in the garage and made crutches out of it. My daddy can do anything."

9

L E L A   W A S   I N the closet when the TV people came. She could hear them talking and laughing, and June was talking to them in a voice that reminded Lela of lemonade, all sweet and sticky but with a sour taste underneath.

"And this is the girls' dormitory. Eight girls in here at the present time. Four boys on the other side of the house."

The closet was dark and smelled of old tennis shoes. There was just the line of light beneath the door to tell Lela it was day. She stared at the light so hard she saw spots. Maybe she had been there two days. Maybe a week. It was hard to remember when June had put her in there and locked the door.

"How do you keep the place so clean?" That voice was so close to the door Lela could almost feel its vibrations.

"The kids do it," June said. "Everyone has their chores."

She was thirsty. She had finished the bottle of water June's husband, Everett, had brought her. And hungry. The bologna sandwich had tasted funny. Old or something. The meat inside was slippery.

"Can you give me a few reasons why you were chosen Foster Parents of the Year? Not too detailed. People don't care about details. Something zingy, you know, like you personally bathe each child every night, you sit up with them when they're sick, you know, et cetera, et cetera."

"Well, I believe in discipline. No child in my care is going to scream and get out of line and demand things. Life is tough. They've got to learn they have to earn what they want. No crying. I can't stand crybabies. Or whiners. A kid that whines won't whine long, not if I have anything to say about it."

"But you're not too strict, right?"

"Oh, no. Lots of love, that's what I believe in giving my kids. And they are my kids, all of them, whether they were born to me or not. If they're in my care—and Everett's, of course—they're our kids."

"Your husband seems to leave the talking to you."

"Oh, Everett talks all right. He just likes to wait till he has something to say."

"Anything else? I'll cull what I want out of it anyhow, so go ahead and kind of ramble, if you want to."

"Well, we keep to a schedule here. There's no other way to run a place like this if you don't have a schedule. And the kids love it. They love the security, the sense of being in a safe and clean environment. You don't know the places these kids have been, the horrendous experiences they've had."

"What's in there?"

"Just a closet."

"Is that where you keep the bodies?" Someone laughed.

"Can we get some footage of the younger kids on the swings?"

"You go on out with Everett," June said. "I'll be right there."

Lela could hear feet scraping across the floor, a door closing, then footsteps coming back. The door opened. For a moment she couldn't see a thing, just little explosions of light in front of her eyes, like firecrackers going off or sparklers on the Fourth of July. She rubbed her eyes. It was lighter than light. Big bowls of light that she couldn't see through.

"They want pictures of everyone out in the back," June said. "Go wash your face and brush your teeth and put on a clean dress."

"I'm hungry," Lela said. "The meat tasted funny."

"That's what liars get," June said.

———

"My husband and I never did this for the money or for recognition," June said. She was talking into the camera, her face as stiff as her starched dress. "We just had so much love to give, and no children of our own to give it to."

"Cut," the woman with the pad of paper said.

"What's the matter?" June said. "Did I do it wrong?"

"You look in pain. We can edit these things, but we can't get rid of expressions like you've got on your face."

"Sorry. When will the program be on?"

"We'll have to edit it first. And then it's up to the station chief. I know it's a big thing to you—businesswise and all—but it's just a local story, when you get right down to it. No fire, murder, mayhem, et cetera, et cetera. We call them feel-goods. Makes people feel good to know there are people like you out there watching out for kids, you know, et cetera, et cetera."

"Well, it hasn't been easy," June said. "I thought you said it was going to be on for sure."

"I didn't say for sure," the lady said. "I said if there's room, and no other story breaking, et cetera, et cetera. So tell me about these kids, who they are, where they're from, et cetera, et cetera." She motioned to the man holding the camera.

"Well, this is Louise. Abandoned as a baby. Been a ward of the court since she was born. And this is Jeff, his mother's in jail for manslaughter."

June was going down the line, telling a few words about each child. Everett walked beside her, head stooped over like a chicken's.

"This is Lela. She's temporary pending the court hearing."

"Hi," Lela said.

"What a sweet smile," the lady said. "How old are you?"

"Almost nine. What's your name?"

"Annette."

"Do you have something to eat in that truck? I'm hungry. I haven't eaten for a week."

"What?"

"She's always doing that," June said. "Lying, I mean. She ate not more than two hours ago. She's a little psychiatric."

"I've been in the closet two weeks," Lela said.

"This is ridiculous," June said.

"I haven't had anything to eat for a month," Lela said.

"She hasn't even been here a month," June said.

"I'm almost nine," Lela said. Annette was wearing a red suit with a white blouse. The blouse had a stiff collar that came up around her neck and then flattened out into two points near her padded shoulders.

"If I had a sewing machine, I could make a blouse like yours," Lela said. "Mama sews all her own clothes, and mine and Jolene's. But June keeps me in the closet all the time. I can't see anything in there. And it smells, too. Sometimes I have to go potty, and I go in the corner, and that makes it smell worse."

"Not true, not true," June said. "Bathroom breaks are always taken care of. The child is just—"

The man with the camera had it turned in Lela's direction, and she could see lights on it and hear a little whirring sound.

June laughed. "She was only in the closet two hours," she said.

"Have you ever been to Huntington Beach?" Lela said.

"Lots of times," Annette said. She had her hand up like she was trying to keep June from talking.

"I can remember the beach and sand," Lela said. "There's no beach here. There are cows, but you can't see them because they're too far away. But no beach. I love the ocean. Do you know what June does?"

"No, what does she do?" Annette said.

"She ties me to the bed. I can't move I'm tied up so tight."

"She lies about everything," June said, "makes up stories you wouldn't believe."

"Call the station, Chuck, and tell them we've got something really good," Annette said. "And get Rich up here to take pictures of the grounds, and someone from editorial to get background on all the kids, et cetera, et cetera."

"Do you have something to eat in that truck?" Lela said. "A pizza or something like that?"

"We'll get you something in a minute," Annette said. She looked like she had a fever, her cheeks were so red.

"Mama always made her own cookies from scratch," Lela said. "Daddy didn't like box mix cookies. Daddy tried to kill us with the car. Then he disappeared, and Kitty brought me here because Mama thinks she floats in the air without a parachute."

"Just a minute, just a minute," Annette said. "What about this place? Tell me more about what they do to you here."

Lela sat down on the wet grass. Her legs felt weak and her head was throbbing.

"Can't you see what she's doing?" June said. "She just wants to get on television." And she looked all shook, like she couldn't believe what was happening.

10

"WHAT'S THAT LIGHT for?" Lela asked.

"You," Annette said. "To light your pretty face when you talk."

"Why?"

"So everyone on television can see you."

"I have no place to put my feet." Lela stretched her legs out as far as they would go, but she still couldn't reach the bar on the bottom of the high stool Bill had put her on. Annette said this was where she made her television show. She said it was the same station they showed cartoons on on Sunday mornings.

"She looks uncomfortable," Bill said. He was Annette's producer, Annette said. She'd called him on the telephone from the foster home and he'd come to get them in a big red truck that had the letters *KOXC* on the sides. He'd carried Lela out to the truck, crutches and all, and put her in the back with Annette and hadn't paid any attention to June, who was standing on the sidewalk and yelling at them the whole time until they drove away.

"Leave her just the way she is," Annette said. "She seems smaller that way. You know, more sympathetic, downtrodden, vulnerable, et cetera, et cetera."

"Five minutes to air time," a man said. He had earphones on his head like he was listening to the radio.

"Can I swing my feet, then?" Lela said.

"What?" Bill said.

"Daddy never lets me swing my feet."

Annette was reading things from the pad of paper in her hand, flipping the pages and saying words out loud, real fast, lips barely moving, head up to the ceiling, like she meant for only the lights to hear her. Lela looked around her. It was like the hospital, nothing pretty in it, not even a plant. Just a long table and behind it a big picture of streets or freeways or something. And across the room a window with people sitting in front of a lot of television screens.

"Where do they keep the cartoons?" Lela asked. "I want to see them."

"They're on tape," Bill said. "You can't see them. Do you want a glass of water?"

"Do you have any chocolate?" Lela said.

Annette stopped what she was doing long enough to say, "No chocolate. She'll get her face dirty."

"Dirty is good," Bill said.

"Chocolate, then," Annette said.

There were all sorts of people in the room now, everyone doing something, pulling lights closer, sliding chairs around, combing Annette's hair.

"Thank you," Lela said when a lady in a short dress with lace around the hem handed her a Hershey bar. "I like nuts. Is there nuts in this one?"

"Two minutes," the man with the headphones said.

"Eat it quick," Annette said.

Lela tore open the package and stuffed half the bar in her mouth.

"One minute," the man with the headphones said.

"Swallow it, for chrissakes," Annette said, and Lela gulped down the rest. It didn't taste good this way, eating it so fast. She liked to nibble at the edges first, all around the sides so she could see her teeth marks on it before she really ate it. Not the way she ate bananas. She ate them like corn on the cob, twirling the banana around and around till it was all squishy and nearly breaking in half. Then, when Mama wasn't looking, throwing it away.

"Good afternoon," Annette said. She was sitting behind the long table, smiling out into the air at no one Lela could see. "This is *News at Noon*, Channel Six, Annette Sullivan reporting. Late-breaking story of June and Everett Raines, just this week named Foster Parents of the Year, now accused of child abuse. Hear it first on *News at Five*. Back in a moment."

"Go to commercial," the man with the headphones said.

Annette waited a second and then got up from behind the desk and came over to Lela.

"You smell like a teacher," Lela said. "Mama doesn't wear perfume. Daddy doesn't like perfume."

"Are you comfortable?"

"Uh-huh."

Bill came over, too. "The Raines have a lawyer, and he's on the phone."

"So?" Annette said. "I'm sure of my facts. I saw the closet with the piss pot in it and the stale sandwich and empty water bottle. The kid's believable. The other kids corroborated. It's good enough for me."

Bill tickled Lela's chin and made a giggling sound, like she was five years old or something.

"Mama killed Daddy," Lela said.

"I just don't need any libel suits," Bill said.

"She shot him," Lela said. "She's been meaning to shoot him for a long time." Lela crossed her good leg over the sore one. It felt better that way, with the stool so high and nowhere to put her feet. "And she finally did. He fell over, with blood coming out of his shirt. There were even holes in his pants, and his legs. Even his shoes. Then she buried him in the backyard. I helped her dig the hole."

"Did you hear what she said?" Annette said.

"Jesus, the kid's a liar," Bill said. "We're in trouble."

"Don't get frantic, Bill. Frantic is death."

"We haven't got time to play around here, Annette. You said child abuse. You didn't say murder."

The man with the headphones came over now. "What's going on?"

Annette's face was real close now, and Lela could see little drops of water growing on her upper lip.

"Did you say your mommy shot your daddy?" Annette said.

"Uh-huh."

"And you helped bury him in the backyard?"

"What did she say?" the headphoned man said.

———————————

Mama was so happy.

"Oh, Lela, oh, honey bunny, is it really you?"

She just grabbed Lela up and hugged her. Just stood on the front lawn and rocked her back and forth in her arms. Didn't even look at Annette or pay any attention to the big truck that pulled up to the curb behind Annette's Toyota. Just held Lela in her arms, right next to the olive tree in the middle of the front lawn, held her tight as a baby, just squeezing her, rocking her, like she hadn't seen her in two years.

"They put me in a closet, Mama," Lela said.

"Oh, honey bunny, oh, sweetie, I won't let them get you again."

Mama finally noticed Annette. "Who are you?" she said.

"Annette Sullivan, KOXC television," Annette said, and she pulled Lela's crutches out of the backseat and put them on the curb. "She must be heavy."

"Television?" Mama said, and Lela felt herself slipping out of Mama's arms and onto the damp grass. "I don't understand. You're going to fix the television?"

"No, we *are* the television."

Mama looked at the truck now, at the two men with cameras balanced on their shoulders standing on the sidewalk in front of the house.

"I was on television, Mama," Lela said.

"I know, sweetie," Mama said, "you're always on my television. I have a picture of you on it, don't you remember?" She helped Lela stand up, then steadied her till she had the crutches under her arms.

"I can run on these crutches now, Mama," Lela said. "You should see how fast I can go, faster than a train, faster even than Superman can fly." Lela could feel the tips of the crutches sinking into the grass, melting into the dirt. Just digging a hole and melting.

The men with the cameras walked across the lawn and put their cameras on some sticks near the grapestake fence, the one Daddy was going to put a swinging gate on for the camper-trailer he was always talking about buying.

"What do you mean, you *are* the television?" Mama said to Annette.

"KOXC news," Annette said.

"Is this about the custody hearing? Did the judge change his mind and give Lela back without a custody hearing? Is that what this is all about?"

"Not exactly," Annette said, but Mama was already swinging Lela around and around and laughing and crying all at the same time.

They sat at the wrought-iron table in the backyard. Lela sat on Mama's lap and Mama kept kissing her neck and squeezing her as if she were a doll or a teddy bear.

"We started out doing a story on foster care, Foster Parents of the Year, et cetera, et cetera," Annette said. "And it looked like it was going to be a bigger story than that, so I thought I'd ask you a few questions, tape some of it if you didn't mind, see what we've got when we get through."

The men with the cameras had stuck their sticks in the lawn between the railroad ties that Daddy put down to step across the yard on.

"The whole thing's a nightmare," Mama said. "I'm hoping it gets straightened out at the custody hearing and I can get my girl back again."

"The foster home was pretty bad," Annette said. "It started out they were Foster Parents of the Year, and it ended up with me thinking we've got a story on abuse of children in foster care. They had her in a closet, with no food and no water."

"Oh, my God," Mama said, and hugged Lela even tighter than she had before.

"I put in a call to child services. I didn't know what to do with her. I sure as hell wasn't going to take her back to where she was. Then when we got to the studio and we were about set to go on air, Lela said you shot your husband and buried him in the backyard." Annette giggled when she said it, but she had her pad of paper out and was holding her pen so tight that her fingers looked almost as white as the paper.

Mama didn't even look surprised. "Does this mean she's out of foster care? She's home to stay?"

Annette slipped the pen into her jacket pocket. "I didn't think the story about her father was true."

"What?"

"Her father."

"Oh, him."

"You didn't shoot him, then."

"I've wanted to more than once."

Mama went inside and brought out some lemonade, and it seemed to Lela like they were having a party. Annette and Mama were talking like old friends, laughing about how Lela always tells stories, and Annette said she knew it was a story all along about Mama shooting Daddy, that she could always tell when something wasn't ringing true, especially the part about burying him in the backyard. That part was a dead giveaway, Annette said. And Mama said are you really going to leave her here, and Annette said I sure am, and then Mama said let me give you some zucchini from my vegetable garden. It's late for vegetables, Mama said, but there's still some zucchini left, and Annette said she had a favorite recipe for fried zucchini, and Mama said she'd like to have it, she collects vegetable recipes, there's never enough ways to cook vegetables, is what Mama said. And then she started telling Annette her recipe for string bean casserole, and the men with the cameras got tired and sat down on the lawn. One of them was leaning against the sticks his camera was on. He looked like he was sleeping, or trying to go to sleep. The other one was reading something out of a small book he must have had in his pocket. It had a picture of a submarine on the front, and he seemed to be really enjoying it.

———————————

One summer there were so many gophers in the yard, Daddy put traps all over the yard. Then he sat out in the yard and every time he saw a gopher squeeze its fat body up out of a hole he banged it on the head with a brick he had left over from making the planter box where the lilies were planted. In just one week he had fourteen dead gophers lined up against the fence. "That's a warning to the others," he said.

So it didn't surprise Lela at all to see Daddy come walking into the yard. It was his yard, after all. The one he killed gophers in. The one he planted lilies in and put the railroad ties in and laid bricks around the planter in. The one he mowed every Saturday. Why shouldn't Daddy come walking into his own backyard?

The minute Mama saw him, she yanked Lela up out of the chair she was sitting in next to the wrought-iron table and headed for the back porch. Annette saw him, too, but she just glanced over at him as if she thought he was someone from the television place who had come to help her out.

Mama was walking faster now that she was on the cement path, nearly running, bouncing Lela in her arms. Then they were on the back porch steps. Mama opened the screen door and nearly dropped Lela on the linoleum inside, she was moving so fast. Then she turned and slid the little metal hook into the ring. Daddy had put the hook and ring there years ago, Mama said, when Jolene was a baby, to keep her from running away.

"What's going on here?" Daddy said. He was standing right inside the fence, not far from where he was planning on putting a gate for the camper-trailer he was going to buy.

Annette had put on her sunglasses, big ones that came down over her cheeks nearly to the points of her lips. Lela couldn't see her face because of the sunglasses, but her voice when she spoke to Daddy had a little shake in it.

"We're doing a little interview. Why? Who are you?"

"What's going on here?" Daddy said again. The man who was sleeping or trying to sleep was standing up now. The other man was trying to shove the book in his back pocket, and it kept slipping out and falling on the grass.

Daddy had replanted the backyard when Lela was in first grade. He'd used a machine that chewed up the old dead grass. A long-toothed black box that unraveled the grass like a carpet, nipping at the edges first before it tore off a strip, like Mama did with the scissors when a hem needed ripping out. Daddy watered the new grass every morning and every evening after he planted it. Daddy loved the grass in the backyard. He never let Lela play on it. He made her play on the cement patio where the wrought-iron table and chairs were. He'd never have let anybody put sticks in it or sleep on it or read books on it.

"Marilee!" Daddy yelled all the way from where he was standing near the pile of juniper bushes that he trimmed twice a year with an electric saw that he said could take your hand off if you didn't know what you were doing.

"Oh, sweetie," Mama whispered, and Lela could feel her shaking.

"Daddy," Lela called out from behind the screen door.

Annette spun around when Lela called out. Her head just snapped up at the sound, and she opened her mouth real wide under the big sunglasses.

"This is my yard!" Daddy shouted. "My house!"

The man with the book and the man with the sticks looked at Annette as if they were waiting for her to tell them what to do. But she was already running toward the back porch as fast as she could. It was the strangest thing watching Annette running through the yard, falling and getting up again. Then she was on the cement path and nearly running on all fours, she was in such a hurry.

"He's got a gun," Annette said. She was out of breath, her mouth right on the other side of the screen door, right about where the latch went into the ring that Daddy had put up to keep Jolene inside.

Annette tugged at the door, and it made a banging noise where the little space was between the latch and the wood of the house.

"Let me in."

"I can't," Mama said. "I can't. He'll come in, too."

Mama had her hand on the little metal latch, was patting it as if it were a dog she was trying to keep from barking.

Daddy was still standing in the yard. He looked like a thin, leafless tree in the middle of the grass.

"All of you are killing me," he shouted. "You're all just trying to kill me."

There was a loud pop and the man with the sticks and the man with the book started running. Like when the gophers saw Daddy with the brick, they all ran every which way, trying to get away from him.

"Let me in," Annette said. It was as if she were begging. Or praying.

"I can't let you in," Mama said even when Annette began to cry. "Don't you see? I just can't."

"This is my home!" Daddy shouted.

Annette said, "Please," in a real soft voice, but Daddy shot her anyway. She jumped a little when he did it, like she was stamping her feet at him. Then she just leaned against the screen and stared into the house for a few seconds before she fell down.

Lela couldn't see anyone in the yard now. Just Daddy. Standing there like he was thinking what to do next. Then he started walking toward the house.

"Marilee, hand Lela out to me," Daddy said. "Open the door and hand her out."

Mama was moaning as though she had banged her toe and couldn't stand the pain.

Daddy was on the step now. Lela couldn't see where Annette was. She just heard funny sounds coming from down around the bottom of the door.

"Donny, I can't give her to you, you know I can't, you know it, Donny, you know I can't."

"Then I'll shoot you through the door."

Lela closed her eyes. It was like sometimes when she had the worst dreams, and she'd call to Mama in her sleep, but Mama wouldn't hear her, and she couldn't get out of the dream, couldn't escape the monsters chasing her. That's the way she felt now, with Mama holding her tight and nothing between them and Daddy but the little metal latch.

"It's your fault, all of it," Daddy said. "You let Jolene go off with that punk. You did that to me on purpose. You knew I couldn't stand it, and you let her do it."

"I didn't, Donny, I swear I didn't. I didn't know anything about it. I didn't even know there was a boy named Glenn. I didn't know Jolene even knew any boys. She was so quiet, Donny, how was I going to know a thing like that?"

"Open the door."

"No."

"Open it, I said."

Mama's hand rested on the metal latch. Lela stared at the fingers. Mama could roll dough so thin you could see through it. Mama could sew a hem so you didn't even see the stitch marks. Mama called her "honey bunny" and "sweetie." Mama loved her.

The latch made a little squeaky sound when Mama opened it. Daddy always oiled everything in the house, so nothing squeaked, everything sounded the way it was supposed to sound. Perfect.

Sometimes time didn't move. Like when you waited for school to be over, or summer to start, or your birthday to come. You could wish all you wanted, but nothing would make that time go by. Then there were the times when you wanted to make it last, couldn't stand for the movie to be over or the ice cream to be gone or another birthday to be a week behind you and a whole year to wait for another one. Now Daddy was moving toward them through the door, and Lela couldn't hold back the time.

"You bitch," Daddy said, and Lela felt Mama fall away. Just fall away. Away, away, away. Lela wished she could take back what she'd said to Annette, wished she could stop everything from happening. But Mama was on the floor and not moving at all, and it was too late to be sorry now.

11

"I TOLD HER and told her," Daddy said. "You let the outside world in, you'll have trouble. She was always wanting to talk to neighbors, wanting to tell them this and ask them about that. It was all I could do to keep her home. Church wasn't ever enough for her. Question, question, question, that's all she ever did. I didn't have answers enough for all the questions she was always asking me. So I told her, I said, the quickest way to doubt me, to doubt the Lord, to doubt the Sacred Word, is for you to get friendly with neighbors. You just stay by my side, and I'll manage everything just fine."

Lela looked out the car window. The road was narrow here, and they were way high up on one of the mountains that she had seen the white stuff on when they stopped at the McDonald's in Riverside and bought the hamburgers and French fries. They were up so high that the cars on the road down below them looked like bugs.

"It isn't so hard to understand," Daddy said, "loving your own daughter. She's my flesh and blood. And I knew what I was doing was sacred, was something special between Jolene and myself, had nothing to do with evil. Evil was what other people did. Evil has to be in your heart, has to be something that hurts someone. How did I hurt anyone? It was love, God's love, that's what it was, all the time, in every way."

Lela picked the last dark bits of French fries out of the bag. When Mama was with them, she always asked for crisp French fries, the kind you could practically build a little house with, they were so crisp.

"I knew when I married your mother that she'd be stubborn and hard to train to obedience," Daddy said. "I told her from the first day —and the Bible is very clear on this—obedience to your husband. 'For we wrestle not against flesh and blood,' like the Bible says. But she was always wrestling against me, testing me, waiting to see if I was weak enough to walk over. I saw that in my own pa's house, the woman pushing, pushing, pushing, till there was nothing left of obedience, nothing left of the man."

The trees grew right up against the mountains. They looked like the kind you put Christmas lights on, big at the bottom and smaller at the top. How did they know what direction to grow? Why didn't they grow down instead of up? Why didn't they bend over so the cars couldn't get through?

"There was no sin in it that I could see," Daddy said. "And don't believe anyone who ever tells you that I didn't examine my soul every day I was alive, every time I touched my child, every time I saw that look in your mother's face. And I told her, I said over and over, Now listen, I'm not out to hurt my own flesh and blood, so don't go thinking I'm doing anything I'm not. But she was always watching, trying to catch me. Well, I made Jolene, she belongs to me. And I told your mother that finally, I said, You're just too stupid to explain things to. Don't watch me anymore. I'll tell you from now on anything you want to know. You want to know about what I do with Jolene? Same thing I do with you. But it's better. More natural. She's part of me and you aren't. What I do with her comes from inside me, from a spirit-filled place, and if it's evil, then why did God put the urge in me in the first place?"

Lela touched the window. It was getting steamed up, and it felt icy cold to her fingers.

"I'm cold," Lela said. She almost hated to look at Daddy, almost hated to speak to him.

"Put this on," Daddy said, and even though he was driving, he pulled off his jacket, one arm at a time, and dropped it down on the seat between him and Lela. Then he put on the windshield wipers, because the windshield was turning white.

"Damn snow," Daddy said.

Lela had never seen snow. She had seen pictures of it. And at Christmas when Mama took her to the mall to sit on Santa's lap and tell him what she wanted for Christmas, there was cotton on the little house in back of Santa, and Mama said that was what snow looked like.

"When I married her, I knew she'd need a lot of teaching, a lot of Bible reading," Daddy said, "so she'd understand right from wrong, so she'd know that I owned her. She came from a house without Christ. She had never been inside a church till I took her there. I could see that my work was cut out for me. And there was her mother and sister standing there always trying to tell her what to do, how to do it. Telling her I was wrong. Telling her I wasn't treating her right. Telling her I was ruining my girls. Too much discipline. Too much

Bible. Too much this. Too much that. I had no peace at all until I got her away from them."

Lela didn't mind so much when Daddy talked about Jolene. It was when he talked about Mama, like right now, that it made her stomach hurt.

Daddy was driving slower now, and Lela sat on the edge of the seat, trying to see what was outside. Everything was white out there now. Where had the trees gone? Where were they hiding?

"I don't believe it," Daddy said, and he stopped the car and rolled down the window. Snow was coming inside now, and Lela tried to catch some of it in her hands. A few pieces stayed on her fingers, but the harder she stared at them, the quicker they disappeared.

"Where are you heading?" There was a man in a police uniform leaning in Daddy's window. His face looked all shiny, and there were bits of snow on his eyebrows.

"Up to Running Springs," Daddy said.

"You'll need to put chains on, then."

"I didn't bring any chains."

"Peter up at Peter's Point can sell you some."

Daddy pulled into the parking lot next to another car. A big station wagon with skis and suitcases on top of it.

"Damn tourists," Daddy said.

"I need my crutches," Lela said.

"I'll carry you," Daddy said, and he lifted her up in his arms.

The snow was coming down faster and faster, and if Lela's stomach hadn't been hurting so much and if she didn't almost hate to speak to Daddy, she would have asked him to put her down so she could crawl around in it and make big balls of it like the little girl standing in front of the store was doing. She looked warm in her hooded jacket and red mittens, warmer than Lela was with just Daddy's jacket over her cotton blouse.

"Cold enough for you?" a man in a plaid shirt said to Daddy when they were inside the store. The man was on a ladder, putting cans up high on a shelf.

Daddy didn't answer.

The store was dark, but nice and warm, and it smelled like new leather shoes. There was another man in a windbreaker standing next to a big black stove in the middle of the store, a tall man, taller than anyone Lela had ever seen. He had a plastic cup in his hands, and steam was coming off the top of it. A lady in a green wool sweater and black pants was sitting on a long wooden bench in front of the stove. She had bright red lipstick on, and her brown hair curled around her shoulders. It looked as if someone had rolled it all in one direction onto a fruit juice can, it was so smooth and even. She looked up and smiled at Lela when the door closed.

"Brrr, that cold air," the lady said. "Makes me think we should have gone to Palm Springs instead."

"I need chains," Daddy said to the man on the ladder.

"I'm all out of chains," the man said. "Expect some in next week."

"What good'll that do me now?" Daddy said. He sat Lela down on the bench next to the lady in the green sweater.

"Not a thing, I suppose."

"You're a store, aren't you? You sell groceries, don't you?"

"Last time I checked."

"You're not too busy to sell me a few things, are you?"

"I guess you weren't expecting snow," the man in the windbreaker said, "dressed the way you are and without chains. It is kind of late in the season for snow, so you've got nothing to be ashamed of. It's happened to me, too, and we've got a house up here. Up at Big Bear Lake. No matter how much you think you can read the weather in the San Bernardinos from down below, you can't. It could be sunny in Riverside and storming up here. You have to be a mind-reader."

"Or listen to the radio," the man on the ladder said.

"Don't mind Peter," the man in the windbreaker said. "That's his way of being friendly." He put his hand out for Daddy to shake. Daddy looked at it a second and then took it and moved it up and down a few times.

"My name's Walter Bingham. This is Kathy, my wife."

Daddy didn't tell them his name. Just kind of nodded his head.

"Are you heading up to Big Bear?" Walter said.

"No," Daddy said.

"So what few things did you want?" Peter said. He was half turned on the ladder, leaning his stomach into the space between the ladder and the shelves.

The lady, the one the man said was named Kathy, reached over and touched Lela's knee, the knee on the leg that didn't hurt.

"What's your name, honey?"

It wasn't the question. It was the honey part that made Lela cry.

"She got her leg broke in a car wreck," Daddy said. "She cries whenever you touch that leg."

"Oh, I'm sorry," Kathy said, and she pulled her hand back as though Lela's knee were hot. Lela didn't care. Didn't even want to explain that it was the wrong knee.

"It's all right now," Daddy said. "She just likes to baby it. My wife babies her, treats her like she hasn't even learned to walk yet. My wife can't figure anything out."

"Oh," Kathy said.

"It's all right now," Daddy said.

"Without chains, it's pretty hazardous," Walter said. "We could give you a lift. We all try to help each other up here. It's not like Palos Verdes. That's where we really live. On the peninsula in Palos Verdes. We hardly know our neighbors there, even though we've been there fifteen years. Everyone keeps to themselves. The gardeners talk to each other, and the maids, but the people don't. Up here, it's different. It feels like real life up here. We do our own cooking and shopping. Everyone knows everyone. If you're going to Blue Jay, I know people in Blue Jay."

"My wife can't even read a map or tell you the names of the states," Daddy said.

"Well." Walter laughed, but Lela could tell he didn't think what Daddy said was funny.

"My wife can't do fractions," Daddy said. "She can't tell truth from lies, flesh and blood from strangers, revelation from apostasy."

Kathy was staring at him with a real strange look on her face. Daddy looked down at the floor, then turned back toward Peter, who had gotten down from the ladder and was looking straight at Daddy now from behind the counter.

"I asked you what few things you wanted," Peter said.

"A pound of ham," Daddy said. "A few loaves of white bread."

"We have a little girl, too," Kathy said. "Deborah. She was six last month. How old's your little girl?"

"You got ammunition?" Daddy said.

"What kind of ammunition?" Peter said.

"For a thirty-eight Smith and Wesson."

"Deborah's outside," Kathy said. "We can't keep her out of the snow. She just loves it. We came up mainly because of her. I like Palm Springs better myself. Deborah would love it if you'd let us give you and your little girl a ride up."

"We don't need a ride," Daddy said.

"There's no hunting up here this time of year," Walter said.

"Maybe he likes to shoot at cans," Peter said. He looked as if he didn't like Daddy, the way his lips turned sideways when he talked to him.

The door opened again, and the little girl came in. Her cheeks were red, and she was holding a ball made out of snow in her red-mittened hands.

"Can you come out and play?" the little girl said. She put the ball on the bench in front of the fire, and Lela watched the water seep out of it bit by bit and drip onto the floor until there wasn't anything left.

"She hurt her leg," Kathy said.

"Oh," the little girl said.

"This is Deborah," Kathy said. "She's our little girl. What's your name?"

"You're in luck," Peter said. "How many boxes you want?"

"How many have you got?"

"Eight."

"I'll take them."

"You planning a war?"

"We can take you where you're going," Kathy said.

"No," Daddy said. He never turned around to look at her. He was just stacking bags of potato chips and boxes of crackers on the counter in front of him while Peter sliced the ham on a big machine behind the counter. The slicer made a whirring sound. And it had a little skip in it, as if a marble or a rock had gotten caught in it somewhere.

"Can you play jacks with a broken leg?" Deborah said.

Daddy turned around and looked at Lela. "I'll be through in a minute, Lela, and then we'll be on our way."

"Her name's Lela," Kathy said.

"Can she talk?" Deborah said.

"I don't know," Kathy said.

Lela stood up. Kathy and Deborah both looked at her as though she had done something magical, standing on her own two legs.

"Oh, my," Kathy said, and stared at the pool of vomit on the wooden floor between Lela's shoes.

"She must have the flu," Walter said. "It's going around. Everyone has it."

Kathy was holding Lela around the waist like Mama did when she was sick. Lela liked the way Kathy held her. Tight, but not too tight.

"She always does that," Daddy said. "Vomits when she wants attention."

Lela watched the yellow-and-green stuff fall onto the floor. She wanted to stop, but it was like a water faucet that wouldn't turn off. She wished she had tried to aim for the bucket where the logs for the fire were, but it just came up too fast for that.

"It's those twisty windy mountain roads," Peter said. He was standing there with a mop, waiting for her to get through. "We get at least one kid a week coming in here and dumping their lunch on the floor."

The water felt good on Lela's face.

"There, now, are you feeling better?" Kathy said. She had brown eyes and a matching brown spot right in the corner of her red mouth. She moved the wet paper gently across Lela's face.

"Yes," Lela said.

"She can talk," Deborah said.

"Of course she can," Kathy said.

Lela was sitting on the edge of the sink with the water running right under her. Deborah pulled a fresh paper towel from the metal box and held it under the water till it was dark brown and soft. Then she handed it to Kathy.

"I used to get carsick all the time," Kathy said. "Deborah doesn't, though. You don't have to be a little girl to get carsick. Anyone can do it. I once vomited at the opera. Stood up in my seat and vomited on the shoes of the woman next to me. I was twenty-four at the time."

The bathroom was painted a light green. There were cracks in the cement floor and cold air coming in from somewhere.

"What grade are you in?" Deborah said.

"Third," Lela said.

"I'm in first."

It was so cold in here, Lela could see smoke coming out of their mouths when they talked.

"Have you ever been up here with your daddy before?" Kathy said.

"No."

"Do you know where your daddy is taking you?"

"No."

"Did he say anything about Lake Arrowhead? Or maybe Blue Jay or Running Springs?"

"I don't know."

"Where's your mommy?"

Lela shook her head.

"Maybe she doesn't have one," Deborah said.

"Bring her out of there now." Daddy was outside the door, yelling.

"We're coming," Kathy said. She lifted Lela off the sink and held her close for a moment, and Lela thought she said something to her, but it was in such a low voice she wasn't sure.

12

THE BUICK SLID a lot in the snow. Sometimes it felt as if they were going down the mountain instead of up, and then Lela would catch sight of the stars, see them coming toward her, and she'd know they were still heading up. Daddy screamed at the car like it could understand English, like it was just being stubborn sliding all over the place, like it ought to know better. But the car didn't listen. It just went where it wanted to go, and Daddy kept turning the wheel and putting on the brakes and yelling, and Lela thought they were going to crash or something, but they never did.

"You don't need the crutches," Daddy said. He had stopped the car, and in the seconds before he turned off the lights, Lela could see a little house, piles of snow all around it. It didn't look like a real house, but something that someone had started and then got busy somewhere else and forgot to finish. The door was the only thing that looked straight. Everything else—roof, windows, and the poles holding up the small porch—was crooked. It looked like if you touched it, the whole thing would fall down.

Daddy opened the car door for Lela and she stepped out onto the snow. It felt all crunchy under her feet. She supposed she could walk on the sore leg. She walked on it in therapy sometimes when the nurse wasn't looking, and it only hurt down around the ankle then. Now it hurt halfway up, a sharp pain when her shoe bent and the toes curled, as if the foot were attached to something that wasn't fixed yet. But it didn't make her cry.

"Go on," Daddy said, his arms full of bags of groceries. "Your leg's as good as mine," and he kind of pushed her through the snow to the little house.

"If everyone stays out of our way, we'll stay out of theirs," Daddy said. And he opened the door with a key, like it was his place, like he lived there.

"There's no TV, no telephone, no stove," Daddy said. "A person doesn't need those things to live."

Lela's leg was really aching now, and she sat down on the floor. There were no chairs, just a table where Daddy put the groceries.

"I guess what happened today scared you," Daddy said. He sat down on the floor, too, and crossed his legs. "But it wasn't my fault. Everything just was happening so fast I couldn't keep up with it. Jolene going off with that kid, leaving me like that, and then the police looking for me, trying to blame me for the wreck. And I took a chance and came home to get your mama and you, bring you up here. I was going to show your mother how we didn't need much to be happy. And then there were all those people in my yard, and then your mama started running, and she wouldn't open the door. I told her to open the door. You heard me tell her to, didn't you?"

"Yes," Lela said. Daddy was talking to her like she was a grown-up.

"What you saw happen today is a good lesson, Lela. That's just how quick things can be taken away from you, how people can interfere in your life and mess it up so you can't fix it again."

And he reached toward her, put his hand on her head, and left it there. Then he smiled at her the way he always smiled at Jolene.

Daddy covered them both with a blanket when he was through. Lela hadn't cried, even when it hurt the most. She had just shut her eyes real tight and tried not to think what he was doing. She tried to count the squares in hopscotch. If there were two up on top, then one, then one, then two, then one, one, one, how many were there?

"I have to pee," Lela said.

Daddy pulled the blanket back. He was almost snoring, as though what he had just done had worn him out.

"Hurry up," he said.

She just had her blouse on, and it was so cold around her bare bottom, and now when she walked she couldn't tell if her foot hurt worse than where Daddy had done that thing to her, or if her head hurt worse, or if she really had to pee at all, or if she was just sick to her stomach and was going to vomit again.

There was still a candle burning on the table. Daddy had made a picnic for them on the floor. Ham sandwiches and pretzels and cookies. There were still crumbs and torn bags on the floor, and she could feel the sharp bits of pretzels sticking to the bottoms of her feet.

The bathroom smelled bad. It doesn't flush, Daddy said. It's septic.

She sat down on the seat. There wasn't any wood, just bare cement. She couldn't pee. Nothing would come out, but it felt like something really was in there and wanted to come out. She stood up real fast and leaned over the toilet and tried to vomit. But that wouldn't come out, either. She just gagged and gagged. Tried to force it out, tried to cough it out. She couldn't, but just trying made her feel better.

Lela could hear Daddy calling her. Over and over and over.

"Lela. Come back in, Lela. I won't hurt you. I promise. Nothing's going to hurt you, Lela. Where are you, baby?"

The snow felt good on her bottom. She couldn't feel any of the sore spots when she sat here on the snow. The sore spots just went to sleep with the cold snow touching them. She settled her legs straight out in front of her. So this was what snow felt like. Like ice cubes. She leaned back and looked up at the sky. There were the stars. What held them up there? Why didn't they fall down, just crash into her? Was there anyone up there, anyone watching?

"Lela, baby, I won't get mad. Just come in now. You'll freeze to death out here. Aren't you cold?"

She could hear his boots making heavy sliding sounds in the snow and see the circles his flashlight made.

"Mr. Benoit!"

"Who's out there? Who the hell's out there?"

Daddy's flashlight couldn't turn the night into day. His flashlight wasn't as bright as the light the stars made. Only God could make stars. Only God could make lights that bright.

"Sheriff's department, Mr. Benoit."

She dug herself deeper into the snow. Oh, it felt so good now. She took her hands and began packing the snow around her. First on her stomach and then on the tops of her legs.

"Get off my property. I own this property. This is mine. I have a gun and I can use it."

"Where's the little girl?"

Daddy didn't answer. He just started shooting. Lela could tell that's what he was doing, because the noise was the same as when he shot Annette and Mama, only louder. That was because it was night-time. On the Fourth of July when Jolene and Mama and Daddy and Lela were sitting in the backyard watching the fireworks being shot off from the pier at the beach, it sounded like that. Daddy said that sounds are always louder at nighttime. Daddy said the air was wetter, and that was why.

She felt so sleepy. She wished she had her blanket from home. She wished she had her Japanese doll, the one Daddy bought in Japan when he was in the navy and the teddy bear Jolene bought her for her seventh birthday. She would have sat them both in the snow beside her, and they could all go to sleep together.

13

KATHY, IN A new red suit with a ruffly blouse, sat to Lela's right, real close, and gave Lela a little hug every time the judge asked the psychologist a question. Walter was at the end of the table near Miss Levinson, the lady who came to the hospital a few times and asked Lela all those questions about Daddy and Mama and Jolene. "I'm your lawyer," she told Lela, "and I'm going to ask the judge to let Kathy and Walter take you home with them." Miss Levinson had short black hair and was wearing a gray suit and a man's necktie, and one of her shoes made a funny noise when she walked.

"She seems not to have absorbed the events in the normal way, Your Honor," the psychologist was saying. Lela looked up at him sitting in that high chair next to the judge. He was nice. He brought puzzles and games and dolls to the hospital when he came to see her. That was fun. But he was always trying to make her remember things. That wasn't fun at all. He always wore Levi's and Hawaiian shirts when he came to see her in the hospital, so she almost didn't recognize him in his brown suit.

The judge was looking at some papers now. The psychologist was sipping water out of a big red paper cup. Lela looked at the flags in back of the judge. They hung exactly the same. Even the way the last little piece of cloth curled around itself and leaned against the pole was the same.

"I made a flag once," Lela said. "Mama sewed it on the machine. It had stars and stripes and everything."

"I bet it was beautiful," Kathy said.

"It was."

Just as Walter was carrying her into the building, a lady Lela had never seen before came up and said, "I pray for you every night." The lady was standing in the back with the rest of the people who couldn't find a seat. Lela turned around and waved at her.

Miss Levinson leaned across the table. Every time she did that she had something to say in a real low voice. She always smiled when she talked, too, like she knew a secret no one else did. "I'm pretty confident now, folks. It's going really, really well. The psychologist, then Walter, and then Kathy, and then it's all over."

"If I have one shoe and you have three, and Walter takes one away, how many do I have?" Lela said.

"Maybe Lela would like to go out in the corridor for a while," Miss Levinson said. "I can call her back in for the last fifteen minutes. That'll be enough for the judge to see, anyway."

"Well? Do you know how many shoes I've got left?" Lela said.

"Eighteen," Walter said.

"No."

"Fifteen?"

"No. Should I tell it again?"

"I know, I know," Kathy said, and she raised the fingers of her right hand and started counting them out loud.

"Well, it's three, if you didn't know," Lela said with a laugh.

"Did you people hear what I said?" Miss Levinson said.

"I heard you," Kathy said.

"Lela's fine right here," Walter said.

"She doesn't like to be away from me for very long," Kathy said, her hand on Lela's arm. Kathy's hands were always so warm. And soft, too, like she dipped them in something oily to get them that way.

"Where's my Eddie the Teddy?" Lela said.

"Right here," Kathy said, and pulled the teddy bear out of her knitting bag. Lela was always waiting to see if Kathy would forget something, but she never did. All those people who came to the hospital with toys, Kathy never lost one toy. Not a teddy bear or a doll. Not even the little pieces that came with the Yahtzee game. She kept all the toys in the cupboard in the hospital room, in neat rows, and helped Lela write notes to everyone who sent something. Lela didn't even know the people, but Kathy said they all felt like they knew her from reading about her in the paper and seeing her face on the television news.

The judge was finished reading, and the psychologist was talking · again.

"I find the child slightly immature for her age," the psychologist was saying.

"Did I tell you what we're going to have for dinner?" Kathy whispered. She pulled a little pillow out of her knitting bag and put it under Lela's feet. Kathy had everything in that knitting bag. Chocolate graham crackers, books, potato chips, a kaleidoscope. And a small green square of blanket and yarn and knitting needles. The blanket hadn't gotten any bigger than it was when Lela first saw it.

"Will she require therapy?" the judge was saying.

"Definitely, Your Honor," the psychologist replied.

"Fried chicken and Jell-O," Kathy said.

"With spaghetti?"

"If you want spaghetti."

"If I have any reservations about granting Mr. and Mrs. Bingham custody of the child," the psychologist was saying, "it would be based on the fact that their oldest daughter died at roughly the same age that Lela is now, and there's a danger of their interest being based solely on their desire to replace that child."

"It appears to me that in that case they will treat her with even more affection," the judge said.

"I'm not talking about affection, Your Honor. What I'm saying is that Lela is a special-needs child who will require long-term therapy and will have to be regarded as an individual with unique problems by any family she's placed with. I'm not certain that the Binghams can provide the proper setting, that is, a neutral one, free of their own psychological baggage, so to speak."

"Oh, my," Kathy said.

"The child who died was treated at City of Hope in Duarte," the psychologist was saying. "The mother stayed there a whole year until the child died. The younger child, Deborah, seems resentful of the mother's attention to anything or anyone else. I worry that the mother's desire to replace the deceased child could have deleterious effects on the remaining child, as well as on Lela Benoit if she is indeed put in the custody of the Binghams."

"There's a boy in my school who fights all the time," Lela said. "He gave me a bloody nose once."

"Oh, my," Kathy said, and Lela knew she hadn't heard what she said.

Miss Levinson jumped up and put both hands on the table in front of her, like she was trying to push it out of the way.

"I object to the characterization of the Binghams as somehow unworthy, Your Honor."

"Oh, my," Kathy said again.

"It's okay," Walter said, and reached for Kathy's hand. "It's okay."

Walter was really smart. He could make any coin you want disappear. He could make a quarter disappear or a nickel. Even pennies. Lela had watched and watched him every time he did it. It's in your sleeve, she always said, but then he'd pull it out of her ear, or sometimes when the nurse was in the room changing the bandages on her toes where the snow bit them, he'd pull it out of the nurse's cap. Sometimes out of her pocket.

"I'm not characterizing," the psychologist was saying. "I'm stating a reservation I have."

"Well, don't," Miss Levinson said.

"He's an expert witness, Counsel," the judge said.

Lela was getting tired. All the voices were the same. Maybe some were low and some were high, but they all sounded the same to her.

The psychologist was finished now, and Walter went up and sat in the chair.

"Can I have a chocolate graham cracker?" Lela said. Kathy was blinking a lot, but she picked up the bag and brought out the box of cookies while Walter was telling the judge his name and address.

"I own Bingham Aviation," Walter was saying. "We make airplane parts."

Kathy was making a lot of noise opening the box of cookies. Walter looked over at her and smiled. He seemed different today. He always wore a Dodgers jacket and tan slacks when he came to the hospital to see her. Now he was wearing a suit, a dark blue one, with a blue-and-red-striped tie that he kept running his hand over, like it wouldn't stay down if he didn't.

"Let's play ticktacktoe," Kathy said.

"We had our suspicions from the first," Walter was saying. "When he was buying groceries. Things didn't seem right. And then later on that night when we got up to our cabin in Blue Jay and went to bed, my wife couldn't sleep, and I knew she was thinking about the little girl. She said she had a feeling that something terrible was going on. I told her she was building things up in her mind, there was probably nothing wrong. Then along about two in the morning the sheriff got us up out of bed and told us they thought there was a fugitive up around Running Springs and he had a little girl with him,"

"I won Deborah three games yesterday," Lela said.

"You're such a good player, that's why," Kathy said. She was drawing lines for the game, putting her *X*'s in so fast it made Lela laugh. Miss Levinson looked over at her and shook her head.

"I know a few things about warfare," Walter was saying. "I was an air force pilot in World War Two and lobbed more than my share of bombs on the Germans, so when the sheriff told me what the man was a fugitive from and asked me if I'd like to help chase him down, I told him hell yes, and I went into the den and got my gun. Having a place as isolated as ours, it's foolish not having something to protect your family with. I never take it out except once in a while to clean it, but I took it out that night."

Kathy was the most fun of anyone. Sometimes she just came in the hospital room and lay down on the bed next to Lela and they watched cartoons. Sometimes all afternoon. Sometimes she read to her.

"There were four of us in all looking for a man in the dark," Walter was saying. "We didn't know what he had done with Lela. We just knew he was dangerous, that he had murdered his wife and another woman in cold blood. And then we heard him calling to her. 'Lela,' he kept saying, so we knew she was out there somewhere. The sheriff hollered to him, called him by name, and that was when he started shooting at us. We were afraid to return fire. We weren't sure whether he'd find Lela before we did and didn't want to take a chance on hitting her. But we knew she was alive then, and we just let him go, hoping if he did have her, he'd be in so much of a hurry to get away he'd leave her behind."

Kathy read all the Jungle Books to Lela in the hospital. Kathy's voice was magical. She could make it go up and down, make it soft or loud, strong or weak. She could sound like an elephant or a wolf or any animal she wanted when she was reading. She knew the exact noises a crocodile would make when he got angry. She knew how a baboon laughed.

"When we finally found her she was naked and bleeding from the vagina," Walter was saying. "There was even blood on her face. She was just lying out in the snow, shivering. Her eyes were opening and closing and she kept saying how sleepy she was. I don't think she knew where she was at that point. She was half frozen. No panties on. Just a little blouse. It was ten degrees out. She couldn't have stayed outside much longer. We're lucky we found her when we did. I'm pretty hard, Judge. Plenty of people have tried to rock me and couldn't. As I said, I was in the war. I've seen a lot of things. I've always prided myself on being unshakable. But the sight of that child in the snow made me cry."

"This is very sad," the judge said. And he cleared his throat and looked over at the flag in the corner. It didn't sound sad to Lela, what Walter was saying. She didn't even know who he was talking about.

She had missed half the words, she was so busy trying to find a piece of paper in Miss Levinson's briefcase so she and Kathy could play another game of ticktacktoe. Miss Levinson was holding her head in her hand and didn't seem to care that Lela was going through the papers in her briefcase, messing them all up looking for a clean piece of paper. What did Walter say that was so sad? The only sad thing Lela could think of was the story Kathy read her from the Jungle Books, the part about Mowgli being left with the wolf pack. There were lots of funny parts to the story, but that part made Lela feel really sad.

"I found some more paper, Kathy," Lela said. It was a little notepad, and it had three clean pieces of paper left in it.

"That's fine, honey," Kathy said. She was hunting for something in her knitting bag. Tissues. She had a box of tissues in there along with the cookies and toys and pillows. She took the plastic off the top of the box and then pulled a tissue out real slowly as if she were afraid it would make noise and upset everybody if she didn't pull it out that way. Her nose was already dripping by the time she got the tissue out.

"Your nose is dripping, Kathy," Lela said.

"I'll fix it, honey," Kathy said, and she pressed the tissue against her nose a few times and then leaned over and kissed Lela on the cheek. Lela loved when Kathy kissed her. Kathy's kisses weren't like Mama's. Mama always kept her lips against your skin for a long time when she kissed you. Kathy's kisses were quick. There were a lot of them, but they didn't take half the time Mama's always did.

"I have something to say about what the expert said about my wife and me," Walter was saying.

"I think Mr. Bingham might be getting too emotional, Your Honor," Miss Levinson said, and stood up again. She was taking long, deep breaths between words, not talking without breathing like she did before. "Maybe we're all getting too emotional. Perhaps we should take a recess."

"I'm not emotional," Walter said. "I want to talk about what the expert said about me and my wife. It needs to be said. It doesn't matter how emotional everyone in this room gets, it needs to be said."

Miss Levinson kind of tossed her hands in the air and then sat down.

"Go on, Mr. Bingham," the judge said.

"What the expert said about us wanting to replace our oldest girl, Anne, the one who died, is plain wrong. Just plain wrong. Kathy's

very loving. So am I. We've got room in our house and in our hearts
for both Deborah and Lela. And I'm not a poor man. We can give
Lela what she needs, including all the psychological help required.
As for Deborah being resentful, she's just a little girl who sometimes
gets jealous, as we all do. She's not going to torture Lela. She loves
Lela. She's looking forward to having Lela for a sister. We're committed to Lela as a family. Not just my wife or me or Deborah, but as a
family. We aren't trying to replace anyone. If we had wanted to do
that, we could have adopted a child any time in the six years since
Anne died. It's Lela we want. You might say we were a family just
waiting for Lela to join us."

Kathy was drawing lines for a new game and wiping her eyes with
a Kleenex in between. Kathy could draw anything. Lela had a whole
notebook full of animal pictures Kathy had drawn.

"The father is still at large, Miss Levinson?" the judge said.

"Yes, he is, Your Honor," Miss Levinson said. She stood up when
she spoke to the judge, and Lela started a game of counting the
wrinkles in the back of Miss Levinson's skirt while she was waiting
for Kathy to take her turn at ticktacktoe. There were so many wrinkles now, she lost count. More than thirty, at least. Kathy's clothes
never got wrinkled like that. She wore soft skirts and dresses that
looked like she just ironed them no matter how many times she sat
down on them.

"The police think Mr. Benoit might have headed for Vancouver,"
Miss Levinson was saying. "There was a map of Canada in his cabin
at Running Springs."

"Are the police actively seeking him there?" the judge said.

"That's my information, Your Honor."

"My question then, Counsel, is whether there is any possibility
that he might still be in the Southern California area, whether there's
a danger to the Binghams if we release the child to their care."

"We can't know for sure where he is, Your Honor."

"We're willing to take that risk," Walter said.

"Yes, we are, Your Honor, we're willing," Kathy said, and Lela
wanted to laugh at the loud way she said it, because Kathy hadn't
said anything louder than a whisper until then.

"Can I talk? I'd like to talk, please."

The voice came from somewhere near the door, and it startled
Lela, made her try to think of something. What was it?

"We're holding a hearing here," the judge said. "We can't just
have people come in here and talk any time they want. If you're
looking for the county clerk's office, I think you've lost your way."

"I'm as lost as I can be."

Lela kept her eyes on the paper with the *X*'s and *O*'s. That voice. It made her wiggle in her seat.

"I came all the way from Camp Pendleton, all the way, and I can't let this happen," the voice said, and Lela knew she had to look. She just had to. There was nothing else to do but look.

"That's Jolene," she said.

"Is this young lady here to testify, Counsel?" the judge said.

"I've never seen her before in my life, Your Honor," Miss Levinson said.

Jolene was walking fast, from the door to where the judge was. Oh, Jolene could walk fast when she wanted to. Lela remembered how fast she could walk. And run, too. She was the fastest runner when she was in the seventh grade. And had the longest legs, too. Lela's legs were too short to run as fast as Jolene. In her sleep she did, though. She could run so fast in her sleep that her feet didn't even touch the ground.

"I won that game," Lela said. She was studying the *X*'s again. Kathy sometimes didn't pay attention when she played ticktacktoe. It was like she didn't care if she won or lost.

"I see that, honey," Kathy said.

"Are you giving my baby sister away?" Jolene said. She was standing right up against the wooden stage in her tight blue jeans and cowboy boots, staring up at the judge. And there was Glenn, too, standing right off to the side by the man typing on the little machine. He was wearing a uniform, like he was a soldier or a policeman.

"Glenn," Lela called out. "I'm over here."

"How's the Olympic swimmer?" Glenn said. He was smiling at her as though he really, truly missed her.

"Let's have some order here," the judge said.

Miss Levinson was on her feet and walking up to where Jolene was.

"She's not a part of the custody hearing, Your Honor," Miss Levinson said.

"What do you mean?" Jolene said. She had turned her face to look at Miss Levinson, and Lela saw the little red line across her cheek from when Daddy had run his car into Glenn's.

"I mean you don't belong here," Miss Levinson said.

"I do. I do so."

"Are you contesting Mr. and Mrs. Bingham's petition for custody of Lela Benoit?" the judge asked.

"If that means do I want to take her home with me, that's what I'm doing," Jolene said. "This is my sister. She belongs with me."

"There's no more paper in the pad, Kathy," Lela said. "So we can't play another game, so I won four, and you didn't win any. Do you have any more paper anywhere?"

"I didn't bring any more paper," Kathy said, tears in her eyes.

Kathy always cried at strange things. Like now, just asking for more paper made her cry.

Lela glanced up at Jolene. Walter was walking back to the table and Jolene was sitting down now in the big chair next to the judge and telling him her name. The judge was acting so nice to Jolene, talking to her in a quiet voice, as if he didn't want to scare her.

"My name is Jolene Colson."

"No, it isn't," Lela said.

"It'd be best if you don't say anything, Lela," Miss Levinson said.

"Well, it isn't."

"It's my married name, sweetie, you know that," Jolene said.

"Maybe you'd better take Lela outside after all," Walter said.

"Don't make me go out now, Walter," Kathy said. "If something happens, and I'm not here to hear it—"

"I don't want you to get upset."

"How much more upset can I get?"

Lela dug her fingers into the box of chocolate graham crackers. The sound of the paper was almost loud enough so she didn't have to listen to what the judge and Jolene were saying.

"Yes, I was abused, too, that's right," Jolene was saying.

"I got chocolate all over my fingers," Lela whispered, and Kathy stuck her hand into the knitting bag for a tissue and wiped her hands.

"Since I was seven," Jolene was saying, "so I was afraid for my sister, I knew he'd try it if I went away. So I took her with me, and then he tried to kill us all, and now he's out there with his guns and who knows what else, and I didn't want to come before this, and when I read about her in the paper, I said to Glenn, I better stay away, or it'll just make things worse, but then I read that they were going to get custody—"

Lela took the plastic from the top of the box of tissues and laid it on the table. Then she took the plastic off the chocolate graham crackers and laid that down on the table, too.

"Glenn's stationed in Camp Pendleton," Jolene was saying, "but we don't know for how long. He expects to be shipped to Vietnam pretty soon, and then I get base housing, and Lela and I can live there till he gets back. It'll be as good a place as you can figure for her to live. They've got PX and movies and slides and swings. There's lots of kids there. Everyone's got kids on the base. There's even a school.

There's everything you need. Just everything. A doctor. A hospital, too, if you need one."

When all the plastic was laid out flat on the table, Lela tore them into strips and started to make a braid out of them. The plastic made a nice rattly sound that kept Lela from listening too hard to what Jolene was saying.

The judge was asking Jolene how old she was.

"Eighteen next January."

"This is November," the judge said.

The braid was tricky to do. You had to shove all those edges into the new part so it looked like it was all one long shiny thing. Mama showed her how to do it when she took Lela and Jolene on that long bus ride to visit Aunt Marge in Wichita two summers ago.

"There's your answer, Your Honor," Miss Levinson said. Lela looked at her, at how she was smiling at the judge. "The sister is a minor. A minor can't take custody of a minor."

"Coal miner, coal miner," Lela said. The braid was looking beautiful. It caught the lights from the ceiling and made all kinds of colors, like a rainbow, like a drop of water in the sun.

"I have to agree, Counsel," the judge was saying, and Jolene was asking what it was he was agreeing to.

"You're a minor. You can't take custody of your sister."

"You're going to give her to strangers?"

Kathy stood up. "Jolene, oh, Jolene, we're not strangers."

"You're strangers to me."

The braid was so long it covered one end of Miss Levinson's briefcase and dropped down over the other side.

"I bet I can make a braid that can go from here to China and back," Lela said.

"You can't do this," Jolene said.

"I'll take Lela out now," Kathy said.

"Wait, I'm not finished with my braiding yet," Lela said. She could see Jolene heading straight for her, looking like she was going to hit her or smash her face, she had such a mad look in her eyes. But when she got to the table, she just knelt down next to Lela's chair.

"Oh, sweetie, oh, Lela, I tried so hard. You know I did, don't you, baby?"

Jolene had her arms around her, was squeezing her. "I'll come back for you, you just wait, you'll see, Glenn will come back from Vietnam and I'll come and get you, and I'll be old enough then, too, and nothing will take you away from me again."

"We're not trying to keep you from your sister," Walter said.

"We want you to come and visit as often as you like," Kathy said.

Jolene wasn't paying any attention to Walter or Kathy, and she just wouldn't let go of Lela, just kept hugging her and hugging her and kissing her cheeks, and Lela saw the braid slip away onto the floor, and all those tiny tucks just gave way, just slipped away, and all the colors, all the rainbows, disappeared. Lela put her arms around Jolene's neck now. It was like she knew something only grown-ups are supposed to know, and that made her cry.

1966

"*A HIGH-STRUNG child, I can see that," the man said. He had long hair and a thin face, and he smelled a little like Walter, like he smoked a lot of cigarettes. He gave Lela a big sheet of paper and a box of crayons and sat her down at a small desk in a room filled with toys and books and then went back and stood in the corner with Kathy and talked about Lela and why she was there.*

"She's had horrific experiences," Kathy said.

Her face was worried looking, and it made Lela's stomach jump a little bit, but the man smiled over at her and said, "Draw something for me, Lela."

Lela could tell that a lot of children had been in the room. There were paper pictures thumbtacked to the wall. Purple trees and green houses and lots of moons and stars and cats and dogs.

"Is she showing any overt symptoms?" the man said. He was looking at Lela over Kathy's shoulder, his forehead wrinkled up the way Kathy's was.

"I can draw an alligator," Lela said.

"Have you ever seen one?" the man asked. He was smiling, but he didn't look happy.

"A million and one," Lela said.

Kathy lowered her head and put her hand to her mouth. She was trying to hide what she was saying, but Lela could hear it anyway.

"That's one of the symptoms," Kathy said. "Stories."

"All children tell stories," the man replied.

Kathy gave him the folder she had in her satchel. The man began to read it, standing there with the folder in his left hand and going through the pages with his right, letting them fall against his chest one by one by one.

"And she vomits," Kathy said.

"Here it is," Lela said, and held up the picture so the man could see.

"That's beautiful, Lela," he said, and his voice sounded all shaky and loose to Lela, not straight and steady the way it was when he talked to her before.

"And faints," Kathy whispered.

1967

I T   W A S   F O G G Y   that last day with Dr. Warren. Lela couldn't see out the windows of the playroom, it was so foggy. They were playing the game of finish the sentence. Lela liked that game a lot. Dr. Warren would start, and she would finish. It was so much fun.

"My favorite thing to do is," Dr. Warren said.

"Ride horses," Lela said.

"The places I ride my horse are," Dr. Warren said.

"To see my mother and father and sister," Lela said.

"My mother is," Dr. Warren said.

"In heaven," Lela said.

"My father is," Dr. Warren said.

"My father is," Lela repeated.

"My father is," Dr. Warren said again.

"Shooting me," Lela finally said. "He has a gun and he's shooting me. And there's blood everywhere. On my dress and on my panties and in my mouth."

When Kathy came to get her, Dr. Warren handed her the folder with all of Lela's pictures and papers and records in it. He didn't take Kathy into the other room to talk to her, didn't stand in the corner and whisper like he sometimes did. He kept blowing his nose and wiping his eyes and stopping every once in a while to cough.

"My wife and I just had a baby," he told Kathy. "Our first. A girl. It's changed my outlook. I don't know what to say, and I'm so sorry, but the way I feel I just won't be any use to her anymore, and it just kills me anyway to look at her."

"I understand," Kathy said.

1971

"WE CAN TALK *in front of you, can't we, Lela?" Dr. Rusk asked.*

Kathy had brought Lela to his office. Dr. Rusk is the best child psychiatrist in the South Bay, Lela's pediatrician had told her.

"You can talk all you want," Lela said, "but I won't listen. I don't need a doctor. I have a doctor."

"Are you comfortable in that chair, Lela?" Dr. Rusk asked.

"It's the hardest chair I ever sat in," Lela said. "It's probably the hardest chair that was ever made."

"Would you like to sit on the couch with us?"

Kathy and Dr. Rusk were sitting next to each other on a black-and-gray tweed couch near the office door. Lela could hear the doctor's nurse in the other room. She was blowing her nose. Blow, cough, snuffle. Blow, cough, snuffle.

"I like hard chairs," Lela said.

Kathy kept looking over at her, smiling little quick smiles, and then turning back to Dr. Rusk. Lela loved the way Kathy's hair swung back and forth when she did that, almost like she was doing it on purpose so she could show off how silky smooth her hair was, how it all went the same direction, whip, whip, whip.

"The pediatrician, Dr. Clarke, thinks fourteen's a crucial age, that if we catch these problems now—" Kathy said.

"I have no problems," Lela said.

"Of course not," Dr. Rusk said.

"She hasn't seen anyone in four years for, you know—for her—for that —for the—"

Dr. Rusk nodded at Kathy. "I think you're doing absolutely the right thing by bringing her to me."

"It's just that she's so fragile emotionally. I mean, she takes the world's cares on her shoulders. Anything will make her cry or vomit or faint. I don't think she's ever gotten over that, you know—that—well, it's all in the records I sent you."

Dr. Rusk kept patting Kathy's arm and smiling at her, as though he were her friend. He looked older than Walter. Lela couldn't tell how much older, though. He had a brown beard that sparkled with shiny red spots where the sun through the window hit it.

Lela looked around the office. Diplomas on one wall and paintings of sailing ships on the other. And then that tall, wide window looking down on Rodeo Boulevard, with all those cars going up and down the street.

"My technique is a little different from most therapists'," Dr. Rusk said. "Some people might even call my methods unorthodox."

"She won't talk about the—you know, what happened to her," Kathy said. "The last doctor tried, and at first she wouldn't, but then she did, and it just about devastated him, and I don't even know what it was she said to him, but she's never talked about the—about—you know—never talked to me about any of that—about what happened. She never really has talked much to anyone about the—about how—about— Lela, do you want to go out in the waiting room?"

"I'm not listening," Lela said.

"Why do you want her to talk about it?" Dr. Rusk said. "Why bring it up? Why pain the child further?"

"You don't think she needs to bring it out and deal with it?" Kathy said.

"I think she needs to bury it, get on with being a child, with growing up."

Lela got up and walked over to the window. Kathy and Dr. Rusk looked comfortable sitting next to each other on the couch, talking, but Lela couldn't keep sitting on that dumb chair with a big window waiting for her across the room, practically begging her to come and look at what was happening outside.

"I've tried to shield her," Kathy said. "Walter and I both—my husband, Walter. He's particularly protective of her. He's the only one who seems able to calm her down at times."

"I'm going to be an artist," Lela said. "I entered one of my watercolors in the art show at the PV mall—not the old mall, the new one—and it won first prize. Someone bought it for fifty dollars, and he left a note with Mary Berger—she runs the art show every year, and this was the first year I could enter, because you have to be fourteen or older, and I was fourteen in November, just in time to do the picture and get my name entered—and Mary said the man said he was going to hang my picture in his office, and I could come and see it any time I wanted to. I said I didn't drive, but maybe I could get my father to take me over. I'm working on another picture now. Irises. The bearded kind, not the day lilies. Day lilies don't last long enough for me to really do a good job of painting them, and I need at least three days to do a picture the way I want it to look. Mary said the man said he was going to

hang the daffodils next to a Miró because the colors blended. That upset me a little bit, putting pictures together on the wall because the colors blend. I told Mary I thought I'd go and buy the picture back from him if that's all he thought art was."

"Like now, you see what she's doing?" Kathy said. She was nearly whispering to the doctor, but Lela could still hear what she was saying. "The talking. It's almost like a trance, the way she starts talking. Off somewhere in her own head. I know she's listening to what we're saying, though. I can break in and tell her to do something right now, and she'll do it, but it's unnerving, and I worry about it, what it means."

"She's attempting to deny reality," Dr. Rusk said.

"But she won't admit she remembers anything," Kathy said, "so what is she denying?"

"It's very complex, but briefly, she's hearing echoes of memory and trying to drown them out by talking over them."

"Of course," Lela said, "Sister Margaret Henry—she teaches third period art at St. Cecilia Martyr—that's the private school I go to, St. Cecilia Martyr High—Deborah will go there next year when she's in seventh—Sister thinks I shouldn't only paint flowers and trees and houses, that I ought to do pictures of people." It was funny how short everyone looked from up here and how their heads seemed to fit right onto their shoulders, with no necks in between. "How many ways can you paint a flower, Sister always asks me, but I never get tired of flowers. I've never, ever seen two flowers that looked alike. Never. Not once. Oh, sometimes I think I've found one that's exactly like one I've seen before, but when I look real close I can see the little details that make it different from all the others. Maybe it's just a darker color than most, or the petals are thinner. You could say that twins are identical, too. Well, I don't know about that, anyway, but I'll bet they're not. I'll bet if you look real close, you'll see they're not."

"Walter can get her quieted down," Kathy said. "Just a few words from him and she turns into a little lamb, will talk to you, not at you. And he can make her listen. Really listen to what he's saying. They can have a conversation. Deborah can talk to her, too. They talk all the time. Deborah doesn't remember a thing about the, you know, the—about what happened. She's two years younger. Deborah is a little outspoken at times, teases Lela about her vomiting and fainting, but I figure that will change as they grow up. But I don't know what to do. I reach and reach for Lela, but she's always just a little too far away from me, and I think it's because of her—you know about her mother, about the—"

"I read about it at the time," Dr. Rusk said.

"It's nearly impossible for me to carry on a conversation with her. She *pulls away. Sometimes I think I'm going to, but it doesn't happen. She always seems to be somewhere else. I don't know how Walter does it. He just leans over and whispers in her ear when she goes off. I don't even know what he says. I sometimes think he doesn't say anything, that he just leans over toward her, and that somehow makes her feel safe."*

"The goal of my treatment of her will be to make her forget what happened," Dr. Rusk said. "I don't believe in integrating bad memories in young people. Perhaps in adults integration works, but not in youngsters. Lela needs to destroy her bad memories, not come to terms with them. In my opinion, her fragility, her symptomatology, all indicate that she's been trying to do that herself, but unsuccessfully."

"Deborah is my own child, I told you that. Didn't I tell you that?"

"You did."

"She thinks I favor Lela, but it isn't true, it's just that she worries me so much that I hardly have time to think of anything else. Or anyone else. I don't know what I'd do without Walter. He's my rock."

Lela pressed her face against the window glass. What if she fell? What if the window gave way and she fell down onto the street, fell onto someone? Like that lady stepping along the sidewalk swinging that big red purse. Or the man behind her, the one in the pullover sweater. She could kill someone if she fell out the window. Just thinking about it made her want to do it.

Kathy was on her way out the door now, stopping, turning around, looking anxiously back at Lela.

"Will you be all right, honey?"

"Umm-hmm," Lela replied.

1972

THERE WAS NOTHING Lela wouldn't do for Dr. Rusk. Gilbert. Gil. She called him Gil.

"Deborah's always saying things to me that hurt my feelings," Lela said.

"You can't change Deborah or control how she behaves," Gil said. He was sitting on a pillow on the floor. He always sat on a pillow at Lela's therapy sessions. Lela always sat on the couch. "The only one you can control is yourself."

"I never say anything mean to her. Why does she say mean things to me?"

"Maybe it's her way of letting you know she's there. She's probably a little jealous of you, too."

"Then sometimes she's sweet as pie."

"Nothing's pure, Lela. Nothing. I told you that."

Gil knew everything. Everything. It was as though he could look inside Lela's head whenever he wanted to check and see what she was thinking. It seemed as though she didn't have to say more than two words before he knew what she was going to say. Sometimes he even told her what her own thoughts were before she knew herself. He didn't make her talk about anything she didn't want to talk about. If she wanted to talk about school, it was all right with him. Or about a movie she saw. Or a song she heard. She wasn't afraid to say anything to Gil. Sometimes they just sat and didn't talk at all. A whole hour they'd sit facing each other without saying a word. She trusted him more than Kathy, more than Walter. She almost never vomited anymore, and she'd only fainted once since school started, and that was because Deborah made up a story about Walter and Kathy getting a divorce, which Kathy said later could never happen, not ever in a million years. And the bad thoughts were gone. No little pictures in her head. No more feeling like she was going to fall off the end of the world. And it was all because of Gil. He knew just what to say to make her feel like everything was going to be okay.

"I'm going to the freshman dance," Lela said. She was still in her school uniform, sitting here in her psychiatrist's office on his nubby couch in her St. Cecilia Martyr plaid skirt and white blouse.

103

"Your first date," Gil said, and he smiled.

"The boy goes to St. Boniface High," Lela said. "He lives in Rolling Hills. I'm not sure I want to go."

"You're really frightened, I can tell." Gil put his hand on Lela's knee. His nice, warm hand.

"Did you know that St. Cecilia died for love?" Lela said. "She refused to worship the Roman gods—St. Cecilia, that is. Her boyfriend was a Roman, and she converted him to Christianity, so the Romans killed her. I don't think I could die for love. If I was St. Cecilia, I'd have converted him back."

"Let me hug you," Gil said. "A hug will help take the fright away. Give me your hand. Come sit on my lap."

Lela felt awkward, the way she had to bend her knees, practically kneel on the floor, then turn around so Gil could help her into his lap. He sometimes hugged her when she was feeling very sad and didn't know what to do about it. But it always felt strange, sitting on his lap.

"The Romans tried to boil her alive," Lela said, "and that didn't work, and then they tried to behead her. It took three days because the ax kept slipping off. The boy's name is Darryl. I don't mean Darryl's the one St. Cecilia converted. I mean the boy I'm going to the freshman dance with."

When Gil hugged her, it felt nice. He was sitting on his pillow and holding Lela in his lap and hugging her and rocking her a little bit. His beard tickled her nose.

"I didn't tell Kathy I was afraid to go to the dance."

"That's all right. You told me."

"He asked me if I wanted a gardenia corsage or an orchid one." Their breaths were mingling, and she felt like a little girl. A very little girl.

"What if something happened to you, Gil? What would I do then?"

"Nothing's going to happen to me."

Walter sometimes held her on his lap when she was thinking thoughts that wouldn't go away. But he held her lightly on the tips of his knees and never let her stay there very long.

"We'll talk some more next week," Gil said, and he made a move to help her up.

"Hold me some more," she said. Gil had his hand on her plaid skirt, the one Sister Caroline in Algebra 1 said was too short. Can't you let the hem down a little? Sister Caroline said.

They were still sitting on the floor a half hour after it happened, with their clothes all around them and Gil asking Lela over and over if she was all right, and running his hand over his beard every time he asked her, and she saying over and over that she was fine, just fine.

"*I don't understand how it happened,*" *he said.* "*I can't imagine how in hell I let it happen, how I could ever have done such a thing to you.*"

Lela knew how it happened. He had put his hand inside her pants and moved his fingers up and down against those soft spots she never looked at, not even in the bathtub, and then lain down on top of her and pushed himself inside her. And she had let him do it. She had even helped him do it. How else to please him, make him love her?

"*I'm so ashamed,*" *he said.* "*So ashamed.*"

She had thought it would hurt or sting, but it didn't. Although he had had to kiss her there with his tongue to make it easier for him to get inside her. Now all it felt was wet. She had put her panties on, and they felt wet, too.

"*I never seduced a patient in my life. Jesus Christ, you're only fifteen years old. Jesus Christ. Are you sure you're all right?*"

He wasn't trying to touch her anymore. He was just sitting on the floor with his pants off, rubbing his beard and shaking his head. He looked as if he were going to cry.

"*I'm glad it happened,*" *she said. She pulled on the plaid skirt and tucked her white blouse inside the waistband.*

"*You're too young to be glad about a thing like this.*"

"*Didn't you tell me I control my own behavior?*"

"*That's not what I meant. Jesus Christ.*"

He was looking at her differently than he had a half hour ago when he was putting himself inside her. He hadn't looked ashamed then. He'd looked happy.

He got up now and put on his pants and started buttoning his shirt, keeping his eyes away from hers. "*I hope you won't hate me,*" *he said. His skin, always a shade lighter than the red flecks in his hair, was blood dark now.* "*I hope it doesn't make you lose faith in people again. I'll refer you out, of course. We can't continue after this.*"

"*It was my choice,*" *she said.*

"*Jesus Christ,*" *he said again.* "*What was I thinking?*" *He started to tremble.* "*What in hell was I thinking?*"

She walked up behind him and enclosed him in her arms, held him as he sometimes held her.

"*If I hadn't wanted you to do it, I could have screamed or fought or run away.*"

"*You don't understand, Lela. You're still just a kid.*"

"*I understand that I would vanish,*" *she said,* "*turn to smoke, melt away, without you.*"

Part
Two

14

1993

"THEY BUILT THIS place of natural Palos Verdes stone," Lela said. "Those were the days when it was still plentiful and not too expensive."

"I don't want no old houses," Mr. Swenson said.

"It's not old," Lela said. "Thirty-five years. Is that too old?"

"Maybe. Just so long as it isn't older than me."

Mr. Swenson was in work pants and a baseball cap and seemed intent on opening every cupboard in the house. Mrs. Swenson had on a flowered dress with a matching jacket. When they came in the office that morning and asked to look at houses in Rolling Hills Estates, Brad had said, "No money. I can smell it a mile away when they have no money."

"I don't see anyone else sitting out in front eating stale Danish and looking at our listing book," Lela had said.

Brad was Lela's partner. And Deborah's husband. He had provided the start-up money for Bru-Bing Realty five years before, in 1988. Two years after Walter lost control of his airplane and flew it into an apartment house and he and Kathy as well as four people in one of the apartments were killed.

"It must get cold in Minnesota," Lela said.

"I like the change of seasons," Mrs. Swenson said. She had left most of the talking to her husband till now.

"I never noticed it that much," Mr. Swenson said.

"It doesn't snow in California, you know," Lela said. "Hardly even rains."

"I read about the floods," Mr. Swenson said. "It was in the *St. Paul Star*. I know all about it. Houses falling down from the mountains, all that stuff."

"We weren't touched up here. Everything up here's built on bedrock."

The house was in Rolling Hills Estates, miles above the San Pedro flatlands, so high up the hill you couldn't see the topless bars and empty stores below. Choice property. Above the clouds. With a view of the ocean. But the house was a mess, the gardens had turned to weeds, and the time when California hillsides were tipped with gold, when houses, even dilapidated ones, with a view of anything—including a freeway or a cemetery—practically sold themselves was over. That time was before the L.A. riots. Before the recession. Before torrents of rain ended the California drought, and hillside houses, sliding along mushy slopes, sometimes came straight down to meet the view.

"I grew up not far from here," Lela said. "In a house on the peninsula. You could see the ocean from there. My sister and her family live in it now."

"Is it for sale?" Mr. Swenson said.

"Oh, no."

"Too bad."

"Actually you can see the ocean from here, too, if you go out to where the pine trees start, then take the path out to the—"

"I don't like water that much," Mrs. Swenson said.

"Do you like clams?"

"Littlenecks," Mr. Swenson said. "The wife makes clam soup out of them."

"There's pismos here," Lela said. "You go out and stand in the surf and wiggle your feet around, you can feel them. Four inches across, most of them. I once found one eight inches. Four of us had it for dinner."

"Small eaters," Mrs. Swenson said.

"I don't know if I mentioned it," Lela said, "but this house won the Architecture of America design award in 1958."

"And I can buy you all the awards you can carry," Mr. Swenson said. "Everyone's always giving out awards for something or other. It doesn't mean a thing."

A man Lela didn't recognize had come into the house and was standing looking out the bay window at the yard. He was just standing there, gazing out as though he had been invited in. He didn't look like he was from the area. His hair was long and caught in a rubber band at the back of his head. That could have qualified him as a local, except that he wasn't wearing torn jeans and an old white T-shirt. He had on a suit, an out-of-date one, but it was clean. He did have a California complexion, though. Sunburned face and sun-squint lines around his eyes.

"I'll let you go and check out the kitchen for yourself," Lela said to Mrs. Swenson. "There's even a little nook off the pantry. The former owners used it as a sewing room. It'd be great for storage. Whatever it is you like to store would be out of the way and yet you could get to it in a minute if you had to. You know how you're always looking for things and they're up high in some kitchen cabinet. In the pantry you've got shelves that start at the floor and don't go any higher than your head. It's perfect for storage. You'll love it."

Mr. Swenson was on his knees, looking up the flagstone fire-place. He stood up now and rubbed the small of his back with two sooty fingers. "I think I'll go see the chimney up on the roof," he said.

"Good idea," Lela said.

Mrs. Swenson headed for the kitchen.

"It must be tough—selling, I mean," the man at the window said, turning around.

"I'm with Bru-Bing Realty," Lela said. "Brad Brubaker and Lela Bingham. I'm Lela. This house is a steal. The owner's in jail. Doug Jones, the doughnut king, maybe you've been watching the trial on television. He lost all his doughnut shops—went bankrupt or some-thing—and killed his wife for the insurance money."

"I'm not from the area. Up north." He cleared his throat as though he weren't used to saying that many words at one time. "A small town up north. Very small. If it was any smaller, you might not even notice it."

"Small towns are nice," Lela said. "You get to know everyone in them. Not like Los Angeles or New York."

"Not like that at all," he said. He was staring at her. Studying her, really.

"Are you doing okay, Mrs. Swenson?" she called out. "Finding everything you need?"

"I don't think she can hear you in there," the man said.

"They're from Minnesota," Lela said. "The Swensons. He's retir-ing. This would be a great house to retire in. Or you could turn the whole place into a studio. Knock out a few walls, and there you are, with a space big enough to do sculpture in or paint murals. And look at that sky, will you. Magical light, I call it. And at night, the jasmines up here just blow you away with the smell. Some of the bushes are overgrown, but it's no trick to cut them back a little. It doesn't hurt them at all. Are you down here looking for a house?"

"No, I'm not." He had a metal plate under the skin of his forehead, right up near the hairline, and the way the sun caught it startled Lela.

"Vietnam," he said. "The plate. It gets hot sometimes, you know, if I'm out in the sun too long. Do you want to touch it?"

"Well—"

"Go ahead. Don't be afraid."

It felt the way a rug would feel if you put a board under it to keep it from slipping. Or the inside of a seasoned frying pan, smooth in the center and a little bumpy at the edges. Lela didn't know what to do with her hand when she pulled it away.

"It freaks most people out," he said.

"Well, I don't know. It doesn't freak me out."

"My name's Ross McGowan. I'd like to talk to you, if you can spare some time. Maybe we could go get some coffee when you're through here."

"If this has something to do with the lawsuits against my father's estate, there's nothing left. No assets, no business, no money. Just the house that my sister's living in."

"Lawsuits?"

"The ones against my father—Walter Bingham. You're not here about the lawsuits?"

He shook his head. "I don't know anything about that." He kept staring at her. "I thought you'd be darker."

"Pardon me?"

"Darker. You know, have dark hair, dark eyes. I didn't expect a blonde."

"I help it a little," she said, and touched her fingers to her hair. "But it's mostly natural."

"You had dark hair in the picture your sister gave me."

Lela smiled at him. "Will you excuse me just a moment?"

"Sure."

"I just want to check something out in the kitchen. See if Mrs. Swenson is finding everything."

"The nook, sure, gotcha."

Mrs. Swenson was turning the jets on the stove on and off, clicking the flames from high to low and back again.

"I'm used to electric," Mrs. Swenson said. "I've got all electric in my kitchen in Minnesota."

"I just want to make a call," Lela said. She already had her cellular phone out and was dialing the number. "Isn't that pantry nook fabulous?" The phone was ringing.

"Looks like a shoebox to me," Mrs. Swenson said.

"You've got to imagine it with your things stored in it. It makes all the difference how you see a house, using your imagination, that is. Go take another look. Go on. I'll just be a minute."

"I looked once, but I'll look again."

Lela stared at Mrs. Swenson's broad back as she walked toward the pantry. It was square from her shoulders down to her hips.

"Hello?" Deborah always answered the phone with a question mark and a nervous tremolo in her voice, as though she half expected a monster to jump out of the receiver and bite her.

"Deb, it's me. Lela. There's a guy in a house I'm showing on Carnation Lane who says you gave him a picture of me. A Ross McGowan."

"I didn't give anyone any pictures. I don't know any Ross Mc-Gowans."

"Are you crying?"

"Oh, God, Lela, I'm pregnant again."

Mrs. Swenson was back.

"You couldn't fit a rat's tit in that pantry," Mrs. Swenson said.

"I'll be off the phone in a second, Mrs. Swenson. If you want to check the bathroom off the master bedroom one more time   "

Lela waited till Mrs. Swenson was out of the kitchen before she put the phone to her mouth again.

"How do you know you're pregnant again?"

"The test kit."

"Maybe the test kit's defective."

"For God's sake, Lela, test kits aren't defective."

"Did you call the doctor?"

"It's only the first month. You don't go to the doctor the first month. Maybe he's there about one of the lawsuits."

"Who?"

"The guy."

"He said no."

"I promised Brad after the twins that was it. No more. What'll I do if he leaves me, Lela?"

"He won't leave you."

Mr. Swenson was making stamping noises on the roof. Lela looked up at the ceiling. It sounded as if he were going to come through any second.

"I called the midget this morning," Lela said. "He'll be at your house at one o'clock, but he won't be a Ninja turtle. He says it's demeaning."

"What *will* he be? I don't want the kids scared. Did you go and hire someone who'll scare the kids, for God's sake?"

"Batman or Superman. Is that too scary?"

"But he's a midget. How can a midget be Batman or Superman?"

"He's an actor. He can play anything, but I've got to let him know which one you want, so take your pick."

"You should have asked me first, Lela. Now we're stuck with whatever he wants to be. You really should have asked me first."

"It seemed so minor, I never thought you'd make a federal case out of it."

"I'm not making a federal case."

"Jason won't know the difference anyway." It was Jason's birthday. He was two. The twins, Tony and Joey, were nine months.

"You pick, then, since you've arranged everything anyway," Deborah said. "I can't. I'm in too much turmoil. The house is upside down. The damn roof is falling down now in the upstairs bathroom. Brad says he isn't putting another nickel into the place. And Rowena doesn't listen to me. She cooks what she wants, even though she knows the twins' skin erupts if they so much as look at peas. And Jason won't mind anyone but her. He kicks me when I try to tell him to do anything he doesn't want to do."

"Maybe you expect too much."

"What?"

"I like Batman myself."

"You don't know anything about raising children."

"I just said—"

"What do you know about how much I should expect?"

"I'll be over as soon as I'm through."

Ross McGowan was still standing at the window in the living room when Lela came back.

"You were gone so long, I thought maybe you couldn't find Mrs. Swenson," he said.

"I had to call my office," she said. "They like to know where I am every minute."

"Sure."

"So you have a picture of me, you said?"

He handed her the photograph. It was of a little girl with curly brown hair and a space where her two front teeth should be.

"I don't think that's me," Lela said.

"You are Lela Benoit, aren't you?"

"Bingham."

"But it was Benoit, right?"

"I don't know what it was." She handed the photograph back to him. "I don't know that girl."

He nodded his head and put the photograph carefully back in his suit pocket.

"The fireplace won't draw," Mr. Swenson said. He had soot in his hair and cold cinders clinging to his eyebrows.

"It won't?" Lela said.

"I'm staying at the Holiday Inn in Wilmington," Ross said. "I'll be there till Sunday, if you want to talk."

"There's birds nests and raccoon crap all up through the chimney," Mr. Swenson said. "You ever look up there?"

"No, I haven't. But that doesn't sound like a serious thing to me. We've got chimney sweeps we can call, can get rid of anything. Mice, raccoons—"

Mrs. Swenson was back from the rear of the house. "The bathtub's too small. I like to take baths. I'd never fit in that bathtub."

Mr. McGowan was on his way out the door.

"Sorry I couldn't help you," Lela called out after him, and he just gave a little wave of his hand over his shoulder.

"I guess that's that," Lela said, and she smiled at the Swensons. "You know this house is in the Palos Verdes postal district," she said. "That makes it more valuable than one down the hill with a San Pedro address."

"A fancy address won't help this house," Mrs. Swenson said.

15

"She did it on purpose," Brad said. He was standing at the sink, watching Lela decorate the cake. "She knows money's tight, and she gets pregnant again."

"I think I'll put a few more balloons coming out of the Ninjas' hands," Lela said. She didn't like it when Brad talked about Deborah that way, as though she were the enemy, as though he had nothing to do with anything involving her. It made her stomach ache when Brad talked about Deborah like that.

"I'd like to dump this house," he said. "Would you believe two thousand dollars to trim the trees last month?"

"I think this is my masterpiece," Lela said. She had done a special job on the cake, made a border of pastry flowers, pink and green roses, brown dogs chasing yellow cats, palm trees, kids on swings, and in the middle the two big Ninja turtles, arms around each other's shoulders, balloons shooting from their guns instead of bullets.

Deborah was back again with Tony, one of the twins, on her hip. She hadn't lost any of the weight she'd gained when she was pregnant with them and was still wearing maternity smocks over her stretch slacks. The door swung a few times behind her, bringing in gusts of children's laughter from the living room.

"Not one of them believes that midget is Batman," Deborah said. The midget had arrived in black trousers rolled to the knees and a cape that trailed behind him like the train on a wedding gown. "Wherever did you get him, Lela?"

"From the Yellow Pages."

"The Yellow Pages? You hired someone from the Yellow Pages?"

"They sound like they're having a good time."

"I asked you something."

"Actually I got him from a friend. She had him at her husband's birthday party."

"Is that the truth?"

"Leave her alone, Deb," Brad said.

"What friend?" Deborah said.

"Rowena, could you give me a hand lifting the cake onto the tray?" Lela said.

Rowena, skin as black as the midget's pants, was at the sink, cutting tuna sandwiches into four-inch squares and shaking her head slightly from side to side like she always did when Deborah was in one of her moods. She wiped her hands on her apron and went around to the other side of the butcher block.

"Just ease it onto the tray slowly," Lela said.

"Did the Swensons bite?" asked Brad.

"Not yet," Lela replied.

"What did the midget do at this friend's husband's birthday party?" Deborah said.

"Impersonated John Wayne," Lela said. "And Madonna. Oh, and Judy Garland."

Rowena was laughing.

"It's not funny, Rowena," Deborah said.

"You should have taken the kids to the zoo instead of letting them wreck the house," Brad said. He was short and muscular and combed his hair to one side to hide the bald spot growing at the top of his head.

"You've been picking at me all week," Deborah said.

"Admit you got pregnant on purpose."

"Tell him, Lela, tell him it was an accident."

"It was an accident," Lela said. She stood back and surveyed her work. "I should get a prize for this one."

"You didn't put artificial coloring in the frosting, did you?" Deborah said.

"Houses aren't selling so fast," Brad said. "How am I going to support four kids and a wife?"

"You can get cancer from food coloring," Deborah said. "I told you no food coloring."

"It's just a cake," Lela said.

"Why don't you ever listen to me?" Deborah said. She turned toward Brad. "She never listens to me."

"This is only the second year she's made a cake," Brad said. "Don't stretch it, Deborah."

"You always take her side."

"Did you leave those kids by themselves in the other room?" Brad said.

"The midget's there with them," Deborah replied.

"I think we ought to stop calling him the midget," Lela said.

"So how did the Swensons look when you left them?" Brad said.

"Iffy," Lela said.

"Maybe they'd like to buy this house," Brad said.

"I'll never sell this house," Deborah said.

"Two thousand dollars to trim trees, Deb," Brad said.

"I'll go to work."

"What as? An Egyptologist? In Southern California, for chris-sakes?"

Lela wanted to tell them to stop behaving like babies, stop snipping and sniping at each other. She wanted to tell them how she thought they ought to talk to each other. Nicely. Sweetly. Lovingly.

"Lela's got a mass murderer following her around," Deborah said.

"A what?" Brad said.

"You know, a fatal attraction."

"He's not a mass murderer," Lela said. "He's just some guy from a small town up north. He's got a metal plate in his head from Vietnam. He let me touch it."

"You touched a stranger's metal plate?" Deborah said.

"It was the weirdest feeling. I can't describe it. The reason I noticed it was the sun was shining on it through the window, and it was giving off like rainbows and things."

"What did he want?" Brad said.

"Oh, he had me confused with someone else."

"There was a real estate agent raped up on Barton Way last week," Brad said. "You'd better be careful, Lela, feeling strange guys' metal plates."

"I think it's done," Lela said, and stood back and stared at the cake. "Well, maybe just a little more green around the border, and that's it."

"It's prettier even than last year," Rowena said.

Brad had his arm around Deborah and was whispering something in her ear that made her giggle. Lela, watching them, could feel the nervous knot dissolve in her stomach.

"I can't stand when you make love in front of me," she said.

"Lela's jealous," Deborah said. She gave Brad a little kiss and then brought Tony over to the butcher block.

"Don't you let him touch that icing, Deb," Lela said. "Not after I slaved over it for two hours."

"It's just a cake that's going to be eaten up in five minutes anyhow," Deborah said, and she held the little boy over it. "Look, Tony, a Ninja Turtle cake, sweetie. Isn't Aunt Lela smart the way she does things?"

The sun had gone an hour before, and Lela could barely see where to dig. A flat of carnations usually took her an hour, if she was being very careful. If she just dug a hole and dropped the root ball into it and sprinkled peat moss over the top, that was one thing. But when she stopped to pick weeds or to lop overhanging branches from the coral trees, it could be midnight, and she'd be out with a flashlight, kneeling, digging, weeding. The snails came out at night, too. That was another thing to take her time. She didn't like to smash them. Smashing them made her feel awful. So she'd lift leaves and poke around the edges of the planters looking for them. Then she'd put them in a sack and empty them into a pickle jar with a fistful of leaves. She had four pickle jars full of fat, happy snails at the back of the house next to the trash cans.

There, the last carnation. She put it in the ground and patted the dirt around it. The garden in the dark seemed so different. She could sense it in the way the leaves sounded with the breeze blowing, a different sound from in the daylight. Not crisp and papery. More like soft curtains flapping at a window. And the grass gave off an aroma that wasn't there when the sun was shining on it. Something between cinnamon and crushed mint leaves. She stood up and stacked the empty flats one on top of the other, then carried them to the back of the house where the snails were. She couldn't see them in the dark but was sure she could hear the sounds of their chomping.

She started up the path toward the house, an airy ranch style with a blue tile roof. There were French doors and picture windows in back looking out on the garden, but none in the front of the house. Just a ten-foot Philippine mahogany door sunk into a Palos Verdes stone wall like a picture in a frame.

Lela liked living in Redondo Beach. She could remember when land was so cheap here that anyone could buy a piece of it. Four walls and a roof, and you had a bungalow. Bums used to sleep in tents on the beach in those days, and fishermen would drive all the way up from East Los Angeles to drop their baited lines off the end of the pier. That was when the Valley was the place to live if you had the money to move out of the inner city. When the Valley filled up, people started moving farther and farther down the coast, crowding into the beach towns, building fancy houses next to shacks.

Lela's closest neighbor, someone she knew by name from the property rolls but had never spoken to, was an elderly woman named Lillian Levine. Lela's stone wall on the south side of the house ran parallel to the rotting fence of Miss Levine's 1930 beach bungalow. Once, three years before, Lela sent Miss Levine a note asking if she minded if the gardener dug up Miss Levine's peach tree, since it was growing under Miss Levine's fence and undermining the stone wall on Lela's property. Miss Levine replied by leaving a basket of peaches in front of Lela's mahogany door. Lela left the tree alone, and now there was a foot-wide space in the wall where the peach tree's roots were tearing it apart.

Just before Lela stepped inside her house, she glanced over the wall to the bungalow. Its roof, rimmed in sea spray and climbing roses, seemed to be sinking into the overgrown culvert to the side of Lela's garage. One of these days she'd look over the wall and see nothing but the bungalow's chimney sticking up.

Lela turned on the light and let down the blinds on the French windows. The interior of her house was sparsely furnished, nearly bare. Her bedroom had a large bed and an eighteenth-century Chinese screen mounted on the wall behind it, a rosewood dresser, and a slipper chair. The guest bedroom had a bed and a few things of Kathy's. Her writing desk. A chintz-covered chair that Kathy used to read in. In the living room a pair of Chinese rosewood chairs flanked the French doors. A tall cloisonné vase perched on an altar table. There was a Korean chest against one wall with a silk-robed samurai sitting cross-legged on top, a stalk of early-budding forsythia in a bronze vase beside him. Wood floors, polished to a brittle sheen, swept from walls to windows.

The house was chilly. It didn't matter how hot it was during the day, once the sun went down, a damp breeze came up from the beach and it felt like the ocean was reaching for the land, touching it with cold, moist fingers. She wished she could light a fire in the fireplace, but there were three Japanese shigaraki jars standing where the logs would have gone, placed there by Dale, her ex-husband. After Lela left him, when he had the house to himself, he had thrown out all of her oak furniture and put Annamese pots and Chinese scrolls and samurai warriors anywhere he wanted.

When Lela got the house and furnishings as part of the property settlement, she left Dale's furniture in exactly the same spots where he had put them. They were never moved, never replaced, never touched, except to be dusted once a week by the cleaning service. It was as though the house still belonged to him. It was as if she were the caretaker, having the floors stripped and rewaxed in the winter, the mahogany door varnished in the spring, the filters in the air-conditioning system replaced at the beginning of summer.

She washed at the kitchen sink and carefully wiped the drips from the drainboard with a paper towel. She had learned neatness from Dale. Now she could spot a crumb or a fleck of dust at twenty paces. She could tell when the cleaning service had been in the house by the way the salt and pepper shakers with the words *Sal* and *Pimiento* faced backward on the drainboard instead of forward. None of it had come naturally to her.

There was a car coming up the drive. Lela could hear its engine, then a door slam, then footsteps on the flagstone walk.

"I thought you might have gotten lost, Mr. McGowan," she said when she opened the door.

"Just Ross is fine," he said.

He looked out of place in the Chinese chair. Uncomfortable. As if he didn't know what to do with his long legs except to kind of bend them at the knees and lay his ankles sideways on the floor. He was in Levi's now and a white shirt, but he still looked like someone who might live in a trailer out in the desert at Joshua Tree, someone who killed rabbits with a slingshot and roasted them, fur and all, over an open fire before he ate them.

"I was adopted," Lela said. "I don't remember any other family but the Binghams. I don't remember any other sister but Deborah. But I told you on the phone I'd listen to whatever you have to say with an open mind. I don't think too deeply about things, though, I can tell you that now. I've never even been a bit curious about that other family, the one I came from, not even a tiny bit curious."

"You live here alone? No husband?"

"What?"

"Alone. Here in this big house? By yourself?"

"No husband. You know, it's so strange you showing up like this. I mean, what this girl, this Jolene, has to do with me—well, if you want to tell me about people I don't know, never met, probably never will meet, I told you, I'm willing to listen." Lela squirmed in her chair. "But that other thing, going to see her, I can tell you right now, I won't. I can't. I said you could come over, but I didn't tell you how squeamish I am about things. Things upset me. Truly. Sad stories, where people get hurt or killed or maimed, make me melt right into the floor. I just can't stand them. I said I'd listen to you, but not if you're going to tell me something that'll make me feel like I'm about to melt into the floor."

He was balancing a half-empty teacup on the one-inch carved-wooden arm of the chair, his finger hooked clumsily into the too tiny handle.

"Because she really isn't anything to me. A sister is someone you know—and I'm not trying to be mean—I don't want you to think that. I could give you some money for her, if that would help. I mean, how would you feel if someone came to your door and said you have a sister and she's in trouble and he wants you to throw some underwear in a bag and go with him to . . ."

"Santa Rosa? I'd want to know what it was all about."

"I've already figured out it must be something awful, or why would you be doing this?"

Ross leaned forward till his knees were nearly touching the floor and he was half out of the stiff Chinese chair, and he just kept looking at Lela with that steady stare of his. It made her want to blink, it was so steady.

"I can tell you've got a good heart and don't want to see anyone suffer," he said.

The phone was ringing. It was Deborah.

"Jason loved the tricycle, Lela. He hasn't gotten off it since you left. I think he's going to take it to bed with him."

"I'm glad," Lela said.

"Is something the matter?"

"I've got company."

She could see Ross through the kitchen door. He was walking around the living room, holding the teacup as if looking for a place to put it.

"What kind of company?" Deborah said. "You didn't tell me you were having company."

"It's a man about the furnace. Remember, I told you how the smoke came out all over the wall every time I turned it on."

"But it's summer."

"That's the time to fix it."

"In the evening? What furnace man comes to the house in the evening?"

"That's when he does his estimating. In the evening. He fixes furnaces during the day."

"What are you talking about? What in the world, Lela, are you talking about? I don't believe you've got a furnace man there at all. I think it's that guy with the metal plate in his head."

"What would I want with him?" Lela replied.

16

"HOW MUCH LONGER?" Lela asked. They had been driving for six hours with only a stop in Bakersfield for gas.

"We'll get something to eat in Stockton," Ross replied, "and we'll be in Santa Rosa by dark."

Ross drove with his arm crooked at the elbow and hanging down the open window of the old Buick. Coming up through the Grapevine, the car struggled to rev itself up to fifty miles an hour on the steep grade. But the way Ross drove, the door tucked under his arm like he was carrying the car, it felt as if they were going a hundred.

"This isn't like me," Lela murmured, "running off with a total stranger just because he said I looked like I had a good heart."

"There's a first time for everything," Ross said.

She laid her head against the broken seat back and stared up at the ceiling. The cloth had begun to come down in places. Someone had attempted to stick it back up with big upholstery staples. And the door on her side wouldn't close, just sort of hung by two or three hinges, so that she could see the road, gray, white, blue, black, spinning by. She hadn't been in a car any older than last year's model for as long as she could remember, and this one, with its oily smell, and the sun glaring on its cracked windshield, and the hot breeze blowing in through the broken back window, was giving her a headache.

"We should have taken my Hyundai," she said.

"I don't like borrowing things from people," he said.

They reached Stockton in midafternoon. Ross got off the freeway and drove through the half-empty streets until they found the small downtown area.

"They've got Valley fever up here," Lela said. "It's in the soil, and when the wind blows, you breathe in those spores, it can ruin your lungs."

"Don't breathe," Ross said.

"Your lungs are really important. I had pneumonia when I was fifteen, and I can tell you it's no picnic. It feels like you just can't get enough air into you. Like you're not even breathing. I lied to Deborah and Brad about where I was going. Told them I was going to San Francisco for a reunion of people I worked with in Hong Kong."

"Why didn't you tell them the truth?"

"I'd have to explain too many things. They'd have talked me out of it."

"There's a Chinese restaurant," Ross said, and he made a U-turn in front of a lettuce truck and parked out in front.

"It's dangerous just being a farmer these days," Lela said as she followed him into the restaurant. "Pesticides in the air and spores in the soil." He didn't walk so much as lope, almost as if he had a limp, but not quite.

The restaurant, windows shaded by bamboo blinds, was a few degrees cooler than outside. And dark. Almost too dark to read the menu. Ross wasn't even looking at his, but Lela thought she ought to at least look like she was. So she stared at it a while and then put it down. "I'll have chow mein," she said.

"Sounds good to me."

Then she excused herself and went into the bathroom. It was a single-stall bathroom. Spotless. Not a wad of paper on the floor, no lipstick writings on the mirror. There was even a soap dispenser. Lela slipped the latch on the door and, although she hadn't eaten since dawn, leaned over the sink and vomited.

"You look green," Ross said when she came back and sat down.

"It's the light in here," Lela said. "You look green, too."

The chow mein came, a steaming hot mound of glistening noodles. Ross put some onto Lela's plate, then some onto his own.

"Like this," he said. He was using chopsticks to pick up his noodles, holding them between his fingers like he knew how. He had a clump of noodles raised in midair, was holding them, waiting for Lela to unwrap the paper from her chopsticks.

"You know what?" she said, staring into the steaming rice, "I'm not even hungry."

"You haven't eaten all day."

"I was hungry before, but I'm not now. I think it was the ride in the car. It was so hot." She blew some air up from her mouth toward her nose and could feel it riffle the hair near her forehead.

"Maybe it's just the air," Ross said, smiling, "all those spores and pesticides."

It was better now at dusk. Not as hot. And the fields sped by more easily. The road even felt smoother, and the car's engine sounded quieter. And Ross's voice was soothing. He never raised it, not even when he told her something that would have raised a normal person's voice. He was telling her now about when he was a kid.

"My mom was raped, and the minute I was born she took off. I never saw her again. My grandma raised me. I was the only grandchild. Spoiled rotten. My grandpa was an architect. Everyone thought he was successful at it, too. We lived in Piedmont. Ever been up there?"

"No. I don't think so."

"Big house. They sent me to a fancy school. Gramps really made his money booking the horses."

"I've always heard that rich people's kids didn't go to Vietnam."

"I just never could stand being part of the pack. Everybody around me in college was getting radicalized at about the same time. Demonstrating against the war. General rebellion. Sheep mentality, is how it looked to me. You said there was no husband. Never?"

"Once."

"He liked Chinese furniture, right?"

"He was an art professor. I was a student of his and he admired my artwork. We got married even though he told me that he thought marriage was a moribund artifact of a simpler time, an anachronism snatched from the sentimentalized past and clutched to our bosoms so as to anchor ourselves in the familiar."

"Is that a quote?"

"An exact quote. What he really wanted was a body in the room. He didn't ask much, just that I clean the kitchen up after myself, not eat crumbly things in the living room, and not leave my clothes on the floor."

The signs were saying "Santa Rosa 40 Miles." Lela's stomach was beginning to hurt.

"I'm hungry," she said.

"You should be," he said.

He stopped at a Sizzler in Sonoma, and Lela went in and ordered takeout from the salad bar. Three teenage boys were sitting in a booth, all eating off the same plate.

"Out! Out, I said." The manager looked really angry, and it scared Lela the way he raised his voice to the boys. Raised voices always scared her. She waited with her plastic takeout dish near the door until the boys were gone, and then she pushed it open. The boys were still in the parking lot, and one of them looked over at her and waved like he knew her, so she waved back and hurried toward the Buick.

"They've been spitting," Ross said, "trying to see who could throw the biggest wad."

"They were inside," she said, "trying to cheat Sizzler out of eight dollars."

"Just being kids," he said.

"You want some pineapple slices?" Lela said when they had found the freeway again. "They're nice and fresh."

"Sure."

"What happened to your grandparents?" Lela asked, holding a pineapple spear to his lips.

"Gramps died of a heart attack when I was fifteen."

Lela watched his jaw move as he chewed the pineapple. He was older than she'd thought at first. At least forty-five. Maybe even a little older. It was funny how a person's face could change right in front of you, grow familiar. She hadn't liked his face when she first saw it. It seemed all right to her now, though. Even the ponytail was all right. Maybe on someone else it wouldn't have been, but on him it was just fine.

"A few years after Gramps died, Grandma went in for a routine workup. She'd been having headaches. Unexplained headaches. She died between X-ray and the emergency room. That's when I decided to go to medical school."

"You're a doctor?"

"I used to be. I graduated from med school and had an office staked out in Sausalito. I was thinking about doing plastic surgery as a specialty." He laughed. "Plastic surgery. Jesus. Then the army said they needed me, and I went, did my tour, and came home. I never thought what going to Vietnam would really mean, that a piece of my skull would get shot off and there wouldn't be enough bone left to cover my brain. Never imagined it would change me the way it did. I just went to Vietnam to prove something. I can't remember now exactly what it was."

Ross got them two rooms in the Holiday Inn in Santa Rosa, and while he made the phone call, Lela went upstairs and took a shower.

"We're supposed to go to a gas station on G Street at eleven to-night," Ross said when she joined him in the coffee shop downstairs.

"Why so late?" Lela said.

"She doesn't get off work till ten-thirty," Ross replied.

———————————

The gas station was closed, and it had begun to rain. Not a heavy rain, but one that kept up a steady rhythm on the roof of the car.

"Is that her?" Lela said when a car pulled in.

Ross opened his window and peered out. The car, a banged-up Camaro, had parked near the rest room. The door opened and a short, slightly plump woman got out, a newspaper in her hands to shield her from the rain. She ran across the lot, past the two islands to where Ross had parked.

"This is one big helluva chance you got me taking," the woman said, opening the backseat of the Buick and climbing in. She had a flat, Hispanic face and a bad complexion. Or it might have just been the raindrops shining on her skin in the station light that gave it a bumpy look.

"This is Lela," Ross said, "Jolene's sister."

"Aha," the woman said.

"I thought we were meeting Jolene," Lela said.

"I never told you that," Ross said.

"But you said—"

"This is Vickie, a friend of mine."

"Wait a minute, wait a minute. You said we were meeting Jolene. You said she didn't get off work till ten-thirty. You said—"

"I got all the stuff in the car," Vickie said. "It's been one hassle after another this whole week. I almost gave up on you. If you hadn't come, I don't know what I would have done. I've only got my lousy job between me and starvation, and I can't afford to feed more than myself. Not to mention if she found out what I was doing, I'd be dead meat in five seconds."

"It's going to be fine now," Ross said, "just fine."

"Where *is* Jolene, then?" Lela asked. "You said I was going to help her, going to do something for her." She felt her pulse starting to race.

"Is she for real, or what?" Vickie said.

"She's just a little nervous," Ross replied.

"Yeah, well, are you going to help me with the stuff or not?"

Ross opened the door and got out. Vickie followed him across the lot to her car and opened the trunk. Lela felt lightheaded, her heart was beating so fast. She couldn't see through the rain what Vickie was taking out of the trunk. It didn't look heavy the way she slung it out of there and dropped it onto the pavement. It was a cardboard box. Just a plain old cardboard box filled to the top with something Lela couldn't make out. She saw Vickie cover the box with the newspaper she had in her hand while Ross opened the side door of the Camaro and bent his head in. He was helping someone out of the backseat. It looked like a child.

Another car pulled into the lot, a Chevy, tires skidding on the oily wet pavement. It headed toward Ross as he ran back through the rain to the Buick, cardboard box in his arms, the child running alongside of him. Lela pulled at the cold metal of the door handle, wrenched it open, and clambered out of the car. It was a reflex the way she got out of that car. As if something were propelling her across the worn seat and onto the pavement, her arms open. As if she had been here before and knew what was going to happen.

"Quick, get her in the car," Ross said. He tossed the box into the backseat. Lela fell into the car after it, the child in her arms.

"This wasn't the way it was supposed to go," Ross said. He was back behind the wheel, starting the engine. "It was going to be easy. Goddammit, why isn't it ever easy?"

Lela got a glimpse of a woman's face in the other car, mouth open, as though caught in midscream. In the headlights she could see a tiny scar, red as wine, running down the woman's cheek.

"That was Jolene," Ross said as he peeled out of the station. Jolene made a U-turn and raced toward them, her Chevy's headlights glaring through the Buick's broken back window.

The little girl had her face pressed against the window now, looking out at the car following them. She was about six years old, very thin, with a small face that had freckles dotting her cheeks and the bridge of her nose. In the shine of headlights Lela saw lice crawling in the child's brown hair.

Ross was pushing the old Buick to its limit, his hands tight on the steering wheel, twisting it hard from side to side. He squealed out of the station, then bumped over a curb onto the narrow street, Jolene following close behind him. He was driving so fast the car was vibrating, the engine wheezing as if it were going to cough and quit.

"You brought me up here to kidnap Jolene's child," Lela cried over the rattle of old car engines and the noise of bald tires racing over rain-slick streets.

"She's my child, too," Ross shouted back at her. He made a sudden turn into a heavy-equipment storage yard and began skidding between skip loaders and earth movers. Jolene was still right behind the Buick, riding its wake, trying to crawl up its tailpipe. And screaming at them through the open windows. Lela grabbed for the child, tried to protect the little girl's head, keep it from bouncing against the metal interior of the car, trying not to hear Jolene's high-pitched shrieks, incoherent and full of fury. So this was it. She had come up here with a stranger to die in an old wreck of a Buick, holding a kidnapped child in her arms.

Then Ross turned off his lights, gave a sharp yank at the steering wheel, and drove off the road. The smell of crushed asparagus suddenly filled the air, and the ground turned springy beneath the car. It was as if they were swinging in a hammock, rocking gently from side to side, dipping up and down in the soft dirt just long enough to mash another bundle of crisp green stalks into asparagus perfume.

When they reached the end of the field, Ross stopped the car. Jolene's Chevy was stuck in the field behind them, her headlights steady and not moving forward. Ross, eyes bright and ponytail still dripping rain, turned around to face Lela in the backseat.

"She can't drive worth a damn," he said.

There was nothing but old clothes in the cardboard box. Children's clothes. Worn underpants, faded T-shirts, ripped pajamas. The child was wearing a grown-up's old sweater, a blue knitted one, with a cable down each side in front. She was barefoot. Not even socks on her feet. She sat on the chair in the hotel room, swinging her bare legs. She didn't seem bothered by how she got here or why. Don't let her off the chair, Ross said when he went off to find a drugstore. We'll burn her clothes and dip her in lindane. But for chrissakes, don't let her off the chair till I get back.

"What's your name?"

"Lela."

"Mine's Sandy. Like the beach."

The sweater was crawling with lice. Lela pulled it over the child's head and got her slacks off. Her white skin was blotched with bites, and she had big bruises on both arms. She had both her front teeth. The picture wasn't of her.

"I'll just put these things in a paper bag, and we'll throw them away later, Sandy," Lela said.

"I don't care. I've got lots of clothes at home. Tons of clothes."

She was wearing women's bikini underpants that were pinned at the waist and fell from her small hips like an apron.

"I have three nephews," Lela said. "They love Ninja Turtles. You're probably too old for Ninjas, though."

"Oh, I have all of them. There isn't one Ninja Turtle I don't have. Mama bought all of them for me. Is that man coming back?"

"What man?"

"You know, the man. He was here. Is he coming back?"

"You mean your father?"

"Who?"

Lela's pulse was racing again. Dancing, actually, erratically, unrhythmically. The child didn't even know Ross was her father. She went into the bathroom and took a vial out of her medicine kit and put one of the pills in her mouth, then went back into the room where the child was.

"Are you hungry, Sandy?"

"Not now. Uh-uh, no, I'm not. Vickie cooked me some hamburger and fried potatoes, and we had chocolate cake with raspberry frosting. It was hard frosting, not wet like you put your fingers in and it's all soft and sticks to you. And she stopped at the market and buyed me jelly beans. Green ones and pink ones. I don't like the black ones. They make the black ones out of dirt."

Lela looked away. The pill was working. She felt calm now, in control of herself. But all sorts of pictures had begun to zip through her head. Little snapshots of people she didn't recognize. She didn't know this child, either. She didn't want to know this child. Then why, when she looked at her, did her heart feel like it was breaking?

17

THEY LEFT SANTA Rosa early in the morning and started back to Los Angeles. Sandy was in the backseat, her head out the window. It had been foggy when they left the hotel, and there was still a fine mist floating across the highway and into the car.

"What's that sign say?" Sandy said.

" 'Drink Pepsi,' " Lela answered from the front seat.

"She can't read or write," Ross said. "She doesn't go to school."

"Six-year-olds go to school," Lela said. "It's state law."

"Not to Jolene it isn't," Ross replied.

Ross had the wipers on. One of the blades was missing a pad, and the rusted steel hopped up and down, alternating silent glides through the air with ear-jarring scrapes across the glass. Occasionally the blade would get tangled in itself and flop up and down uselessly until Ross stuck his hand out his side window and unjammed it.

"Well, I'm certainly glad the fog's lifting, anyway," Lela said. "I hate fog. Sometimes at the beach it's so foggy I have to drive with the car door open so I can look down at the road to see where the white line is. Once it got so bad, I just stopped the car where it was and got out and sat at the side of the road and waited. Four cars piled into mine. It was a Honda. Just smashed it to pieces. I had to fight the insurance company to get them to pay me. They said I was negligent, abandoning the car that way. Hasn't anyone ever tried to get Jolene to put her in school?"

"You have to find Jolene first to do that."

"Chick promised to take me to school," Sandy said.

"He's the boyfriend," Ross said.

The wind was blowing sand now, kicking it up from the artichoke fields and mixing it with the remnants of fog so that the air looked like brown spray paint coming in waves across the road.

"I once had a whole car stripped in a sandstorm," Lela said.

"She'll need some clothes," Ross said. He glanced at the child in the rearview mirror. "Goddamn rags she's wearing makes me sick. The whole thing makes me sick."

"I was coming back from Yuma," Lela said. "I'd never been in a sandstorm before. It stripped the whole car, like some big hand of God had come down and dipped it in a vat of lye. Didn't leave a speck of paint on it. I couldn't believe it."

Sandy was bouncing up and down on the seat now, shaking the whole car.

"We'll stop in Santa Barbara and buy her some clothes," Ross said, "and some shoes."

"I can't keep her very long," Lela said. "You'll have to figure something else out."

"How long?" Ross said.

The question gave Lela a sudden pain deep inside.

"Brad's had bad luck with cars, too," she said. "He had a BMW, and we just had this rain coming down for a week without stopping, and it was high tide, and the drains couldn't handle all that water, and it just backed up on the streets. Our office is in a minimall just before you start up the hill, and the rain and the high tide and the plugged-up drains just all came together and flooded the whole block in front of the office. My car was in back of the building, but Brad's was out in front, and the water went all the way up to his dashboard."

Maybe the pain was in her liver or her pancreas, not in her stomach.

"It was so funny. Brad put on scuba gear and tried to get his briefcase out of the trunk, but the water pressure against it was too much. A year-old BMW, just ruined. The water hitting the dash blew out the electrical system. The insurance company tried to dry it out, but it didn't work. They had to give him a new car."

Maybe it was what the doctors called referred pain. Maybe it wasn't in her vital organs at all. Maybe it was radiating upward from her feet. Or her knees.

"How long can you keep her?" Ross said.

"How do I know how long?" she said. "You haven't given me a chance to think. You never told me we were going to steal a child."

"I don't have custody. There was no other way. I couldn't leave her where she was."

"Jolene looked like she wanted to kill us."

"She probably did," Ross said.

"Pink," Sandy said. "Oh, I like pink so much." She had the dress up against her chest and was dancing from side to side in front of the mirror. She was wearing new white sandals with slick leather soles and was sliding along the carpet as though she were ice-skating.

"She's sure an energetic little thing, isn't she?" the saleslady said.

"What does that sign say?" Sandy said.

" 'Back-to-School Fashions,' " Lela told her.

Ross was in the car, waiting. She could see him through the racks of little-girl dresses, just sitting behind the wheel, as though he had nothing to do with any of this, just sitting there and staring straight ahead.

"We'll take that one, and the overalls and the two pair of jeans," Lela said. "And the socks and underwear and pajamas. And how about T-shirts, something colorful."

"T-shirts, T-shirts," Sandy singsonged.

The saleslady disappeared down an aisle and was back in a few moments with a pile of T-shirts in her arms. She smiled at Sandy.

"You're lucky to have such a nice mother, buying you all these clothes so you'll look nice when school starts."

"I'm not her mother," Lela said.

They had lunch in Ventura, in a coffee shop near the railroad tracks.

"I stayed in Ventura overnight once," Lela said.

Sandy was standing at the table, kicking at the legs of her chair with her feet and eating potato salad off her plate with her fingers. Holding her fork in her left hand and picking up glistening bits of mayonnaised potatoes with her right.

"Use your fork," Ross said.

"I am," Sandy said. "See." She put the fork in her right hand and began sliding potato salad from her plate right into her mouth.

"Jesus, she eats like an animal," Ross said.

"The Holiday Inn," Lela said.

"The Holiday Inn?" Ross said.

"The place I stayed when I was here. The railroad tracks outside reminded me of it. There are railroad tracks not more than a hundred yards from the hotel. I didn't notice them when I checked in. I thought there was just the ocean on one side and on the other a line of trees. The trees were hiding the tracks."

The child was staring at Ross. The animal part. She had stopped chewing at the animal part, was staring at him, the fork in her hand.

Not budging now. Not fidgeting. Not swallowing, either. Not even what she had in her mouth.

"I was attending a textiles conference," Lela said. "I was based in Hong Kong, traveling here and there for the company. Europe, the States, the Orient. It was after my divorce."

"You're not my father," Sandy said. "You aren't. I don't have a father, and you aren't him." Her thin chest was going up and down in little spasms, as though she were crying. But there were no tears, and she wasn't making any noise.

"I'm your father all right," Ross said. He reached one hand out toward the child, tried to pat her head, but she jumped back a step and began to tremble.

"In the middle of the night, in my dreams, there was this horrible rumbling noise, as if I were on a train going through a tunnel," Lela said. It was too much having to sit here and watch this child suffer. "I didn't know whether I was dreaming it or there really was a train going through my room." She wasn't an animal. All you had to do was look into her eyes to know that.

"The next morning a man in the elevator said, 'Did you hear that train go through your room last night?' And then I remembered the dream." She knew exactly what the child was feeling, and she wanted to tell her it was all right, that she'd help her, she'd fix everything that was wrong, she'd keep her safe. "It was so weird, how I just accepted that noise, how I felt that room shaking—I mean, it shook like a dog shakes a house slipper—and I never even gave it another thought until that man in the elevator said that."

"I want my mama," Sandy said, and she turned and walked away from the table.

Lela sat, unable to move. Sandy was nearly to the door when Ross reached her. He knelt down, was talking to her, telling her something, and she was nodding her head. Then he picked her up and she put her arms around his neck and held her face to his. Lela felt her breath catch as she watched them there by the cash register, holding each other tight as if there were no one else in the coffee shop but them.

It was almost midnight when they got to Lela's house. Sandy had fallen asleep in the backseat and Ross picked her up and carried her into the house. They put her down on the bed in the guest room, and Lela covered her with a quilt she had designed when she was working in Hong Kong. An Oriental-themed fabric. Orange peonies and yellow stalks of bamboo. She had copied it from an antique kimono she'd bought in a shop in Kyoto, Japan.

"I'll make some coffee," Lela said.

Ross followed her into the kitchen.

"This house doesn't feel like anyone lives in it," he said. "All this stiff furniture and hard edges." He sat down at the round, glass-topped rosewood table in the kitchen. A delicate Chinese table with heavy armchairs that had dragons and birds carved into their backs.

"Dale believed in form over function. I was surprised when he said he'd take the bank account and give me the house. I keep thinking I'll sell it. Trouble is, I'd get less than what I owe on it. Property values aren't what they were when Dale and I bought it. We paid five hundred fifty thousand for it, and I'd be lucky to get three hundred out of it now."

He had tilted the chair back on its rear legs and was watching her as she stood at an open cupboard. There were all those bags of special coffee beans lined up on the shelf.

"I have vanilla bean coffee, hazelnut, chocolate raspberry, macadamia . . . Do coffee beans rot if they get too old?"

"When were you divorced?"

"Four years ago."

"Is that how old the coffee is?"

"Probably."

"They just lose flavor."

"I don't drink coffee at home myself. In the morning I always have breakfast in the coffee shop next door to the office, and I don't drink coffee after six in the evening. If I do, I can't sleep. I don't sleep that well anyway. Sometimes I think I don't sleep at all. The doctor says I'd be dead if I didn't sleep, that I just sleep on a different level. Lighter. He says it's like twilight sleep. Dale liked flavored coffees, and he bought all these bags."

"How about regular coffee?"

"Nope. I don't have any of that."

She shut the cupboard and sat down at the table. "I'm truly sorry," she said.

"I don't need any coffee anyway."

"I mean, I can't keep her here. It's not feasible. As much as I want to help, I just can't."

"I'll pay you for any damage she does."

"That's not what I mean. I have to work. There's no one to take care of her during the day. People will find out she's here, and first

thing you know they'll be asking me who she is, what she's doing
here, how she got here, when, where's her mother, her father. It's too
complicated. I have a life, you know. And Deborah. I could never
explain it to her."

He pressed his lips together and nodded his head once, then
looked around the kitchen at the shiny white doors of the cupboards.

"Do you have any liquor?"

"Kahlúa."

"That isn't liquor."

He got up from his chair and stood at the sink, staring at the drain.
Then he turned on the water and poured some into a glass.

"I can't drink anyway," he said. "I'm in AA. Did I tell you that?"

"No."

He sat down and sipped at the water as though it were a rare wine.
"Drugs and alcohol. I've been sober now for five years."

"I can't keep her. I just can't."

"I didn't say you'd have to keep her forever."

"Why did you have to kidnap her? Why didn't you go to court, get
custody, fight it out there?"

"I have visitation rights. I never exercised those rights. I've never
seen her before the other night. I wanted to stay as far away from
Jolene as I could. And if I tried for custody now, she'd run with her
to God knows where."

"I have to show houses in the morning. Brad's alone. And the
Swensons are hot, so hot I can feel it, and if I let them cool off,
then they'll find another broker, and I'll lose them. They're the best
prospect I've had for a sale in a month. Prospects don't grow on trees
when the economy's down. I'd be sick all the time if I kept her here.
I can't do it. Something about her makes me want to die. I can't
explain it. I just can't."

"Don't you want to hear what happened?" he said. "Don't you
want to know why I came down here and dragged you to Santa Rosa
and pulled the kid away from her mother? Aren't you even a little bit
interested?"

"It was a foolish thing, my going with you, and I'm sorry, I really
am. For all your troubles in looking for me, and any expense I've
caused you, I'm truly sorry."

"I told you I was an army doctor. I was on a Huey feeding glucose
to a dying kid when I got shot in the head. Danang is where it was.
Hot as hell. That's about all I remember, is how hot it was and what
a terrific headache I had. They flew me out with my brain covered

with a piece of what felt like plastic wrap. I was in a VA hospital in San Francisco for almost a year while they tried to fix it. Tried every damn thing you can think of. A piece of my femur. A piece of a cadaver's skull. Nothing took. Stainless slid right in there like it belonged. You ever been to Cazadero?"

"No."

"How about Guerneville?"

"No."

"The Russian River?"

"No."

"Beautiful country up there. A lot of Vietnam vets, war resisters, draft dodgers, war widows, homosexuals, malcontents. We're all up there together. No one bothers you. I had a habit when I got out of the service that should have killed me, but it didn't. I used marijuana in Danang, but the year in the hospital was one long drug trip. I came out of there a junkie. I never liked to sniff or inject anything, but I'd put a line of speed in my coffee and I could stay awake for twenty-four hours. The most I ever went without sleep was two weeks. Ever done drugs?"

"No."

"They say once you're an addict, no matter how long you're sober, the desire never leaves you. I'm living proof. I still think about it. Sometimes I yearn for it. Dream about the high, the rush to the head. The energy. God, the energy and stamina. You think you can conquer the world. Only you can't."

"I can't turn my life inside out. Not for strangers."

"She's your niece."

"She's a stranger."

He got up and walked around the room, opening cupboards like he was looking for something. Then he sat down again.

"Cazadero's rural, isolated, with a lot of mean and unhappy people in it. You can buy any drug your heart desires. The biggest damn drugstore of a town I've ever seen. Everyone's into pharmacology, homemade cures, holistic medicine. Herbs. Herbs are really big up there now. Jolene was living in a shack in Cazadero when I met her. On a widow's pension. Her husband got his head blown off in Vietnam. I'd buy an eight-ball for twenty-five dollars and divide it into quarters—two lines for Jolene and two for me. We'd alternate speed with liquor. Sometimes we'd drop acid together, but we'd only do that in the house where we'd be safe—so we wouldn't try to do something like jump off a building to see if we could fly, or anything stupid like that. We'd just listen to music, watch TV. And laugh. I remember laughing a lot with her. But mostly I was just freaked out. She had a capacity. It floored me to see the amount of drugs that girl could put in her system and still stand up. After a while the drugs made me so paranoid that just a car coming down the street would set me off. I'd go get my gun, sure the VC were after me. Even a star in the sky made me crazy. I'd think it was a police helicopter following me around."

"What was that?"

"What was what?"

Lela got up from the table and walked into the dark living room. She thought she had heard a noise. She had. It was the sound of the front door closing.

18

"WE SHOULD CALL the police," Lela said. She was shivering so hard it felt as though she had the flu.

"No police," Ross replied. "We'll find her. I'll go up to the corner and down the other side of the street. You take this side."

Lela had taken the flashlight out of the drawer in the kitchen, and as she walked up the sidewalk toward the north, she played its beam crazily in front of her, up and down, around in circles, catching nothing but tree shadows and slices of neighboring houses. She caught Ross in the thin beam of light. He was across the street, moving swiftly through the dark. And then he was gone. Quick as a magician's stunt, his slim form vanished behind night's black cape. Now you see him, now you don't.

"Ross!"

"I'm here. Keep looking."

The lights were on in Lillian Levine's bungalow. Maybe Sandy had crawled through the hole in the wall and was right now in Miss Levine's kitchen, eating cookies. Lela ran the flashlight across the bungalow's picture window, saw the figure of a gray-haired woman in an easy chair, roses in vases, photographs on tables, a line of trophies of some kind lined up on shelves on both sides of the fireplace. The woman was reading a book while a television flickered unwatched in a corner of the room. Lela flashed the light across the window several times and the woman got up from the chair, placed the book carefully on a side table, and came to the front door.

"Miss Levine?" Lela said. "Lillian Levine?"

"Yes?"

"I'm your neighbor, Lela Bingham, the one you gave the peaches to."

"Won't you come in?"

"Oh, no, I can't."

It was past midnight, and the woman was inviting Lela in, didn't even seem surprised to see her there on her doorstep, having never spoken a word to her before, having lived silently next door to her for five years.

"A little girl is missing," Lela said. "We've lost her. We don't know where to look, don't know where she could be."

She had hardly said the words when Lillian turned, plucked a corduroy jacket from a closet beside the door, took hold of Lela's hand, and stepped briskly down the steps.

"She was in the house. Asleep. Really dead asleep. We'd been driving all day. And then I heard the door close, and she was gone."

They were on the sidewalk now in front of Lillian's house, walking rapidly out of the thick vegetation of the culvert, away from the scent of night-blooming jasmine that the cool evening had trapped and held, like tiny pearls, in drops of ocean spray.

"Her name is Sandy. She's six years old. She doesn't know the neighborhood. Anything could happen to her. She could fall into a culvert, drown in the ravine."

The woman could walk fast. Her legs didn't look strong enough to move that fast.

"I told her father I didn't want to keep her. She might have heard me. It's making me sick to think she might have heard me."

"It does no use to worry about things like that. Play the flashlight over there, near those bushes. I saw something shiny."

Droplets of water glistened in the flashlight's beam.

"Just wet leaves," Lillian said.

"I always tell my clients to keep their kids in the house at night," Lela said. "Just because the hills are so pretty and innocent looking during the day, you just don't know how dangerous the nights can be. God, I'm cold. I should have put on a coat or a sweater. I didn't think. I heard the door shut, and I just ran out of the house."

"Here, you take this," Lillian said, and she took off her jacket and draped it around Lela's shoulders.

"There are rattlers in these hills, too," Lela said. "They like to coil themselves beside swimming pools. Sometimes they squeeze into old tires so that they look just like an inner tube." Lela's teeth were chattering so loudly they sounded like castanets. Or window blinds knocking against one another in the breeze.

Ross was crossing the street toward them now, his dark figure bouncing with the weight of the child in his arms.

"I've got her," he said.

"My house is closest," Lillian said. "Bring her inside."

Sandy was on the couch in Lillian's living room, Lela kneeling on the floor beside her. Ross had hold of the child's hand, was checking the beats in her wrist against his watch.

"Her pulse is okay."

"It could be epilepsy, petit mal," Lillian said.

"No history."

"Sandy, are you awake?" Lela said. Sandy's eyes appeared fixed in place, her gaze snagged by the broken plaster hanging from a corner of Lillian's ceiling. Lela moved her hand slowly in front of the child's face. Not a flicker.

"A sphygmomanometer would help," Ross said.

Lillian left the room and was back in a few seconds, a black blood pressure cuff in her hands.

"Do you have high blood pressure, Miss Levine?" Ross asked as he wrapped the cuff around Sandy's upper arm.

"I was a nurse."

"Pressure's normal." Ross removed the cuff and handed it to Lillian. "Breathing rate is fine, no sign of hemorrhage. No convulsive seizures."

"Sleepwalking?" Lillian said.

"I don't see anything else."

"Sleepwalking," Lela said. "Well, I wouldn't have thought sleepwalking. Deborah used to sleepwalk when she was little. One night she came down the stairs, and Walter said, 'Are you all right?' and she didn't answer, just went out the front door and into the garage, got in the car, and lay down in the backseat."

Sandy's eyes were closed now, her face peaceful.

"I must have startled you, Miss Levine," Lela said, "knocking on your door so late at night."

"Please call me Lillian."

"Barging in the way I did," Lela said. She was trying to get up off her knees, but they felt glued to the floor, stuck there. She tried to pull them away, but the effort made her head slump forward on her chest.

"I've always meant to come over and speak to you," Lillian said, "ask you how you liked the peaches. Some years they're sweeter than others."

"That's life," Ross said.

"The peaches were great," Lela said, "but I can't seem to get up off the floor."

Ross was beside Lela now. "Take deep breaths."

"She's a little shocky," Lillian said.

"It's just so hot in here," Lela said.

Lillian had poured something into a thin crystal glass and was holding it out to Lela. Lela stared at the glass, at how the liquid seemed to cut it in two. A nice, straight, razor cut. She was sure that if she had a ruler small enough to fit inside the glass, she'd find some imperfection, some bumpiness, some unevenness, in the surface of the brandy. Nothing was that straight, that perfect. She put the glass to her lips and swallowed. The liquor burned her tongue and left a tingling trail of heat that ran from the sides of her mouth down the back of her throat.

"I noticed outside that she was very upset," Lillian said to Ross. "I thought she was about to faint."

"She's very high-strung," Ross said.

"I've only seen her outside, at a distance," Lillian said, "zipping in and out of her driveway in a little gray car. She always seems so busy, in a hurry."

Lela let her head fall sideways against her knees. She couldn't lift it. There was no way she could lift it. Ross and Lillian were talking about her as if she weren't there. As if she were a chair or the broken spot in the ceiling. Ross had his arm around Lela's waist to keep her from sprawling onto the floor, but he wasn't paying attention to the fact that her head was trying to leave her body, was wobbling on her spinal cord as though it wanted no part of her. He and Lillian were exchanging backgrounds now, chatting the way people did at the scene of an accident after the ambulance left. Freely. Intimately. Like old friends. Certain that what they said to each other would be forgotten the moment they parted.

"UC Davis Medical School, 1970," Ross was saying. "I don't practice anymore."

"Queen of Angels Nursing School, 1938," Lillian said. "I retired from Cedars-Sinai surgery team when they started doing heart transplants. It was too much to learn at my age."

The terrible heat that had passed through Lela's body was ebbing, and her head felt steady enough to raise up so she could look around the room. The trophies on the shelves beside the fireplace were little statuettes. Couples dancing. Caught forever in midglide. On the table beside the couch there was a photograph of a young man and woman in formal dress on a dance floor, balloons dangling overhead. A small photograph on the mantel was of the same young woman in a nurse's uniform. Next to it was a larger photograph of the dancing man. He was grinning at the camera, as though he had just heard a good joke. Lillian's husband, probably. He had a small mustache and kind eyes. Where was he? Had he awakened one day, eaten breakfast, then looked at Lillian through his kind eyes and danced out of her life?

Ross turned and smiled at her. "Feeling better?"

"Much."

"Neighbors should help each other more," Lillian said. "We all stay to ourselves too much."

Lela awoke suddenly. Disoriented. Then she remembered. The sleepwalking. Ross had put Sandy in Lela's bed this time, and he and Lela had lain down on either side of her, as though to guard her in case she tried to escape again. But she was hardly moving. Hardly breathing, it seemed. She was so still that Lela leaned over her, put her face close to the child's cheek to feel her breath.

"She's alive," Ross whispered.

"I was really frightened tonight."

"I'll have to put a hook and eye on the front door for you."

"She could go out the sliding glass door in back."

"I'll put metal bars in there. That'll keep her in."

Lela got up, stood at the side of the bed. Ross was looking at her through the darkness. She could see his eyes, the whites intensely white, not moving away from her face.

They were in the guest bedroom where they had first put Sandy, on the bed with the quilt Lela had designed when she was working in Hong Kong.

"Oh, yes, like that," she said. He was heavy against her, had her legs spread and was trying, she knew, to please her. Why did it disgust her so, the feel of his tongue moving in and out, the pressure of his fingers? She was dry there except for the moistness of his mouth. She should have taken a minute and used a lubricant. Oh, how could she have forgotten to use a lubricant?

"That's wonderful," she said. "Oh, yes, yes, really wonderful."

She had undressed for him, lain down beside him, offered herself to him.

"Right there," she said. "Oh, don't stop, don't stop now. Oh, yes, there."

She was good at deception. She knew what the sex manuals had to say about erogenous zones, about orgasm, about where it occurred and how in the female body. She knew all the appropriate sounds to make, how many strokes of a penis inside her before she had to squeal with pleasure. She had learned from Gil how to make a small vacuum of her mouth when she sucked him, how to hold her wrist tight when she masturbated him, how to wiggle her hips for the tightest fit when she was on her knees.

Ross was on his elbows, his bare shoulders glistening with perspiration. Was he happy? Had she made him happy? Had he finished? She hadn't felt any rush of liquid when he'd inserted his penis. Had he stopped without finishing?

"You're dry," he said. He had a wild look in his eyes. A sad, wild look.

"I'm sorry."

"What are you sorry about?"

She sat up and pulled the silk robe that matched the quilt around her. The colors in the fabric seemed to dance in and out in the dim light, blossom into full-blown peonies, then shrink back into tight little buds.

"It's almost morning," she said.

19

"YOU SHOULD HAVE called first," Deborah said. "Why didn't you call first, Lela? Then you'd have known the elephant was sick. What's a zoo without an elephant?"

"Two adults and three kids," Lela said to the man in the ticket booth. She had Jason with her in his stroller. Deborah was pushing the twins in their double-seater.

"They look like they're under three," the man said. "There's no charge if they're under three."

"I don't think we ought to go in if the elephant's sick," Deborah said.

"I've already paid," Lela said.

It was a pocket zoo near the Vincent Thomas Bridge, between the shipyards and the harbor. An underprivileged zoo for underprivileged kids, with donated animals and untended grass and a half-finished miniature Amazon River. Lela was one of the zoo sponsors. She ran pancake breakfasts for the Palo Verdes Chamber of Commerce to raise money for the elephant enclosure. She had talked a car dealer in Cerritos into raffling off one of his Chevies to buy the elephant.

"Birds," Jason said.

They were on the little bridge over the Amazon, which in the wintertime was full of silty water but now in the summer heat was a dried-up, weed-choked muddy gulch. The tropical birds were caged here. Bootleg birds from Costa Rica that the Department of Animal Regulation kept demanding documentation on.

"How does a canary go, Jason?" Lela said.

"Cheep, cheep," Jason said.

"I missed you while you were off at that reunion of yours," Deborah said. "Did you have a good time?"

"It was fine," Lela said.

"How did everyone look?"

"The same."

"Don't put your hand on the bird's cage, Jason. He thinks you're going to feed him. What did you do at the reunion, anyway?"

"It was really kind of boring. I'm sorry I went."

"Jason, take your fingers out of your nose."

There were no fair-skinned, blond children like Jason and the twins at the zoo. Only Hispanic children. Dark-eyed boys in faded T-shirts. Girls with black braids pulled tightly back from smooth brown foreheads.

"I don't think it was such a good idea coming down here," Deborah said. "There's a perfectly wonderful zoo in Palos Verdes. And everyone speaks English."

A young girl of about twelve was kneeling beside Jason's stroller. She had her hands out to him, about to pick him up.

"Don't let her do that, Lela," Deborah said, but the girl already had Jason out of his stroller, was holding him close to her face and cooing to him in Spanish.

"She could have TB, Lela. For God's sake."

Lela eased Jason from the girl's arms. "She didn't hurt him," Lela said.

"She could have."

"Do you want to see the snake house, Jason?" Lela said.

"Umm-hmm," Jason said.

A few palm trees, trunks scuffed and fan leaves frayed and brown, hung forlornly over the reptile enclosure. Lela lifted Jason up so he could see a king snake slither over crushed rock behind green-tinted glass.

"You know, Brad and I were talking just the other day about how attached you are to our kids," Deborah said. "I told him it's not really that healthy for you—being so attached to someone else's kids."

"What did he say?"

"He doesn't agree. He thinks it's great. I think you should be married, have your own children."

"Where the snake?" Jason said.

"Look in the corner, sweet face," Lela said. "The tree growing in the corner, near the bowl of water. See it? Look hard, Jason. He's there. All twisted around in a ball, but he's there."

"You're holding him too close to the glass," Deborah said. "It could break, for goodness' sake."

Lela backed away and Jason started to cry.

"More snake, Mom. More snake."

"See, I told you he calls you Mom," Deborah said.

"It was just a slip of the tongue," Lela said. "I've heard him call me Aunt Lela. Say 'Aunt Lela,' Jason."

"No," Jason said.

The twins were crying now, too, hanging over the side of their double stroller, tiny fingers reaching for the dirt.

"They haven't slept through the night this whole week," Deborah said. "I think they're teething. Being pregnant and them not sleeping, and Jason cheeping like a canary all day is my idea of hell. I was thinking that Brad and I'd get away this weekend. Let Esther run the office, leave the twins with Rowena, and take Jason over to your place."

"My place?"

"If you keep the crayons locked up, he won't write on the walls this time."

"I'm busy this weekend."

"Esther's in the office. There are no open houses. Busy doing what?"

"Things."

"Things?"

"House cleaning."

"You have a cleaning service."

"They don't clean everything. You should see the dust in my closets. An inch thick and growing."

"Did you meet someone up in San Francisco? Are you involved with someone? Oh, my God, you met someone and brought him home with you. I knew it. I told Brad, I'll bet our Lela's going to meet someone at that reunion of hers. And I was right. Do I know you or do I know you?"

"Lela wore them out," Deborah said. "We marched around that awful zoo like there was really something to see."

"You know I can't stand kids in the office," Brad said. Jason was ripping up one of the magazines in the bin next to the couch in the reception area.

"Give me the magazine, sweetheart," Lela said. "That's a good boy. Any calls for me?"

"Here," Esther said. She had a tuna sandwich on her desk, and the oil had leaked onto the message pad. Every paper that went through Bru-Bing Realty had the imprint of something Esther ate. Brad had wanted to hire someone young and pretty to answer the phones, but Deborah had done the selecting and picked Esther, who was middle-aged and fat.

"Come down off that chair before you fall," Deborah said.

"Why don't you take them home?" Brad said.

"Because they never get to see you," Deborah said. "You're always in this stupid office or sitting at an open house."

"What does this say, Esther?" Lela said. "I can't read it."

Esther's mouth was full of tuna. She chewed a moment, swallowed, then took the stained paper out of Lela's hand. "Sylvia Delaney, 313–8900."

"She's the one that wants a presentation," Brad said. "It would be a terrific listing."

"We'll need an exclusive if we're going to go to the trouble of doing a brochure presentation and the whole works," Lela said.

"I thought you'd try to sell her on the exclusive when we got there."

Deborah had the twins out of their stroller and was holding one in each arm while Jason ran from one end of the narrow office to the other.

"The Swensons were in again yesterday," Brad said.

"Good Lord," Lela said.

"They really liked you, wouldn't even let me show them anything. Said they'd wait till you got back."

"Thanks a lot."

"A strange Mexican kid picked Jason up at the zoo," Deborah said. "She might have kidnapped him. Or given him TB."

"I could run the comparables for Sylvia Delaney if you get up a list of possible places to show the Swensons," Lela said.

"I don't have a problem with that," Brad said.

"If that kid kicks my shins one more time, I quit," Esther said.

"Come here, Jason," Lela said. "Sit up here at Daddy's desk and draw me a picture of the snake we saw."

"No, Mom, I don't, Mom."

"See, he calls you Mom," Deborah said. "I told you he calls you Mom."

"Someone's opening the door, Deb," Brad said. "Jason's going to run out in the street."

"You could do something about it," Deborah said. "My hands are full with two babies as it is."

Lela caught Jason up in her arms. "I'm going to squeeze all the air out of you and roll you on the floor and slide you around, then scrape you up and eat you, you sweet pie."

Jason was screeching as Lela spun him around in her arms.

"Is he crying or laughing?" Deborah said.

"Can I help you?" Brad said. Ross was standing inside the door with Sandy, just standing there, holding her hand. His war-wounded forehead, caught in a shaft of sunlight, shone as bright as the chrome on a headlight.

"Ross McGowan," Ross said. "How do you do?" He stuck out his hand and Brad shook it.

Lela stopped spinning. Jason's hair, smelling of baby soap, suddenly made her feel sick.

"The metal plate," Deborah murmured, her eyes on Ross's head.

Lela put Jason in one of the gray chairs on the far side of the office where all the pictures of old Redondo Beach were hung. His head was right under a 1945 picture of Tony's Fresh Fish House on the pier.

"We ate in McDonald's," Sandy said. She was wearing her new overalls with the flower buds on the bib, her hair in a ponytail like her father's. "I ate French fries and chocolate yogurt." She let go of Ross's hand and came over and put her arms around Lela's waist. Deborah was staring at Ross's shiny square of skull. Brad just looked confused.

"Ross and Sandy are from up north," Lela said. She hadn't seen Ross since breakfast and hadn't looked him in the eye then, just busied herself pouring Cheerios into a bowl and fiddling with Sandy's hair, looking in all the kitchen drawers for a rubber band to hold up her ponytail.

"Brad's my partner," she said. "We're partners. We sell houses. This is our office." Why did she sound like such an idiot? She knew how to talk to anyone about anything.

"Were you interested in living up in the hills or on the flats?" Brad finally said.

"He isn't looking for a house," Lela said. "He's got one. I mean he's staying at my place. He's not a prospect, Brad. He just came down here, and we went up north, and we brought Sandy back, and she's going to stay—and why did you come down here, anyway, Ross?"

"Because your sister's incompetent, isn't fit to take care of her kid," Ross said. He looked wary now.

"I mean to the office. I told you I'd be home about four." She was whispering now. "Why did you come here?"

"Is that your little boy?" Sandy asked.

"I wanted to see where you worked," Ross said.

"What's going on, Lela?" Deborah said. "You don't have a sister. I mean, you do, but it's me, and I'm not incompetent, so it can't be me, and I don't have a little girl. Are they both staying at your house?

I was with you all morning and you never said a thing about anyone staying at your house. This is a big thing, keeping a secret about two people actually staying at your house as if it were a motel." She paused. "My God, it's the furnace man, the guy that came that night, isn't it, and the house on Carnation Lane, he had a metal thing in his head and he showed you a picture. He's the same one, and you never even said a word to me."

"I think I better go," Ross said, and he took Sandy's hand and walked out the door with her.

"He drove that old car down here from Santa Rosa?" Brad said. He was standing in the doorway watching Ross drive away.

"You told me you went to a reunion," Deborah said.

"He's really staying at your house?" Brad said. He was back at his desk looking through the prospects file.

"Till I get someone to take care of Sandy during the day," Lela said. "Then he's leaving."

"He looks kind of left over from the sixties to me. What does he do?"

"You don't have any other sister but me," Deborah said.

"He could be a criminal," Brad said. "What do you know about him? Have you checked him out? I could call the sheriff's department and see if he's wanted somewhere."

"What do you mean, he's leaving the girl with you?" Deborah said. "Who's going to take care of her when you're working? And don't look at me, because I don't intend to baby-sit every strange child you pick up and bring home. And don't expect me to let Rowena do anything, either. I think you've gone crazy, Lela. What kind of story did he tell you to get you to do this? And who is he, anyway?"

"He's her father."

"I'm lost," Brad said.

"Well, it just makes me sick," Deborah said. "Why did you tell me you were going to a reunion when you didn't go? I think you need to go back into therapy, Lela, that's what I think."

"I don't like cartoons too much," Sandy said. "Everyone gets hurt in those things, but no one dies."

"Because it's make-believe," Lela said. Sandy was on Lela's bed, watching television, a box of graham crackers beside her, while animated rabbits jumped across the television screen on the bureau across the room.

"I watch *All My Children* every day. Mama sleeps most of the time, and I can do what I want. I can cook and watch television and play with my cat. Misty is my cat. Maybe Mama can mail her to us. I bet they have boxes you can put cats in and send them through the mail."

Ross came in after Sandy fell asleep. The television was still on, but Lela had turned the sound off. Humphrey Bogart was fighting off German tanks and artillery in the Sahara desert.

"Bogart had a lisp," Lela said. "Did you ever notice that? I've always wondered why no one ever took him to a speech therapist. Don't you think there were speech therapists who could have fixed Bogie's lisp? He certainly made enough money to afford someone to get rid of it for him."

He was watching her from the bedroom door. He seemed always to be standing in or near doorways, always in a spot between rooms. As though he wanted no one at his back. As though he wanted to be free to run if he had to.

"I always watch Bogie's movies with the sound turned off," she said. "I'd rather read his lips than listen to him lisping."

He was beside her on the bed now, his rough cheek against her ear, his soft breath tickling her neck. He put his arm across her, rested his hand lightly on her breast.

"I'm sorry about showing up at your place today," he said. "I didn't know what a lock on you they had."

She lifted his arm from across her body and got up.

"You're just trying to wreck my life," she said.

———————————

Lela was in the dark living room, in one of the stiff Chinese chairs. She had been sitting there for hours, it seemed. Ross had fallen asleep next to Sandy, but now he was up, roaming around in the kitchen, opening cupboards, running water in the sink. He was making coffee in the middle of the night. She could tell by the sharp clank of the metal pot against the sink. He had bought regular coffee, the kind that smelled like coffee instead of fruit when you opened the can. And he had moved the Japanese jars out of the fireplace and bought a cord of wood for her so she could start a fire when the weather got cold.

"If Jolene's such a terrible mother, why don't you have custody?" she said. He couldn't hear her. Or he didn't want to. She was facing the garden, but it was almost too dark to see anything. The bulb in the Japanese lantern Dale had hung from the silk oak tree had burned out long ago, and she had never replaced it. But she knew where everything in the garden should be, and there was enough moonlight so she could pick out the contours of the fire red bougainvillea, could tell that the carnations she had planted were spreading across their bed.

"Because it would be a fight, and I don't know whether I'd win," he said from the kitchen.

Roses didn't grow too well in Lela's garden. Not like the roses climbing all over Lillian's roof. Lillian's roses bloomed all year round, big as cabbages. They mingled with the honeysuckle vines and wound themselves into the branches of the lantanas. They weren't tender like Lela's were. Lillian's roses had no names, no patents, never turned speckly with rust.

Ross came into the living room with his coffee. He hadn't used one of Lela's dainty cups but had poured it into a water glass. He sat on the floor now, not even attempting the Chinese chair. "I haven't been an angel, either, Lela. I told you I was an addict and a drunk. As for Jolene, she's been arrested twice now using forged credit cards to get cash for drugs. When she isn't high, she's sleeping. I don't want Sandy to grow up like that. With her. That way. She won't look here for her. She'd never think to look here. Why did it scare you seeing me in that office today?"

"You're very blunt."

"I don't keep secrets, if that's what you mean."

"I knew having Sandy here would upset them, so why tell them anything about it? It doesn't matter now. They'll get used to it."

He held the glass in both hands, kind of rolled it back and forth against his palms, watching the way the steam curled and twisted above the rim of the glass.

"You remind me of someone I knew," she said. "He was like you, sure of himself. He never had any doubts about anything."

"Not your husband."

"Oh, no, no. My psychiatrist. His name was Gil Rusk. He had never been in a war, but he was solid, like you are. He died in 1986. We were lovers from the time I was fifteen. It continued until he died. Even when I was married."

Ross got up now and went into the kitchen. He was at the sink. She could see his back through the door.

"I thought I loved Gil more than anyone in the world. I even slept with him the night before my wedding to Dale. It was a beautiful wedding at the Wayfarer's Chapel in Palos Verdes—it's a really beautiful chapel, Ross, you ought to see it before you leave. All glass and wood reaching toward the sky, and the brilliant bluc of the ocean down below."

He had his hand on the handle of the coffeepot and was staring at it, not pouring coffee, just staring at the pot. After a few minutes he sat down at the kitchen table. She could barely see his face.

"I had four bridesmaids, all of them girls I went to St. Cecilia Martyr with, all in pink Scarlett O'Hara dresses, carrying pink baby roses in their hands and wearing pink baby roses in their hair. Deborah and Kathy wore lavender and carried bouquets of baby's breath. Dale invited his ex-wife and her parents. I asked Gil if he wanted to come. He said inviting ex-spouses to a wedding was one thing, but having him there would be a dangerous, perverse thing to do, and I'd better not. So I didn't."

Ross had his hand palm down on the table, the fingers spread out like a child who is about to trace his fingers on a piece of paper.

"At the rehearsal dinner Deborah was being so sweet and helpful, I almost told her about Gil. I started to, was about to, and then I just couldn't do it. Gil's always been a burden. Mentally, I mean. I've never been able to figure out why I needed him. Before Deborah left for graduate school at Stanford I thought I'd tell her about him and see what she thought. I had never told anyone about Gil, not even Walter or Kathy. But then I remembered how Deborah is, always using things I say, hurting me with them. So I didn't tell her. Deborah's so funny. She chose a field she knew she'd never have to make a living at. Biological demographics with a special interest in Egyptian mummies. Nothing so mundane as mine. Art. All the way down the line, even for my master's.

"I remember seagulls were diving close to the windows of the restaurant the day Gil told me he was dying. Their feathers would brush the glass before they veered away, as though knowledge of broken wings on glass was bred in them. Cano's. We sometimes drove down the coast and had lunch at Cano's and then spent the afternoon together in a hotel. Usually the Surf and Sand. Gil was never afraid we'd be interrupted in a hotel, the way he was when we made love in his office. The office was for my therapy, and he liked to separate the two things. Doctor and lover. I think it made him feel less guilty taking me somewhere else. And he didn't have to worry about being interrupted, or that he had to hurry before his next patient appeared, or that his wife might call. Or even that he might leave a wet spot of semen on the couch."

Ross's face was angular, one cheek cut by shadows. He was listening.

"I'm making Gil sound like he wasn't wonderful, when he was.

You'd have liked him. Reality and the moment are all that matter, he always said. His wife didn't know he had cancer. She was for good times, he said, for spending money, for going to the theater. Cano's was crowded. It was the lunch hour, and there were salesmen from the boat basin next door having some kind of celebration at the next table. Probably who had sold the most yachts that month. They were all in white. White shoes. White pants. Gil was trying to look as though he were eating his food, shoving bits of grilled halibut from one side of his plate to the other with his fork, and the sun was low in the sky and there was a veil of red haze, sheer as smoke, trailing behind it."

Gil could turn moon into stars, water into air, nightmares into dreams. He could change memory into ashes. Gil knew everything about everything, everything about her. What did this man know? What could this man do?

"He said he felt better just having me with him, but the skin on his neck was loose and hung over the collar of his shirt, and his hands shook as he worked at the food with his fork. We left the restaurant and went to a hotel in Dana Point. The bellman brought a wheelchair and asked if Gil would need a doctor, and Gil laughed and said he was a doctor. Then he went out on the balcony and watched the waves while I lay on the bed and watched him through the open door."

She stopped talking. Ross hadn't moved. Had he heard her at all? "Go on," he said.

"He talked about going to Scripps and starting some experimental treatment there. He told me he could beat it. He was optimistic. He said he wanted to make love. I could always fool him, but he couldn't fool me. He tried, but all he could manage was to hold me in his arms and stroke my hair.

"Sometime before morning he awakened me. I had been dreaming of flying. I was flying around the room and everyone was saying, Look at Lela, how high she can fly. He had a bottle of pills and he said he wanted to die, but he was afraid. He asked me to make him take the pills. A glass of water was on the nightstand. It was strange how he could talk for hours about reality and the moment, about facing what you had to do head on, and when it came to his own life he didn't believe any of it. He lay down like a child on the bed, arms curled to his chest. I brought the pills and the water to him and watched while he took them."

The nausea hit her too fast to hold anything in, too fast to run to the bathroom. She had only enough time to make it to the kitchen sink before she gagged and vomited.

Ross was beside her, holding her head, cool hands firm and dry against her forehead. He didn't seem to mind that she was bringing up everything she had ever swallowed in her life and dumping it in the sink in front of him. He was being tender with her. Sweet and tender. Wiping her face with a towel. Holding a glass of water to her lips.

"I don't always feel it coming," she said, and retched again.

"Do you take anything?"

"A tranquilizer. Xanax."

"I mean for the nausea."

"Compazine."

"Where is it? In your bathroom?"

She began to tremble, then bent toward the sink again. He held her tighter now, didn't walk away, just waited while her stomach turned itself inside out.

"Don't worry, I'll find it," he said.

———————————————

Ross left in the morning. Sandy and Lela walked out to the car with him. It had been cool the night before, but it was warm now, and there was a thin film of dew on the grass. Sandy was in her bare feet, running across the grass doing cartwheels, leaving dark prints of her feet and hands in the smooth green thatch.

"She's a handful," Ross said.

"Lillian's going to help with her," Lela said.

He had sat with her in the kitchen all night. She had said she was all right, that she vomited when she was upset, that he should go lie down, get some sleep. But he said no, that was all right, he wasn't sleepy, wasn't tired, and he sat there drinking cup after cup of coffee and looking at her without even commenting on what she had told him, and now he was leaving.

"I'll be back in a couple of weeks, and I'll bring Sandy's birth certificate with me if I can get a copy of it," he said. "She'll need it for school."

He seemed preoccupied when he hugged Sandy and told her to be good, and he didn't kiss Lela good-bye at all, just held her hand tight and told her to take care of herself, and then he was gone, and the way he left, without telling her what he thought, made her feel like he'd never be back.

20

"THIS IS ONE of the loveliest houses in Rolling Hills, Mrs. Delaney," Lela said. She and Mrs. Delaney sat side by side on a worn couch, so close that Lela could smell her cologne, a sickeningly sweet powdery scent that reminded her of perfume that had sat on a dressing table for too many years.

"It sure is," Brad said. He was sitting on a yellow plastic kitchen chair, his Italian-leather-booted feet coiled around the chair's tubular steel legs. He was mainly listening, nodding his head occasionally, smiling at Mrs. Delaney when she looked his way. Maybe sticking in a word or two to bolster what Lela was saying, but otherwise leaving it to her. This was Lela's part. She shone in selling the listing.

"And all the antiques and paintings, why, it's like a museum," Lela said. "So much of everything, it takes my breath away. I'm overwhelmed, just overwhelmed."

The house looked as though a van had driven up and disgorged its contents and no one had bothered to arrange anything. It made Lela dizzy. There was no place to rest her eyes. There were some good things, like the bronze cranes in the entry. And the English tall clock and Chippendale chairs and Spanish refectory table in the dining room. And the collection of majolica plates covering one wall of the cluttered library. But there was also the black-and-white television on the wrought-iron stand in the middle of the sunken living room, with the wire stretching across the bare floor like a dried-up strand of spaghetti. And five worn-out couches lined up doilied arm to doilied arm in front of the cold fireplace. And the awful yellow plastic kitchen chairs, one of which Brad was sitting on, that were spotted here and there among the pots of dead and dying plants. And there were empty bird cages everywhere. On the floor, on tables, in the kitchen, in the bathrooms. Some of them looked valuable, like the one that was a replica of Buckingham Palace and was made of teakwood and bronze with Chinese porcelain fittings. The rest of them were the twenty-dollar pet store variety, just plain old twisted-wire cages hanging from metal stands.

"Wherever did you find all these lovely things?" Lela asked.

"It was really my husband who collected," Mrs. Delaney said.

Lela had sized up the house weeks ago when she first heard that Sylvia Delaney was thinking about selling it. It was on the high-priced side of the hill, where wild-branched coral trees wept red blossoms across the shadowed roads and mansions guarded their fortress walls behind armies of white-spiked oleanders and squadrons of bougainvillea. The house looked pretty from the road, with its spring blanket of wisteria draped across the entry gate. But the trees along the drive were overgrown, and the house itself was nearly buried in untended vines that had crept up the stone walls and lifted up the roof tiles so that they seemed to tremble on a moldering bed of dead leaves.

"My husband had a perfect eye," Mrs. Delaney said. "He could tell when something was good a block away. He was always buying, collecting, accumulating. I've never had the talent myself. Things just manage to come into the house by themselves now. I don't even remember buying some of these things."

"Well, I'm just stunned by it all," Lela said. "That cabinet, is it French?" The cabinet was in a recessed nook beside the fireplace, its gold ormulu bonnet nearly hidden by a half-dead ficus tree.

"Yes. Eighteenth century," Mrs. Delaney said. She was a tiny woman in a flowing caftan, her thinning white hair secured to her head with rows of bent hairpins. She had powdered her face, but it hadn't covered the dark shadows in her cheeks. She was dying of something, was what Lela had heard.

"You'll have to excuse me if I'm having a hard time concentrating on the presentation," Lela said, "but I'm really—I mean really—overwhelmed by this place."

There were marble floors throughout the house, but they were gouged and stained. The frescoed ceilings were a little old-fashioned. No one wanted cherubim and clouds overhead these days.

"Anyone who looks at this house will be amazed," Lela said. "Have you called in any other brokers?"

"Williams Brothers Realty. Mr. Williams was one of my husband's investors. He trusted him. I trust him. Who did you say you were with?"

"Bru-Bing Realty," Brad said. "You can trust us, too."

"You can never be too careful," Mrs. Delaney said.

"You certainly can't," Lela said.

"How did you get my name?"

"You called us."

"I did?"

"We'd be happy to take the listing."

"Oh, I don't know about that. Mr. Williams is a dear friend. Did I tell you my husband built this house in 1938? Drew the plans and hired the workmen? Of course, Richard Wright gave him some needed advice, but he did it mainly by himself. Of course, you noticed the floors. The marble came from Carrara, handpicked. The man who laid it was Veronese and had done work at the Vatican. And the ceilings, the pride and glory of the house, were painted by Edward Hopper. Did you know he could paint angels? He came all the way from New England and painted them on our ceiling. His train fare and fee came to three hundred fifty dollars. If you look carefully, you can see my face and my husband's on two of the angels. I don't remember calling you. My memory is so poor lately. Did I really call you?"

"Yes," Lela said. "We had a conversation about traffic. Do you remember?"

"There's no traffic up here."

"That you don't like to go to Los Angeles because of the traffic. We talked about Grauman's Chinese Theatre, and you told me you were with Gloria Swanson when she put her hands and feet into the cement there."

"If you say I did, I must have. But I don't know why I'd call you. I really hate the thought of selling. My husband before he died said, Sylvia, don't sell the house until the market goes up, but the taxes are getting so high—and I'm in my eighties, what do I want with a house this big?"

"It's always a wrench to sell the place you've lived in for most of your life."

"Oh, I'm not particularly fond of this house. I don't form attachments to objects like my husband did." Mrs. Delaney motioned toward a framed black-and-white squiggle that hung crookedly over the fireplace mantel. "Picasso did that sketch of me when I was a girl in Paris. I modeled for Coco Chanel, you know. I was on the cover of *Life* magazine right before the war started. My husband was a Spanish diplomat. Picasso was our dear friend."

Paintings hung in odd places. Near the ornamental frieze that banded the frescoed ceiling. Above the heavy mahogany doors.

Inches from the marble floor. Although it was daytime, the lights were on, all sunlight cut off at the windows by vines that had crawled across the screens and stuck their tentacles tight into the mesh, trying, like tiny burglars, to reach the glass. Overhead spotlights designed to illuminate the art wasted their wattage tracing haphazard smudges of light on the shadowed walls and ceilings.

"I hope everything's insured," Lela said. "I wouldn't want to be responsible for people coming through to see the house and maybe taking something valuable away with them."

"Do people do that?" Mrs. Delaney said.

"You bet they do. But we've never had a problem."

"Never," Brad said.

"Some realtors aren't careful," Lela said. "They just don't pay attention to what's going on. We take an inventory and give you a copy, and we escort the prospective buyers into the house and out of the house and walk them to their cars. We're supercautious. We treat the houses we have for sale as though they were our own. Are you getting tired, Mrs. Delaney?"

"A little."

"I'll hurry it up, then. I'd love to look at your things more closely another time, though. I'm very interested in art and antiques. I was a textile designer before I went into real estate."

"Such a talented girl."

"Not really."

"And modest, too. I'll bet people love to be with you, listen to you talk. You have such a charming way of talking. But you must know that, don't you? Surely you must. People must have told you that a thousand times."

"Everyone loves Lela," Brad said.

Mrs. Delaney turned toward him, head stiff on her shoulders, as though neck and body were fused. "I have psychic powers, you know," she said. "I can tell when someone is sincere by their eyes and their facial muscles. Their cheeks tighten when they're insincere. Like yours are doing now."

"He's had a toothache all day," Lela said. "Haven't you, Brad?"

"I'm serious," Mrs. Delaney said. "Sincerity is in the cheekbones, nowhere else."

"The comparables," Brad said, and handed Lela the presentation brochure. She had put it together in a week. Photographs and figures, comparable real estate prices, all laid out on slick paper in booklet form and placed in a mock-leather binder.

"Here are the comparables, Mrs. Delaney," Lela said. "They're the prices houses like yours sold for this past year in the Rolling Hills–Palos Verdes area."

"There *is* no house like this," Mrs. Delaney said. "This is a unique house."

"This *is* a unique house," Lela said. "There is no house like it anywhere. But houses with approximately the same square feet are what we tried to pick out for you in the comparables. Now, you can see this one on Flora Drive sold for five hundred thousand, this one on Santa Clarita sold for four eighty-five, and—"

"I want a million dollars for this house. Mr. Williams said all he could get me was eight hundred thousand top price. I want a million."

"Sometimes it's best not to deal with good friends in business," Lela said. "They say things to please you. It doesn't always work out the way they say."

"It's not a good idea to deal with friends when selling real estate," Brad said.

"This is a million-dollar house," Mrs. Delaney said.

Lela reached across the narrow expanse of worn silk and took Mrs. Delaney's hand. It felt damp and cold in her warm one. She wanted to drop it, to say to Brad, Let the old woman be and let's go. But they were still in the middle of the game. The old woman was playing it well. Lela couldn't let a sick old woman beat her at the only thing she did well.

"I would buy this house for myself if I could afford it," Lela said. "And I'd pay you a million dollars. And I wouldn't change a thing in it. It's beautiful, homey, a perfect family house. Did you and your husband have children?"

"One son. He lives in Vienna."

"Then he wasn't born in the States?"

"He went there to study and met an Austrian girl and married her. He visits me once a year. Why would I have called you, of all the realtors in the book? I would have called Coldwell Banker. Why would I call a small realty office that no one ever heard of?"

"And does he have children?"

"Three. Two boys and a girl. The girl is like you, sweet and lovely."

"And you believe me when I tell you I want you to get a million dollars for this property?"

"Yes, I do. I do believe you."

"The problem is you have no built-ins in the kitchen. The house on Santa Clarita has built-ins. And a gazebo in back. And a sunroom added on. The house on Flora Drive has solar heating, and the sprinkler system is on a timer, and the roof has been replaced."

"We've brought a listing agreement for you to sign," Brad said.

"I want a million dollars for this house," Mrs. Delaney said.

"The marble is beyond saving," Lela said. "Too old and stained. And I don't think anyone wants a Sistine Chapel ceiling, even if it was painted by Edward Hopper. Especially with your face and your husband's as angels. It's tacky. Very tacky. But believe me, this house, in any other economy, at any other time, would get you that million dollars." Lela snapped her fingers. "In a minute."

Brad moved his plastic chair closer. "Prices could slip farther, Mrs. Delaney," he said.

"I don't think we should rush Mrs. Delaney into anything," Lela said. She stood up. The sofa had a small dent in it where she had been sitting. She bent forward and plumped the pillows with her hand, then put the comparables back in the mock-leather folder.

"Are you leaving?" Mrs. Delaney said.

"We have other appointments," Lela said.

"But Williams Realty said the house is worth at least eight hundred thousand."

"I loved our visit," Lela said, "and your house is marvelous. I wish you all the luck in the world in selling it, no matter who gets the listing."

"The Swensons might be interested in it at four seventy-five if we move some of the junk out of there before we show it to them," Lela said.

"The outside will need a flame thrower just to clear out the vegetation," Brad said.

They were in the Cheesecake Factory at a window seat overlooking the yacht harbor in Redondo. It was between lunchtime and dinner, and there were only a few people in the booths. Across the highway the old power plant's blank-faced stacks of concrete and rusting steel girders stared blindly at the ocean. And beyond the yacht harbor was the pier with its funky shops hanging out over the waves. Lela knew their merchandise by heart. Abalone jewelry. Seashell ashtrays. Carved-wood fish glued to plaques that said "I caught this in Redondo Beach."

"I didn't think I was going to get an exclusive," Lela said. "The most I was hoping for was a listing, the way it was going. She was very good."

"And you were better."

"We can get a marble man in there to fix the floors, that's no problem."

"Do you think Edward Hopper really painted the ceiling?"

"On one of his bad days, maybe. It can be painted over easily."

The waitress brought iced tea for Lela and a glass of wine for Brad. Brad waited till the waitress was gone, and then he leaned across the table.

"I'm not one to give anyone advice, but what are you doing, Lela?"

"I thought I handled it great. She didn't know what hit her. And it was fair, Brad, you've got to give me that. I may be firm, but I'm never anything but fair. She was just too stubborn. The way she was going, the house was going to go into her estate, not on the market."

"I mean the kid and that guy with the chromed head."

"Oh."

"How come Deb and I never saw him before? How come you never talked about him or a sister or a niece?"

"I didn't know anything about them before."

"How could you not know you had a sister? No one forgets a thing like that."

"Well, I forgot. I don't want to talk about it."

"Why not?"

"I don't know. I just don't. It upsets me, and I can't tell you why. Deep down upsets me."

"You mean like not getting a listing? That kind of upsetting?"

Lela smiled at him. "Yes, something like that."

"Whose idea was it, him bringing her to you? I mean, the kid's mother knows about it; it's with her permission—it's legal, on the up and up?"

Lela shook her head. "No."

"Terrific. You've got someone else's kid, took her without ask-ing—"

"I told you, Ross is her father."

"Does he have custody?"

"No."

"Great. So you've got a kidnapped kid—"

"She's not kidnapped. Don't be melodramatic."

"Where are you keeping her? I haven't seen her all week."

"Do you want to?"

"No, I don't want to. I'm just asking."

"She's at home. My neighbor watches her while I'm working."

"You don't know your neighbors."

"Lillian Levine. The peach tree that made a hole in my fence. The one you told me to sue."

"Oh, that neighbor."

"You haven't noticed any difference in my work in the office this whole week Sandy's been with me, have you?"

"I noticed you were a little distracted."

"I pitched Sylvia Delaney, didn't I? Did you see that pitch I gave her? Was it the best you ever saw? And I got the listing. I'm not distracted."

"Well, I don't like any of it. And neither does Deb. You know how she gets when you don't call or come over a couple times a week."

"I'll call her tonight."

He reached for the bill, studied it a moment, then pulled a couple of bills out of his pocket and put them on the table.

"Well, it sounds like you're asking for trouble, if you ask me."

"Someone has to save her," she said.

21

"Imagine you and Lela being neighbors all this time and never speaking," Deborah said. She and Lillian sat side by side on a stone bench beneath the eucalyptus tree in Lela's yard. Leaves, bright and shiny as silver dollars, blew around them, the September breeze piling them in one place, then lifting them up and piling them somewhere else. Brad, in a canvas deck chair, had his face up to the sun, eyes closed. Lela was playing ring around the rosie with Jason and Sandy on the far side of the yard.

"I'm not the friendly type," Lillian said.

"Well, I won't believe that."

Lillian had crossed from her yard to Lela's through the hole in the stone fence early that morning and started the chili in Lela's kitchen while Lela showed Sandy how to make radish roses and carrot curls to decorate the tossed salad.

"You're a nurse, you said?"

"I was."

"What about swollen feet?" Deborah lifted one leg, held it in her hands like a baseball bat.

Lillian bent toward the leg and pressed two fingers into the heavy ankle.

"There's a slight edema," she said. "See the way the skin stays indented where I pressed it? That means you're retaining fluid. It could be an early sign of toxemia. I'd stay off my feet as much as possible."

"With three kids?"

"All fall *down*." Jason's high-pitched squeal joined Sandy's whoops and Lela's laughter as they fell backward onto a soft heap of fallen leaves.

"Eucalyptus oil," Lillian said.

"For my feet?" Deborah asked.

"No. The eucalyptus leaves. They're crushing them and releasing the oil. The smell is wonderful. Sharp as needles. Good for clogged sinuses. Tell your doctor about the swelling. You shouldn't be asking the advice of a retired nurse when your health and your baby's is at stake."

"Oh, I wasn't asking for your advice. Not seriously. I have a doctor. A good one."

"He costs enough," Brad muttered from the lounge chair.

"Look at you," Lela said as Sandy did a cartwheel across the yard. "You're just a natural acrobat. Where did you ever learn to do that?"

"Mama showed me," Sandy said. "Mama can do fourteen hundred cartwheels without stopping."

"Again," Jason said.

Sandy did one cartwheel after another. Lela and Jason clapped their hands each time her feet touched the ground.

"I think Jason's getting tired," Deborah called out across the yard.

"Ring around," Jason said.

"One more time," Lela said, and she and Sandy each took one of Jason's hands.

"Ring around the rosie, pockets full of posies. Ashes, ashes, all fall down."

"Look at Lela," Deborah said, "rolling around in the leaves in a sunsuit and ribbons in her hair as though she were three years old. Isn't she pretty? I've always wanted to look like her. She's naturally thin, can eat what she wants and not gain an ounce. Did she really just go over and speak to you, out of the blue?"

"Sandy was sleepwalking. I helped Lela look for her."

"Well, aren't you sweet."

"I was glad to help. She was quite frantic."

"I'd have been over in a flash if she had called me."

"There wasn't time for that."

"I'd have made time."

"I don't mean time in that way."

"Mother always said to take care of Lela, because she had a bad life before she came to live with us. You know she's adopted?"

"I didn't know that."

"We always tiptoed around Lela. Don't upset Lela. Don't say that to Lela. Even though she's older than I am, I've always felt like the older sister, trying to protect her. If anything or anyone ever hurt her, I'd probably kill him with my own two hands."

"I can't imagine anyone ever wanting to hurt her."

"I don't pretend to be as good as she is. It used to make me envious, how good she is. She has a Christmas list longer than the Redondo Beach phone book. Sends cards to everyone on the list, every person she's ever met—the girls who work in the dry cleaners, gasoline station attendants, a dentist who pulled an infected tooth for her on a Sunday in 1978. She sends them all Christmas cards. She reads the obituaries and sends wreaths to funerals of people whose names sound even vaguely familiar. Can you imagine what people must think when they get a card or wreath from someone they don't even remember?"

"I like her very much. It's been a lonely life for me up to now. I feel as though she and Sandy are my family."

"You have absolutely no family at all?"

"None."

"I think one of the twins is crying," Brad said. Deborah had put them to sleep in Lela's bedroom, and a single thin wail was drifting out through a rear window.

"Will you check on the twins, Lela?" Deborah called out.

"Exercise will do you some good, Deb," Brad said.

"No, I'll go," Lela said. As she passed the picnic table, she gave Deborah's shoulder an affectionate squeeze and smiled at Lillian. "I'll heat the chili."

"Don't pick them up, Lela," Deborah said.

"Is everyone getting hungry for lunch?" Lela said.

"I do, Mom," Jason said.

"Don't pick them up," Deborah said again.

"But they're crying."

"They're not crying. That's one voice, probably Tony's, and it's just a whine, not a cry."

Lela went inside, and Deborah said, "Lela doesn't believe that babies learn fast how to manipulate you."

"I love when the weather turns cool like this after a hot summer," Lillian remarked.

"Can I show Jason how to do a somersault?" Sandy was standing right next to Deborah now, bits of silver leaves clinging like paper hearts to her ponytail.

"He's too young for that, Sandy," Deborah said.

"I was a baby when I did my first somersault," Sandy said. "Younger than Jason. Younger than the twins. I couldn't even walk or crawl, but I could do twenty somersaults in a row. I bet Jason could do one if I showed him."

"I said no."

"Come sit with me," Lillian said, and pulled the child onto the bench beside her. "You have leaves in your hair. They smell nice."

"Do you watch Sandy every day for Lela?" Deborah asked.

"Yes. Yes, I do. We have an arrangement. I do the cooking for all three of us. Lela buys the food. I have a small income, but it's been difficult making ends meet. The arrangement serves us both well."

"Isn't that nice," Deborah said.

"Why don't you go in and see if you can give Lela a hand, Deb," Brad said.

"She can handle it."

"For chrissakes, Deb."

"Lela and I are very close," Deborah continued. "Closer than real sisters could ever be."

Jason was trying to crawl up onto Brad's lap, climbing up his pants, little fingers grasping at the material.

"Jason looks like a spider," Sandy said. She turned her head and looked at Deborah. Squinted at her from beneath a shower of silver-tipped hair.

"I had a pet spider once. It had a pink bow with shiny sparkles on it and streamers. I used to take it for walks. His name was Leroy. Mama killed it on accident when she wasn't looking. Just stepped on it and squished it all to pieces. She was sorry, though. She told me she was."

"I knew you'd pick them up," Deborah said. Lela was on the bed, a twin in each arm.

"Tony needed changing. That's why he was crying. Look how sweet he is now."

Lela could see through the bedroom window into the yard. Sandy, cheeks flushed, ponytail undone, was helping Lillian set the picnic table. Lela felt a rush of warmth for the child, watching her place knives and forks so carefully beside the plates, little fingers brushing away fallen leaves, lips pursed in concentration.

"Can't you see that everything's falling apart?" Deborah said.

"Didn't I get the diaper on right?"

"Not the diaper. Your life."

Deborah kicked off her shoes and lay down on the bed. "A man you never met dumps his kid on your doorstep."

"My niece."

"You don't know that."

"She looks like me."

"So what? What does that prove? I can find three hundred children who look like you. And your neighbor is weird. I think you'd better watch out for her. She's the kind that will come into your life and take over. Lonely people are like that, lying in wait, then pouncing on the first person who's kind to them. I'm warning you, Lela, you know how you are about people, about not being able to say no, about wanting to please everyone. And that kid—that Sandy—she lies about everything. Is her father ever going to come back for her? I mean, really, what are you doing, Lela?"

"I'm going to enroll her in school here."

"School? She's going to stay?"

"She needs me."

"Oh, I see. Well, I suppose if you went to Bangladesh, you'd find hundreds of thousands of children who'd need you, too. My children need you. I need you. God, I'm exhausted."

"Why don't you try to sleep. I'll take the babies outside and I'll wake you when lunch is ready."

"Blood ties go only so far, if you ask me."

Lela had papers spread out on her bed. The Swenson escrow on the Delaney house. Finally. If she could get the Swensons through the last round of meetings, get them to sign the final papers, and Sylvia Delaney didn't back out of the deal, she'd have some cash to redo Sandy's room. She already had sketches drawn of how the room was going to look. She didn't want white furniture or canopies, nothing obviously childish that Sandy'd outgrow in a few years. Something light, but not featherweight. Something solid, timeless in design, but youthful, that would last till she went off to college. Maybe English oak. The idea made Lela smile. Just right. Barley twist bedposts with carved pineapples on top.

There was a cozy snugness in the house. Sandy asleep down the hall, Barbra Streisand on the stereo. Time to think. About fabrics and furniture. About changing this house, making it a happy home.

Lela lifted her head up. *Whoosh*ing sounds on the monitor that Ross had put in Sandy's bedroom. Flapping noises. Not too remarkable. Nothing to be alarmed about.

If she were in Hong Kong, she'd design the fabric for the drapes and bedspread and have the silkscreen team there make it for her.

But she wasn't in Hong Kong. She'd have it done here at that silk-screen place on La Cienega. Capricorn Gel. They did all of Dale's lithographs. They had even done a few of her designs when she was trying to freelance, before she sold her first house and didn't know where the money was going to come from to live on.

What was that *whoosh*ing sound? Lela had learned to interpret the monitor's wheezes, whistles, hisses. The random movement of one of Sandy's arms or the bounce of her body as she turned in bed made a noise like wind rushing through the trees. Rhythmic kicking at the covers and thrashing sounded like thunder, like a storm in the making, and would make Lela walk to Sandy's door. But what was that *whoosh*ing sound? She turned down the volume on the stereo. Stillness. Nothing. Just restlessness. All those cartwheels.

Of course, she'd consult with Sandy first, ask her what colors she preferred. She'd ask her every step of the way if she liked the way the room was shaping up. She wanted Sandy to be happy. Would stars and moons make her happy? Not realistic stars and moons. Stylized ones, cartoonlike, but small, so you couldn't really tell what they were unless you looked closely. Lela took a scrap of clean paper out of the Swenson escrow envelope and began sketching miniature moons and stars and suns.

A man's voice burst out of the monitor. Then a woman's.

"Lela!"

Papers flew off the bed.

"Lela!"

A man wearing a yellow raincoat stood in the doorway of Sandy's room. Jolene, in jeans and a long, furry-looking overcoat, a hand on each of Sandy's arms, was half dragging, half pulling the child through the bedroom door into the hallway.

"What are you doing?" Lela cried.

"Police," the man said, and he held a long sheet of white paper out to Lela. It was smooth and cold and flitted briefly against her fingers before it fluttered to the floor.

"Lela!" Sandy shrieked.

"What are you doing?"

"Stay away!" Jolene said, and kept yanking at Sandy's arms.

"She has a custody order," the policeman said.

Lela lunged at Jolene, felt the curly fibers of Jolene's coat, stiff as bristle, scratch her fingers.

"You're making it harder," the policeman said.

Lela had hold of Jolene's collar, clutching at bits of fur.

"She's my child," Jolene screamed. "Mine."

"Don't make me hurt you," the policeman said. He looked as though he were waiting to catch a ball, the way he held his arms out, the way he kept bending at the knees trying to grab hold of Lela.

"Are you crazy?" Jolene screamed.

"Lela!" Sandy shrieked. "Lela!"

Lela's fingers were caught now, tangled in Jolene's hair.

"Shoot her!" Jolene said.

"I can't shoot her."

"Then give me your gun, and I'll shoot her."

"Lela!"

Lela could see his face through Jolene's fur collar. Little snippets of face that needed a shave. And when he pinned Lela to the floor and stepped over her to lift Sandy into his arms, she saw the dirty white sneakers on his feet.

––––––––––––––––––

Lela stood at the open door and watched them leave. They had come in that same Chevrolet Jolene was driving up in Santa Rosa. The rear fender was battered in, and it was missing a taillight. Sandy looked out the rear window at Lela as the car moved slowly away from the curb and headed toward the corner. It hesitated at the stop sign, turned right, and was gone. Lela imagined it in the darkness, making a left turn at the next corner and heading toward Pacific Coast Highway.

She had tried. Oh, how hard she had tried. She walked out into the street and stood there in the dark, looking at the starlit sky, letting the damp air cool her cheeks where Jolene's fingernails, as pointy and sharp as a cat's, had drawn blood.

The man with Jolene had been expecting rain. He had even thought to wear a raincoat when he left Santa Rosa and headed south to take Sandy away. It was raining a little. More mist than rain. She sat down on the curb, her bare feet in the oily sludge Jolene's old car had left behind. She hoped it would pour. She hoped it would rain so hard that it would bore holes in the sidewalks and strip paint from the houses. She hoped it would rain hard enough to scare the birds out of the trees. Hard enough to break the planet in two. She put her head in her hands, fingers clamped tight against her rain-damp hair. Falling apart, Deborah said. Your life is falling apart.

22

"LET ME IN, Lela." Brad was at the bedroom window. "Come on, don't be like that." Lillian had pulled the window blinds all the way up, and here was Brad's face, a dirty spot against the glass, obliterating the carnations that were in bloom, blocking the sun. He was the one who had phoned the clerk at Sonoma County Superior Court and told her where Sandy was. I did it for you, he told Lela. I did it for you.

"I don't think he's gone home at all since yesterday afternoon," Lillian said. "Unless someone picked him up and brought him back, I think he's been in the backyard all night." She stood in the doorway of Lela's bedroom, an apron around her waist. She had done that often during the day, stopping what she was doing in the kitchen and looking in on Lela. Saying something to her. Maybe coming over to the bed and rearranging the covers. She had come right over when Lela called two nights ago. In her nightgown, with a blue-checked bathrobe over it and slippers that had a row of sheepskin around the ankles.

"He just doesn't know when to give up," Lela said.

Lillian had slept in Sandy's room the past two nights, in Sandy's bed, the one Lela was going to cover with moons and stars. She wouldn't go home, no matter how many times Lela told her she should, that she'd be all right, she'd get over it.

"You were asleep, but I could still see him out in the dark smoking cigarette after cigarette at midnight," Lillian said.

"He doesn't care about his lungs," Lela said.

"They had chicken on special at the market. I thought I'd make some fried chicken for dinner."

"You really shouldn't be doing this. You're making me feel awful that you're going to all this trouble for me. I'm just tired, that's all. And miserable. I can fry eggs for dinner. I don't care what I eat."

"I loved Sandy, too, you know. I could roast the chicken if you'd like that better."

"We were only thinking of you, Lela," Brad said. He had his hands up against the window, trying to see inside. His face looked metallic in the fading sunlight, his hands cupping the sides of his jaw as though he were about to hand his head to someone.

"Deb and I both. We couldn't stand by and watch you get involved in something that could only hurt you. I didn't know you'd take it this way. I didn't know, I swear, or I'd never have done it. If I thought it was going to make you sick, I'd never have made that call, Lela. Believe me, I'm sure sorry now. Do you think if I wanted to hurt you, I would have told you I did it? I'm not that stupid, Lela. Are you going to at least come to the office and get the Swenson escrow started? They won't deal with me. I talked to the old man, and he said you were the only one he'd let handle the sale. Come on, Lela. Be reasonable."

"I was going to make tomato soup," Lillian said, "but the tomatoes at the market were hard. They were red, but not soft. They're taste-less when they're like that."

"They pick them green," Lela said.

"If they'd let them ripen on the vine, they'd taste like tomatoes. Oranges, bananas, the same thing. Nobody can wait for anything to ripen these days."

"Maybe you should give him a sandwich. He probably hasn't eaten since yesterday."

"There were some McDonald's bags and wrappers in the trash when I went to the market this morning."

The phone was ringing again. Lillian glanced over at it on the floor beside Lela's bed, waited for the answering machine to pick up the call. Deborah's voice came on after the message, nasal sounding, as though she had been crying.

"Lela, please pick up the phone. Aren't you ever going to speak to me again?"

"I should get one of those machines where you don't hear your message over and over and you can turn down the volume so you don't hear who's calling," Lela said to Lillian. "It's state of the art now to have those features, but when I bought the machine four years ago, this was the best they had."

"Say 'I love you, Auntie Lela.'" Lela could hear Jason's voice in the background. "Come on, Jason, Auntie Lela's waiting."

"I could turn it off, if you tell me what buttons to push," Lillian said.

"Wait," Lela said.

"Love, love, Mom," Jason said.

"Isn't he adorable?" Lela said.

"You could just pick up the phone and talk to him if you like," Lillian said.

"Deborah will get on if I do."

Deborah was back on the phone. "He called you Mom, Lela, and it didn't even bother me. I think it's cute. See, I can be generous, too. I can share. Please pick up the phone."

Brad looked as though he needed a shave. Looked as though he were really and truly sorry. Why did people always do that? Commit a crime and then say they're sorry, as if just those few words would cure everything.

"We didn't mean any harm, Lela," Deborah said. Her voice, magnified on the answering machine's speaker, filled the bedroom. Breathing sounds. Deborah's or Jason's breaths, Lela couldn't tell which. Loud whispery rushes of breath that someone with a cold or asthma would make.

"Jason is always sick," Lela said to Lillian. "Always sneezing, blowing, coughing. Allergies run in the Bingham family. Deborah was always sneezing when she was little. And getting rashes. She'd eat something and it wouldn't be two minutes later she'd turn red and start itching."

"My husband had allergies," Lillian said. It was the first time Lillian had ever mentioned a husband.

"We just couldn't sit by and see you taken advantage of," Deborah said. "You don't know this man or his child. They tell you a sad story and you just jump in with both feet. You have a family already. You have us."

There were banging sounds, as if the phone had dropped out of Deborah's hand and hit the cupboard or the floor. Jason was screaming now. Loud, short shrieks. "Well, see if I care," Deborah said. "See if Jason or Tony or Joey cares. We don't need you. Do you hear me, Lela? We don't need you."

"Is there some way to shut the machine off?" Lillian said.

"Pull the whole thing out of the wall," Lela replied.

It was dark now, and Brad was gone.

"He left a little pile of cigarette butts by the French doors and another pile on the right side of the lounge chair," Lillian said.

"I gave him a gift certificate for the smoke clinic for his birthday, but he wouldn't go," Lela said.

"They were cold when I swept them up."

"I spent five hundred dollars for the smoke clinic and he wouldn't even go to one session. Did you know he has a degree from Cal Tech in chemical engineering?"

"I didn't know."

"He's really not as dumb as he acts."

Lillian had turned the lights off after dinner and now sat at the foot of Lela's bed. The room was sunk in darkness, soft shadows of eucalyptus trees still clinging to the window.

"Are you going to stay in bed forever?" Lillian asked.

"I don't know. It's an idea."

"Did I ever tell you about my husband?"

"No."

"We were dancers. Not professionals. We just danced for fun. Max was a cattle rancher in New Mexico when I met him. I was working at Santa Fe Charity then—1943. Then I got an offer to come to Cedars for surgical nursing training, and Max went into the army. He was in the Battle of the Bulge. Parachuted right into the middle of the German army and lived to come home. My father was alive then, and when Max's train came into Union Station and Max came running toward us with all those medals on his chest, my father said to him in Yiddish, 'Out of all that fire, my child, you returned whole.' "

It was quiet in the house. Just the sound of Lillian's voice, high pitched, with a slight loss of breath weaving in and out of her sentences.

"Max got a job at the L.A. Department of Water and Power, and we were married in 1945. I was pregnant once when I was twenty-six, but the child died in the womb and I nearly bled to death. Max and I planned to dance all over the world when he retired and I put down my nurse's cap. We were going to start in New Zealand. Max had a cousin who settled there in 1938. A refugee from Germany, a sheep farmer who wrote us letters about the beauty of the countryside. He sent us pictures of his stone house high on a green hill in Auckland. His farm was on the side of an extinct volcano, rich with ash. He said the grass was as green as emeralds."

Lela kept glancing at the window as Lillian talked, as though she expected Brad to be there again, expected him to break the glass with his fists, jump inside, and demand that she forgive him.

"We were close friends with our neighbors in those days. One couple in particular lived in the same apartment building we did, 414 North Curson in West L.A. Jack and Sarah. Jack worked at the Pan Pacific Auditorium as an events man, did the ad campaigns for the ice shows and the circus. A redhead. Shocking red hair. And a mustache. Sarah was a housewife. A pretty little thing. Jack and Jill, Max called them."

The idea of staying in bed forever was appealing. She'd get up for meals and go right back to bed. She'd have her groceries delivered and let the rest of the world take care of itself.

"Things began to go wrong in about 1970. Max started staying away from home some nights. And he would argue over nothing. He accused me of things. Of throwing away his clothes, of hiding his mail. He said I wrote letters to Jack, love letters. I said, Why would I do that? And why would I need to write letters when he lives right down the hall? I tried reasoning with him, but it was like parts of his brain were missing. I'd say one thing, he'd say another. There was never any connection between what I said and what he said. He just wasn't the same man I had married. He wasn't the Max I knew from before, the one I loved and trusted. Some nights he just sat at the dinner table and stared at the food. 'You're trying to poison me,' he'd say. 'You want me dead.'"

"He wanted you dead?" Lela said.

She hadn't been listening very closely, hadn't really heard much of what Lillian said until that moment.

"Sarah said, 'Come over anytime, don't hesitate. If you need help, we're here for you.' Jack said some men went through a stage like Max was going through, when they think they haven't lived the life they wanted, when they realize their dreams are never going to come true. 'It'll pass,' he told me. 'You'll see.' I said I thought he was having a breakdown of some sort. Why else would he say such things to me?"

Lillian's voice was quavering.

"My father, the man who thought Max could walk through fire, said, 'Leave him. Come live with your mother and me.' My parents had a grocery store in Boyle Heights. They lived in a cottage in the back of the store. A small store, with a few crates of fruit along one wall and a barrel of pickles near the front door. You didn't even have to walk into the store to smell the pickles. Just pass by the front door. My father was the best pickle maker. I can still feel how cold the brine was when you reached into the barrel, how the salt stung the scratches on your hands. The store didn't have refrigeration. My father kept meat on ice in a glass case and salted his fish and then layered it between waxed paper in a cardboard box."

There were sounds outside. Was it the shuffling of shoes across the

flagstone patio? Had Brad found a ladder and climbed onto the roof?
Could he fit through the attic window, through that small crawl space
the air-conditioning man said was causing hot air to come into the
house in the summer and heat the attic and radiate down, and there
was nothing wrong with the air conditioner, it was the best on the
market, and no amount of air-conditioning would help if that hot air
kept coming in from that attic window? Would he squeeze in through
there and cry and plead with her and make her feel worse than she
already did?

"I asked my doctor what I should do," Lillian said. "He said Max
was suffering from the beginnings of dementia. 'You should leave
before he harms you.'

" 'I can't leave,' I said. 'He's my husband. If he's sick, then he
needs me more than ever.'

"One night Max didn't come home. Nor the next night. Nor the
next. He hadn't been at work, his boss said when I called. And I
hadn't seen Jack or Sarah for several days. I thought Jack might have
heard from him, might know what had happened.

"Their door was open, just standing ajar, so I walked in. There was
a quiet in the apartment that wasn't normal. Their television was
always on. If it wasn't, then they were out. But the door was ajar. And
it was quiet inside."

It was tree limbs, that's all it was. Brushing against the eaves. In
the same spot they had brushed last year before they were trimmed.
And here they were back again, all branched out and sharp as bristles,
making that awful grating sound, wearing a groove in the wall of the
house, scraping the paint away.

"I walked toward the back of the apartment where the bedroom
was. Jack's body was in a chair and Sarah's was in her bed. Max was
in bed beside her, the covers up to his chin. I had never seen so much
blood, not even in an operating room. Max had been a rancher. I told
you that, and he knew how to slaughter cattle. He had slaughtered
Jack and Sarah. Gutted them. Like you gut a steer in a slaughter
house. Just gutted them."

Lillian had put a bowl beside the bed in case Lela vomited. She
had vomited once right after Lillian came over in her nightclothes.
She was vomiting again now. Into the bowl. Fiesta ware, the vomiter's
choice. Retching into its red depths, her lips close to its sleek rim, her
hands holding tight to its smooth sides.

Lillian brought a washcloth and wiped Lela's face. Then she took
the bowl away and brought a cup of tea and stood by the bed while
Lela drank it.

"I tried to stop Jolene from taking her," Lela said. "I had hold of her coat and was pulling and pulling. It's my fault, not Brad and Deborah's. My fault. I wasn't strong enough. I didn't pull hard enough. I let her go. I should have taken her somewhere, run away with her before Jolene could find us. It's no one's fault but mine."

"I used to say that about Max," Lillian said. "I should have insisted the doctor do something. I should have warned Sarah and Jack not to let him in their house, told them not to talk to him. I beat myself up for years thinking of what I should have done, of what I didn't do. I sat in my little house by myself, the way you're doing now. Oh, I didn't get in my bed and I didn't vomit. I just turned inward, studying all the ways I could have stopped him and didn't. I let twenty-three years of my life go by wishing things were different. Twenty-three years."

Lela leaned back against the pillows and closed her eyes. "Where is he now?"

"In Camarillo State Hospital. I visit him sometimes. On his birthday and our anniversary. He doesn't know me at all. I had no one I cared for until you and Sandy. I hope you don't intend to stay in bed forever."

23

"N o B I C Y L I N G O N the pier." The voice was on a loud-speaker. "No dogs on the pier. No skateboarding on the pier."

Lela parked her car in the lot across from the Huntington Beach pier and walked across Pacific Coast Highway to Main Street. She had lost Brad somewhere near Signal Hill when she took the right turn into the oil field, and he kept on going down Atlantic. "Give up," she had wanted to scream at him through her car window. "Leave me alone."

She looked over her shoulder now, expecting his car to pull into the lot. Checking for Brad's car had become a habit in the past few days since she had got out of bed. "I'm not coming back, I'm through," she told him when she went into the office to clean out her desk and sign the Swenson escrow papers. "I don't want to sell real estate any-more and I especially don't want to be in business with you."

That was when Brad started following her in his car. Following her to the market, to the cleaners, to the drugstore. Leaving notes in her car begging her to change her mind. "Think of Deborah. Think of Jason and the twins. We need you."

He followed her to the garden shop, turning up once in the flori-bunda roses and nearly scaring her to death.

"Do you know how selfish you are? Do you know how selfish?" he said.

She had started working in the garden again. Gardens, like life, needed maintaining if you didn't want good things to go to seed and bad things to sprout. Besides which, gardening and thinking went hand in hand.

"The gun shop's the only old building left in town," the man on the telephone told her when she had called. "You can't miss it. We're the dirty gray building halfway down the block on Main Street. Every-thing else is puking pink."

Lela and Deborah had summer beach parties in Huntington when they were in high school. Deborah liked surfers then, blond boys with boogie boards and callused knees. Lela's boyfriends were always older, the kind who would come to a beach party in slacks and sports jacket and not join in when it came time to throw the girls into the water.

The town was all beach then, except for the oil wells and the rusted remains of Henry Huntington's railroad tracks. In the twenties Huntington Beach had the makings of a seaside resort, with a small hotel on Main Street and a train running all the way to Los Angeles. The hotel and shops were dilapidated by the fifties and abandoned to bikers and surfers by the sixties. Hobo beach, people started calling it, because of the bums. Or tin can beach, for the garbage the bums left behind. Now there were pink condos, cineplexes, a Hilton Hotel, and new souvenir shops that had restaurants on their roofs and tourists sitting under the umbrellas, looking like they had come to Huntington Beach intentionally and not just because they couldn't find a room in Laguna.

A metal sign pounded into the door of the gun shop said "Please check in firearms with person at the door."

"Your purse, ma'am, if you don't mind," the person at the door said. He was wearing a thick leather belt with a turquoise buckle and had a pistol on each hip.

"Walk your skateboard off the pier." The voice was at Lela's back now, the breeze carrying the words over her shoulder into the open door of the gun shop. "No dogs allowed this side of Pacific Coast Highway. Walk your dog and your skateboard off the pier."

"You can go on in now," the man said, and handed Lela back her purse. The door closed behind her, and the loudspeaker voice and sea air and sunshine were cut off.

She took a number from the machine next to the bulletproof vests. All the clerks were wearing cowboy hats and, like the man at the door, at least one pistol apiece. There were no windows in the place, and it felt like night, with guns displayed like jewelry in glass cases that glowed in the light of overhead neons. There was no fancy decor. Black carpeting. Cardboard signs. The cement walls weren't even painted. Just plain gray cement. And the room was a perfect square, with a door to the front and a door into the stockroom and, Lela supposed, another one out into the alley. A square cement-walled room. Square, Lela imagined, so no one could hide in an alcove, load a gun, and start firing. Unpainted cement so that if someone did, the clerks could just hose the blood off the walls afterward.

Men, some of them in camouflage pants and flak jackets, were hunched over the glass gun cases. Two or three women were trying to squeeze in between all that macho burliness, trying to catch a glimpse of a few guns before the number on the little slip of paper they were holding was called. Youngish girls, in blue jeans, hair straight down their backs. The men didn't notice them. Guns were sexier. *Clack-choo.* A guy at the rear of the store was testing the breech on an AK-47, holding it straight up, sighting with his right eye and *clack-choo*ing at the ceiling.

"Twenty-one."

"That's me," Lela said.

"What can I do for you, little lady?" He was wearing a checked shirt and Levi's and had a red, white, and blue bandanna tied around his thick neck. A row of medals were pinned to his cowboy hat.

"I want to buy a gun."

"Ever owned one before?"

"Never." She felt embarrassed, as though she had stepped into the men's rest room by mistake. "Guns scare me, as a matter of fact."

He smiled at her. A friendly smile. "Okay," he said. "A forty-five is real cost effective, real accessible. A hog of a gun. Sound baffler's extra."

"Baffler?"

"Silencer."

"Oh."

"But it's a big piece for a woman to handle. A Ruger four and three-quarter and five and a half is good. Or the Bounty Hunter, it's a real Colt-looking son of a bitch. A German company. Real, real Coltish looking, better than the Army's San Marcos, all case-hardened frame —and if it's not, they're keeping it a secret. The price is there, and it looks like it's more machine than it really is. Reconditioned. You want it new, this gun loses three hundred bones when you put the first load in the barrel. A real buy. You can hang a pair of ivory grips on it and give it a custom look. Or how about this forty-five Smith and Wesson? Reconditioned, spiffy, hog of a machine, and it's got night sights. It's almost a Glock, without the price. Are you hooked on polymer?"

"What?"

"Does it have to be plastic?"

"I guess not."

"Then how about a Beretta? It's a little tricky. Nine millimeter. To utilize the double action, you have to find a way to lower the lever without firing the gun. Then again, the Glock 21 is a little slimmer, not as chunky as the other models. The Glock 21's $529.95 cash or five forty on a credit card. So do you want me to pack it for you, or do you want one right out of the box?"

"I just need a basic gun, one that's easy to use."

"Fair enough," he said, and took her over to another case and sold her a Lady Colt, a thirty-eight, small enough to fit in her purse, for $395. She paid with her credit card. Then he started filling out the papers. "Pick it up in twenty days."

"What?"

"State law."

"But I need it now."

"You got someone special you want to kill this afternoon?"

"No. It's not that."

"Because if you do, I can sell you a rifle and ammo right now, and you can walk out of here, all perfectly legal. Tell me your problem, honey."

She leaned forward over the counter, and he leaned down to meet her. Shoved the rim of his cowboy hat into her forehead.

"Someone's following me," she said.

"You mean like stalking you?"

"Yes. Everywhere I turn he shows up. Even at the garden shop. At the market. I thought about getting a restraining order, but there are all those stories in the newspapers about women being stalked and killed even with restraining orders."

"They're no good. No damn good at all."

"Then I thought self-protection. I'll get a gun for self-protection. Do you think I'm right to want a gun to protect myself from someone who's following me?"

"My wife sleeps with one under her pillow."

"I think he might even be out in the parking lot. I think he followed me here."

She could feel him believing her. It was in the way his shoulders relaxed when she was talking, the way he kept smiling at her.

"Well, you don't look like a criminal, I'll say that much."

"I'm not."

"Ever been in jail?"

"Never."

"Any history of mental illness?"

"None."

"Well," he said, and stared at her for another few moments. "Well," he said again, and then he looked over her head to the man who was helping the guy with the AK-47. Something passed between them.

"Come on out back," he said.

Lela followed him through the storeroom, past all the boxes of ammunition and guns.

"I could get in trouble," he said. They were at the back door near the toilet, and there was no air, and Lela felt sick, but she didn't faint and she didn't vomit when he handed her the gun.

"I appreciate it," she said.

Brad was in the parking lot when she came out of the gun shop.

"I just bought a gun," she said.

"You want to shoot me?" he asked, a horrified look on his face.

"Don't be silly," she said. "I'm going to use it to get Sandy back."

24

H E H A D B E E N in the sheriff's department, he told Lela. An unlikely-looking gun instructor, in tan slacks, his white dress shirt starched, neatly pressed, the sleeves rolled to the exact same spot on each forearm.

"Women are better shooters than men," he said. "I've had men bring their wives in and tell me in private how they had to drag her here, she was so afraid. And I got them both out on the range, and she whipped his ass with the accuracy of her shooting. Makes you think, you know."

She put on the ear protectors and went through the double doors into the anteroom and then through another set of doors into the shooting range.

"Keep your knees locked," he shouted to Lela. Everyone was separated by baffles, each person to his own target. She was doing what he had told her in the little room where the Coke machine and the T-shirts were. Face straight, feet shoulder-length apart, arms slightly bent to act as a shock absorber, both hands holding the gun, left thumb resting on right thumb, palms together. Sighting on the front sight of the gun, not the far sight of the target. Closing one eye. Aiming in.

"Hold your breath and squeeze. Squeeze the trigger. Slow, slow."

"I can't hold the gun still."

"It doesn't matter. Sooner or later it's going to shoot. Just keep your wobble area centered. Don't resist the recoil. Ninety-eight percent of misses are in anticipation of recoil. Remember what I said about Zen. Observe and go with it. That's it. Keep it coming. Keep it coming. Slow, slow."

Pops all around her. Was that hers?

"I didn't hit anything," she said. After each shot he said you check the target, then eyes back front for sight alignment.

"You will."

It was hers that time. That pop that sounded like a heavy chain whipping the lid off a metal garbage can. She had gotten an ear, nowhere near the upper chest that she was aiming for. The smell of gunpowder was stronger now that she was the one shooting.

It took twelve pounds of pressure by her finger to pull the trigger back, he said. It felt like fifty.

"Not bad. You're doing all right. Now get centered as you raise your hand again. Then follow through and leave everything unchanged. Consistency is the key. First stance, then consistency."

Suck air in while aiming, he had told her, then let out half a lung full when you shoot. She couldn't breathe at all.

"You did good," he said when they were through. "Two through the neck, one in the heart, four in the extremities."

He filled out a certificate of basic marksmanship for her, then walked her out to her car.

"Remember what I said. Visualize a six-inch spike sticking into the beast's stomach. Then fire."

It was afternoon, and the fog was starting to come across the highway from the ocean, and for the first time in a week she hadn't seen Brad's car.

"You'll do fine. Just remember, aim sure and true when you decide to shoot. You never want to hurt anyone you aim at. You want to blow him away."

"Thanks for everything," she said, and shook his hand.

He watched her unlock her trunk and put the gun case in there, watched her smooth the blanket around it, as though she were tucking a child into its crib.

"Won't do you any good in the trunk," he said. "Keep it in your purse. Assume the worst can happen."

"It's against the law, isn't it?"

"I'd rather twelve judge me than six carry me," he said.

———————————

Once she reached San Francisco, Lela drove up the coast, Highway 1, to Jenner. Below the highway, where the Russian River stalled on a fan-shaped beach at the mouth of the sea, sea lions, a cold gray in the late summer sun, lay sleeping on the rocks in the estuary. Lela resisted the temptation to pull off the road and go down to the beach, lie down with the sea lions, and not go any farther. What had seemed so reasonable when she began her journey in Los Angeles had started to make her feel demented by the time she reached San Francisco and absolutely insane by the time she crossed the Golden Gate Bridge.

Walter always used to talk about points of no return, about making sure, in case of trouble, he had enough gas in his plane to get back to where he started. There are no gas stations in midair, he would always say. The Golden Gate Bridge had been Lela's point of no return. The baywater was running swift and cold below the bridge, and the Windsurfers were out, full sails angling toward the sun. She had felt a charge of exhilaration watching them skim the water. She could have gone back then. Easily. Told Brad she accepted his apology, checked the listings that had come in over the weekend, and taken Deborah and the kids to Chuck E. Cheese for pizza. It was a fleeting thought, a possibility, and she drew strength from it and kept driving.

It was still daylight when she turned onto Fort Ross Road. The ocean and seals were behind her, and the road, wide at first, with rolling hills painted bright yellow by drifts of wild mustard, narrowed after the last sliver of sea disappeared. She rolled down her car windows and let in the cool air. She had eaten a fried-clam sandwich at a roadside stand in Bodega Bay, but it wouldn't digest, just sat, a leaden lump, on her stomach.

She was driving through redwoods and Douglas firs now, small shafts of sunlight breaking through the giant arms of the trees. There were bushes with clusters of bright red flowers at the sides of the road. What were grevillea doing this far north? She thought they needed a warmer climate, couldn't withstand a prolonged freeze or even an early frost on tender shoots, thought they'd turn black, wither up. Fragile plants, beautiful to look at, with firlike needles sharp enough to cut your hands.

There was an occasional horse ranch, but otherwise the landscape was dense with forest, the road empty and unobstructed. She hadn't seen a town or another car for half an hour, and the thought that she was on the wrong road began to nag at her. She was about to turn back when a sign popped up at the side of the road, "This Is a Nuclear-Free Zone." Then a shack with a brick chimney. A split-wood cabin perched on stilts. An old green bus with curtains in the windows. A clearing filled with abandoned cars. A man sawing firewood. A fruit stand selling seedless grapes and cantaloupes. No master builder here. No plan. Just people setting themselves down randomly, sprouting like wild mustard at the feet of the redwoods. Sharing space.

The town itself appeared almost as an afterthought, and Lela nearly missed it. There was a general store, a church, a lumber yard, a garage, and a post office. A building with no name had pickups, bikes, and cars scattered around its wide-mouthed open door. Inside, two ponytailed mechanics sat on a redwood log, as though posing for a picture, eyes dreamy as they sipped their coffee and stared at the wrecks in the yard.

Lela parked the car beneath the trees, not far from the general store, and walked up its wooden steps onto the porch. Cards and notices and ads were pinned on the log wall beside the front door. "Visit the Eternity Store on King Ridge Road, tarot cards, drums and rainsticks, astrology and channels." "Organic alfalfa and wheatgrass and sunflower our specialty." "Wood stoves repaired." "Used bicycles." "Woodworking." "Russian lessons." "Healing arts festival, healers and psychics." "Rooster to good home, preferably vegetarian."

Inside, it was warm and dark and smelled of raisins and nutmeg. A heavyset young woman wearing a man's golf sweater over her cotton dress was at the cash register. The only other people in the store were two women in matching Pendleton jackets who were looking over the titles on the video rental shelves.

"I'm looking for Austin Creek," Lela told the woman at the cash register.

"Lower or upper."

Lela handed the woman the card Ross had given her before he'd left.

"Oh, Ross McGowan," the woman said. She handed the card back to Lela. "Why do you want him?"

"I'm a friend."

The woman seemed hesitant.

"He gave me the card," Lela said. "This is his handwriting. This is his address. Austin Creek, Cazadero."

"Anyone could have written that."

"Anyone didn't. He did."

"How do you know him?"

"I'm his daughter's aunt," Lela said.

"Well. So." The woman looked at one of the women at the video rental shelves and said, "This lady wants the McGowan place. Did he get back from Santa Rosa yet?"

"He's really tall," Lela said when the women didn't answer. "He was wounded in Vietnam, has a metal plate in his head."

"Oh, they know him," the woman at the cash register said. "Everyone knows him. They're just shy of strangers. He pulled an abscessed tooth for Rebecca. Didn't he, Rebecca? Didn't Ross pull one of your teeth?"

"It's all right if he didn't," Lela said.

"You caught them at a bad time. They've seen all the videos at least twice. People get depressed around here just before we get the new videos in."

The woman took Lela out onto the porch.

"I'm sorry I wasn't too friendly. I thought maybe you was from the health people over in Guerneville. They come here once in a while and ask if Doc McGowan's still practicing medicine without a license. He usually sends people over to Monte Rio to the doctor if they need a hospital. That is, if there's time. If there isn't, he takes them over to the hospital in Santa Rosa, on account of they're not so particular as the hospital in Guerneville is about checking to see if the doctor sending them's got a license or not. Once in a while he's got an emergency case—usually one of the loggers takes off a finger with his misery whip or lops off a toe with his ax, and then there's no choice but for Doc McGowan to sew them up the best he can and send them to Guerneville because it's closer than hauling a body all the way to Santa Rosa. I don't know why they pick on him. He's the best we've got." She pointed up the road.

"Keep going to Austin Creek Road about four and a half miles till you come to the Boy Scout camp. Take the bridge over the creek. Ross usually goes to see his patients in the hospital in Santa Rosa on Monday and comes back on Tuesday. He should be home. You better get going before it gets dark."

You don't know what dark is till you've driven through the redwood groves after dark, Ross had told her. Only moonlight and the light from a half-hidden structure kept Lela from driving into the creek. Her front wheels were nearly over the embankment when her headlights caught the moon's reflection in the uneven surface of the creek. The water was lapping at her tires, and the stars were bright in the sky, as bright as stars can be when there is no other light, when it is truly dark. She sat behind the wheel, wondering where she had lost the bridge, thinking she would just stay where she was until daylight. Not even get out of the car.

Then the door opened on the other side, and Ross was leaning toward her.

"I've been wondering when you'd come," he said. "I heard that Jolene's got Sandy."

It was a split-log house, with a porch that held a few pieces of weathered redwood furniture. There was a couch and a bed in the main room and a blackened stone fireplace.

"I wanted to telephone you, but you didn't leave a number," she said.

"When people want me, they know where I am, they just drive over the bridge."

He brought her into the kitchen and heated a can of soup and toasted two slices of bread in the broiler of his two-burner stove. The kitchen looked like a small hospital laboratory, with Bunsen burners and glass-fronted cabinets filled with medicines.

"I'm so glad to see you," she said, and started to cry.

He put a box of Ritz crackers on the table. "It's not your fault."

"I'm a doctor, but not according to state law. In my salad days as a druggie I'd dispense drugs to whoever wanted them. That's how I lost my license."

He was very neat. Logs piled at the side of the fireplace. His clothes hung on a wooden rack. Medical journals stacked against the wall in tidy three-feet bundles.

"Didn't stop people from wanting me to take care of them. They think I'm eccentric, some brilliant guy from San Francisco driven crazy by the Vietnam War. They're not too far wrong. I don't have a fee schedule, don't even discuss money. They just leave something in the jar by the door. Whatever they want. Five, ten dollars. I never check to see who leaves what."

She reached for his hand. It was warm, and his fingers were blunt at their tips, the nails short and smooth.

"There used to be more logging in the old days, more injuries, but I wasn't here then. They'd take their injuries over to the doctor in Guerneville. Now they come here. They know about my drug problems. Most everyone here has had problems with drugs. I warn them maybe all those drugs I took have fried my brains. They just laugh. People don't listen. They'll make their mind up about something or someone and stick to it, no matter what. They're just lucky my brains didn't get fried. I'm still a pretty good doctor. I used to do a lot of reading when I first got sober. There weren't too many patients then. I don't have time to read much anymore."

He lit a fire, and they sat on the couch in the dark.

"I still have the cord of wood you bought," she said. "It hasn't been cold enough to light it."

"It's all right if you only came because of Sandy."

"Deborah bought a fireplace video that she puts on when company comes. Real fires are dangerous, she says, especially around children. And you have to buy wood and have the chimney cleaned every once in a while, whereas a video is a onetime investment, no upkeep, no mess. She has a video fish tank, too. Very soothing, just watching the fish swim around, if you don't mind that they do the same thing over and over. You don't have to feed them or clean the tank. And the cat can't get at them. The water won't spill. She has an ocean video, too. Crashing waves. Some people like the sound of the ocean. They say it's better than sleeping pills, just put on the ocean video and in minutes you're asleep."

He was on his knees, bare body lit by firelight, smoothing the skin of her stomach, unknotting the tightness there with his fingers. Then her waist, gently, gently beneath her ribs. Now his tongue warm against her nipple, the tug, very soft, almost imperceptible, of his mouth closing around her breast. She felt an unfamiliar warmth between her legs even before he touched her there. He stayed inside her a long time, and she stroked his back and kissed the metal plate until it was as warm as her lips.

"I'd never hurt you," he said.

25

THEY STARTED THE morning by arguing. Lela said she was going to go look for Sandy, and Ross said it was too dangerous, and she told him she didn't care, and he told her she was just trying to be a daredevil, to prove she wasn't afraid, to prove she wouldn't vomit or faint the minute something scary happened. And she told him just because you fucked me doesn't mean you know all about me, even though she knew he did, and he said, Oh boy, the spunk is streaming out of you now, but you just don't know what you're in for, and then they drank their coffee and ate some dry toast and made love again, and Ross told her she was the best lover he'd ever had, and she said she had never been good before, that it was because she loved him, and then she was sorry she said it, and they got up and got dressed and the patients started coming in.

"Hold still now," Ross said. "It'll be over in a minute."

"He doesn't know what minutes are," the mother said. She was holding the sobbing child on her lap while Ross sewed the hole the dog had chewed in his wrist.

"See that clock up on the wall," Ross said. "Watch that big hand move, and you tell me when it goes to the next mark. When it gets to the next mark, I'll be through."

Lela stood out of the way, near the white cabinets, and watched. Ross acted as if he had all the time in the world, as if there weren't three patients already waiting on the couch in the main room of the cabin. He didn't seem to mind that no one had an appointment, that they just showed up. He didn't get rattled when he had to stop what he was doing every few minutes to answer the phone or give advice or measure out pills or liquids into bottles for someone to take back to town. He didn't look as if he had noticed it was raining outside, didn't even blink when the lights in the kitchen flickered at each clap of thunder.

"How's Howard's gout, any better?" he asked the little boy's mother.

"He says the blankets hurt his toe in bed," she replied, and Ross took a bottle of pills out of one of the white cabinets for her to take home to her husband, then gave the little boy a sucker from the metal pail next to the cotton swabs, patted the mother on the back, and said, Say hi to Gordon for me, and when the mother and little boy were gone went and washed up at the kitchen sink.

The Russian River rolled right past the door of the restaurant, and the cook, a fat woman in a big white chef's hat, looked out from behind the kitchen partition and said Vickie was due in at any minute; her shift started at eleven. She came out from behind the tall oak serving counter and without even asking Lela if she wanted some poured her a cup of coffee and then went back to the kitchen.

A row of ripped Leatherette booths lined one wall of the restaurant, and there was a candy counter with a few bars of chocolate in it next to the cash register. An old Coke sign that looked like the one Lela had seen go at Butterfield's in Los Angeles for fifteen thousand dollars was hanging next to a piece of cardboard that announced in handwritten letters "Open 8 to 8, When We Feel Like It."

"You're lucky we're open," the chef said. She was eating French fries from a plate on the oak partition and cooking something below it that Lela couldn't see but that was steaming up the place and making a sizzling noise.

"You talking to me?" Lela asked.

"No one here but you, honey. We usually take off in the winter and don't open till June or July. That's when the queers come up from San Francisco, in June, when the weather starts to warm up. They love it when it's warm. Got a bar up the street called the Cattleman. Folks call it the queer steer. Winter's dead around here."

Vickie showed up a few minutes early. Lela recognized her bad complexion and the peculiar way she walked, picking up her feet with a little sticking motion, as if she had stepped in some chewing gum. She wore a sweater over her brown uniform, and she went back to the kitchen, where Lela could see her put the sweater on a hook, and then the chef, who had turned her back to Lela, started saying something to Vickie. Lela was sure it was about her, because Vickie kept looking over at Lela, then back to the chef, and then looking at Lela again, and then finally she came back out with a cup of coffee and a lit cigarette and sat down.

"I remember you," Vickie said.

"I remember you, too," Lela said.

"So how's the kid?"

She really didn't know. Lela was looking her right in the eye, and there wasn't a sign that she knew. And when Lela told her, she stubbed out her cigarette with her foot, the way you'd squash a bug that had just bitten you. The chef yelled out from the kitchen to watch the goddamned floor, vinyl doesn't grow on trees, and Vickie just shook her head, kept saying damn, damn, and shaking her head.

"Was she alone?" Vickie finally asked.

"She was with a man."

"Ugly-looking guy?"

"He needed a shave. He looked dirty."

"That would be Chick. He's a cooker. The two of them are pretty tight, seeing as he's the one supplies her with speed in exchange for a place to cook it."

"You'll have to speak English."

Vickie pulled another cigarette from a pack in her uniform pocket and lit it.

"I met Jolene in 1978. She was living on a war widow's pension in one of those canyons in Cazadero. There used to be a commune there, some professors from Berkeley bought up a cattle ranch and divided it up amongst themselves and their friends, forty acres apiece. My dad was building sewers in through there for the ranchers, and he used to come and tell us about those Berkeley guys moving down here and bringing all those books with them on how to raise rabbits and chickens. They had themselves a school for their kids, and there was a big lice problem when they'd come to town. All you had to do was brush up against one of them and you'd catch the buggers yourself.

"My dad was in the CHP in those days, the California Hippie Patrol, and they'd catch those professors and cut off their long hair, and Daddy'd come home as happy as if he'd scalped an Indian. Then after a while the hippies just wanted to reach into a refrigerator and eat a piece of chicken without having to feed it first, and so they took off and went back to where they came from. The county hired Daddy to check out all those wells they dug and close up their cesspools and what-all, and I used to go along with him on the truck, give him a hand with the digging, and that's how I met Jolene. She was living in one of the shacks the hippies left behind.

"Daddy said stay away from her, she's no good. You don't have to look twice to know that, he told me. She was kind of young to be a widow, just about thirty, I'd say, the same as me, and there was a bar in Monte Rio where we'd hang out. I liked her right away. Real wild. Could think up the craziest things to do. Of course, I don't remember too much of what it was we did do, since we were high most of the time on meth when we did it."

"Meth?"

"Methamphetamine. Speed. Brain drain, I call it. About that time Ross came to Cazadero, and the three of us would go tootling around through the canyon floor in his Jeep. He had a red Jeep then, I remember, and he could do drugs as good as anyone I ever knew. He used to like to mix his. Some heroin, some speed, some LSD. He could take a witch's brew that'd launch a spaceship. Him and Jolene both.

"I got married in between, had a kid, a boy—Lennie, I named him —got divorced and lost Lennie to my ex-in-laws. That's when I went home to Daddy, and that's when I stopped doing drugs. Jolene didn't, though. She was doing them right up until the second she had Sandy. She was such a speed freak, I thought the kid would come out with a buzz on. But she didn't. She was fine. Cute kid. She's cute, isn't she?"

"She's very cute."

"Ross got clean about that time, and Chick moved into Jolene's place with her and Sandy and started cooking speed for sale. Built a little laboratory there and pretty soon was selling his own brand of shit. Chick's recipe, he calls it. Cold medicine and swimming pool acid. He cooks it up into pure crystal powder in a bug spray tank.

"I kept telling Jolene what she was doing to Sandy was a crime. Half the time she was freaked, thinking she was Wonder Woman, not sleeping, all excited and hyper. The other half she spent sleeping it off. For days she'd sleep. That's the way you get, and when you wake up you're so depressed you can't stand it. The stuff stays in your body, though, and you think maybe you can lick it, stay away from taking any more ever again, and then your body tricks you, gets clean, and you really need it then just to stay sane.

"She looked real bad last year about Easter time. I saw her in the general store in Cazadero, and I hardly recognized her. She was so thin and had all these sores on her face—sketching, they call it, when a speed freak starts freaking out thinking he's got bugs under his skin and he tries to dig them out with his fingernails. She dug so hard she had scabs. I told her, I said, Jolene, let me help you. Come on and stay with me. She was rock bottom then and she said she'd do it, she wanted to go over to Jenner to that rehab place. I made an appointment and went over to get her at her place, but Chick wouldn't let me in, and Jolene came out on the porch and said she'd blast me with a shotgun if I came any closer. Speed makes you paranoid, makes you crazy. That's when I gave up on trying to help her. I just kind of stayed where if she needed me for Sandy, I'd be there. But it killed me how that kid was living in that hellhole of a place. I kept telling Ross what was happening with the kid, and then he said he was going to take her to you, that Jolene had a sister. I said I'd do whatever he wanted to get her out of there."

"I need to find her. Can you help me find her?"

"They moved out of the place they were at. Jolene passes stolen credit cards for food for the kid. Chick doesn't give her much, figures he'll keep her close that way. The last I heard he had moved them all up to Red Oat Mountain. There's nothing there now but an old shack where the old fire lookout used to be. I gave up on Jolene a long time ago."

26

I T W A S S U N D A Y , an overcast day with dark gray clouds moving fast over the tops of the redwoods.

"People don't get sick on Sundays around here," Ross said. "And if they do, they've got the good sense to leave me alone till Monday. Unless they're dying. Then all bets are off."

Lela packed a basket with sandwiches and they drove out along Austin Creek, then took a side road up out of the canyon. When they passed the treeline, the road suddenly shrank to one lane with sheer drops on either side. Ross drove his battered car over it nearly as fast as the engine would go, looking neither to the right nor left, but, it seemed to Lela, at the sky, as though the rain clouds were guiding him.

"In the twenties you could drive an automobile up this highway from San Francisco," he said. "Most people never made it, though. They'd get halfway, look over the side into the canyon, scare themselves to death, and walk the rest of the way down."

They ate their sandwiches in a grove of Douglas fir, then lay down on a bed of fallen needles and made love. He was patient with her, staying inside her but holding off, kissing her breasts and telling her he loved her, and she telling him back, and neither of them looking into each other's eyes when they said it. She climaxed with just a touch of his fingers, and they lay down together afterward and let the rain pelt them until they were soaked and then made love again. Then they went back and sat in the car, and Ross wrapped an old blanket around them.

"I went over to Guerneville and talked to Vickie," she said. He moved away from her. Imperceptibly, but definitely moved away, pulling the blanket from his shoulders, smoothing his wet hair with his hands, looking out the window.

"She told me where Jolene's living now, told me how Jolene gets, how bad it is."

1 9 5

"I told you, I don't have custody. Jolene does."

"You could get custody."

"Fat chance."

"You could at least try."

"Okay. So I go in and tell the judge Jolene's an unfit mother. I've got witnesses, I'll tell him. I can prove it, I'll say. Then he'll ask me what I do for a living. Then what? You think any judge in his right mind would take the kid away from Jolene and give her to me, a beat-up Vietnam vet practicing medicine without a license? And where were you when the child was born? he'll ask me. Oh, you were zonked out of your mind on drugs, you say? Sounds like a perfect place for the little girl to me."

"I've decided to go up there and get her myself."

"I can't stop you," was all he said.

The air at the top of Big Oat Mountain was remarkably clear, no wind blowing. The ocean was out there at the foot of the redwoods, out past the logging roads and the patches of clear-cut land, past old logging ponds, now silty green with decayed wood. The ocean looked different from up here, a dark blue sheet that seemed to mirror the sky, with only a slim yellow line of sun on the horizon separating the two.

She parked her car at the top of the grade and started up the dirt road. It might only have been a fire break snaking through the trees, or the tamped-down aisle of gravel and dirt from the runoff of a mountain stream, and not a road at all. She could feel the chill of the elevation through her pullover sweater now, and it was raining again, a shower of icy drops that made a tinkly sound in the branches of the trees and turned the dirt beneath her feet slightly spongy. It was a road. She could see that now. There were car tracks in it and the footprints of someone who had walked up it after the last rain.

It wasn't hard to spot the cabin. First she saw Jolene's car, its white paint like a beacon at the top of the rise, and then the cabin, a meager log structure with a tilting porch and a stack of firewood that reached nearly to the tin roof. A shack in back of the cabin had a sign hammered into the ground in front of it. "Keep Out," it said. "Mad Dog on Premises."

The door to the shack was unlocked, and she gave the metal handle a twist and walked inside. The first thing that hit her were the fumes, acrid and sickeningly sweet.

There was no one inside. Just a mess of plastic bags filled with white powder, an old iron bathtub rigged with a network of stained plastic tubing that trailed, like pieces of an old string mop, into an assortment of containers on the dirt floor. A Bunsen burner was cooking up a gooey brown mass, and Lela supposed that the fumes were coming from that. Plastic containers littered the floor, some of them empty, some filled with an oily red liquid. Two shotguns stood against the wall.

It must have been Chick who came up behind her and said, "Who the hell are you?"

"We could kill her and bury her back of the shed," Chick said. The cabin was just one room with mattresses on the floor and an old wood stove.

Jolene and Chick both looked crazed. Jolene's eyes jittered and danced, and she kept jerking her head to the left and scratching at her arms, every once in a while looking down at the gouged skin and examining it before she gave a little shudder. Chick was kind of dancing in place, shifting his weight from one foot to the other as if the soles of his feet hurt.

"Did you bring me something to eat?" Sandy asked. She was wearing a tattered sundress, even though it was a cold day and there was no heat in the cabin. And she had a dirty white cat in her arms that looked as undernourished as she did. Lela didn't see any signs of food anywhere, not on the oilcloth-covered table or on the wood stove. There were open shelves with a few dishes on them, but no food. The refrigerator was the motor-on-top kind and had no front door. It had no food in it, either, just bags of powder and jugs of oily red liquid.

"I think she's from the CIA," Chick said.

"I've just come to get Sandy and take her back home with me," Lela said. She couldn't keep her voice from going up and down and all over the place.

"I asked Mama to take me to Vickie's to get a doughnut," Sandy whispered. She and the cat smelled bad. The whole cabin smelled bad. Jolene looked dirty, from her bare feet to the greasy hair that had fallen out of its rubber band and was hanging in her face. Chick was wearing stained jeans and no shirt.

"Did the police send you?" Jolene asked, and Chick went to the front door and looked out.

"I hear helicopters," he said. "I bet she brought the police in those damn helicopters. Maybe they followed her up here. You know how they do that, get the dogs on your trail, pick up your scent from your clothes, your shoes, track you up a tree if they can't find you in a car or on the road walking."

"I'm really hungry," Sandy said.

"Oh, sweetie," Lela said, and made a move toward the child, held out her arms.

"You leave her alone, leave her alone," Jolene said. Lela stopped moving and let her arms drop to her sides.

"I could blow you away right now," Chick said. He put a finger up in the air. "*Kerchoo*, you're dead."

"Oh, you don't want to do that, Chick," Jolene said. "She'll be good, won't you, Lela?"

"I'll try."

"You should have seen her when she was little. Really cute, Chick. A really cute little kid, like Sandy almost. Oh, she was so cute, cute, cute, she could talk, talk, oh, she was something else. I just loved listening to her talk and tell stories and jokes. Talk, talk, it never stopped, and I was always sitting and listening and doing nothing, nothing. She was something, Chick. You should have seen her then."

"Well, she's boring now," Chick said.

Jolene came over to Lela, so close Lela could feel the heat from her body. "You can't steal people's babies, Lela. Didn't anyone ever tell you you couldn't do that?" She was having trouble keeping her head still. "See, I can take care of my own kid. If I want, I can go over to Shop Rite in Santa Rosa and cashier. They're always looking for people as smart as me. I can add and multiply. I don't even need a machine. Every teacher I ever had said, Such a smart, smart girl, and I could pick out clothes for people, and I even could cook, if they asked me to, you haven't tasted food till you taste mine, because if I'm not hungry, I don't cook, because what the fuck's the use of cooking when you're not hungry, you don't do it right, don't think of the seasoning or salt or pepper or sugar, you know, spices, they came from the West Indies, and I think Columbus should have stayed where he was, don't you, Chick? I mean, we'd all be better off, since Indians are smarter anyhow, and who wants to learn Spanish when all I know how to speak is English. Do you want some speed, Lela?"

"No, thank you," Lela said.

"Chick mixed a fresh batch. Good stuff. Isn't it, Chick? Isn't it the best stuff you ever made?"

"Those damn helicopters come one inch closer, boom, I'll go get my shotguns and blow them away," Chick said.

"I'll go climb on the roof and see what they want," Jolene said.

"Maybe I'll just move the business over to Sebastopol," Chick said. "There's a guy owes me money in Sebastopol."

"I could walk ten miles, I feel so good," Jolene said.

"We can go by there, give him a chance to pay me back," Chick said, "or let him know what I think of deadbeats."

Jolene was dancing now, trying to get up on her bare toes, her thin, scabby arms up and twirling over her head. "Did you bring the CIA and a bunch of helicopters with you, Lela? Did you go and do that?"

"I don't think there are any helicopters out there," Lela said. "And I don't think the CIA even knows I'm here."

"I'd give her some speed," Chick said, "but she's so bor-r-r-rring. She's the most boringest person in the world, could bore right into you, she's so boring. I don't think speed would even do her any good."

"You ever been high, Lela?" Jolene asked. She stopped dancing and came over to Lela, looked in her eyes. Jolene's eyes were skittering from side to side in their sockets. "I mean really gut-busting high, so you don't know your insides from your outs, your nose from your foot, your toes from your ears, your ass from your tits?"

"I've never been high, Jolene," Lela said.

"God, I feel good." Jolene danced away again. "Don't you feel good, Chick? How about a little wrestle?" She gave Chick a punch on the side of his arm, then danced around him, scratching and sniffing and jabbing at the air.

"What the hell are you doing?" he asked.

"Come on, put up your dukes."

Lela had Sandy by the hand and was leading her to the door, when Jolene turned and shrieked, "Hey, what the fuck do you think you're doing?"

"Go on down to my car," Lela said to Sandy, and gave her a little shove with the palm of her hand. "The door's open. Just get in and wait for me."

Then she took the little Lady Colt out of her handbag. She felt silly doing it, kept thinking of all the movies she had ever seen where the heroine or the hero or the villain whipped out a gun and said stick 'em up.

"What's that?" Jolene asked.

"It's a gun, stupe," Chick said. "She's got a gun."

"You're crazy," Jolene said. "Looks like a pencil sharpener to me."

"It's a gun," Chick said.

"It's a gun," Lela said.

"You gonna let her do this?" Jolene said. She was getting agitated, scratching at her arms with both hands. "First she brings the CIA in and the helicopters, now she has a gun?"

"I'll go get mine," Chick said.

"Stay where you are," Lela said. "Don't move."

Chick was running around looking for his shotguns, and Jolene kept screaming at him that they were in the refrigerator, and he kept saying you stupid bitch, what are they doing in the refrigerator? They got to arguing so much that they didn't pay any attention to Lela at all, so she just walked out the front door and out to the shack. She opened the door again and the fumes hit her. It wasn't really thought out what she did next, but the minute she did it she knew it was the thing, along with coming up here to get Sandy, that she had intended doing all along. She aimed the little Lady Colt at one of the bottles of red liquid and fired. The explosion knocked her nearly ten feet back, and she barely had time to run before the whole shack was burning as nicely as any bonfire she had ever seen.

27

"RIGHT OFF AND before we start these proceedings, I have something to disclose." The judge, a round-faced Hispanic woman, had come into the courtroom late, holding up her robes so that she didn't trip on them in her high heels. She looked out of breath, tired before the morning even began.

"And at the outset, before I make my statement, I say to both Counsel that I will recuse myself if there is any objection."

A policeman had brought Jolene from jail to the Santa Rosa Superior Court for the custody hearing, to a courtroom with corkboard walls and a dingy gray rug. Jolene, wearing clean sweat pants and a Sonoma County Jail T-shirt, her face scrubbed and her hair shiny clean, had wobbled a few times on the way to her seat. The policeman grabbed at her arm to steady her, then sat her down in the first row and bent over her, seemed to be giving her instructions about something, lifting her chin up with his index finger to make sure she was listening. He was now in the back of the room, sipping coffee and looking bored.

Most of the seats in the courtroom were empty. Ross and his attorney and Lela were in the third row. Sandy and her court-appointed attorney were at the counsel table. Someone in a fire chief's uniform was sitting in the last seat to the right in the fourth row, a briefcase on his lap. A matronly woman, a cardboard box full of files at her feet, was reading a document, every once in a while looking up, listening. Jolene was sitting by herself in the first row, and the only part of her that Lela could see was her head, which was nodding up and down as though she were fighting sleep.

"I represented Ross McGowan on a misdemeanor charge in 1985 when I was practicing law in Guerneville," the judge said. "I've had no contact with him since then, and the matter was plea-bargained, no time served. Since he's brought the action for custody, I will recuse myself if either Counsel objects to my hearing the case."

"What do you say, Ross?" Ross's attorney, Barry Spiller, had come up from San Francisco the day after the fire and looked out of place in his pin-striped suit. Sandy's attorney, Jane Gibbons, hair loose and straight to her waist, was wearing a two-piece squaw dress with Indian jewelry on her neck and wrists.

"I just want the kid, that's all," Ross said. "I'll do whatever you think."

"Do you question my ability to be fair to you, Mr. McGowan?" the judge asked.

"I don't question your ability at all," Ross replied.

"It's fine with my client, Your Honor," Spiller said.

"We have no objection, Your Honor," Jane Gibbons said.

"Can I go down and sit with Sandy?" Lela whispered to Spiller.

"I don't think it's such a good idea."

The judge was handing a sheaf of documents to the clerk, a stocky man in a golf sweater and hiking boots, when Jolene slipped out of her seat onto the floor.

"Will the police escort please straighten the respondent in her chair," the judge said.

Miss Gibbons, who was closest, struggled a few minutes, trying to get Jolene up off the floor, and then the policeman put down his coffee and came over and lifted her up with one arm and kind of slapped her shoulders a few times as though trying to stick them to the back of the seat.

"I don't think Jolene should have to hear this," Lela said.

"She's a party to the action," Spiller said.

"I think it's cruel."

"She doesn't know where she is, anyway," Ross said.

"Can we consolidate the exhibits, Counsel?" the judge said.

"Fine, Your Honor," Spiller said.

"We're all right with that, Your Honor," Jane Gibbons said.

"Daddy." Sandy was crying. The clerk kind of waved the exhibits at Jane Gibbons, who went out into the hall and came back with a cup of water. Sandy drank the water and then started crying again, her sobs the only sound in the courtroom aside from the drone of the air conditioner.

"Can I go down and sit with her?" Lela said. "I won't make a sound, I promise."

"I'll go," Ross said.

"You stay here," Spiller said.

"Is there someone who can calm this child down?" the judge said.

Lela got up and went and sat next to Sandy.

"I'm here, sweetie," she said, and put her arm around the little girl. "Do you know how to play ticktacktoe?"

"I never did," Sandy said, sniffling.

"The psychiatric report is in evidence, Your Honor," Jane Gibbons said. "We do have Selma Woods from child services here who'll testify in the matter."

"I'll show you," Lela said, and pulled a piece of paper out of her purse.

"Do you have a pen?" she asked Jane Gibbons.

"What?"

"What number is the exhibit, Counsel?" the judge asked.

"Or a pencil," Lela said.

"The respondent has fallen out of her chair again," the judge said.

"Here, use this," Jane Gibbons said, and handed Lela the pen she had been using to mark exhibits.

"Oh, red," Sandy said. "I like red. Chick bought me crayons and I only used the red ones. They're the best."

Ross beat the policeman to Jolene. He picked her up and gently eased her into her seat.

"I could have handled it," the policeman said.

"That's all right," Ross replied.

"You son of a bitch," Jolene said.

"Him or me?" the policeman said.

"She means me," Ross said, and came back and sat down.

"You will be decorous in my courtroom, miss," the judge said. Lela could see the side of Jolene's face now. She was grimacing, as though about to cry, and Lela looked away because she was getting a pain in her stomach just being here, not to mention having to think about Jolene and what she must be thinking, what she must be feeling.

The judge was asking the fire chief to come up and sit in the witness chair.

"I'll take *X* and you take *O*," Lela said.

"I like *O* better," Sandy said.

"Then you take *O* and I'll take *X*."

"The respondent has been charged with arson, Your Honor, and is presently incarcerated in Santa Rosa Jail pending arraignment," the fire chief was saying.

"I'm not very good at this," Lela said. Sandy had a third *O* in place and was beaming.

"I learn everything in a minute," Sandy said, "in a second. You want me to tell you what time it is? I learned all by myself."

"You're so smart."

"The drug trafficking charge has been dropped, I see," the judge said.

"To my knowledge, the respondent's co-defendant on the arson charge is being held on the drug trafficking charge," the fire chief said. "Arson is what we're concerned with."

"That's two games you won," Lela said.

"I'll let you win one, too. Can we buy tacos for lunch, the kind that have the cheese and tomatoes inside?"

"We'll buy anything you want."

The lady from child services was in the witness chair now.

"There is no home life, Your Honor."

"You've been inside the home?" the judge asked.

"What's left of it. The fire destroyed one wall. I saw enough, though."

Jolene had begun to wail. Sandy looked over at her, surprise in her face. Lela felt sick now, wanted to vomit, wanted to faint, wanted to scream.

"We'll get tacos for lunch," she said, her voice lost in the noise Jolene was making. "And ice cream and candy."

"I want Misty," Sandy said. "I want to go home."

———————————

Ross carried Sandy out of the courtroom as if she were a baby who couldn't walk, his face lit with happiness, or maybe it was victory, Lela couldn't tell which. He put Sandy down on a bench in the corridor and she threw her arms around Lela's neck and pressed her lips to Lela's cheek and held them there, pressing the skin, kissing, pressing, pressing as though imprinting herself there.

"It was pretty cut-and-dried, Ross," Spiller said. The attorney had them in a corner near the courtroom door, knuckles on hip, explaining things. "No one could have presented a better picture of an unfit mother than what that woman did all by herself in the courtroom today, drugged out of her skull. In jail two days and managing to get drugged."

"Speed lasts a while," Ross said.

"Be that as it may, she hung herself. Poor bitch. Short of you being a murderer, this was all by the numbers, straight down the line."

"I'm not that great, either. If she's a bitch, I'm a bastard."

"That drug stuff you're talking about? Forget it. If that social services woman had brought it up, I'd have flattened her. I'd have cried foul, prejudice, cited case law. Even quoted the Constitution, if I had to. But the judge likes you. It wasn't even a fair fight."

"She didn't have a chance."

"Whose side are you on?"

"It didn't feel right, her not having an attorney to represent her. Where the hell's her attorney? You told me she was being taken care of, no problem, so why in hell did he hang her out to dry, put her in a position where she had no one?"

"He knew he'd lose on the custody phase. I'd have stayed away, too. What's the use of showing up and making a fool out of yourself?"

Jolene, hands manacled, came out of the door with the policeman, who had put on dark sunglasses. She passed within two inches of Lela's face. So close Lela could see the scabs, like pepper flakes, on the sides of both cheeks.

"Well, you got her now," Jolene said, looking straight at Ross. "And what do I care about it? What does it matter, anyway?"

And then she was gone, the oak double doors swinging behind the policeman's broad back.

"Is Mama going back to jail?" Sandy said.

"For a little while," Lela said.

"What about the arson charge?" Ross asked Spiller. "How's her lawyer on that? Is he going to let her defend herself on that one, too?"

"He's good enough," Spiller replied. "There was an indictment for commingling client funds a few years back, but he beat it. He's cheap. Good and cheap. He'll do all right for her."

"I told you I burned the place down," Lela said. "Jolene didn't have anything to do with it. You should have let me tell the judge that. I shouldn't have listened to you. I should have told him."

"We went through that already," Ross said.

"But she didn't do anything," Lela said.

"Here's the way it works," Spiller said, looking impatient. "Jolene'll be found incompetent and they'll let her off. If I'd let you tell the judge you shot the hell out of the place and set the fire on purpose, with all these save the foresters, all these environmentalists, running around in Sonoma County giving names to the trees, they'd lock you up and throw away the key. You want that? 'Cause if you do, say the word, I've got a pipeline into the judge's chambers, can get you booked and arraigned and convicted within, oh, say, two weeks tops."

"I want Misty," Sandy said, and started crying again.

"Misty's at home," Lela said.

"The trouble with you two," Spiller said, "is you want your cake and want to eat it, too. That woman's done for, fucked and refucked, and the two of you did it. Be grateful."

It was possible to pretend to forget about everything, just kind of float from day to day. Help Ross with his patients, drive Sandy over to the school out on Fort Ross Road. Even go over to Guerneville to the Sonoma Artists Supply and buy a $12.99 watercolor set, then take Sandy hiking out along Austin Creek to a place where the water and the bridge and the trees merged, where the sun slipped through leafy branches to make patterns of light on the shadowed creek.

Trying to get the look of Austin Creek, the way the sun hit it, seemed impossible. How had Matisse done it, all those lily ponds with the color spectrum cut into fractions as fine as shattered glass? Why was sun so hard to capture? Especially when it was shining directly on the water. Not early morning or late afternoon sun. That was easy. The creek was dark and mysterious then, and the sun was only a suggestion. But in early afternoon, when the sun was so brilliant that the stones in the creekbed turned red and purple and the surface of the water broke warm and gentle over them, and there were no mysteries about anything, why couldn't she capture it then?

Sandy seemed able to get the way the sun looked. She could take a few paints and mix them together, and even though the trees looked like mossy sticks and the bridge was lopsided, her water was just right. Incandescent.

Why was it so hard to catch the essence of things? And life, what about that? Even the sun had nothing on life when it came to being difficult, stubborn, hard to catch. Sandy could catch it. She seemed happy now, not speaking about Jolene, just concentrating on painting sun on water.

Gil used to say, Close your eyes, Lela, and say, "It doesn't matter, I don't care," and everything fuzzy will become clear, everything nasty will be gone. So why couldn't she just do that with Jolene?

She'll be all right, Ross said when they got the news from Vickie that Jolene was out of jail. An incompetent, not responsible for her actions, her attorney had argued in court. Why, she couldn't even raise her own child, wasn't even responsible enough for that, the attorney said. Lost custody. Can you imagine? She's to be pitied, not put in jail.

Not thinking about Jolene became a chore, something Lela worked at every day. At night it was different. At night she dreamed of her parents. Her real ones. Something she had never done before. At least she couldn't remember ever dreaming about them. But they had no faces, and they didn't speak. Her mother just sat on a chair with her hands in her lap and her head down as though she were praying. Her father was always walking, his back to her, so she couldn't see what he looked like, either. Sometimes in her dreams she would run after him, try to catch him, but he never turned around, never seemed to hear her.

When Lela was little people would always say, "You look just like your daddy." But they were talking about Walter. "My, isn't she just Daddy's little girl," people would always say. But she wasn't. She wasn't his little girl.

One day, when the sun was doing flip-flops on Austin Creek, Lela drove Sandy to school and told her to be good, that everything would turn out fine. Then she went back to the cabin. There were two patients waiting, two women reading magazines as though that were why they were there, and Ross alone in the examining room, drinking coffee and looking out the window. Probably thinking about Jolene, too, Lela supposed when she saw him there so still and quiet, or maybe studying the water of Austin Creek, wondering about its secrets, about the difficulty of capturing the sun in paints. Or maybe not thinking of anything at all.

"I'm going back to Los Angeles," she told him, and he turned and didn't look surprised at all.

28

"Y O U   D O N ' T   F O L L O W   through, Lela," Deborah said. She was on the couch in Lela's living room, feet up on a stack of pillows, eating chocolate-chip cookies.

"We each have to live our own lives," Lillian said.

"She's my sister, Lillian, and I'll tell her what I want to tell her, if you don't mind." Deborah had a soft cervix and was in danger of dropping the baby on the sidewalk if she didn't sit down and stay down, the doctor said. Don't you have someplace to go where there are no kids yammering for you to get them things? he asked her. Well, there's my sister, Lela, she told him. But she hates me.

"I came back because I wanted to," Lela said. The door was open to the garden. There was a stick propping up the white oleander that, even before Lela left, had begun to lean into the rose bed. Lillian must have done that. And the leaves of the roses had no speckled spots on them now but were as green as new grass.

"You know how you are, Lela," Deborah said. "You never finish anything you start."

How had it happened? Why had she asked Deborah to leave Jason and the twins and Brad to Rowena's care and bring her soft cervix and swollen belly here? And not a word said about how she screamed at Lela on the telephone, told her she could do without her, didn't need her.

"It's always the same," Deborah said. "You make people love you and then you disappear. So now Ross loves you and Sandy loves you, and here you are, back with me, who understands you only too well. I suppose I should be glad to have you back. And I am. I keep telling Lillian that of all the people in the world—besides my husband and children, of course—I love you best. Lillian, a cup of decaf, please."

Lillian had kept the potted plants watered, too, and even torn out the fading, leggy carnations and planted bearded iris. They were beginning to bud now, little lavender knuckles of bloom peeking out of the green stalks.

Lillian was back with a cup of decaf. "What are you going to do now?" she asked Lela.

"Find out about my family," Lela replied.

"I don't think Brad's ever going to forgive you, Lela, running off the way you did," Deborah said.

"At least he isn't following me around in his car anymore or camping out in my yard."

"Well, he doesn't understand you like I do. He thought he'd push. I told him, Brad, don't push Lela, it's a mistake. The soft approach is best with Lela, I said. If you look like you're pushing, she runs the other way. He's got a man he's considering bringing in to replace you, anyway. Claims he sold ten million dollars' worth of real estate in Encino last year."

Lela came and sat down on the end of the couch next to Deborah's propped-up feet. "I've been thinking a lot lately."

"A first for you," Deborah said. "You're not exactly the thinker of the world."

"I think I'm realistic."

"It's not the same thing. But we've got you back now, and if you act sweet with Brad, tell him you're sorry, you were temporarily out of your mind, he'll forgive you and take you back into the office."

"What about the ten-million-dollar Encino man?"

"What about him?"

"I've never sold ten million dollars' worth of real estate in a single year in my life. I think Brad ought to grab him."

"Are you just trying to argue with me? Is that what it is?"

Lillian, in one of the straight Chinese chairs, started fiddling with the hem of her apron, pulling at a loose string till the material puckered, then straightening it out, pulling it and straightening.

"I'm simply stating a fact. Brad ought to hire him."

"He wants to be a partner."

"Better yet."

"Brad prefers you. He knows you're unreliable and will probably fly off on some errand of mercy or other in another few weeks, but you might have a chance if you play your cards right. The first thing you have to do is apologize to him." Deborah glanced up at Lillian. "Would you get me a glass of water, Lillian?"

"Lillian's not your maid," Lela said.

"It's all right," Lillian said, and let the apron drop.

"No, it isn't," Lela said. "I'll get it."

The washer on the kitchen faucet was almost gone, and the water sprayed up over the faucet and misted the labels on Deborah's medicine bottles above the sink. Lela filled and refilled the glass. All her life, all her life, all her life, the water said. What about all her life? She leaned forward and put her head under the water, felt the shock of the cold on her scalp, felt the washerless faucet soak her blouse. Her shoes were getting wet, and when she moved her feet they made squishing sounds on the floor.

"Did you fall in?" Deborah called from the living room.

Lela left the glass on the sink and came back into the living room.

"What have you done to yourself?" Deborah looked confused.

"I'll get a towel," Lillian offered.

"No, don't," Lela said, and sat down on the couch.

"You're getting the couch wet," Deborah said.

"It's my couch," Lela replied, and she leaned over the pillows and took Deborah's hand. "I want you to stay here, Deb, and I don't want anything bad to happen to you, and I think Lillian is being very kind and you're taking advantage of her. And this is my house, and if I want to get the couch wet and bathe an elephant in the sink, I will do it, and I will do it without any remarks or comments from you." And she said it all in the most loving voice, gently pressing Deborah's fingers all the while. It was the kindest way she could think of to let Deborah know she still loved her, that she was welcome to stay in the house and keep her medicine bottles on the ledge above the sink, and even to ask Lillian to bring her coffee and water, if she was polite about it, but that she'd better get used to the idea that things between them were not the same, would never be the same.

"I don't remember any murders in Huntington Beach in the seventies where a man shot his wife in his own backyard," the librarian at Huntington Beach Central Library told Lela. "I'd remember a story like that. Are you sure it wasn't the wife who shot her husband and his lover? Seems I remember something along those lines."

"Benoit is the name of the family," Lela said.

"Relatives of yours?" The librarian was in her late thirties, too young, Lela thought, to remember much of anything that happened in Huntington Beach in 1965.

"My mother and father."

"Oh, Jesus, you poor thing."

The librarian set up the microfiche for Lela and showed her how to run it.

"Just kind of graze along the headlines till you see a name you recognize, and if you need anything, just holler. Not literally holler, I didn't mean that. After all, we are in a library. But holler metaphorically if you need to."

"I'll certainly give a metaphorical holler if I need something."

Film zipped by, too fast to decipher anything. Nothing but a blur. Lela felt herself getting lightheaded. She sat back in the padded chair and took deep breaths. It was a beautiful library, with windows overlooking a park. Jogging trails circled the lake, and a man and a little boy stood at the edge of the water, throwing bread crumbs to the ducks from a plastic bag.

"Let's not talk about it," Kathy would say when Lela asked about her mother. "It's better forgotten," Walter would say when she asked about her father. And, of course, Gil showed her how to get rid of unpleasant memories. Hypnotized her, lectured her, gave her pills, fucked her.

A jogger was doing stretching exercises against a tree, clutching it as if he were standing in quicksand. First one foot back, way back, stretch, look up at the sky, feet together, now the other foot back.

"Are you working the machine all right?" The librarian was back. She held her pencil in a peculiar way, as though she were about to lead an orchestra. And she dyed her own hair. Lela counted at least five shades of brown radiating out from the woman's crown.

"I think I'm pressing the button too hard," Lela said. "I have a heavy touch, I suppose."

"Like this," the librarian said, and bent over Lela and jabbed at the button with the eraser end of the pencil.

Lela smiled, and the librarian smiled, and then someone came and called the librarian away, and Lela was alone again, the newspaper on the screen in front of her out of focus and sideways, for which she was grateful, because then she had to fiddle with the focus button and reinsert the tape, and that took ten minutes, and then she sat and looked out the window some more, and that was another ten minutes.

"The bathroom, where is it?" Lela asked the young girl at the machine next to her.

"Down the hall, past the mysteries."

Just one pill wouldn't mean she was weak. Everyone took pills for some malady or another. There was someone washing out a coffee cup in the sink in the bathroom, swishing water over it, swinging her elbows from side to side. Lela held the green tablet in her hand and waited until she was gone, then put the pill in her mouth and cupped her hands beneath the faucet.

Memory can be like a wild beast, Gil used to tell her. If you stalk it too hard now, you'll only have to kill it later.

The film on the microfiche slipped by. Nothing. Nothing. Nothing. Then a story on a television newswoman caught her eye.

> Annette Sullivan, Channel 6 *News at Noon*, was shot to death on the back steps of a house in Huntington Beach while attempting to film a story on a suspected murder. See page 4, Sullivan.

Lela spun the film expertly now to page 4.

> A woman identified as Marilee Benoit, said by police to be an occupant of the house, was also killed in the gunfire. Her husband, Donald, is being sought for questioning.

Well, that wasn't so hard. It really didn't have anything to do with her. Not really. Not anywhere inside of her. Her heart was beating less rapidly now. It was like stepping into the ocean on a cold day, afraid of what it's going to feel like, standing there and shivering for a few minutes until your body becomes accustomed to the chill.

And there was a photograph of Marilee Benoit, a tiny one next to a big photograph of the newswoman. Lela couldn't make out Marilee's features too well, couldn't tell if her eyes were light or dark. She had a big smile, though, and a dimple in one cheek, or it might have been a smudge on the microfiche. She didn't look familiar.

On the fifth page was a larger story about the newswoman, her background, where she went to school, the fact that she was engaged to be married the following month. The broadcast awards she had won. Lela smashed her whole palm down on the button, made the film spin, looking for something more about Marilee and Donald, but there wasn't anything.

It was the same for the next day's newspaper. More stories about Annette Sullivan, then about her funeral and the city dignitaries who attended the service at Saint Bonaventure Catholic Church. A small bit about the continuing police search for Donald Benoit. Then a week later an article on journalists who had been murdered on the job and a smaller picture of Annette Sullivan alongside the story on her.

There was a tiny notice in the obituaries in the second week's newspaper.

Marilee Benoit, age 35, survived by daughters Jolene and Lela, sister Marjorie Jamison, mother Renee Sweetzer. Services at Bethany God the Creator Universal Church 1:00 p.m. Wednesday. Burial at Olive View Cemetery, Costa Mesa.

And then a small article on the very last page with the picture of a little girl with a shy smile and a gap in her front teeth.

Newsmen were barred from Judge McKinney's courtroom today due, court watchers informed this paper, to the sensitive nature of the testimony in a custody hearing concerning eight-year-old Lela Benoit. TV newswoman Annette Sullivan was killed in a shooting that also took the life of the child's mother. The child's father, Donald Benoit, wanted for questioning in the murder of the two women, is still at large.

The pastor was kneeling on a rotting rubber pad, weeding a bed of daylilies in a small garden near the side door of the church.

"I used to have daylilies in my yard," Lela said. "They'll take over if you let them."

He pushed his glasses back with one dirty finger and looked up at her. "Rhizomes. Nasty things, those."

"Bamboo, the same thing," Lela said. "I once saw a yard taken over by bamboo, growing everywhere, popping up even in the cracks in the patio. They had to use a bulldozer to get rid of it."

She knelt beside him, feeling the damp of the grass pass through her slacks. "Let me," she said, and began digging at the dirt with her fingers.

"Oh, no, take this, you'll ruin your hands," the pastor said. He handed Lela the trowel he had been using and started slicing through the lily root stalks with a little pocket knife.

"I love to garden," Lela said. "I sell houses—or I used to—and it was always easier for me to sell a house if it had a beautiful garden. Some people don't care about them, take them for granted, but I just love growing things, watching how they change, the stages they go through. If you take that knife and slice on an angle, it'll be a lot easier."

"Like this?" His hands were arthritic, and he grasped the knife with difficulty.

"That's it. See how clean it cuts? Like an onion. You have to find the seam." The dirt was soft, separated easily from tangled roots. "I sold a house once with a yard overgrown with bamboo, and the owner swore she only planted one. I'll never forget that yard, feathery bamboo all over the place. It was a sight. The people bought the house anyway. They put in a swimming pool."

She could see through the open door of the church all the way down the aisle. There must have been a wedding or a funeral recently. Bouquets of flowers stood wilting at the sides of the altar. A wreath of limp violets was draped over the lid of the pipe organ.

"Did you sell many houses?" the pastor asked.

"Not too many. Not enough." She turned toward him. "So," she said.

The pastor brought Lela into his office and she sat in a chair while he stood at his desk and flipped through the funeral record book.

"Benoit, Benoit, Benoit." Half-glasses stuck on the bridge of his nose, he kept repeating the name while he looked through the register. "You say she died in 1965. I came in '72. I don't remember the name, but it should be here."

There was no way to know what part of her brain still knew things and what part didn't. The picture of Marilee Benoit in the newspaper could have been that of a stranger. The name of the newswoman was one she had never heard before. But the pipe organ with its sad-looking flowers atop it made her say, "I think she played the organ here."

The pastor shut the book, went around behind his desk, and sat down.

"We had an organist murdered by her husband," he said. "I wasn't here then, but of course I heard about it."

"That was my mother," Lela said.

29

IF YOU START at the ocean in Santa Monica, you can take Venice Boulevard all the way to downtown Los Angeles. On the way you'll pass through Culver City. Nothing much has changed in Culver City since the twenties, except that the old Red Car no longer rumbles past, wheels striking sparks on the streetcar tracks. But people still raise rabbits in their backyards and repair their own cars in their driveways and make things for their stucco houses on lathes in their garages while they watch basketball on portable TVs. Venice High School still has the seminude statue of Myrna Loy on the front lawn that was sculpted by a teacher in the twenties when the actress was a sixteen-year-old student there. The statue has been vandalized, taken down, restored, and put back up so many times that school authorities finally put a metal cage around it. But it's still there.

Lela's check of 1965 telephone books showed Renee Sweetzer, Marilee Benoit's mother, living in a house on Beethoven Street in Culver City. According to the entry in the 1993 book, she was still there.

The old woman held the screen door open a couple inches and fanned it back and forth in front of Lela's face. Lela knew about how people did that. When she went after a listing, they sometimes did that, trying to show you they were in control, this was their house, if you didn't like someone fanning a door in your face, then leave, who the hell asked you to come bothering them anyway.

"Are you Renee Sweetzer?" Lela asked.

"I am."

"I got your name from Marilee Benoit's death certificate."

"Marge!" The old woman was calling to someone over her shoulder, someone who came out of the kitchen wiping her hands on a dish towel. She looked a little like the old woman, same round face ending in a pointy chin. But Marge had a dimple in one cheek and was younger. So it wasn't a smudge on the microfiche. Marilee Benoit had a dimple, too.

"What's the matter?" Marge was at the door now, ready to shut it. Just about, in fact, to say we don't want any when Lela put her hand out and grasped the knob.

"She's come asking about Marilee," Renee said. There was a walker behind the door, and she reached for it and leaned forward, then clump-clumped away into the dark interior.

"Are you Marilee's sister?" Lela asked the younger woman.

"Well . . ."

A small dog was at the screen door now, yapping at Lela.

"Here, pooch." Lela bent down and petted its ears, and it growled softly, its neck muscles stiff. "She looks like a Pekingese. I'll bet she's won a few prizes."

"She's a mongrel," Marge said.

"Mongrels make stronger stock. Some of these purebreds you see are sickly and don't live long and don't make good house pets. I used to sell houses, and I'd see it every day, how the purebred dogs have to be pampered. People would tell me they're at the vets with the thing three days out of five, and they cost a fortune in dog pills and special diets. If I were going to have a dog, I'd go out to the pound and get a mongrel. None of those fancy dogs with papers for me. I think it's all just trying to one-up people having papers on a dog, anyway."

She straightened up. The porch was small, with two steps and a wrought-iron railing. Built in the forties, Lela guessed, with two bedrooms, one bathroom, stall shower, and no tub.

"I'm here from the *Los Angeles Times*," Lela said. "I'd like to talk to you about Marilee Benoit."

There was the smell of dog in the house. On the cushions of the couch Lela was sitting on. Marge and Renee smelled of dog, too. And there was too much furniture in too small a space. Big square pieces of furniture. An old blond square box of a television in one corner, a green vinyl lounge chair, where Renee was sitting, in another corner. The dining room was part of the living room. Just a jog in the wall and there it was, carved oak table with lion feet sitting a few feet from the kitchen door, pressed-back chairs squeezed so tight under the rim of the table that they resembled oak fence posts surrounding a bare yard.

"We've never talked to anyone about Marilee before," Renee said. She had her metal walker next to her and was holding on to it with one hand.

"Let me handle it, Mother," Marge said. She was sitting next to Lela on the couch, the dog on her lap.

"Especially not any newspaper reporters," Renee said.

"Women are murdered every day," Marge said. "Why does the *Los Angeles Times* want to do an article on Marilee? What's so special about her?"

"It's not just an article," Lela said. "It's a series. California women who have been murdered by their husbands."

"You want to know how he killed her?" Renee said.

"No, that's all in the police reports. I want to know about her as a person. I like to flesh out my stories with human interest details, you know, like where she went to school, what her hobbies were, what happened to her children."

"Marilee's dead," Renee said.

"She knows that, Mother."

"Then it's all right if I ask you a few questions?" Lela said. Her fingers shook slightly as she took the notebook out of her purse.

"I don't like it," Renee said.

"I suppose it's all right," Marge said.

"I hope you don't mind if I take notes." She fumbled with the pages of the notebook. There were descriptions of houses she had listed for sale in 1992, some mortgage interest calculations, and a few blank pages toward the back. "I wouldn't want to depend on my memory."

"You look familiar," Marge said.

"People are always saying that about me," Lela said. She smiled, and it felt like her teeth were stuck to her lips. "I would like a glass of water, if you don't mind."

Marge went into the kitchen and came back with a green plastic tumbler of water. Lela took a few sips of the water and then put it down on the blond coffee table in front of the couch.

"Are you going to use our names?" Marge asked.

"Not if you don't want me to."

"Well, I don't."

"Then they won't be in there. The *Times* doesn't want any lawsuits. They're very careful about respecting people's privacy. Marilee had two children, didn't she?"

"Two girls," Marge said. "The older one was married, I think. It was the little one, Lela, that was left."

"Marilee was murdered by her husband," Renee said.

"She just got through telling you she was doing a story on murdered women," Marge said. "Why else would she be here asking questions? You'd know what's going on if you'd just listen."

"I've never gotten over it," Renee said. "He left that little girl orphaned, and not a soul in this family wanted to take her except me. I cried every night about wanting to, but my husband wouldn't allow it. He said, 'After all these years of Marilee ignoring us, I'm not about to clean up the mess she's made.' He was very stubborn that way. I asked Marge to take the child, but she wouldn't."

"She doesn't want to hear about that, Mother."

"I'd like to hear about everything," Lela said.

"She twists things around," Marge said. "Jim and I were barely getting by on what he made, and we had the twins to raise. She makes it sound like I didn't want Lela, but the truth of the matter is I'd have taken her if I hadn't been so strapped for money. I didn't even have the money to travel from Wichita to California for the custody hearing. Where was I going to get the money for that? And where was I going to get money to hire a lawyer?"

"I raised three kids when your father was making twenty-five dollars a week," Renee said.

"She's been living in the past lately," Marge said to Lela. "Putting the blame on me for what happened. She was the grandmother. She should have done something herself."

"My son was generous," Renee said to Lela, "always handing out money to his friends. My husband would say, Well, Bill, let's see if your friends hand *you* money when you need it. Bill left home after high school. He heard they were mining for diamonds down in Venezuela. I tried to find out where he was when Marilee died. I know he'd have taken the little girl. He loved children. I think he and the woman he was living with down there—an Indian woman—or Chinese, or something—had five or six. He would have taken another one, as generous as he always was. But the letters came back, and I didn't know what else to do to find him. I don't know to this day."

"The two of you live here alone?"

"Since eighty-three," Marge said. "Dad died, my kids were grown and out, and my husband the same, so I came here to take care of her, see to things. A house needs taking care of, just like people do, only more so. She'd never paint the place or put down new carpet if I didn't see it needed doing. You aren't putting in the bad things, are you, the things she said about me?"

"Of course not," Lela said. "Any time you don't want something in, just tell me and I'll put a star by it to remind me not to use it. How did Marilee meet her husband?"

"In a gas station," Renee said. "We were getting gas, and he was in the next car, and he came over and started talking to Marilee. She was still in high school. She didn't even graduate, just ran off and married him. He was a few years older, and my husband said he thought he probably had a wife or two somewhere, the way he acted. He was peculiar right from the beginning, always spouting off on religion—'The Bible says such and such,' was his favorite way of talking. My husband just hated that. He was an atheist and he always said he'd go to hell in his own way, he didn't need anyone to tell him how.

"But Marilee was sorry later, I can tell you that. She cried plenty over the way he treated her after they were married. But it was too late. My husband said let her drown in it, and I had to live with him, so what could I do? I gave her a little money now and then, but God knows what that husband of hers was doing to her and those girls all those years. But what could I do to prevent anything? You can't keep a child from doing what they're going to do when they're determined they're going to do it."

"What happened to the little girl?" Lela asked.

"I keep thinking I know you from somewhere," Marge said. She was petting the dog, rubbing her fingers over its oily coat. "It's the strangest feeling."

"That happens to me sometimes, too," Lela said, and took another sip of water. She could feel Marge's eyes on her, examining her hands, her face.

"Strangers took the little one," Renee said. "Just took her. Like that. Like you'd see something you like in a store and just pull out the money and buy it. Oh, they had plenty of money, I heard, so that part was a blessing. But not to ever see my grandchild again, that was a bitter pill. But I had to swallow it and not say anything to my husband or he'd have killed me. He never laid a hand on me in his life, but he could shrivel your soul the way he talked. It always frightened Marilee. Marge never seemed to mind when he yelled, but Marilee, I could just see her turn pale when he raised his voice. So what did she go and do? Married a man who hit her and finally murdered her. And I couldn't even get my own grandchild afterwards.

I had to let her go to strangers. Marilee would have turned over in her grave, she loved that little girl so much."

"Mother, that's enough," Marge said. "I don't think any of this needs to be in the newspaper."

"She could have had any boy in high school that she wanted," Renee said. "She was homecoming queen and played the organ for all the school plays. You know how they used to do. Background music, like in the silent movies. Of course, we had movie movies then, and Marilee just played the organ for fun. And then at church, of course. No one could play an organ like Marilee. Things were tight sometimes, but I never begrudged the money for her lessons."

"No one said you did, Mother," Marge said.

"What happened to the father?" Lela said.

"Disappeared," Marge said.

"Gone," Renee said.

"He was a maniac," Marge said. "They lived up near us in Wichita when Elaine, that was the middle girl, was born. Put him in jail for child beating on that one. Beat her so bad she had his handprints on her face. Two years old when he did that. She died when she was three, and we always thought he did it. Maybe you better not put that in your story."

"I won't if you don't want me to," Lela said. "I'll write it up first and send you a copy and you can edit it and what you don't want in you can cross out. How did she die?"

"They were on their way to California. No one ever told us exactly what did happen to Elaine, just that she died in a motel they were staying at."

"She drowned," Renee said.

Marge turned toward her. "How do you know that?"

"Marilee told me. She said he dumped her in the swimming pool because she wouldn't eat her supper."

"Well, I didn't hear about that one. But I think he did terrible things to those other two girls of his."

Lela could hardly see the notepaper. The lines seemed to crisscross the page. Up and down and sideways. There was no room to write. She scribbled something in the corner of the page. Marge's eyes were devouring her, and there was no air in the house. It had been warm outside, but the heat in the house was oppressive.

"I didn't eat breakfast," Lela said, and she just put her head down on her lap, didn't think she was going to faint, but the next thing she knew she was lying on the dog-smelling couch and Marge had a glass of water pressed to her face, dribbling it down her cheek, not even trying to get the lip of the glass in the right place.

"I knew you looked familiar," Marge said. "You must think we're the dumbest people in the world, that you could come in here and tell us a story about being a reporter. Hating us enough to do that, when it wasn't our fault what happened to you, what your father did. Coming in here and making up stories about how you're writing an article on Marilee and you're going to send us a copy, and being so sweet it makes me sick to think about it, when we told you and told you we couldn't have done anything different than we did. You came here just to trick us into telling you things, and it's very sneaky and underhanded and I don't appreciate it one bit."

"Oh, Lord," Renee said, and she got up and grabbed her walker and went through the jog that was the dining room and through the door into the kitchen, and Lela could hear her crying at the sink.

"When you feel better, you should just get up and leave," Marge said.

The Police Records Bureau of the Huntington Beach Police Department had no record of Marilee Benoit's death. Murder or otherwise.

"I'm sure sorry," the lieutenant said. He was in a blue suit, white shirt, and no tie, and his hair was spiky, like a punk rocker's hair would be, not a policeman's. "We moved into the new headquarters in April 1975, and it's just possible that a few murders got lost then. We were on computer then, too, but your mother's death could have been in one that crashed during the move. It happens, you know. Computers are like people, not completely reliable."

"What about my father? Donald Benoit. What about him?"

"If we don't have anything on your mother's murder, I don't see how we'd have anything on your father. Was he murdered, too?"

"No, he was the murderer."

"Oh." He looked real sorry now, like he had made a mistake in handling this routinely, that he should have put on his tie and met her in the lobby and had a sad face on, and told her he had gone through every computer in the place and there was nothing there, and how could he help her, and you know how life is, so unpredictable, so unfair, and the police do everything they can, but sometimes there are things that even the police can't do, with all their resources, and it's a damn shame, and if there's anything else we can do for you, don't hesitate to come back in. But she hadn't told him her father murdered her mother, so he had looked at her in her nice blue blazer and tan skirt and thought it was a random thing, her mother getting murdered, and he knew how those things went, you never could find someone who committed a random murder. Shot in the supermarket or on the freeway or in the parking lot at South Coast Plaza. So he obviously hadn't looked too hard, was only in that room with the bank of computers for a few minutes before he was back. Now he was looking at her differently, his interest obviously up. Way up. He was even breathing a little quicker.

"That's pretty unusual, you know—for 1965, anyways," he said. "It happens now once in a while, but in 1965—"

"His name is Donald Benoit," Lela said.

The policeman went back into the computer room and was gone a long time this time. When he came out, he looked disappointed.

"All I've got is a description on him that they used for the APB— all points bulletin. It doesn't mention your mother. It just says he's armed and dangerous, wanted for murder. I don't show a resolution of the case. That doesn't really mean anything. He could have been apprehended in another jurisdiction or another state and we wouldn't necessarily have his whereabouts or whether he was arrested or not. Of course, we should be able to plug into the network of computers, but that information doesn't always get on line. I do have a contact for him, though. His mother lives in Gardena."

30

"T H E D O C T O R S A Y S I can get up a little each day," Deborah
said. "I should get home."

Brad was there, looking uneasy, sitting on the floor in front of the
couch, his hand resting on Deborah's fluid-retaining leg.

"You don't have to go home," Lela said. "Take advantage of being
here."

"There's no rush," Lillian said. She was coloring with Jason in an
Aladdin book, sitting at the kitchen table in a chair near the door to
the living room while Jason sat atop the table.

"Jason, you're not coloring the table, are you?" Deborah said.

"It's an old table," Lela said. "I've been thinking of getting rid
of it."

"Are you sure?"

"She ought to know what she plans on doing," Brad said.

"Don't snap at her," Lela told him. This was going to be hard,
making all of them over. She didn't even know whether that was
possible.

"I told Brown I changed my mind," Brad said, "that I don't think
a deal between us is in the offing."

"I hope you didn't do it because of me," Lela said, "because I'm
not coming back."

"There you go," Deborah said, "being obstinate, being—"

"You come back and I'll give you the top listings for yourself, no
split, for a year," Brad said.

"That's pretty generous."

"More than you deserve, after what you—" Deborah stopped herself, bit her lip.

Oh, it was hard to change yourself. All those patterns we make in
our behavior. Push this button, I say this. Push that button, I say that.
No thought. No will. No control.

"I've still got some things to take care of, and they'll take time," Lela said.

"I could float you a small loan in the interim," Brad said, and Deborah opened her mouth to say something and then didn't.

"I'm taken care of for at least another six months."

"Then what?"

"Maybe I'll come back then. Maybe I'll do something else. I don't know yet."

"That Ross is the one who did it," Deborah said. "He's the one who—"

"Oh, Deborah," Lela said.

"Once a bitch, always a bitch," Brad said.

Deborah was crying, holding her hand over her nose and mouth, not making any noise, just letting the tears roll.

"I'm trying so hard," Deborah said.

"I know you are," Lela said.

Grace Benoit's trailer was at the far end of the park, up against the cinder-block wall. It looked as if it were growing out of the ficus trees that had been planted around it. Great weeping trees in plastic paint buckets, with a long green hose dribbling water into the one next to the steps.

The trailer was an old one and kind of bounced as the nurse let Lela in.

"You can only talk to her a little while. She's nearly ninety and might go to sleep on you in the middle of a sentence." The nurse looked elderly herself, her curved back carrying her chin so far downward into her chest it seemed as if she were studying the spots on the collar of her white uniform.

The bedroom was dark, trees mashed against the single window and shutting out the sunlight. A little lamp with a ballerina base was on the table beside the bed.

"Grace, this lady wants to talk to you," the nurse said.

Lela sat down on the chair beside the bed and waited for the bluish lids to raise up.

"I'll be out of a job soon," the nurse said. "Medicare wants her in a home, would rather pay them than me."

"Who wants me?" Grace's eyes were open now. She coughed lightly, then reached over and turned on the ballerina lamp.

"I want to talk to you about Donald," Lela said.

"What for?"

"She'll die in two months in a home," the nurse said, "but they don't care." She cranked the bed at its foot until the old lady was in a sitting position.

"You look like Donald," Grace said.

"I suppose I do," Lela said. "I don't think I look like my mother."

"What's one more old person dying, is the way the government thinks," the nurse said. "You know what I make a day? One twenty-five. You know what they'll have to pay in a home? Try to guess. It isn't no one twenty-five a day, I can tell you that."

"Go on outside," Grace said. "You talk too much."

"He was the best boy, the best son, any mother ever had," Grace said. "Mowed the lawn, went to church, made his bed. And he'd clean up after himself, you never knew there was a boy in the house. Liked to collect things, I remember."

She coughed a lot. Said a few sentences, then coughed, then spit into a tissue, then continued. Lela bent close to the bed to hear her better.

"Played water polo in high school. Got all sorts of medals for it. And his father said he could go to practice after school, but he'd have to bring money in, too. My husband was a strong man, knew how to raise a boy. Donald—Donny, everyone called him—worked out at the airport cleaning airplanes up. He used to bring home uneaten dinners." She coughed again and the nurse came in with a bottle of green liquid and a spoon.

"Did she fall asleep on you yet?"

"She's fine," Lela said.

"I told you to stay out," Grace said.

"You were coughing."

"Well, just go out and stay out."

She leaned back against the pillows and shut her eyes, and for a moment Lela thought she was asleep. Then she opened her eyes again and kind of lifted herself up with her knuckles.

"Where was I?"

"He worked out at the airport."

"Saved all his money, too. Went to school all day and worked all night and played water polo in the afternoon. I remember one time he wanted to buy a radio, a portable radio to take to the beach. And my husband said no, it was a waste of money. So I bought him the radio, but we didn't tell my husband. It was just our secret. And he kept it in his locker at school. We were very close. He was a wonderful son.

"Only once, only one time in all his growing up, did I ever see a bit of temper in him. That was when he was eighteen and going to go into the navy. It was at dinner, I remember that. He said he wanted to buy a car and leave it at home so he'd have something to drive when he came home on leave.

"My husband said he thought that was a waste of money, the car'd get old by the time Donny got out of service, and we didn't want a rusting piece of junk rotting in our driveway. We lived in South Gate then. We had a nice house, too. I had a vegetable garden. Grew all my own tomatoes and corn, beets and peas. I just loved to garden. If I don't have things growing around me, I don't feel alive. The day my last tree dies outside, that's the day I die, no matter what that old lady says.

"So my husband said no, you can't buy a car. And I remember it like it was yesterday. Donny got up out of his seat, and his face was all red, and he was mad, like I never had seen him mad before, and he said, 'I'll buy any damn car I want,' and I said, 'Listen to your father, Donny, he knows better than you do.'

"And Donny gave me a look that struck me to the bone. Ice cold it was, like he wasn't even related to me. 'It's my money,' he said, 'and I'll do whatever the hell I want with it.'

"And my husband stood up, and he—I remember this like it was yesterday—he stood up and he made a fist and he shook it at Donny, and he said, 'You don't ever speak to your mother like that. You do, and I'll put this fist right in the center of your face.' "

"Where is he now?" Lela said.

"My husband died in sixty-five." She looked over at the window, at the way the pattern of shadows kept changing with the wind. "My husband wouldn't let me take you. He said you were tainted." She turned to Lela. "You poor child. Nobody wanted you, did they?"

"I mean Donald. Where is Donald now?"

"The same place he's been for the past fifteen years and will probably be for the next fifteen years. He strangled his wife and they put him away for it."

"He shot her, you mean."

"Oh, no. That was your mother he shot. This was his second wife. He strangled her."

31

S H E   W A S   O N the Vincent Thomas Bridge now, driving over its graceful span. Up here, the shipyard and docks and Ports O'Call Village seemed very small, the water of Los Angeles Harbor so blue she could see the submerged rocks that bordered the shore. Lela had never had a listing in this part of San Pedro, where the houses were wind battered and sea worn, and the stores had black iron grilles that rolled across the windows at night.

Up a ways, where Western Avenue met Paseo del Mar, the houses got a little better. Lela had sold a few there. San Pedro's really a romantic place to live, she would tell prospective buyers. Serb and Croatian fishermen settled here at the beginning of the century and ran their family fishing boats up and down the coast. She never told them that the ones with the biggest fleets had moved away, now lived in Rolling Hills Estates or Palos Verdes.

There, flashing beneath the bridge, was Ports O'Call Village, a touristy harborside clutch of shops. The parking lot was full for this time of morning. She often took clients there, sat with them on the patio of one of the restaurants and watched the container ships move in and out of the harbor. It made the area seem better than it was, made San Pedro not such a dirty word, sipping drinks and talking real estate next to water. Especially when private boats pulled up dockside and tanned people in white ducks and deck shoes emerged from belowdeck to wrestle fiberglass hulls into watery parking spaces, then jumped off, grabbed a nearby table, and ordered drinks. It was a known fact that tanned people in white ducks and deck shoes lashing fifty-foot boats to mossy pilings gave seedy harbor areas a certain panache. Lela never told clients to be careful about where they drove when they left the parking lot, just made sure they followed her to the freeway and she saw them safely on it.

She was past the dockyards now, past the containers waiting to be unloaded. Right below were rows and rows of brightly painted Japanese cars. Then she was off the bridge, on flat land. Exit at Ferry Street, then right on Terminal Way, the community relations man at the prison had told her. You'll see trucks and warehouses. Keep going on to Seaside, then straight. You can't miss it.

———————————

She walked through the compound, across the cement strip, past the garden where vegetables and shasta daisies grew side by side. A guard opened a gate and had her sign an admittance sheet. There was another gate after that one.

"Name?" the guard said.

"Lela Benoit," Lela replied.

———————————

It was almost October, but there were women in T-shirts and strapless dresses, little kids barefoot and fidgeting.

"Are you carrying anything in the bag?" the matron said.

"Nothing."

It was like a doctor's office. Strip down to your panties. Then put on a bathrobe while they check your clothes for smuggled-in weapons or drugs. They didn't do this for everyone, the matron said, just the visitors who came to see the dangerous prisoners.

Dress again. Button the blouse. She wished she had a T-shirt on instead of a blouse so she wouldn't have to fiddle with buttons.

He was waiting for her on his side of the mesh screen, the diamond design making little dark imprints on his face. His hair was short and nearly white. Eyebrows grew up at the sides into his hairline, and his nose, meaty at the tip, was a straight slash of bone.

"Keep your hands away from the mesh," the guard said as she sat down on the bench.

Her handbag was in the visitors' locker. Her clothes had been shaken and examined. Even her hose had been turned inside out in case she had sneaked razor blades into the feet. What in the world could she do to him if she touched the screen with her hands?

"You got the Request to Visit form all right, I see," her father said. His voice startled her. His lips hadn't moved. At least she hadn't seen them move.

"Yes," Lela replied.

The matron who examined her told her he never had any other visitors. Not even at Christmas. Not one in fifteen years. It was a surprise, she said, when Lela's request came in.

She shifted on the bench, crossed her leg, made herself more comfortable. He was so still. Not even a muscle twitch. But she could see him studying her, assessing her.

"You think I'm a lunatic, don't you?"

"I don't know what you are," she said. She felt very small and insecure sitting there. Not like a grown woman. Like a child.

"So you've come to see the beast. Well, look at him. This is the dungeon where the beast is kept. Do you want to shake my cage? Go on, shake it."

She turned away, stared for a moment at the woman at the next bench. Serious conversation, face as close to the mesh as the guard allowed. A row of benches. There was no shortage of benches here.

He was stretching his neck now, looking around. Then he settled his eyes on her again. The overhead light was breaking the gray of his eyes into green-flecked marbles.

"I had a fight with an inmate a while back," he said. "What month is it now?"

"September."

"It was March I had the fight with him. March. Isn't that the one comes in like a lion? He tripped me in line. What's that movie about a man who flies?"

"*Superman.*"

"No. The other one."

"*Batman.*"

"Right. We were waiting in line to see that one, and he tripped me. I don't allow anyone to trip me. I don't allow anyone closer than one foot to me. That's my rule. You come into that one-foot spot, you're mine. Do you have pictures?"

"Of what?"

"Kids. Anyone. I don't care."

"No."

His voice was making her sick. What was it about his voice that was so sickening?

"The prison doc says I've got arthritis in my feet and hands. I told him he's crazy, there's no arthritis anywhere in my family. My mother's dying. Did you see her?"

"Yes."

"I had a brother. Max. It was my dad's kid from another marriage. Max didn't stick around like I did. Smart. Joined the marines when he was eighteen and died at Guadalcanal. Where's Jolene?"

"Up north."

"They said I strangled my second wife. Betty. All I did was give her a hug. Squeezed her too tight, I told them. They didn't believe it. There are a lot of guys in here like me who didn't do what the judge said they did. Innocent as babies. You turned out all right. How's your sister?"

It was as if she had fallen into a pit and was trying to crawl out, but the sides of the pit were like glass.

"You don't talk much, Lela. Cat got your tongue? Your mother talked a lot, I remember that. See, she was stubborn beyond words. There are women like that, who get a notion and stick with it, no matter how hard you try to reason with them. And pretending she was better than I was. If she was so good, why'd she lay down with me in the first place without even being married? 'I never did it before, Donny, I swear.' Shit. She knew how to fuck before I got there. I could tell. She wasn't so pure. Anything I hate more than a liar is a faker, pretending to be something you aren't. I could have put up with it, though. I was putting up with it. Then she let Jolene run away, just let her go, didn't even try to stop her. Well, I can tell you that little girl was better than her mother any day, knew how to please me better than your mother ever did."

She had the mesh in her fingers, was squeezing the metal, could feel the dents the wire was making in her flesh.

"You weren't bad, either, for a little kid. God gave you both to me for my use, and your mother couldn't see it. She killed herself the same as if she'd got the gun and pointed it at her own head."

"Come on, honey, the visit's over." The guard who had brought her through the inner gate into the visitors' section was trying to pry Lela's fingers away from the mesh.

"Now the second wife knew better. But she had a habit of talking out of turn. She'd already buried one husband when I met her."

"You get her on one side, I'll get the other." The matron who had taken Lela's purse and her clothes was pulling at her other arm, trying to get her feet down from the ledge where she was starting to climb the mesh.

"I put her in the trunk of my car and took her to Texas where she was from. San Antonio. I offered her body to her folks, but they didn't want it, so I brought her back to California. They'd never have found me if I hadn't done such a stupid thing as that. I was here for five years and no one thought to look for me right here in California. Working on a ranch on the Irvine spread. Even now, you think they care that your mother's dead, and I might have done it? Hell no. Not saying I did, mind you. But might have. It's the bureaucracy, it can't get anything straight."

There was a third guard there now, and Lela wasn't sure, but there might have even been a fourth. They were trying to tear her apart, pull her arms out of their sockets, everyone trying to take a piece of her for themselves.

"If your mother hadn't said that one last thing she did about getting a divorce, about being glad Jolene got away, there wouldn't have been any problem at all."

"Maybe you ought to tell the warden we have a problem in here with a visitor," one of the guards said.

"The second wife was another case. Your mother obeyed most of the time, most of the time knew her place, but the second one, that was Betty, she was a pistol. I told her, I said, Betty, you disobey me one more time, you're dead, and she didn't believe me. I told her. I warned her. I don't know what more I could have done. God, why don't women believe you when you tell them something?"

"Honey, come down from there," the matron said. Lela could see over the mesh now, see over the top of it, could see the shiny bald spot on her father's head.

"It was a foggy night, and I said you aren't going to town in this fog, and she said then drive me there, and I said you know I can't leave this place, I've got problems with the law, and she said what kind of problems, and I told her it was none of her business, and she said she'd go to town anyway, and if I stopped her she'd call the cops and tell them whatever I did, whatever problem it was, they could come and get me."

"Take him back to his cell, and maybe she'll come down. She's holding so tight I'm afraid we'll hurt her."

"I was pushed into that one, too. Women don't realize how they push men into things. It's so simple to obey. My God, I've got rules the same as any country, any Bible. Know my rules and live by them, I give you no trouble. But pass over that line, get in my face, and you're dead."

"Are you all right, honey?" the matron asked.

"I'm fine," Lela said. They had laid her down in the warden's private lounge. It was like a house here. She could have been in a house anywhere, lying on this green print couch with the ruffly throw pillows. She sat up. They had taken her shoes.

"Where'd my shoes go?"

"Everything's back in a locker in the dressing room waiting for you when you're ready to leave. But you can rest a while longer.

The prison doctor's going to come down and talk to you in a few minutes."

She stood up.

"I'm sorry," she said. "I'm really sorry I caused you all this trouble. Tell the doctor thanks, but I had to leave. It's really an emergency, and I hadn't thought of it before I came, and I shouldn't have just made an appointment and come here without thinking about this other thing I had to do."

"You kind of fainted when we pulled you down off the screen."

"I do that sometimes."

"We've never had anyone try to climb the mesh before. It was quite a sight. We'll be talking about it for a good while, I can tell you that."

"I wanted to kill him, but I didn't have anything to do it with, and if you'd all have cooperated and given me a gun, I wouldn't have had to climb the damn screen in the first place. I'm a good shot. I have a certificate of marksmanship."

She swept past the matron and stood at the closed door.

"Please get my shoes now. I want out of here."

———————————

She caught the Harbor Freeway south to Costa Mesa, to the cemetery where Marilee was buried.

Someone had put a small cement plaque in the ground. "Marilee Benoit, Beloved Wife and Mother, 1930–1965." She was thirty-five years old when she died. A year younger than Lela. What was it like, knowing your husband, the one you loved, the father of your kids, was killing you?

Lela smoothed the plaque with her hand, then sat down and stared at it. Marilee Benoit. She played the organ in church and had a blue bow in her hair with streamers that ran down her back. She called Lela "sweetie" and "honey bunny," and she had soft skin and didn't talk about bad things, ever, but was always happy, always talking to people with a voice so sweet that it sounded like at any moment she was about to sing.

Lela lay down and covered the plaque with her body, put her arms out as though to embrace the grave. She remembered her. How could she not? How could she have forgotten, even for a moment, how much she loved her?

32

"I've been retired since 1978," Mr. Durbin said. He lived in Pasadena, next to the 210 Freeway. He had fruit trees in his yard, and the San Gabriel Mountains, rounded tops nearly obscured by smog, rose up behind his garage as if they were growing out of its roof. "How did you find me, anyhow?"

"You were on microfiche in the superior court records department," Lela said. She was sitting at a rosewood picnic table, going through yellowing, cobwebbed, dirt-spotted packets of stenotype notes. Fruit trees nearly hid the whole rear of the house, and there were rows of wire-fronted hutches full of fluffy white rabbits next to the hedge of eugenia bushes at Lela's back, but the chain-link fence on the freeway side of the lot was bare, and she could see cars speeding by and could hear the buzzing of their tires and smell their exhaust.

"Too bad," Mr. Durbin said. He was plucking oranges from one of his trees and dropping them into a plastic market bag for Lela to take home with her. "Not that I don't like company now and then, but I like to think I never heard of court reporting. I like to think I've been raising rabbits all my life."

Lela had helped Mr. Durbin sort through the bags of clothes and discarded furniture in his garage to get to the cardboard boxes where he had stored the stenotype notes. The two of them then dragged the boxes out onto the grass next to the picnic table beneath the orange trees.

"I don't go to court reporter reunions or picnics or luncheons," Mr. Durbin said.

Some of the note packets had fallen out of their rubber bands and were trailing off the end of the table, unraveling like spools of thread. Lela took off one of her shoes and put it across the loose notes to keep them from flying away.

"I don't go to their funerals, either," Mr. Durbin said. "When I retired, I never thought anyone would find me. I hoped they wouldn't, anyway. Twenty-five years of sitting in the same chair in the same courtroom and banging away at a stenotype machine and wishing I were somewhere else. I was the fastest shorthand writer in Los Angeles in the forties. But I saw those judges looking at me and thinking I wasn't getting everything down, so I went to school and learned the box. I hated it. There was no beauty in it. I wrote classic Gregg, every symbol the way the book taught you. Beautiful. But those twenty-five years of banging that box bored me to death. I've washed my mind of every single hearing I ever reported. I certainly don't remember the one about you."

"I don't either," Lela said. "I guess I was too young."

"Eight isn't too young to remember things. I can remember things as far back as four and a half."

"I just don't remember," Lela said.

She certainly didn't remember Mr. Durbin. But how could she have forgotten someone as tall as he was? His head would have been higher than anyone else's, even sitting down. And that tic, did he have that tic when he was taking notes in that courtroom in 1965? Did his head snap to the side every few seconds the way it did now? She tried to imagine him younger, with dark hair and no tic, wearing a suit and tie and clacking away at a stenotype machine, but all she saw was a tall old man in tan slacks and a golf sweater who needed to trim the hairs in his nose.

The superior court clerk had told Lela there never were any transcripts made of the custody hearings unless someone requested one for some reason. No one had requested one. But the final order showed that the proceedings had been reported, and as far as the records went, they showed that the court reporter was still alive. Cecil Durbin. He retired to Pasadena, she told Lela. That's in the foothills near the Rose Bowl—you know, where the New Year's parade is every year, where the car exhaust gets trapped below the mountains and you're not supposed to breathe the air. He'd know about hearings in 1965, she said.

"My name was Lela Benoit then," Lela said. She handed Mr. Durbin a stack of notes from the pile to her left, the ones she hadn't gone through yet. "The Binghams were petitioning for custody. I just want to know what happened, who was there, who might have objected."

"Well, here's one for June 1965. They're all mixed up. I didn't think anyone would ever want to see any of this mess again. Most reporters don't keep tapes longer than five years. I just hate to throw things away. June, June. I can see I was certainly busy in June. God, it's awful to think I sat in that chair in that courtroom and churned this stuff out and don't even remember any of it. I might have been out that day and there was a pro tem in my place. That could have happened, too. I don't think there's even a record anymore of my sick days in 1965 or whether I had any pro tems sit in on any hearings. I don't think they keep records like that."

"Bingham was the petitioner."

He started flipping through the tapes. "Staten. That isn't it. McBride."

"Bingham."

Lela could see how expert he must have been at one time, slapping the tapes down on the picnic table and tucking the fragile paper just so in the fingers of his right hand while he scanned fold after fold.

"Bingham?" he said.

"Do you have it?"

"Walter and Kathy Bingham, Petitioners, Superior Court Case Number SOC 389465."

Lela got up and walked around to the other side of the picnic table and looked over Mr. Durbin's shoulder. She couldn't make out anything that was on the stenotype tape, just odd combinations of letters, but she kept looking at it anyway, hoping something would pop out at her, something that would make sense, that she would recognize.

"It looks like an ordinary custody hearing to me," Mr. Durbin said. "Here's the psychiatrist. His testimony. Okay. The child is immature, he says." He was going through the folds rapidly now. "Child welfare worker off the stand. Okay. Walter Bingham on the stand now. BB for Bingham. I always gave everyone arbitraries, something I made up out of their name—like BB for Bingham—so it'll stand out if I have to read back. So it's BB on the stand. There's JJ—that's for the judge—well, all I see is the normal stuff. BB is saying something about the social worker said the Binghams were trying to replace someone."

"They had a daughter who died."

"Right. Trying to replace their daughter. JJ—that's the judge—he thought that was okay, so that's that part."

"No one objected?"

"Can't see any objections. Oh, yes, here it is. LEV LEV. That must be the attorney for the child. She objected."

"Did the judge ask anything about where my real family was, why they weren't there?"

"Let's see. BB, JJ, BB, LEV LEV—okay—nothing there, argue, argue— Hmm."

"What?"

"Here's something funny."

"What?"

"Someone came into the courtroom." Mr. Durbin was reading the tape now as if it were interesting. "Judge Feinberg tried to shoo her out. Told her she was in the wrong courtroom. She said she wasn't. The little girl said something."

"The little girl. That's me. What did she say?"

Mr. Durbin hesitated, pondering, his juice-wet finger right on the spot. "She said 'Jolene.' No, she didn't say it exactly that way. She said, 'That's Jolene.' "

"Spaghetti. My favorite," Deborah said. She was eating lunch, sitting sideways at the table, her legs up on the chair next to her. "You are the best cook, Lillian. What's that spice I taste in the meatballs?"

"Oregano," Lillian said. She moved around Lela's kitchen as though it were hers, talked to Deborah as though she were her mother. Indulgently. Sweetly. When she wasn't cooking, washing, cleaning, or putting away, she was knitting an afghan for the new baby. She kept the yarn and needles in a cotton drawstring bag that she hung on the knob of the kitchen door.

"No, that's not it," Deborah said. "I know oregano when I taste it."

"Basil."

"Right. Basil."

"I've decided to go back up north," Lela said.

"Whatever for?" Deborah broke stride momentarily, held her fork with the hanging strands of spaghetti away from her mouth.

"I'm going to see if I can help Jolene."

"Jolene? That's the craziest thing I ever heard. She tried to kill you."

"She only wanted Sandy back. She wasn't going to kill me."

"How do you know that? Do you know that? This is so crazy, Lela. You don't even know her." She slid the spaghetti expertly from the fork into her mouth. "Anyway, I need you here."

"Lillian's with you."

"But you just got back." She was eating more slowly now.

"I know it, and I wouldn't leave if I didn't have to."

"But I'm really frightened on this pregnancy, Lela. My legs are as big as tree trunks. They were never like this before."

Deborah put the fork down, and Lela could tell by the way she was looking at the wall next to the refrigerator, her eyes fixed on the same empty spot, that she was making a list in her mind, thinking of things to say that would make Lela do what she wanted. "Rowena's got three babies to take care of," she finally said, "and me over here lying on my back like a lump because I have a soft cervix and balloon legs, and Brad working so hard to support us all he can't even think straight. You can't leave me now. You'll just have to change your plans. You don't owe this Jolene anything. What has she ever done for you? What could be more important to you right now than this baby? You know how you love Jason and the twins, how you were when they were born, taking pictures every day, buying things for them. And if this is a girl, you'll love her even more. You can take her to ballet lessons and design pretty dresses for her. You remember the fabric you designed for me that I had made into a dress and took on my honeymoon and everyone said where in the world did you get that dress, I want one exactly like it?"

"I'll be back when you have the baby, Deborah. I promised you, and I will. What you need to do is what you've been doing, to stay off your feet. I can go up north, and you can still do that. My leaving won't prevent you from lying down until the baby's born."

"But I've made my sonogram appointment with the doctor for next week. You can't go away when I need you for my sonogram."

"Brad can go with you."

"You're the one I want with me. Brad's a man, he doesn't know, he doesn't care. He didn't even want this baby."

"I'll go," Lillian said. She picked up her yarn bag now and sat down at the table and began slipping streams of blue and pink yarn over and under the steel needles, over and under.

"You're always delegating, Lela," Deborah said. She had started twirling spaghetti around her fork again and eating steadily. "Always going off and leaving someone behind to do what you should be doing. And now you're putting the burden on Lillian when she's got enough to do for me as it is watching me swell without having to go with me to get my sonogram, too.

"The problem with you, Lela, is that you're not ever satisfied with anything for very long. That's why you got a divorce. You've always been changeable. I'm not criticizing you now, so don't get angry at me." She glanced at Lela's face as if there were a gauge there to tell her if she was saying too much. "I'm just saying that if you'd stay in one place for a little while, you'd find someone to make babies with, too, and won't have to be always running after other people's."

Deborah's voice hummed in Lela's ears, one moment wheedling, the next moment instructive. It wasn't an even voice, without emotion, like Mr. Durbin's. He had lifted all those plain words off of the yellowing notes with the straightest voice Lela had ever heard, saying them as if they weren't words at all, but symbols of something he didn't understand and didn't want to understand. He had read the whole custody hearing out loud in that flat, straight voice, sitting at the picnic table in his yard, reading and eating oranges, and Lela crying all the way through.

"You know, Lela," Deborah was saying, "the mistake you made was in opening that can of worms in the first place, going around and talking to all those people who didn't want you when you were a kid and don't want you now."

"Jolene wanted me," Lela said.

"What?"

"Jolene tried to get custody of me when I was eight years old. But she was too young. Just seventeen. Can you imagine, Deb, a seventeen-year-old wanting to have custody of a child, not thinking a bit about herself, about what it means to take responsibility for someone else's life, but just worrying what was going to happen to her sister? Seventeen. Well, she didn't get custody, and if she had, I wouldn't be sitting here. We wouldn't be having this conversation."

"What's that supposed to mean?"

"It just means that I'm going to go and see if I can't help her out of the mess she's in. She needs someone to care for her, someone she can depend on. I've asked Brad to list the house. I'll need money if I'm not going to work for a while."

"You're going to sell your house? I don't believe it."

"If it's sold before the baby's born, you won't be able to stay here, of course. You'll just have to go home and stay in bed there. Rowena's very capable, and I'm sure Lillian won't mind spending time with you there, cooking, knitting, keeping you company."

"I don't mind at all," Lillian said.

"But she's a dope addict," Deborah said. "What in the world do you know about dope addicts?"

"I know you get upset with the kids," Lela said, "and that's not good for you, but they'll be quiet if you're firm with them. And Jason will pick up his toys if you're consistent. Reward him when he cleans up after himself. Put him in his room when he doesn't. He'll soon get into the rhythm of things. The trouble with you, Deborah, is you don't follow through. And he doesn't have to play ball in the house or write on the walls if you take the balls and the crayons away from him until he learns to be civilized. You just can't expect children to know what you want without telling them."

Deborah looked around her now, and it wasn't as if she had even heard what Lela said, but that she had just discovered she was sitting at the wrong table in the wrong house, that she had mistakenly opened someone else's door.

"It's about time to think about what we're going to have for dinner," Lillian said.

33

THE ROAD INTO Cazadero was flooded, highway patrol cars parked to the north and south of the washed-out stretch of road. Lela could see a patrolman at the head of the line of cars she was in flagging people down, talking into side windows, then standing back and pointing his arm back in the direction of Guerneville, turning everyone around, away from the river of water sloshing across the road and into the trees. There was a line of cars, disembodied headlights piercing the afternoon's wet gloom, on the other side of the water, their drivers wanting to get across to where Lela was. A patrolman was turning them around one by one, pointing them toward the coast, toward Jenner.

"One sixteen's closed," the patrolman said when Lela reached the head of the line. "Where are you heading?"

"Austin Creek," Lela said.

"Can't."

He started to stand back, began to raise his arm to point her in the direction of Guerneville, when she said, "I'm sick. I need to get to Dr. McGowan's place on Austin Creek."

He leaned back in the window, the sleeves of his rain slicker splashing icy darts of water in her face.

"Really sick?"

"Really sick."

Cars were backing up behind her now.

"Go back up a few miles," he said. "The service road may still be open. Take the bridge over and look for a dirt road. Any road."

———————————

Lela once told Gil about a dream she had. In the dream she was in a car going up a road into the mountains, and a man was driving, and there were circles of gray, crusty snow embracing the trunks of the trees and glitteringly white snow clinging to their needled branches.

In her dream she kept looking up at the trees and wondering why they grew up instead of down. Her father was driving, and they had left her mother behind in a puddle of blood, and there was a girl with bright eyes and curly brown hair who kept telling Lela to wait, that she'd come back for her. Gil said he could give her any dreams she wanted. They don't mean a thing, he said. They're just thieves that will rob you of sanity if you believe them.

———

There was no one on the road. Just the bridge ahead, glistening in the steady downpour, the river racing by beneath it, logs and twigs caught on the rocks. Along the banks the water moved fitfully, seeking quiet in dark, stagnant pools. In the center of the river the water was turbulent, leaping up in little waterspouts, moving fast, a train of water gulping rain and rising.

———

"You were crazy, driving over that bridge, coming out here in weather like this," Ross said.

"I told Daddy you were coming," Sandy said. She was jumping around, first hugging Lela, then jumping some more. "I said, Daddy, you wait, Lela won't forget us, and you didn't. Look at her, Daddy. She's here. I told you."

———

"I kept saying to myself, What the hell, who cares if she comes back or not. Life goes on. But it didn't. I've been holding my breath the whole time you were away."

His legs were warm against hers, and everything in the room felt right. The hard bed, the lumpy pillows, the quilts that smelled faintly of formaldehyde. And when he slipped inside her, it felt right, too, as if he belonged there, and she couldn't even think clearly, the sensation was so sweet, so hard and sweet. All of it just right, nothing between them but moist skin, warm bellies, his penis inside her, pushing through her reserve, her fears, joining that intimate spot she had never let anyone enter before. Not really enter. Not with her permission, with her wanting them to. Never before thrilling, as she was now, to the sound of a man's voice telling her how much he loved her.

———

The bridge held, but all along the bank and around the cabin the water rose.

"I hope it stays this way forever," Lela said.

"It won't," Ross said. He was at the bedroom window, watching the water. "When it rains steady like this, the creek goes wild. We once had twenty-two inches in a twenty-four-hour period. Coming over that bridge it could have gone out with you on it. It's happened before. The river can rise up so fast you don't know what hit you. In fifty-five it rose to forty-nine feet. Washed out a string of cabins and took the bridge with it. Took the flooring right out of this cabin, they tell me. I didn't think you were coming back. Why did you come back, Lela?"

He was framed there in the window, lean torso, slim hips, the long clutch of hair caught in a strip of leather.

"Everything went so wrong," she said. "For a long time I couldn't figure what I could have done differently. I kept thinking it's all my fault. A sick empty feeling, as if I'd gone off and left something burning on the stove or forgot to turn the water off in the bathtub, and it's flooding the house, drowning everyone inside."

He turned toward her. "My God, you came back because of Jolene. It wasn't me or Sandy at all. It was Jolene."

"All the years I was having it easy, she was suffering, and I'm going to fix it. I'm going to help her."

"Jesus Christ," he said.

Lela was getting ready to leave, was standing at the cabin door, her suitcase on the porch. She had waited for Ross to say he knew how she felt, that he'd help her, he'd do whatever he could, they'd save Jolene together, turn her around, make her whole. But he had watched her dress, lain in bed and watched her, hadn't spoken through breakfast at all. All that coldness in him, that anger. She'd known he'd be that way. Everyone but Gil had been that way. Sweet until you let them know who you were, what you wanted, what you thought. And then they got the look that Ross had right now, arms folded as if he were trying to keep from hitting her. She had been waiting for that look, and there it was.

"Jolene was here," Ross said. "You don't have to go running around Sonoma County looking for her." She turned toward him. The water was receding, just a cold drizzle left behind, and Sandy was down by the riverbank, calling for her cat. Lela could hear her childish voice calling over and over, "Misty, where are you, Misty?"

"Jolene was here?"

"She showed up here one day stoned, said she'd used the month's pension money and had gotten thrown out of the place she was staying. Her boyfriend's still in jail, so she wasn't getting the stuff from him. Normally, I would have sent her packing—the best, most honest thing to do with someone who doesn't want to be sober. But I could see she hadn't been eating much, wasn't taking care of herself, and Sandy was . . . well, you were gone, and Jolene was here, even in as bad shape as she was, she's the kid's mother, so I said okay, you can stay here for a while.

"But I'm no one's fool, I've seen it all. I know when someone's using and when they're not. She was using the whole time she was here. Injecting. Go fast, she calls it. 'I've got to have my go fast, Ross,' she said. Her arms were like pincushions. I don't know where she was hiding the stuff, but she was keeping herself high, and it was upsetting Sandy, and I didn't want that, she's been upset enough by her, so I said that's it, no more, and I gave her some money and told her to go."

"You threw her out? Just like that?"

"Don't get all soppy on me, Lela. You think you know things, but you don't. You think you're going to patch up your past by saving Jolene, but you're not. Jolene's responsible for herself. She's a junkie. I was one, and I know how they are. You want to know what it'll be like if you try and help her? Right after a binge she'll seem all right, and you'll look at her and think, Hey, she's beat the devil, pushed back the ocean, drained the bucket. Cured. And she'll feel that way, too. Like no one can touch her or tempt her. She'll feel safe. Smug. It's easy to feel that way when you're still wired for sound, when the stuff's still lurking somewhere inside you, keeping you even. But that won't last long. When the body starts sucking air and crying gimme, you'll do anything you can to put something in it, anything to make it purr again."

"Where is she now?"

"For a while she was just crashing anywhere she could, but that got old. There was a resort in the highlands at Black Rock Creek where the fags used to hang out. There was a summer music camp up there, too. Little cabins for the students to live in. That was in the sixties. The resort was fire-bombed in the seventies, and all the cabins in the music camp burned up. Except for one not far from the bird camp in Austin Creek Park. You want to save her? Well, I won't have any part of it. I won't have any part of you if you try. I mean it, Lela. I love you, and I want you here with me. But if you go after her, that's it. I'm finished. Because Jolene's a holey sack. You can put everything you've got in the top, and it'll just run out the bottom."

34

THE ROAD WAS covered in snow. To the right of the road was a frozen pond, a sleek sheet of silver. It was cold here, much colder than Cazadero had been. Lela stopped the car, then went around to the trunk and got out her suitcase. She pulled galoshes on over her shoes and mittens on her hands and began to walk. She couldn't be sure, of course, but it seemed that what looked like black toothpicks sticking up out of the snow must be the charred remains of the summer music camp.

There was no smoke coming out of the chimney, and the door had icicles clinging to its hinges, but Jolene's white car was sitting a few yards away, snow up to its windows.

Lela knocked at the door, then took off her mittens and knocked again, this time giving the peeling wood a sharp rap with her bare knuckles. There was no sound from inside, and she was really feeling the cold now. Her slacks, wet with snow, had begun to freeze and felt like dozens of icy forks stabbing at her legs. She pulled at the door, but it was locked.

"Jolene."

Maybe Jolene had gone off in someone else's car and left hers behind. Lela stamped her feet on the wooden floor of the cabin's porch and slapped at her shoulders with her arms, then went down the steps and around to the back of the cabin where the snow had drifted against the splintery logs nearly to the roof in places. The single window in back was up high, out of reach. Lela climbed on top of a rusting garbage can and then stepped onto a plastic-sheeted stack of firewood beneath the window, clung to the shifting wood, and looked inside. It was a bedroom, and there was a bed in it heaped with blankets.

"Jolene!"

The blankets moved slightly. Or was it her breath thawing the ice on the frosted window that made it appear they had moved? She rubbed at the window with her bare hand, tried to blow the distortions away with her breath.

They had moved. She was sure they had. She pounded on the window, let her body fall against it as she pounded, made a bridge from the pile of wood to the cabin wall with her arms and legs as she pounded.

"Jolene!"

She felt herself falling, was about to fall, when Jolene sat up, gaunt eyed, and saw her there.

"My God, it's as cold in here as it is outside," Lela said. "I'll have a fire going in a minute."

Jolene had draped a blanket around her and was standing uncomprehending, staring at Lela.

"At least the wood isn't wet," Lela said. She didn't look at Jolene as she piled the wood onto the grate. The smell of her was awful. Even in the clean cold of the cabin Lela could smell her.

"Don't touch my house," Jolene said. "This is my house, mine." Her eyelids were going up and down, sliding toward her cheeks suddenly, then jerking up again. "Don't touch my house, my fireplace, my wood, I said."

"I'm not going to let you freeze, so keep quiet."

The place was a disaster, a filthy mess. Jolene was sitting on the floor now, cross-legged on the blanket, shivering, struggling with her eyelids and swaying from side to side.

"Do you have anything I can fix for you to eat?"

"Don't touch anything, I said. It's mine, everything's mine, and I know where every goddamn thing is in the world, in this house, in this place, in this shitty cabin, in this room . . ." Her voice trailed off.

The kitchen was a four-by-four square off the main room of the cabin. Trash, empty liquor bottles, wads of Kleenex, dirty rags, were in the sink, on the floor, on the small oak table, on the single rickety chair. Lela started tossing everything that was on the cracked kitchen counter into one of the empty plastic buckets she found stacked on the table: a rat-gnawed stale loaf of bread, moldy cheese, a few bananas that had turned black and hard, plastic bags of white powder, brown-stained plastic spoons.

"Those buckets are Chick's buckets," Jolene said. "You ruin Chick's buckets, he'll ruin you when he gets out, I promise he will." She flailed her arms as though trying to reach across the room and hit Lela. "Chick's no one to fool with, I mean it. I told you I mean it. I do."

"I'm sure you do."

"What are you doing with my go fast? You give me my go fast."

"No more go fast," Lela said. "It's in the garbage."

"Nooo!" Jolene was on her knees, head down, wailing.

There were canned soups and vegetables in the cupboards, some of them so old the labels had crinkled to brownish parchment. But no dishes to wash. It looked as though no food had been eaten or prepared in the kitchen for a long time. Water trickled out of the corroded faucet when she turned the handle, but no light came on when she flipped the switch on the wall.

Jolene was flat on the floor now, had wrapped her feet in the blanket, covered her face with it. She wasn't wailing anymore.

"Jolene."

There was no answer. Lela bent down and held her face close to hers. The source of the smell was in Jolene's hair, in her mouth. That would be next. Melt snow and boil it and wash all the smells away. Lela picked her up in her arms. It was easy. As easy as picking up a child. Blanket and all, she hardly weighed anything, probably less than ninety pounds. Eighty-five pounds, at the most. And she wasn't moving. She was limp, eyes closed. Asleep. Or unconscious. As Lela laid her down on the bed and piled the blankets over her, Jolene mumbled something. So she wasn't dead.

It was like taking care of a baby, except that this one was toilet trained. Jolene could get up and stagger to the bathroom, which was little more than a closet with a commode and corroded stall shower in it, then stagger back to the bed and go to sleep.

"Come on, eat the soup while it's hot," Lela said. "I heated it especially for you. It took me an hour to figure out how a wood stove works, and you better eat it."

"I don't want any." Jolene's words came slowly, bubbling their way up out of some deep, overwhelming sleepiness. It was evening now, a whole day gone, and Jolene's mood was different from what it had been when Lela arrived. No more railing about her go fast, about what she had had to do to get it, about how no one should have to do what she had had to do to get it. No more rambling on about Chick, about his buckets, about what he was going to do to Lela when he got out of jail, about how he was going to shoot her, kill her, murder her. She had run down, not gradually, the way a windup toy does, but suddenly, the way a car does when there's not a drop of gas left in it. She gave Lela no resistance when she gave her the sponge bath, didn't say the water was too warm or too hot, didn't say the soap was in her eyes when Lela poured water over her head and scrubbed at her scalp. Didn't say anything. And she made no sound when Lela pulled a clean nightgown out of her suitcase and put it on her, was barely even conscious by the time Lela put her on a chair and cleaned the trash from around the bed and stripped the dirty sheets from the mattress.

"Open your mouth a little wider, Jolene. I can't get the spoon in if you don't open up."

She was thinner than when Lela had seen her in the courtroom the month before, her bones so near the surface of her skin that Lela thought she could see the whiteness showing through.

Each spoonful dribbled half down Jolene's chin.

"You haven't even eaten a thimbleful of soup," Lela said. "You'll never get your strength back unless you eat."

"What the hell are you talking about?" Jolene said.

———————————

For a week Jolene slept steadily. There was a stack of old Ellery Queen mysteries beside the bed and Lela read them all while Jolene slept. How could any one man be as clever as Ellery Queen? He could tell a phony just by listening to a man talk, could spot a grifter by the tilt of a man's hat on his head, could see a con game forming a mile away. The books weren't very good. Dated. Men wearing hats? And what in the hell was a grifter? But she read them anyway. To kill time and because it made her feel good reading the same books that Jolene had read. It was like getting inside Jolene's mind in some way.

When she wasn't reading, she'd sit out on the steps of the cabin and watch the weather, try to figure out by the shape of the clouds and the color of the sky when it was going to rain. And she kept a pot of soup cooking on the stove in case Jolene woke up and said she was hungry. And every hour she'd go into the bedroom and lie down beside Jolene on that dirty mattress and listen to the breaths Jolene took, try to measure the length of the pauses against the beat of her own heart.

At the end of the week, during a night in which rain beat so hard on the roof of the cabin that shingles fell off in places and water dripped through right onto their heads, Jolene opened her eyes and looked at Lela in startled comprehension.

"Are you still here?"

"I'm still here."

Jolene yawned. "You always were stubborn," she said.

"Kids used to stay here and play music," Jolene said. "I found piles of sheet music when I first got here. Thousands of pages with little black marks and dots on them, little notes all over the paper. Slow down. Speed up. Don't rush. Loud. Soft. It seems no one could make up their mind how to do anything. I threw everything away." She was sitting at the table, sipping a cup of soup, eyes bright, focused, the stupor gone. Except for her extreme thinness and a strange air of detachment, she looked healthy. "Did you ever wonder about me?"

"I didn't remember you at all until a few months ago," Lela said.

"I remember how you used to eat a banana. You'd bite it round and round till it looked like a flute. Then you'd throw it away. Mama always said you were the most original eater she ever saw. Do you remember Glenn?"

"I remember a long trip in a car, and a boy was driving."

"That was Glenn. The army sent him back to me in a little box. Hardly bigger than a shoebox. His folks said, 'It's a good thing you had no kids. At least you had no kids.' I was a widow at twenty-two. I hardly remember Glenn now, it was so long ago. He was a good guy, but he just didn't understand. Went to Vietnam without understanding a damn thing about anything. When those people went to court to get you, he said, 'Let them take her, what are you going to do with her, you're just a kid yourself?' And I said, 'You don't understand a thing about it, you don't know what we know, what we've been through, what the hell do you know?' Did I tell you they sent him home to me in a black box? No, it was white. A white metal box, like one of those safes they give you in the bank. He was just a kid when they mailed him back to me. I wouldn't even look inside that box to see what he looked like all burned up. He had blue eyes when he was alive, the prettiest blue, bluer than a blue sky, nothing but blue skies. I didn't know what I was supposed to do with those ashes. There weren't any instructions with them, so I thought about sending the whole box to his folks, but I didn't know how to mail it, what you were supposed to wrap a box of ashes in, and so they hung around and hung around, and every time I moved I put them in the suitcase with my underwear, and then one time I ended up in Oceanside in some guy's apartment and the ashes were gone. Then I started getting checks because I was a war widow, and I forgot all about the ashes. I forgot all about Glenn."

Lela could see little tears like shiny rhinestones sticking to the ends of Jolene's eyelashes.

"You remember me in the courtroom with my cowboy boots on? Shit. I forget where I lost those boots. They had nail studs in them set by hand. Like a jeweler would do it. Expensive boots. I wish I had them now, I could sell them for some go fast. But the judge said I was too young, and it's a good thing, too, because Glenn's dead, and I'm a junkie, and I'm always sorry for everything and never do a damn thing to change."

"I once showed a house to a couple," Lela said, "and they loved it and wanted to buy it, but the wife said, 'We can't buy this house. I can't get my bedroom set into the bedroom.' And I said, 'It isn't the end of the world. I'll figure out a way.' So I bought the bedroom set from them and they bought the house. But the point is that there was a way. There always is, Jolene. There's always a way."

"You shouldn't have taken Sandy away from me, Lela. She was all I had."

"No, she wasn't," Lela said. "You have me."

35

THEY LEFT THE cabin at the end of the week, and Jolene didn't even ask Lela where they were going. She just got in the car and shut her eyes and let Lela drive.

"I thought sure the road would never open up," Lela said, "that the storm was going to last forever." She was driving at a steady speed, as though she had a destination. "I suppose that's a normal feeling when you're in the middle of a storm and the skies are dark; it feels like nothing's ever going to change. You should have seen it, Jolene. Cars lined up. Police directing traffic. You couldn't even get to the coast from Cazadero. We might never have gotten out if it had kept raining and the bridge went under. I suppose we could have hiked out through the mountains, but my sense of direction is kind of shaky and I've never been much of a hiker."

They were going through a town now, Monte Rio, the sign said, population 1170. A small main street with a few shops. The street needed repaving, the signs on the stores were faded. Jolene opened her eyes and sat up.

"So do you feel like throwing away what you're wearing and getting some new clothes?" Lela said.

"I don't care," Jolene replied.

The store said "Women's Fashions and Sundries" but carried mostly rubber rafts and beach umbrellas. Some tables at the rear held folded jeans and sweaters.

"Don't you love this weather after all that rain?" the owner of the store said. There were no salespeople, just the owner and a young girl restocking cosmetics in the glass cases beneath the hanging beach umbrellas.

"It sure is a break," Lela said. "I never thought it'd let up. What size do you wear, Jolene?"

"Six, I think," Jolene said.

"You are tiny, aren't you," the woman said. "Well, help yourself. There's a dressing room behind the curtain. Rafts are half price. Stock up for the summer."

There were no size sixes. Everything was too big. Jolene started trying on jeans and sweaters. Pant waists stood stiffly away from her body and seats bagged out. None of the sweaters fit her, either, but sagged at the neck, exposing the sharp outline of her shoulder blades. And the sleeves hung down over her wrists and nearly covered her fingers.

"You need a children's store," the woman said. "I haven't got anything smaller."

"Where's the nearest children's store?" Lela asked her.

"A ten is fine, Lela, really," Jolene said. "I like my clothes loose. I don't want to shop anymore."

From Monte Rio Lela drove west on 116. She felt good driving, holding the wheel steady, glancing at the speedometer and the gas gauge, watching the signs as though she cared what they said about exits and towns. None of that was important. Heading somewhere, doing something constructive, was what was important. Just putting distance between where she had found Jolene and where they might end up could cure everything.

When they reached the coast, she turned north and drove along the beach. There was no sand here, just a layer of multicolored shells that in the sunlight sparkled like a blanket of sapphires.

At Jenner she stopped at a gas station.

"Do you need to use the rest room?" she said.

"Not really."

"Well, why don't you come in with me, anyway? We may not find another rest room for quite a few miles."

Jolene stood near the sinks while Lela used the toilet.

"Isn't it funny how everyone talks about the weather?" Lela said from behind the closed stall door. "Who was it said everyone talks about the weather but no one does anything about it? He was so right. You'd think there'd be other things people could talk about, things in the newspaper or on television or— Jolene, are you there?"

"I'm here," Jolene said. "And I won't run away if you leave me in the car next time we stop. I promise."

When they were driving again Jolene hardly spoke. She didn't seem angry or sad, just apathetic. They stopped at Sea Ranch for lunch. Lela had a hamburger. Jolene ordered a bowl of clam chowder and didn't even pick up the spoon, but stared out the window at the ocean.

"At least eat your crackers," Lela said, and Jolene pulled the plastic off one of the packets and set the crackers down beside the soup bowl.

"What do you think of these?" Lela said. She had picked up some brochures at the reception desk. Sea Ranch Condos. Two stories, gray wood siding, sundecks facing the water, spas.

Jolene barely glanced at the pictures. "Very pretty."

"We'll take her soup," Lela told the waiter. "Maybe she'll feel like eating it later."

When they left the dining room they walked down the path to the bluffs above the beach. The ledge was rock hard and fissured where the sea had once carved its way onto the land.

"When my house sells, I'll buy a place for us," Lela said. "Something pretty. Not too big, not too small. Built-ins in the kitchen, but I won't be stubborn if something great comes our way without them. I'm pretty realistic about real estate. I don't let myself get seduced by appearances. If the house is a bargain, I don't quibble about whether the appliances are new or old or whether the kitchen needs remodeling. The main thing is if the house is bolted to the foundation and the pipes aren't too old to run water through. Near the beach, though. It'll have to be near the beach. On the sand, if possible, although prices really shoot up when you get that kind of access. Still, I think it's worth it, don't you? I've always loved being able to look at the ocean. Even when I'm not looking at it, I like to know it's there."

The breeze was blowing hard off the ocean and wrapping the legs of Jolene's jeans around her thin legs.

"I'm really nervous, Lela, really nervous," Jolene said. She was trembling. "Nervous and afraid at the same time."

"Oh, honey," Lela said, and put her arm around Jolene's shoulder. There was hardly enough shoulder to grasp, and it folded up against Lela's side as if there were no fat to cushion the bones or keep them from being crushed. "I told you we'd do this together, and I meant it."

"That's not what I'm afraid of. It's being me without anything added. I don't know about this life, what to do with it, how to act. I watch you and you know who you are. I see other people. Like the ones in the restaurant, eating their meals, not thinking about anything special, and they know what to do, how to act. They know who they are. Sometimes I think I remember myself the way I was a long time ago, and I try to catch it, try to trap it in my head, but it won't stay, it just goes away. That girl I was just goes away, Lela."

"We'll keep driving," Lela said. "We've got the whole country left to drive in. We don't have to buy a place on the ocean. We don't have to buy a place anywhere. We can just float across the United States, doing what we please, staying where we want. We can do that for as long as it takes, Jolene. We can go to the desert. Or how about the East Coast? Maine. Lots of beautiful trees and flowers in Maine and not many people. How about that, Jolene, does that sound like something you'd like to do? I've got enough money to take us anywhere we want to go."

"I just don't want you to think I'm going to run away the first chance I get," Jolene said. "You pick the direction and the place. I don't care where it is. I'm hollowed out, Lela, empty, so it doesn't matter. Plant me in the dirt, for all I care. You can light in one spot and I'll be there in the morning, or you can keep driving and I'll stay with you. I won't take off or do anything stupid, because I know when I'm being given a chance, and you're giving me one, and I don't deserve it, and I'm so ashamed I could die that you saw me in the shape you did, and I'll prove to you that I'm strong enough to be good and stay good and never be bad again."

That was when Lela turned the car around and headed back toward Guerneville.

"Like I say, the downstairs apartment is good if you can't walk stairs, but this one's a bit more private, being upstairs and at the end of the hall," the manager said. His name was Paxton. People call me Pat, he said, even though my first name is Bob. He was standing near the door, waiting for Lela and Jolene to make up their minds, emptying coins from one hand to the other impatiently. "They're both vacant now, but they might not be tomorrow," he said.

The apartment was reasonable, as apartments in Guerneville went. This one was in a converted hunting lodge not far from the banks of the Russian River and had two couches that turned into beds.

"You better grab now when the grabbing's good," Pat said. He had a full beard and was in overalls and looked like he could have been one of the hunters who had once occupied the place. "The minute the weather warms up, the fags will be piling in here in full stream, and then you'll be out of luck. So which one is it, this one or downstairs?"

"Which one do you like, Jolene?" Lela asked.

"I like them both," Jolene replied.

"The couches are cleaner in the downstairs one," Pat said. "This one up here they used to cook a lot and the grease settled on the couches. They're not dirty enough to throw away yet. But the Coke machine's on this floor. You'll have to drag your groceries up, though, unless I'm around, and I'm not always. If you take the upstairs, you can hear the floor on the balcony squeaking even with the door locked, so you'll know if someone's coming, so that's an advantage, but if you have kids coming in, there's nothing between here and the first floor except that rail, and they could fall through, so that's something you can think about. But you've got no one clomping their shoes on your head like you have if you take the first floor. I myself would take this one, but that's my personal taste."

"We'll come down in a minute and let you know," Lela said. When Pat left, he closed the door behind him, and Lela could hear the floor squeaking on the balcony, just as he said she would.

"Should we take this one?" Lela said.

"Well, it's nice," Jolene said.

There was a portable stove in the tiny kitchen and a single cabinet that stood on the floor next to the sink. There was no room for a table and chairs, but someone had built a crude bar out of plywood. It was fastened to the wall next to the bathroom door and had two tall knotty pine stools standing in front of it.

"I want you to be comfortable," Lela said.

"I'm comfortable," Jolene said.

"You can see the redwoods from the window if we take this one," Lela said. "Then again, if we take the downstairs apartment, we'll be able to see the rhododendrons."

Jolene was peering out the window now, leaning on the windowsill. "Well, the trees are nice," she said, trying to sound enthusiastic.

"Which one do you like better?"

"I like them both."

"You pick it, Jolene. Either one is fine with me."

Jolene turned around. "Oh, Lela, can't you see how hard I'm concentrating? I'm trying to think of redwoods and rhododendrons and upstairs apartments or downstairs ones, and all I really want to do is get some go fast. You won't abandon me, will you, Lela? You won't give up on me, will you?"

"Never," Lela said.

Lela left Jolene in the lobby, with its log walls and dusty lamps and old magazines, and went into Pat's office.

"We'll take the upstairs apartment," she told him.

"Two and a quarter a week, two weeks in advance, fifty dollar cleanup fee, nonrefundable," Pat said. "There's a Washeteria down the street. If you need a phone, you can call in here free for local calls, but not too many or I'll have to charge you. No eating in the lobby, no leaving garbage around." He had a small TV going, and he was searching for a key on the pegboard behind his desk. "Has she been sick?" He motioned through his office door toward Jolene, whose small figure was nearly lost in the cushions of a cracked leather couch. "Lot of sick people coming up here nowadays. She isn't contagious, is she? TB? AIDS?"

"Oh, nothing like that," Lela replied.

Lela tried to make every day different. Some days they would drive up to the Armstrong Redwoods State Reserve and hike for a while and then picnic beneath the trees. Or they'd go over to the Russian River and rent a canoe. They went to Fort Ross one day and toured the museum there, and Jolene was so fascinated by the story of the Russian settlement that when they went into the store just outside the fort, she said she'd like a set of the little Russian dolls that nested one inside the other. Lela bought her one, and Jolene held it in her hands all the way back to Guerneville, taking the dolls apart and putting them together again. Lela wanted to ask her what she was feeling, what she was thinking. Was she feeling better? Was this the kind of therapy she needed to get well? But just looking at Jolene, she could see how fragile she still was and how hard she was fighting. It seemed to Lela that whatever delicate mechanism was holding Jolene together would fly apart if she asked her anything.

36

JOLENE USUALLY TOOK her shower before Lela did. It was a routine they had settled into. Lela would hear the shower running, and then she'd look at the clock. It was always six-thirty when Jolene got up, not a minute earlier or later. Then Lela would get up and pour some orange juice into a glass for Jolene and make some toast and butter it. She'd set the four vitamins on the plate beside the toast. Vitamin C, vitamin E, betacarotene, and calcium. By the time that was done, Jolene was out of the shower and it was Lela's turn.

This morning Lela hadn't heard the shower, and when she woke up, the clock radio on the bar next to the kitchen said eight-thirty.

"Jolene, honey?"

She knew she wasn't there even when she called out to her. Way before she called out. Probably knew it in her sleep. She went into the bathroom and stared at the shower curtain. No drops of water on it. She felt it to make sure. Dry. Marking time until it happened was all this whole exercise had been about. She was gone.

She got dressed and went downstairs.

"Have you seen Jolene?"

Pat folded the newspaper he had been reading. "She used the phone this morning."

"The phone?"

"She said it was a local call, so I let her use it."

Lela walked to the door and looked out. The rhododenrons were blazing red, so red they made her eyes throb.

"Then about fifteen minutes later a guy came and picked her up."

Lela could have left Guerneville the minute Jolene disappeared. She didn't have to stay with her suitcase packed, sleeping in a chair in case she showed up again. She didn't have to drive up and down the

Russian River looking for Jolene, as if she'd be there on a beach blanket on the sand.

And so she hung on. Ready to go, but not going. She wanted to call Ross, tell him he was right, tell him she was giving up on Jolene, too, that it was no use with someone like her, you offer your life to them and they don't even want it. But she didn't call him and she didn't leave Guerneville. And at the end of the week Pat came upstairs and told her there was someone on the phone who wanted to talk to her.

The house was in Armstrong Woods, with a creek running alongside and horses in a stable. Neatly trimmed hedges and a smooth green lawn ran from the drive out to the tennis courts, where two couples were playing doubles on a sun-dappled court.

"I'm Curtis," the man said who came to the door.

"I'm Lela, Jolene's sister."

He looked as if he had just come from playing tennis, too, except that he had blood spots on his white shorts and on the sweatband circling his steel gray hair.

"She's in the bathroom," he said.

The house was sparsely furnished. A few couches and end tables that didn't look used. But a stepdown well in the center of the living room was lined with big floor pillows that were worn and stained.

"I've called a doctor," Lela said. "He should be here any minute."

He was leading her down a long hall. The house was quiet, except for the sound of a television playing in one of the rooms. A teenage girl was on the telephone in the kitchen. It seemed like a normal house. But Jolene was in it somewhere, so it couldn't be a normal house.

"When she called me I didn't know who she was," Curtis said. "Then she told me, she said, you know Chick, don't you, and I said sure I know him. Well, I'm with him, she said, and I need some speed. And I said isn't he in jail, and she said she was with him before he went to jail, and I said sure I've got stuff for you if you've got the money. She said oh sure, she's got money, her sister was holding her money back at the apartment."

A man and woman were playing backgammon in a sunroom that had potted palms and a view of the redwoods. They didn't look up at Lela as she passed. She wondered if they knew about Jolene, if they had seen her, talked to her.

"She's been in there for two hours," Curtis said when they reached the bathroom. The door was open. There was blood on the marble floor and on the sink and on the commode where Jolene was sitting. There were smears of blood on the mirror and a spray of blood behind her on the little shelf where the perfume bottles were and smudges of blood on the wall above the bathtub.

Curtis stood with his arms folded and a disapproving look on his face, as if he had walked down the hall to use the bathroom and just found Jolene in there messing up his towels and walls and floor. "Junkies who inject think they're going for a ride in a Rolls-Royce, that they're the top of the line," he said. "That's a bunch of bull. I snort. That's as big a ride as I want."

Lela didn't know what to do, where to start. She didn't see blood spurting out anywhere, but what had made all those explosive red dots on the wall? Jolene's shoes and socks were off, and even her feet were bloody. The instep. Between the toes. Lela got down on her knees, started mopping blood from Jolene's face and arms and feet with the bloody towel.

"My veins collapsed, Lela," Jolene said. She was looking at her arms, pinching the skin with blood-tinged fingers. Everything was red. Her sweater, her too big jeans. "Not a good vein anywhere. I've poked and poked and I can't get a needle in anymore."

"I told her, you keep injecting every hour like you're doing, you're going to get into trouble," Curtis said. "But she wouldn't listen. She keeps going in the bathroom, and I tell her to leave, get out of here and take the stuff with her, I'll get the money later, but she doesn't go, just keeps going into the bathroom and coming out again, and then she says she wants eight quarters, so I give it to her, and the next thing I know she tells me she's dizzy, going to faint, and there's blood all over the place."

"I was trying to go out with a bang, Lela," Jolene said. "I got so tired of trying. You saw me trying, Lela, didn't you? You know I was trying."

"You were trying harder than anyone I ever saw."

"You'll have to pay for the damage, stains to the towels, and the drugs she used," Curtis said. "I won't charge for the needles."

She was such a mess, such a skin-and-bone bloody mess. There was even blood on her scalp. Little drops of blood as red as strawberry jam. And on the tips of her hair, as if she had brushed her head against the bloody mirror.

"I don't think I want to live," Jolene said. "But I'm not sure. I'm not sure about anything." She was weeping softly. "I didn't want to disappoint you, Lela, I tried so hard not to disappoint you."

Lela stopped wiping blood away and just put her arms around Jolene and held her tight.

"What did you do to yourself, Jolene?" It was Ross. He looked angry, but his voice didn't show it. Jolene's in real trouble, Lela had told him on the phone, and he'd said Jolene's always in real trouble. He had sounded like he wasn't going to come.

"Couldn't find any veins," Jolene said.

He was checking her eyes, her pulse.

"I kept sticking the needles in every vein I could think of," she said, "but they were all flat, just laid there like dead things."

"I don't think she can walk," Lela said.

"I can walk," Jolene said, but she fainted when she tried, and Ross picked her up and started carrying her through the house.

"I told her that I didn't have any better needles," Curtis said, following close behind, "and she said the ones I gave her were no good, and I told her they were the best ones I had."

"Just shut up," Ross said.

The couple playing backgammon came to the front door and watched Ross put Jolene into the front seat of his old car. Spectator sport, Lela thought as she looked at their faces. Jolene dropped her racket on the serve and has flat, dead veins she can't push any more speed into.

"I was going to kill myself," Lela heard Jolene say as Ross put her into the front seat of his old car.

"Who's going to aggravate me if you kill yourself?" Ross told her, and then he started the car and drove away.

37

ROSS WAS INSIDE with the therapist and Jolene. Lela could see them from the hospital patio, Jolene on one chair, Ross on another, the therapist sitting on the edge of his desk, looking intently into their faces, as though he could drill the truth of the hospital's program into them with his eyes. And Jolene seemed well, really well, her cheeks filling out, the sores gone, just red circles where the scabs had been. Someone had given her a permanent, and her hair lay in soft curls on the collar of her print shirt.

"Would you like some coffee?" One of the orderlies—she actually looked like a cheerleader in her Mickey Mouse T-shirt and lace-up shoes—had come out onto the patio and, Lela supposed, felt sorry for her sitting outside alone.

"I'd love some," Lela said. "Black, please."

It was more like a hotel than a hospital, with the sea down below and the rhododendrons heavy with red and white blossoms. The orderlies and attendants wore ordinary clothes and walked down the halls as if they were merely guests looking for their rooms. But at the edge of the green lawn, just beyond the mass of color and right before the first glimpse of sea, there was a wall. And the orderlies had notepads in their shirt pockets, and they didn't look out the windows at the brilliant sea and flashing flowers, but checked their notes and licked their lips and sighed before they opened a door.

There were other people on the patio. Some were sitting at round stone tables beneath striped umbrellas. Some had brought picnic baskets and spread blankets on the patch of grass. Children played on the slide and crawled through a large yellow plastic tube. It all looked so homey, so natural.

"We've brought so much chicken, I don't know what I was thinking of. Won't you join us?" The woman, stout, with heavy eyebrows and a toothy smile, was talking to Lela. "We have enough chicken to feed an army, maybe two armies. If you don't eat some with us, I'll just have to take it home and feed it to the dog."

Lela smiled at her. The woman had three small children with her. Probably her grandchildren. They were sitting cross-legged on the flagstone patio floor, playing a whispering game and giggling.

"I am a little hungry."

The woman pulled a crispy thigh out of the box and put it on a paper plate and placed it in front of Lela.

"My son is a doper," the woman said. Lela noticed the nonchalance with which she said it, as if she had resigned herself to the words a long time ago. "My daughter-in-law, too, but that's another story. Who are you here for?"

"My sister." Lela nodded toward the figures on the other side of the window.

"Is that her husband?"

"Not really. He's a doctor. Sort of."

"It's a shame, isn't it, what happens to people?"

"Yes, it is."

It was the first time they had let Ross and Lela come to see Jolene. And now they wouldn't even let Lela inside, made her wait on the patio, eating a stranger's chicken leg.

"At least you're sticking by her. Some don't, you know. Especially the sober addicts, they're the worst, not wanting to see when they're sober what they thought was so hilarious when they were stoned. Like my daughter-in-law, she took off without even a by-your-leave. Sixty-four, and me and my husband raising three kids again."

Ross was leaning toward Jolene, talking to her, and she was murmuring something back to him. Ross had said he didn't want to come, said it was useless, said Jolene was in such a mess she'd never get out of it.

"Are you just visiting, or do you live up here?" the woman asked.

"I'm just visiting," Lela replied.

"I got custody. The daughter-in-law tried, but not very hard. You know how people are when they're pretending to be something they aren't. Well, she could pretend to love these kids all she wants, but I knew better. So did the judge."

"They're lucky to have you."

"But my son doesn't know. He'd have a fit if he thought I got these kids away from her. He thinks they're just staying with me. My husband's in there with him now."

"I think you're very wise not to tell him," Lela said.

"I've even got a guardian picked out in case something happens to me and my husband. Does your sister have any children?"

"A little girl. She's at a friend's in Guerneville."

"It upsets the children no end, doesn't it?"

And then the idea struck. It came over Lela so suddenly, she felt a chill. The woman was smiling at her, and the sun was bright, and the rhododendrons looked as though they'd bloom forever, and Lela knew, as she had never known anything in her life, that Ross could make Jolene well. My God, it was so simple, such a brilliant solution. Ross and Jolene and Sandy. A whole family. Why hadn't she thought of it before? And why hadn't she realized before now just how much Jolene had suffered? It was so obvious, so clear that she had suffered more than Lela had. It didn't take a genius sitting down and making out a list of sufferings to know that. Didn't take a genius to know that on any list like that, Jolene would win by a landslide.

"If you're going anywhere near Cazadero," Lela said to the woman, "I'd sure appreciate a lift."

Mary Ann, the clerk in the general store, remembered Lela from the time she'd come in there looking for Ross, and she asked Lela if she had found him, and Lela told her yes, and Mary Ann brought her a Coke from the red Coke box near the front door, and Lela told her she could probably get five thousand dollars for the box, that it was an antique and there were Coke stuff collectors out there, and Mary Ann said then what would she put the Cokes in. Then Lela asked her if she could get a taxi to Santa Rosa, she wanted to catch a plane to L.A., and Mary Ann told her the taxi company didn't come as far as Cazadero, that if Lela waited till she closed up, she'd drive her over to Guerneville and she could get a cab from there to the airport in Santa Rosa.

Lela sat down on a hard oak chair next to the antique Coke machine and sipped the Coke.

"I close at dark," Mary Ann said.

"I can wait," Lela replied. Waiting was no problem when you felt as empty as she did. Felt so dead deep inside.

"There's cookies on the counter," Mary Ann said. "Samples."

"I'm fine," Lela replied.

No one bothered Lela while she waited for Mary Ann. People came in the store and brushed by her. Right by her over to the video racks or to the dark corner where the freezer was.

"Gave you a ticket for running a stop sign in a parking lot?" Mary Ann said to a guy in a leather jacket with a metal cross around his neck.

Her father. That's where it all started. And whose fault was it that he did what he did? Maybe if she hadn't kissed him so much, loved him so much. And Gil. She must have enticed him. Why else would he have done what he did to her when she was just a kid?

The guy in the leather jacket was gone, and the trees were laying a shadow down on the road now, and the light in the store was growing dim. Mary Ann was talking to two women at the counter.

And maybe Gil wouldn't even have killed himself if she hadn't helped.

The sounds the women's voices made was harmonic. Tones that twined into one another. Like a barber shop quartet. Like organ music in church. And the smells in the place were familiar, kitchen spices and old wood floors and washing powder, and Lela thought she heard Mary Ann say something about closing up, heard one of the women say she'd better get some help. Help closing up? It just takes a key to lock a door. Then Mary Ann was standing over her. Hovering, actually. What did she want? It couldn't be too important, or she'd talk louder, make Lela hear what she was saying.

There was no one in the store now. The chair was hard beneath her, and one leg rocked slightly on the warped floor. Lela pushed at the unevenness, rocked gently against it, and stared at the way the dust slanted in the light, the way the particles kept their distance from each other. She wondered how they did that, how they managed.

Mary Ann was gone, and the women, too, and the dim light grew fainter and fainter until it was dark, and Lela still sat on the chair, and now the dust was invisible, and she wondered where it went, wondered if she'd ever be able to get up off the chair, if she'd ever be able to move again.

"Lela."

Ross was talking to her, kneeling on the uneven floor and looking into her face. Mary Ann had her keys in her hand and was telling him to pick Lela up if he had to and carry her out, that she had to get home, she was late for supper.

"What are you up to, Lela?" Ross said.

"Oh, Ross," she said. "You're not supposed to be here. You're supposed to be with Jolene, taking care of her. She won't get well without you."

"Is this something you just made up?"

"You two can argue out front just as well as in here," Mary Ann said, and she walked Ross and Lela outside, then got into a pickup truck that had a big dog leaning out the driver's window and drove away. Ross stared after her car for a long while, and then he sat down on the porch.

"Jolene needs you," Lela said, and she sat down beside him.

"You really've got to get rid of that stubbornness, Lela. It won't do you any good, especially with me. I told you I love you, and you won't listen. Now, you can come home with me and lie down with me and make love with me, or we can stay here on this porch till someone comes and carts us away. It doesn't matter to me. I'm willing to grow old sitting here."

"You don't know what happened to us, Ross. You don't know how horrible it was, how it hurt us."

"And I don't want to know. What good's it going to do if I know?"

"You don't understand. My father—"

"You just can't give me to Jolene because you want to, Lela. I'm not medicine. It doesn't work that way."

"I never told you what happened, what he did to Jolene, what he did to me."

"I don't care what he did."

"How can you not care?"

"I just don't. Because it doesn't matter anymore. Smell that? It's redwood bark. It's stronger at night when there's more moisture in the air."

"And then Glenn going to Vietnam and getting blown to bits."

"Jolene's a junkie, Lela. You're not. I'm not. Not anymore I'm not. People turn out all kinds of ways for all kinds of reasons. If we knew which reason did which thing, there'd be a book, and they'd give it out at the hospital whenever a baby was born. Do this, do that, and the kid'll turn out all right. But no one knows, so people do all kinds of bad things and blame it on everything they can get their hands on. Your father, someone else's father. A war. What's the difference? You turned out all right. You can't help Jolene. She's got to help herself. I told you before, if I wanted to, I could spend the rest of my life regretting things. But I don't. I just take it one day at a time. That's what I do. That's all in the world anyone can do."

"I promised I wouldn't abandon her," Lela said.

"And you didn't. You did the best job you could in the world. God, look at that sky. I've never seen the stars so clearly. Really bright tonight."

He put his arm around her and laid the tip of his chromed head on the side of her cheek. He felt solid beside her. Unbending. As though he were part of the porch. She could tell now by the way he sat there that he wasn't going to give up on her. He wasn't going to take his arm away or stand up suddenly and walk down the steps and disappear the way everyone else did. He was going to sit there and look at the stars and enjoy the peppery scent of redwood and talk to her in that patient voice of his till the sun came up.

"Whatever you want to do," he said. "It's up to you."

Acknowledgments

My love and gratitude, as always, to my husband, Marvin Vida, who is my research assistant, my first line editor, my friend.

Thanks also to Lois Wallace, the best agent and most enthusiastic, sharp-eyed reader a writer could have.

And special thanks to Ann Patty, my editor at Crown, whose editing pencil is feather light, but deadly accurate.

Nina Vida
Huntington Beach, California